THEY BREAK BEAUTY

VICIOUS THINGS, BOOK ONE

LEIA KING

 Created with Vellum

THEY BREAK BEAUTY Blurb

I've caught the attention of the most dangerous men on campus.
And they've vowed to make my life a living hell.

Coming to Stonewell University was the beginning of a fresh start.
But in my second year, all of that changes.
Because of *him*.

The moment we collide, everything is put in jeopardy.
He wants to burn down what I've built.
He wants me corrupted and dragged into blackness just like him.
And he's not alone.

His two dark soldiers are right by his side.
Together, they're known as *Hex*.
Once you're marked by them, your life is cursed beyond saving.

Levi Knight – *Hellraiser.* Volatile and tormented, vengeance courses like poison through his veins. Wearing his pain like armor, he's feral and malicious to those who cross his path.

Mason Hall – *Scourge.* Controlled and scarily patient, he masks his cold-hearted brutality behind a boy-next-door façade. Calculative and vicious, he's a devil in disguise.

Colton Sharp – *Maverick.* The life of the party, the wild player on campus. But beneath the shiny surface, he's dangerous and unhinged. His reckless and erratic nature makes it impossible to see him coming before he strikes.

Cruel. Toxic. Soulless.
There's no limit to their maddening fixation.
They're pulling me back into savagery and shadow.
I spent years running from that old life.
But returning to that nightmare might be the only way to survive them.

Welcome to Stonewell

Happy Reading, Wildflowers!

Author's Note

This is a dark college bully reverse harem romance with scenes of M/M.

A list of TWs can be found at www.leiaking.com

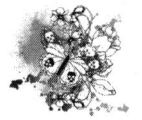

~Levi~

Take your punishment, bitch.

Blood sprayed.

The crunch of bone sounded.

The arousing cry of pain rang out, rolling right through me.

Fuck, yeah, that's the stuff.

I was surrounded on all sides by vultures.

Fucking savages who got off on blood being spilled, men breaking before their eyes.

I wasn't judging what got their rocks off, just that they were mere spectators, never getting in on the action, needing others to give them what they needed.

Namely, the likes of me.

I crooked my finger at my opponent as I bounced on the balls of my feet, sweat dripping down my bare chest and along the waistband of my black cargo pants.

The guy snarled and it turned into him choking on account of me just shattering his nose.

He had about thirty pounds of muscle on me and

while I was barely six-foot-tall, he boasted another six inches easy on me.

Shame he relied way too much on that.

It was really biting him in the ass tonight with going up against me.

Not to mention, I was no stranger to this shit.

Although, it had been a while since I'd been in the street fighting game.

And I was making one fuck of an epic return.

One for the goddamn ages, in all honesty.

He came at me, his movements lethargic and strained. It had him throwing a punch with no aim and finesse whatsoever. It went wide, completely missing me and he staggered at the weight of the miss.

A simple knee to the gut from me had him grunting and doubling over.

I followed it up with a hammer fist to the back of his neck, driving him down to his knees.

I moved in to finish it.

I'd gotten what I'd needed from the fight already.

I'd reached that high that only a brutal bout of violence could provide.

I'd tasted blood, basked in the pain I'd inflicted.

And, most of all, I'd exerted complete and utter domination over a threat.

He groaned, turning so his back was to me.

On a first look, it would have appeared that he was taking that position to make it easier to get back to his feet.

Fortunately, I never just stopped at the surface with anything.

That was how fools were made.

So I had an eagle-eye focus on him, enabling me to see his fingers trying to delve discreetly into the front pocket of his bulky, oversized sweats.

He was retrieving something.

A weapon, no doubt.

Something that was outlawed in these fights.

It was bare-knuckle all the way.

Sure enough, as he made a show of pushing to his feet, I caught sight of the glint of metal, noticeable even through the dark of night and the back alley only being lit by a couple of muted streetlights, one constantly flickering because it was on the verge of burning out entirely.

He spun and swung his fist—too slow as usual, as he had been this entire fight—and I was ready, snagging his wrist and stopping what would have been all that metal slicing my face open enough to permanently scar. *Been there, done that. Not looking to repeat it.* The jagged scar down the left side of my throat told that story all too well.

"You're humiliating yourself," I spat, as I took in the brass knuckles now decorating his right fist. Pimped out ones at that, all fucking polished to the point that they were sparkling, which had given their presence away far too early for him to make the sneak attack he'd clearly intended with them.

"*Hellraiser,*" he growled back at me.

I hadn't heard that name in a long time.

I grinned, baring my teeth. "That's right, motherfucker."

In the next beat, I shifted my grip on his hand, avoided all the metal, then I yanked it down, while driving my knee up at the same time.

A telltale snap sounded as the strategic impact broke his wrist, the weak bastard shrieking out down the alley.

Those shrieks only intensified as I yanked him around by his damaged wrist, kicked his legs out from under him, then forced him into a sleeper hold, while he flailed uselessly on the ground.

It wasn't long before I heard that expected slap on the rough ground as he tapped out.

I held on a little longer than was necessary, reveling in the sight of him turning purple and coming close to taking his last breath.

"Lev!" the ref and fight organizer called, and I looked out to see the familiar figure of Sammy Higgins shaking his head at me, his long dirty-blond hair whipping around him from the vehement movements.

With a grunt, I released the sorry shit in my hold, then rose to my full height.

The crowds parted and Sammy strode into the fray, then grasped my hand and held it high, solidifying that I was the victor.

Roars, applause, and high-pitched whistles rang out.

But I was only focused on one particular aspect of the celebration.

The chants.

"Knight! Knight! Knight!"

They worshipped me.

Damn fucking straight.

As it started to die down a little and Sammy's two *assistants* dragged my opponent away to get him the medical attention he most definitely needed, Sammy guided me off to the side where I'd left my black hoodie earlier.

I snatched it up and shrugged it on, flipping the hood up.

"I asked you to own the trumped-up shithead and put him out of the street fighting racket for a good long while, not kill him, Lev."

I shrugged. "I got a little carried away."

"Don't get me wrong, Alec's been causing me a load of bullshit. The punishment you delivered was warranted and a sight to behold. Really put him in his place. While you were gone, a bunch of these up-and-comers thought they could take control, even challenging me. And Alec was the worst."

"Unfounded arrogance was their mistake. Also, coming at you."

Sammy was a lot more than the organizer of the these fights in the college town of Stonewell. He was the lifeblood of the criminal underground here. Small-time stuff, sure, but a lot of it. He also had his ear to the ground in a major way, and he'd proven to be a font of information.

"You sure you don't want the cash?" he asked, pulling it from his pocket and making a show of counting the thick wad of bills. "It's a major payday. It being your first street fight in over a year brought in a massive crowd."

I looked him up and down.

He hadn't changed at all in the time that I'd been gone, still wearing those velour tracksuits of his, currently a navy one that blended well into the night.

The same couldn't be said for the thick, gold chains hanging around his neck, nor the bling decorating his fingers.

"What I *want* is for you to fulfill your end of our deal."

He stowed the money away. "Of course. Just checking."

"Do you have it?" I pushed.

Him not offering it up immediately pointed to him wanting to engage me in a conversation to catch up since I'd been away. Unfortunately for him, I had no desire to do that right now and no patience for it.

I was laser-focused on one thing only.

He gave a nod. "Yeah, I've got the street level intel you wanted, the kind you can't get via your usual means. As promised, I've had eyes on the girl." He lowered the zipper of his jacket and reached in, pulling out an unmarked envelope. Handing it over, he told me, "This is everything."

I took it and shoved it into the back pocket of my cargo pants. "Good."

"You want me to continue watching?"

"No. Have your people stand down. I'll take it from here."

"All right. I'll be seeing you around now that you're home, yeah?"

"In all likelihood," I responded, non-committal. I didn't like to shoehorn myself in.

He grinned. "Some things never change."

I merely smiled, then turned on my heel to go.

"Hey, out of curiosity, what's your fixation with this girl? Seems pretty damn inconsequential, especially to the likes of you."

I stopped in my tracks, his question cutting into me.

I ground my teeth, then sucked in a breath, and only just managed to answer steadily over my shoulder, "She's far from inconsequential."

"How's that?"

"She's an angel among demons."

His brow furrowed with confusion.

All right, it was much closer to shock.

He knew, just as well as anybody I allowed to become a familiar of mine, that I didn't see the best in people.

Far from it.

I'd learned well not to.

The nightmare of six years ago had solidified that.

But when it came to *her*, it was different.

Everything was different.

She stood apart from all of that.

I turned away and continued out of the back alley, leaving Sammy stumped.

It had taken a great deal of self-control—something I wasn't exactly known for—not to return home the moment I'd gotten word that *she'd* been walking the halls of Stonewell University shortly after I'd left. I'd had to resist the overwhelming urge to make contact. I'd had to stay the course with what I'd been embroiled in at the time, over the entirety of the last year actually.

But that was done with, that phase complete.

I was here now.

And one reason was because of her.

For her.

It was finally time.

I smiled to myself as the anticipation coursed through me.

Brace yourself, Stonewell.
Levi Knight is back.

2

~Brianna~

Life was good.

I was smiling brightly as I strolled down the corridors of Stonewell University, excited to be in my second year now and majoring in Software Engineering.

I'd spent the summer working freelance coding jobs online as well as software troubleshooting, while also kicking ass developing another app to add to my portfolio.

I now had three under my belt, the first being an educational game for young kids, the second enabling you to electronically tag and track important belongings like car keys, phones, and anything else considered vital for daily use without the need for attaching a tracker to each item. The third one was convenience-based too, but for the user's closet. It was in the testing stages by yours truly and a few students on campus. It was named *Style Swipe*.

Everything was right on track, things falling perfectly into place.

So much so that it no longer mattered to me that I was twenty-four years old and only in my second year of college.

Sometimes plans didn't follow the timeline you'd initially intended, but they worked out all the better for it.

My heels clacked down the hallway, the sounds of students rushing by to get to their first classes of a brand new year muffling the sharp click of my gray knee-high stiletto boots. I breathed in the anticipation and intensity swirling all around in equal measure as I made my way to the computer lab at the far end of the Science and Technology building of the campus.

I was just a few steps away when somebody cut right into my path.

I jolted back, my furry pink messenger back almost falling from my shoulder from the sharp movements.

As I adjusted it on the shoulder of my gray and pink checkered jacket that matched my skirt, I found myself looking up at a friendly face.

Chloe Anders.

We'd hit it off in my first year here.

She'd started here at twenty because she'd been getting work experience as an intern at a mid-level fashion magazine. She was doing a double major in Fashion and Mixed Media, now in her second year like me. We'd hit it off when we'd both attended a dorm party back when I'd lived there as a freshman, and a guy had gotten too handsy with her. So I'd done what anybody witnessing such a thing would do—I'd smashed his face into a wall and broken his nose, wherein he'd run off crying like a little bitch. *Good times.*

Of course, that had been when I'd still been trying to shake off my old life and reinvent myself. That violent reaction had been a bit of slip, so I'd made sure I hadn't done anything like that since.

I threw my arms around her, hugging her tightly.

It was the first time I'd seen her since before summer

break. She'd been off at a high-elevation ski resort with her well-to-do family. We'd texted and video called a lot, but it wasn't the same as being in person.

"Long time," I spoke into her shoulder.

"Way too long."

As we eased apart, I took her in.

Her hair was edgier than it had been last year. While still dyed lavender, short—just extending down to her chin —and feathered, she'd also now had it shaved on one side. It definitely fit with her rocker chic vibe.

"Wow, it looks amazing," I said.

"Thanks." She gestured at her black denim dress that had buckles and studs all over it. "You like?"

"Did you make that over the summer?"

She winked. "Did you really think I could go months without designing something? You know it's like an addiction to me. Just like you and your apps."

I chuckled. "Too true."

My gaze dipped to her shoes. They were a unique mix of platform heals and sneakers. And these ones were half denim and half leather. "Those are really something."

"I'm making you a pair. Gray and pastel pink. You can wear them to the joint homecoming party a bunch of the frats are throwing."

I hugged her again. "I love it. Thank you."

"It's the least I can do after you gave me *Style Swipe*. It's the shit, Bree! I've already got the next two weeks set outfit-wise. Talk about a time-saver."

"I'm glad you like it. But, remember, any bugs, let me know."

"Will do." She gestured behind me as students started filtering in to the room I'd been headed to for my first class. "You'd better get to your snake coding class."

I grinned. "Python." Among other things.

"Right. Sorry, it's difficult remembering all of them."

"Believe me, I know." It took hours of practice too. Constant as well. Fortunately, when you enjoyed something, effort wasn't really a chore. "See you for lunch later?"

"Definitely."

She took off back down the hallway and as the crowds swallowed her from view, I went to make my way into class, only to be pulled up short by my phone buzzing in my jacket pocket.

Expecting it to be her texting me, I was more than a little surprised when, not only wasn't it her, but it was an unknown.

Blocked ID: Same hair, new look. Suits you.

I frowned down at the message.

I'd reinvented myself since coming to Stonewell last year, so the people who knew about my *new look* could only be from my past.

One of them who I'd been close to, yet hadn't spoken to in that same amount of time came to mind the most.

Brianna: Tommy?

We'd agreed we wouldn't talk, that we'd needed to make a clean break. But maybe he'd had a moment of weakness.

That theory was shot to hell in the next moment when a response came right back.

Blocked ID: Guess again.

Brianna: No games. Who are you?

Instead of answering, whoever it was redirected.

Blocked ID: You look well. Happy. Is it real?

Brianna: Until I know who you are, no personal information.

Blocked ID: Smart woman. Enjoy your first class.

When I didn't respond—because this was super weird

and no small amount of creepy, honestly—he continued sending texts in spite of it, not the least bit put off.

Just adding to the creepiness.

Blocked ID: Loving the boots.

Shit. I shot my head up and rapidly scanned the immediate area, trying to locate anyone suspicious through the crowded hallway.

It was impossible. There were just too many people, too many possibilities.

Another text notification jolted my attention back to my phone.

Blocked ID: Don't go to the homecoming party.

My eyes narrowed at the message.

Brianna: Excuse me?

Who the hell was this stranger to tell me what I should and shouldn't do?

Blocked ID: Don't go.

Brianna: I don't take orders. Especially not from a creepy stranger texting me out of nowhere.

Blocked ID: Creepy? No. Concerned? Yes. Too many of the frat members aren't safe. Especially at that party.

Brianna: I can take care of myself.

Blocked ID: Don't put yourself in a position to test that.

Brianna: We're done here. Don't contact me again.

Blocked ID: I can't agree to that.

Brianna: It wasn't a request.

Blocked ID: I don't take orders.

Brianna: Neither do I.

Blocked ID: Love the fire. You'll see me soon, Wildflower. Until then, behave.

I stared at my phone for several moments in utter disbelief.

What. The. Hell?

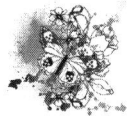

3

~Brianna~

"Wowzer, this party is really something!" Chloe exclaimed as we strutted along the walkway toward the mansion that was hosting the joint frat homecoming party.

It certainly was something and it was already well underway.

On the lawn to the far-right a crowd was gathered around a guy doing a keg stand.

A little closer and to our left there were six people lined up and shooting BB guns at beer cans they'd positioned on the fence.

And there were a whole lot more students looking on and drinking away.

Last year, we hadn't gotten invitations, because for some reason freshmen weren't allowed at this particular event. It wasn't stated why, but Chloe and I had reasoned that it was some rite of passage to make it through your first year before being allowed in.

"And we haven't even made it into the house yet," I breathed, taking it all in.

"Or the patio and pool area!"

I frowned. "There's a pool? Open for this massive party that's gonna be full of drunk-off-their-asses college students tonight?" That seemed like a crazy liability.

She shrugged. "Yeah. They go all out for this thing."

"Did you bring a bathing suit?" I asked.

I didn't see how she could have. We'd both agreed not to bring purses with us. That was just a disaster waiting to happen with a crazy party like this. I had a pink three-quarter length light coat over my gold and pink sequin romper with zipped pockets where I'd stowed my phone and the keys to my Charger that I'd driven us here in. But the jacket she was wearing over her black and red feathery mini-dress was a cropped leather thing with no pockets. She had a holder attached to the studded belt at her waist, but that only fit her phone and the key to her on-campus apartment.

"Nope. What's the fun in that? At a party like this, it's skinny dipping all the way."

I frowned at her as we entered the mansion itself. She was more out there than usual at these sorts of things. Usually, she was more closed off and guarded. But right now she was almost giddy and literally talking about getting naked in front of a bunch of strangers.

Something was off with her.

As we progressed further into the mansion, bodies slamming against one another and grinding on pretty much any available surface, while others gyrated to the dance music with the heavy bass, I considered turning back around immediately and getting us out of here.

That lasted about ten seconds when she suddenly bounced on the balls of her feet, then made a straight run for the bar, disappearing into the crowds in the process.

I sighed.

I had a feeling it was going to be one of those long-ass nights.

―――

"HERE," I said, rushing back to Chloe who was sitting forward on one of the pool loungers clapping her hands and bouncing way too enthusiastically as she watched the naked volleyball match taking place in the largest pool.

That's right, it turned out that there were three altogether.

There was a smaller one just behind it near a long bar, which was where I'd been getting rid of Chloe's beer, then grabbing her a water bottle.

Then over on the opposite side of the area, there was one that was more of a hot tub—a massive one with fake mini-waterfalls pouring into it.

"I'm good," she said, trying to wave me off as I went to hand her the bottle of water.

"Take it or we leave right now."

She started at my stern tone.

Yeah, I didn't bring that out much.

All she'd seen from me was pretty much my *reinvented version,* consisting of the bubbly and happy-go-lucky disposition I worked hard not only to put out there, but to keep feeling myself.

I had to.

When I didn't, when I slipped a little, it… it hurt. The dark memories tried to dig their claws into me.

Chloe snatched the water from me, giving me a pout for good measure.

"Slowly," I warned her, as she started gulping it down.

She took my advice and shifted to taking sips.

It was the first of my advice that she *had* actually taken tonight.

And that wasn't like her, like us.

I eased myself onto the edge of the lounger by her feet. "What's going on with you tonight?"

"Nothing," she said, still sipping at her water, while looking at the naked show behind me in the pool.

"You were worked up when I picked you up. On edge in a hyper, nervous energy sort of way. Then as soon as we got here, you downed two of those mini bottles of vodka that are all over this house like freaking decorations and basically dry humped the first frat guy you saw. And since then you've been knocking back beer after beer."

"Hey, that guy was hot. And he really turned it on."

"He welcomed you to the party and asked for a dance."

"He was wearing leather pants. You know I'm a sucker for those."

"Chloe," I pushed, tapping her ankle.

She shoved a hand through her hair and stared at me with her glazed, pissed-drunk eyes.

It looked like she was actually on the verge of confiding in me like she always did.

But then she blinked, put the water bottle down and jumped to her feet. "We're here to party, not for a fucking therapy session, Bree."

She staggered in her step, headed for the pool.

I reacted quickly before she reached the edge, just as she was moving to lift her dress up and flash everyone.

"Uh uh," I said, grasping her hand before she could expose herself.

She pouted at me again. "You're no fun tonight. I mean, you've barely even had a drink."

"I'm the designated driver."

"It's more than that. I thought we came here to have fun."

"We did. But it's hard to enjoy anything when you're drunk off your ass and barely even aware of anything around you. Did you even see the food they have here? It's high-end stuff, not just chips and dip. There are games happening in a couple of massive rooms downstairs. A karaoke competition in another."

"Well, my idea of fun is stripping naked and playing with the girls and boys in the pool."

"That's the alcohol talking. You don't even like showing too much cleavage with what you wear. I'm not about to believe you'd really be fine with exposing yourself—not in the light of day when you've sobered up."

"Urgh," she groused. "Let's at least go back to the dancefloor then."

"Fine, but just dancing. No hooking up."

Mischief shone in her eyes, but she did move away from the pool, and then we were heading back inside to the main house, the thumping of the bass guiding the way to the dance area that the frats had set up, even along with some strobe lighting.

She jerked her hand free of mine, then pushed her way toward a group of guys and started getting her dance on with them. I stayed near a group of sorority girls, moving to the slow jam beat while keeping a close eye on her.

I hated dancing around guys.

I didn't like being touched.

Not by men.

Fortunately, the sorority girls must've seen the nervousness all over me, how uncomfortable I was, because one of them took my hand and the other three welcomed me into their group. They were dancing in a fun, hilarious way, just living it up.

Exactly what I'd been going for when Chloe and I had been headed to this party earlier.

I'd wanted to let loose a little and have fun.

But with the way she'd been, it had forced me into the role of babysitter.

One of the girls—one with beautiful long black curly hair—leaned in and told me in a serious tone that cut into the revelry, "You should get her home."

Her friend in a romper a lot like mine added, "Right now. She's what they're looking for."

I frowned. "What?"

Another one with straightened brown hair and a gold mini-dress told me, "Look, we like you. And your friend. That style app you made? Ah-mazing!"

"And you want Chloe to make you an outfit for that gala you've got coming up," the one in a romper said.

"Well, that too."

"What did you mean that she's what they're looking for?" I pressed.

The one with the amazing curly hair told me, "It's a sick game with a couple of the frats. Let's just say they use tonight to reach a certain quota."

"Of hookups," another added.

"We're here trying to figure out who's involved in this sick game and we've got a couple of members from another frat helping us. So far we've only got a few ID'd and tossed out, so there's still a lot more here."

"They want the inebriated ones, like your friend right now."

I screwed up my face. *Urgh.* That was beyond sick and twisted. "Shit, thanks for the heads up."

"No worries."

I went to get Chloe just as she was grinding her ass against a guy behind her, while she linked her arms around another in front of her, but the sound of the music suddenly stopping startled me, pulling me up short.

"Let's take this party up a notch!" someone called out, and I followed the sound to see three guys taking position on a raised platform with a drum kit and microphones. One sat behind the drums, while one holding a bass guitar took position at one of the microphones.

But the one who really caught my eye—and whose presence caused a whole lot of commotion and the crowds rushing over to the makeshift stage—was the one in the leopard print shirt and black leather pants who had an electric guitar strapped to him.

He was a very familiar face around Stonewell—especially the college campus.

Colton Sharp, playboy extraordinaire.

His platinum-blond wavy mohawk was styled to perfection, his toned body emphasized by his form-fitting clothing. He was clean-shaven with so many hoops and studs in his ears that there were too many to count.

Shrieks and applause erupted as he took position. "This is a new one. Just for you," he spoke, making the crowd go even wilder.

Then they launched into hard-rock anthem.

His voice was gritty with a sexy rasp, and the confident way he moved and the seductive way he rolled his hips and grasped the microphone as he got into the song, his passion pulsing forth… it was intense and one hell of a pull.

He had the place enraptured in mere moments, that charisma of his and that powerhouse voice taking control of the whole place.

It was staggering.

I'd never seen him live before. I'd only heard one of his songs from Chloe after she'd worked with him on some branding related to that specific song during her mixed media class.

He stuck out his tongue during a guitar solo and a tongue piercing glinted under the muted lighting in the space. *Whoa.*

Speaking of the lights, they started to dim when he reached the end of the song and a slower, more intimate melody began.

A chill rolled through me as they dimmed too much for my liking.

I didn't... I didn't like the dark.

As if that wasn't bad enough, the sorority girls around me had disappeared into the crowd which had shifted when Colton had taken the stage.

And Chloe was gone!

Shit!

I spun around, trying to locate her through the dark, crowded space.

I tried to make my way through, but I had to push through the throngs that felt like they were closing in around me.

Heat rose to my face and neck, my chest.

My pulse spiked.

My breathing became unsteady and a strain.

I was about to suffer one hell of an anxiety attack.

Making it to the wall, I managed to navigate around the outside of the space and make my way out into the lobby.

The dark lobby where no one was hanging out now that concert was underway and had focused everyone's attention.

My phone buzzed in my jacket pocket and I pulled it out with shaky fingers.

It took me three tries to swipe it open.

Chloe: Sorry I disappeared. Threw up in bushes. At your car. Drive me home.

Relief coursed through me. She was okay.

Brianna: Be right there.

I pocketed my phone, then slumped against the wall, needing to take a beat before I headed outside and saw her. I didn't want her to see me like this. She didn't know about these… episodes. No one did. Not even my dad.

They weren't a regular occurrence, so it wasn't a big deal.

Besides, I could handle it.

Right now, I just needed a moment.

Unfortunately, I wasn't even granted that as a booming voice sounded, followed by what appeared to be two sets of screams, a moment before two bodies rolled down the stairs over on the other side of the lobby.

I watched, stupefied, as the two guys scrambled up in obvious pain, beaten and bloodied, just as a hulking mass of a man stomped down the stairs.

"You're done. With your fraternity. With this campus," he spoke in a fierce and uncompromising tone.

I took him in and the recognition set in right away even in my current discombobulated state.

Mason Hall. The best friend of Colton Sharp. He was the eerily quiet one who projected a fearsome edge.

Just like he was now.

His caramel-brown hair was thick and shaved short on the sides. He was way over six-foot and broad too with linebacker shoulders. His left arm was covered in tattoos all the way down. And his right shoulder down to the top of his elbow was inked with a skull tattoo with wings and the snarl of a lion. He was wearing a black button down short-sleeve shirt that highlighted all that ink, but also had him partially blending into the dark, especially when combined with his navy designer jeans.

"You're marked," he rumbled.

The two guys nodded frantically, then hurried off, stumbling in their step from their haste and their injuries.

Mason cursed, then headed back on up the steps murmuring something about rooting out the rest of the filth.

Wow.

I leaned my head back against the wall and tried to concentrate on my breathing, when somebody barged on in from outside and came to a sudden stop just as they were about to pass by me to enter the *concert space.*

"Lost your way, hottie?" he spoke.

"No. just taking a breather."

"Too much cheap beer, is it?" he asked, his voice taking on a taunting tone.

And something else.

Something I had an instinct for. Something dangerous and threatening.

That was proven right in the next second when I went to push off the wall and he slammed me back against it with a hand to my chest, the jarring impact making me choke.

"Mason can't stop us all," he muttered to himself as he sank his hand into my hair. "Thinks he's a fucking god."

I went to turn my head away, but he fisted it, holding me in place.

Adrenaline thrummed through me, but its power and my reaction was muted too much in my current state.

He shoved his knee between my legs making me grunt. "Your friend was our target. Easy prey all fucked-up like that. But her throwing up was a major turnoff. But now you're here. Dazed and looking like a lost little lamb. And alone in the dark."

A growl sounded from the shadows.

"She's *not* alone," someone rumbled.

The asshole in my space jolted and swung his head around.

He didn't get much further than that before a hooded figure launched himself from the shadows, snagged the guy around the throat and ripped him from me.

He was pounding on him then with fists of absolute fury.

He slammed him into the side of the stairs, then wrenched his shoulder, making the guy scream, before knocking him out with a knee to the face.

"Piece of shit," he ground out as he smashed his boot into the guy's ribs even as he was already sprawled out unconscious on the lobby floor.

"All right, *Wildflower?*" he asked, leaving the guy and coming back to me.

A chill rang down my spine as I made the connection.

The Blocked ID who'd texted me the first day back.

"He won't touch you again. No one will," he went on, as I stood there trying to make out his identity beneath that low-hanging hood he had up and the dark of the lobby.

He got up close, but didn't reach out, or actually touch me at all.

"I'm back. You're safe now."

What the—

"Who are you?"

He flipped his hood down.

Oh. My. God.

I couldn't... I couldn't believe it.

Trying to process it was a whole other thing.

Those eyes of his, a rare shade of pale blue, burned

23

into mine with an intensity that couldn't be denied. His black, curly hair was wild and piled on top, some strands falling over the left side of his face and obscuring his eye.

And most prominent of all was that jagged scar down the left side of his neck.

A scar I knew the story of. Every disturbing detail of it.

He was just under six-foot with a boxer's toned and muscular physique.

Levi Knight.

It was everything I could do to conceal my true shocked reaction.

More than that, to conceal the recognition.

I managed to force a frown of confusion instead.

"It's been six years, but that shouldn't matter," he said, his eyes narrowing a little at my reaction, or lack thereof.

"Six years?"

"You know very well." He shifted his weight and thumbed himself. "Levi? Levi Knight?"

"I don't—wait—you used to go here before I showed up, right? You were a member of *Hex*? The disbanded secret society here at Stonewell U?"

"It wasn't a *secret society*, but, yes. That's not how *you* know me, though."

"I'm not sure what you're getting at, but that's all I know of you." I pushed off the wall and sidled past him. "Thanks for your help with that rape-charge-waiting-to-happen, but I need to get my friend home and—"

He dodged into my path up so close that his appetizing sandalwood scent rolled through me.

My breath hitched, a noticeable gasp escaping me.

It had his eyes darkening.

"Admit that you remember me."

"I—"

A curse from the top of the stairs thankfully saved me from having to answer at all.

And in the next moment, rushed footsteps sounded, and I looked out to see Mason dragging somebody who looked half-dead, the guy barely able to stand. That was proven in the next second as Mason hauled him across the lobby toward the entrance doors and the guy collapsed halfway out.

Mason stilled on the last couple of steps as he noticed Levi there.

He looked *almost* as shocked as me.

"Fuck me! *Lev?*"

Levi finally took his intense gaze off me and turned.

In the next moment, Mason was there, slap-shaking with him, then pulling him in for a tight hug.

"You didn't give us a heads-up or anything. No one knew you were coming back. Not even me and Colt."

"Let's get you both out of here," Levi responded in an eerily calm tone.

"What?"

Levi gestured to the sprawled-out guy. "This place is done. There are five more around the east side who've been put down."

"You took care of some of those fuckers?"

"I had time."

"I'm more concerned with how you even knew about it."

"How do I know anything, Mason?"

"Lev, what's going on? What are you doing back here?"

"I have my reasons. Pack up, get Colt, and come with me. Then we'll talk."

As Mason tried to dig for more information, I'd heard enough.

I slipped out while they were talking and took the meandering, out-of-sight route to my car.

Holy hell. This had been a complete nightmare of a night out.

And, with Levi Knight now here, I didn't doubt that this was just the tip of the iceberg.

A brief nightmare was about to turn into an absolute hellscape.

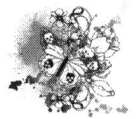

4

~Mason~

I didn't like it.

Not the way Lev had shown up back in Stonewell.

Not how he was being evasive and less than forthcoming.

The calm coming off him was definitely also a chief concern.

He didn't do composed and rational as a rule, and I certainly wasn't fool enough to think that had changed for him in one single year.

He was up to something.

He had big plans.

And with him that meant danger and a mammoth headache for *me*.

Keeping the likes of Colt in line was no small feat, but Lev was several levels beyond that. At least Colt was capable of listening to reason, of being talked down. At least *he* could recognize when he was out of line or headed down a dangerous path.

But Lev… he just couldn't.

Not anymore.

Ever since what had happened to him six years ago, he hadn't been the same.

He'd returned with a few screws loose.

He'd returned damaged.

I sipped at my glass of scotch that he'd served me—another suspicious thing with him being so attentive—and took in the lounge he'd led me to. Colt was still over on the other end of the house being obsessed with the recording studio Lev had set up for him. There was no question that Colt would definitely want to move in here now, no questions asked. It certainly was the way to his heart—and everything else—and Lev knew that all too well.

"Sorry about that," Lev said, striding back into the sleek room with light-gray walls, black leather furniture and a frosted glass coffee table, along with black and white artwork of prized cars and motorcycles lining the walls. "Couldn't get all the blood off. I used the last of my special solution a few days ago."

Fuck me. "How?"

"How what?"

"How did you use it all? You've been street fighting again? Already?"

He lifted a shoulder. "A little. And it's not *already.* I've been back in town for a couple of weeks."

"What?"

"Chill. I didn't tell you, because I wanted to get this surprise ready. This house for the three of us to move back in together. I get that you and Colt needed the whole brotherhood thing while I was gone, but joining a frat? Come on, Mason, that's weak."

I ground my teeth. "You weren't here. You don't know what—"

"I *know* the fraternities around here are infected with

entitled shitheads, sexual predators that are under the false assumption that they're above the law."

"There are a select few. I've been taking care of it."

"Right, in your usual cautious and slow way."

"You mean, the safe way."

"I mean, the ineffective way. Instead of just dealing out a beating, you should've made an example out of them, outed them to everyone at that damn party. Rather than that, you had Colt distract everyone with that crazy-ass charisma of his and an impromptu concert, while you took care of it in the shadows."

"They weren't just roughed up, they were also marked."

"By *you*. It's not enough."

"You don't know—"

"Mason," he said, coming closer and snatching up a bottle of vodka. "You've gone soft. That's the rep I was hearing all about since I've been away." He screwed off the top and downed a couple of large gulps. "Those five assholes I put down? They were gonna come at *you*. They knew you and the sorority heads were behind rooting out the bad elements at that party, and your position and reputation has been so incredibly weakened that they thought they actually had a good shot of succeeding in putting *you* down. You, brother. Jesus fucking Christ."

"Things have been in a peaceful state over the last year."

"Which has given these shitheads time to gather and delude themselves into thinking they have power and invulnerability, that they're untouchable." He took another gulp of vodka. "*When the world is at peace, a gentleman keeps his sword by his side.*"

"Wu Tsu." I rolled my eyes. "Something you quote all too often."

"I quote it as necessary."

It was clear what he was getting at, even though he hadn't actually stated it outright.

We were both great manipulators, albeit I was much more calculating.

I had the patience there where he didn't.

And I knew him well. The three of us had been the best of friends—brothers, really—since we were kids.

"You want me to resurrect *Hex.*"

"I want *us* to."

"Lev—"

"I'll be the public face. I'll take the heat."

"That's not how it works, you know that. And how does Roman feel about what you're suggesting?" I gestured around our surroundings. "I assume this was his doing? He wanted you back here, so he made *this* happen, bought it for you?"

"Dear Old Dad had no hand in this. I have access to my trust. *I* bought this place."

"You… what? There were contingencies upon you receiving all that money. Well, barriers, so that he could keep delaying it and exert control to keep you in line."

"And me taking that internship to put my network security skills into practice for the last year mowed down all those *barriers.*"

"I don't believe you."

He smirked and laid his hand on my shoulder. "Ah, Mason, I've missed your extreme paranoia and gift for smelling smoke when there isn't a fire, nor even a spark."

I grasped his hand on me and loomed over him, my mammoth form and six-foot-eight height completely eclipsing his five-eleven. "Lev, what are you doing back here? Really?"

The whole looming thing didn't faze him in the least.

Of course not. This was Lev we were talking about.

"The internship came to an end, I missed this place, I still have my degree to finish." He leaned in and kissed my cheek. "And I missed *you*. My boys."

He pulled away and took another swig of vodka, then swept his arm around the room. "I mean, look at this place. Don't you love it? It's a fuck of a lot better than the frat accommodations and without all the bullshit commitments and things you had to adhere to, all that fakery shit. Did you see what I set up for you? Your bathroom has a top-of-the-line Jacuzzi bath, the kind you go weak in the knees for. There's a library off your room with all your favorites stocking the shelves. Colt's got that recording studio. I've got the workshop outside for my woodworking. We're all set."

It would seem so.

He'd gone all out.

He desperately wanted us here, the three of us back living together as it used to be before he'd had to leave at his father's behest.

That desperation was what worried me.

I couldn't determine where it was coming from, what it was truly rooted in.

While I didn't doubt that he *had* actually missed us, it clearly also wasn't the extent of it. Things were never that simple when it came to Levi Knight. They were always multifaceted and they came with a multitude of complications.

But having him right here in the same place as us, living together again, it would give me the opportunity to find out what was truly going on, what he was really focused on beyond the surface level, why he wanted *Hex* revived too.

And, yeah, I'd missed him, despite all the rest.

There'd been a hole without having him here with Colt and me.

"You've gone to a lot of effort. It hasn't gone unnoticed," I offered up.

A genuine smile spread over his face. "Yeah?"

"You heard me," I said, smiling back at him.

"Sweet place. Real ace, Lev!" Colton cried, bursting into the room, then running at Lev and throwing his arms around him. "Can't believe you're here with us! It's been way too long! Shit, we've missed you!" He lifted his head and looked out at me. "Right, Mason?"

"We have, yes."

"Hasn't been the same without me, huh?" Lev said, as they eased back, and he flashed us a self-satisfied grin.

Of course.

Colt ate it up like he always did with him. "Shit, no, brother." He guided Lev over to us then pulled the three of us into a group hug. "You're never leaving again, you hear me?"

Lev looked out at me and answered Colt pointedly, "I'm here to stay for a good, long while."

"Hell, yes! Just like the good ol' days!" Colt cried excitedly, tightening his hold on the both of us until he was almost cutting off our breathing.

Lev smirked at me.

Son of a bitch.

Colt was prone to seeing things through rose-colored glasses. Especially when it came to that. He focused on the good only and either forgot or buried the bad beneath it.

But I hadn't forgotten it, not by any means.

I remembered everything.

And as much as it was amazing to have our missing third back here with us, it was also a grave concern with the way he'd come back and the veil he was determined to pull over our eyes as to the reason for it.

Once the shock of him showing up so unceremoniously and throwing me for a loop wore off, I'd begin the process of untangling the tangled web he'd woven, and get to the bottom of it all.

But for now, without knowing all those details, I *did* know one thing for sure.

The peace and quiet of the last year was about to be blown to smithereens.

5

~Levi~

I sat astride my Harley Softail Deluxe as I waited off the dirt road obscured by the heavy foliage.

Usually waiting wasn't my scene, nor my forte.

But in this case there were rewards to be had.

The first was observing Brianna Walker in her natural habitat.

Well, what had become her natural habitat over the last year. Something she was clearly intending to keep to.

Not if I have anything to say about it.

Which, of course, I did.

Her apartment building ten miles from campus wasn't a shithole, but it was modest, to say the least.

I'd initially been surprised when I'd investigated and delved into every little thing about her, because her old man had money. Despite the major setback he'd had a few years ago, he'd pivoted and found success through other means. Curt Walker owned a very profitable series of small businesses—a motorcycle repair shop, two luxurious lounges, and a chain of diners called *Penny's*. He'd done very well for himself. She had the means to be living in the lap of luxury, yet here she was residing in a humble one-bedroom apartment instead.

Hmm. She didn't want anything to do with her old life, she'd intentionally separated herself, even financially.

On the surface, it was admirable, a move of strength and independence.

But with the depth of my research, I was aware that it was closer to the opposite.

She was running.

Running scared.

Of the shadows of her past, of the trauma.

Unfortunately, that was often paired with a great deal of denial.

And barriers.

Barriers that threatened to get in *my* way.

I wouldn't allow that.

In fact, I was already in the process of removing some other *barriers* on her end.

I shifted my weight as I watched her through her bedroom window and she finally moved from working away on her laptop.

I'd been here for almost two hours and she'd been sitting there the whole time working, shifting between coding one of her apps and then doing her coursework. Every twenty minutes on the dot, she'd reach out beside her and drink from a mug of hot chocolate topped with whipped cream and a great deal of mini-marshmallows.

She walked to her bed that was covered in hot-pink silk and lace—some hardcore Barbie shit going on, just like the rest of the space.

She snatched up her phone and as she did, I could see the screen flashing with an alarm.

Putting it down, she walked back to her laptop and

shut down her work for the night, then she crossed to her dresser and pulled out a pair of little shorts and a tank.

She eased off her fluffy pink cardigan and for the first time, I was able to see a purple and blue watercolor butterfly tattoo on her left inner arm. I couldn't make out the intricate details from this distance, but it was enough to at least discern.

I got even luckier as she turned around and I saw a black dandelion tattoo on her right upper back.

I stilled. *She* saw it too. She saw that she was my wildflower.

Well, she didn't know that she was mine yet.

But she would.

Very soon.

I ground my jaw as I watched her start to strip off her gray scoop neck top too.

No.

I didn't want to see her like that, stripped down and bared to me, not like this.

It wasn't the way.

When that happened, she needed to be looking into my eyes, right there up close wanting it as much as I did.

This… this cheapened it.

If that was all I wanted, I could've used other means to get it.

Besides, I also needed her out of that apartment.

So, I pocketed my lighter, then pulled out my burner, firing off a text.

A text she would believe was from her friend, her only friend here.

Chloe: I'm ready to talk. I need to. Can you meet me tonight? My place?

The notification thankfully pulled her up short and her top didn't come off.

Instead, she picked her phone up again, read my message, then hurriedly responded.

Brianna: Of course. I'm leaving right now. See you in fifteen.

Nice.

Chloe: You're the best.

And she really was.

The lengths she went to in order to be a good friend to that trainwreck was worthy of sainthood. I knew from my research on Brianna, that she was putting forth a bubbly and excitable persona wanting to enjoy life and have fun, so it made sense that she'd be pulled to that in Chloe Anders. However, Chloe took it too far the majority of the time and it had put them in volatile and sometimes outright dangerous situations. Fortunately, as soon as I'd found out she'd been here at Stonewell U, I'd had eyes on her and people strategically intervening when those sorts of incidents had occurred to ensure nothing had come of it, that Brianna hadn't been harmed.

She hastily pulled on her cardigan, rushed out of the bedroom and I shifted to watch her grab her three-quarter-length pastel-pink coat, then head on out, locking the door behind her.

I noted that she didn't turn the lights off on her way out.

She didn't want to come back home to the dark.

As soon as I saw her charcoal-gray Charger driving out of the parking lot, I headed for the apartment building.

───

COCONUT.

That was the scent that had infused me when I'd gotten up close to her during that party.

I smiled at the shampoo bottle in my hand and opened it, sniffing it. Sure, enough, it was the same scent. As I'd already found out her body wash was as well.

Mmm.

It smelled best when it was on her skin and in her hair.

I continued around the bathroom, taking in her glittering silver electric toothbrush, a hair straightener and a curler too.

I opened the cabinets and found the standard toiletries to be expected.

A hot-pink silk robe was hanging off the back of the door. I stroked the sleeves, then breathed it in, smelling her scent all over it.

I opened the mirrored doors of the cabinet above the main vanity mirror, taking in her makeup. Silver eyeshadow, the expected pink too, a lot of lip gloss.

And then I caught sight of something behind a box of tampons and her birth control meds.

Vials of medications.

Anxiety meds. Heavy-duty sedatives. Sleeping pills.

Hmm. One of the things I hadn't been able to determine was this. Reading the name on the prescription vials, it made it clear why. She hadn't used her real name to acquire them. Likely her father's doing then.

I made my way back into the bedroom.

I liked to start from the farthest point then work my way back out. Not that I had a lot of experience with breaking and entering people's homes and going through their possessions. Of course not.

Ribbons hung from some sort of organizer just to the left with a jewelry tree beside it full of beaded bracelets and rings, but no necklaces or earrings. I knew why there were no earrings—she didn't have her ears pierced. And the lack of necklaces, I had a strong theory for.

I continued around the bedroom, finding a thick book of fairytales on her bed, a couple of faux-crystal silver and pink lampshades on her nightstands. I'd also seen some origami creations around the open concept space of the living room and kitchen before I'd walked into the bedroom.

That, combined with her studies for her Software Engineering degree, and the fact that she was out a lot socializing with Chloe, made for an extremely busy life with barely any time to rest.

Very little time to think was more like it.

Her closet was no surprise at all. Bright and bubbly. There was nothing hidden in the far back either.

But then I went for her nightstands.

The first one had just a single box of tissues in the top drawer. But then I opened the door beneath and pulled up short as I took in a bright purple dildo and a bullet vibrator.

Good for her.

I moved to the other one and opened the bottom door.

A safe greeted me. *Getting to the good stuff now.*

I crouched down and studied it.

The familiarity of it couldn't be denied.

It was one of my father's next-gen products. Well, his corporation's creation, *Knightsridge Engineering.* He used a couple of them in his own home.

As such, I knew well how it worked.

The passcode changed daily and it was randomized and sent to the user's phone.

Considering I had access to said user's phone, it was child's play to determine it.

I pulled my real phone from my pants pocket and fired it up, accessing what I needed to, and it didn't take me more than a few moments to acquire the code.

I punched it into the safe and, sure enough, a high-pitched beep sounded, along with a mechanical whirring as the door clicked definitively, then sprung open.

Smiling to myself, I opened it all the way then peered inside to see two shelves.

On the bottom one was her passport, thick wads of cash, and a burner. Emergency items should she need to leave in a hurry. So she was still concerned about that then. All these years later. Beside it, nestled in the corner was a Glock 26. Yeah, definitely still concerned.

I focused on the top shelf and found a fuzzy rainbow-colored unicorn journal.

I frowned. In a safe? That was a bit much.

But as I pulled out my pocket knife and used it to open the gold padlock attached, then started rifling through it, it became clear it was much more than a journal or a regular set of diary entries.

It was research.

So she didn't just use her highly accomplished coding skills to create apps. She'd been using them in a similar way to that which I did. Illicitly. She'd been conducting her own investigation that mirrored mine.

She'd been trying to find the same people I had.

But then she'd abruptly stopped.

Why?

It didn't say.

I flipped through, trying to determine why.

Nothing. No reason given.

A couple of photos slipped out and I caught them, taking them in.

A growl rumbled in my throat before I could check myself as I studied the first one. It was a photo of Tommy Dixon, also known as *Hawk* in Brianna's previous circles. He used to be one of her father's top enforcers. And there he was in the photo sitting astride his Harley and grinning at the camera, well fucking beaming at it—beaming at *her*.

I looked at the other photo, which was far worse. It was clear she was holding the camera as the two of them snuggled together and Tommy kissed her cheek.

These weren't the first I'd seen of them, evidence of the illicit affair they'd had for a couple of years. There were more on her phone and of a much more *compromising* nature. But having them here in my hands and seeing them again and kept in her book of secrets… it had my gut twisting.

I slotted them back in the page they'd fallen from.

If she'd launched this investigation, it suggested that she *did* remember what had happened.

That had to mean that she actually remembered me too.

So her response at the party had been a load of crap?

There'd been nothing about me in the book, nor of the events concerning that fucked-up time, though.

Had the trauma made her repress the specifics of it?

Was the investigation just built on bits and pieces that she remembered?

Or had it come from what had happened to her mom, which had been closely related to that nightmare?

Had it come from her father's reports, rather than her own recollection?

As much research as I'd done, the only way to know the answers to *that* was to approach her directly, to ask outright.

But given what else I knew about her—creating a new life to run from the past—it stood to reason that she'd want to continue in that vein and do everything she could to avoid venturing down that dark road.

That asshole at the party who'd tried to assault her had

made things even worse in that capacity, freaking her out and causing what had looked very much like a panic attack.

So now she would be more skittish than ever.

More fucking barriers.

It was all right, I could muster patience where this was concerned for a little while longer.

It definitely wasn't my thing, so there was a time limit on it.

But the way things were, combined with my *harsher* and, according to Mason, *volatile*, nature, this situation would require a different approach.

Rather than confronting her directly or getting in her face, she needed to be lured carefully and with a whole lot of charisma and incentive.

Fortunately, I knew just the person for the job.

And then, finally, Brianna Walker would recognize the truth I'd allowed her to avoid for far too long.

She. Belonged. To. Me.

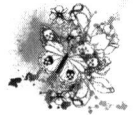

6

~Colton~

"I'm doing some of my best work here, darlin'."

I licked up the length of his cock again, his only semi-hard cock, then raised my head to see Mason staring pensively up at the ceiling as he laid there on the crimson sheets of his bed. He was deliciously naked with his Greek God-like musclebound torso on display, his biceps bulging as he had his hands folded behind his head, and his thighs spread wide for me.

"Mason?" I pressed when he showed no sign of hearing me, *or* of even noticing that I'd stopped teasing him in the way that usually drove him crazy for me and made him putty in my hands.

"Huh?" he murmured, his gaze finally leaving the ceiling and connecting with mine. "Yeah, you know I love you in those leather pants," he said, his eyes roaming over me, my mohawk all mussed from playing with him for the last ten minutes.

"I do know that, yeah. But you're barely reacting to that *or* what I've been treating you to." I wrapped my fingers around his cock. "You're only sporting a semi."

He shifted on the bed and brought his hands to his face. "I'm sorry, I'm just distracted."

I released his shaft. "Because of Lev?"

"Because of him suddenly being back here with no real explanation."

"He missed us. He needs to finish his degree. His internship came to an end."

"All surface-level excuses."

There it was.

I hadn't seen it from him in a while, because things had been all smooth-sailing.

Well, aside from the whole frat debacle of the last couple of weeks when the sorority heads had come to him with evidence of all the sick shit some bastard members had been up to.

But here it was now out in full force.

A whole load of worry.

That part of him that couldn't let go of even the smallest thing, who took on the responsibility of everything.

Mason was two years older than mine and Lev's twenty-one years, so he'd naturally fallen into the role of our unofficial leader. But it had gotten worse over the years and moved beyond that to the point where he needed to exert control over everything, to make sure nothing and no one could touch us. To do that, it had caused him to also exert control over us, to going to every effort to keep us in line.

That had calmed down during the last year with Levi away.

But now he was back, it seemed Mason was already falling right back into it.

Well, Lev kind of brought it out in him.

It was largely because of the *incident* that had happened about five years ago.

That fucking nightmare had almost broken all of us, and it had completely fucked with Mason's life, even turning him from his artistic side to a boring-ass law student who was just doing it for his big-shot lawyer daddy.

Maybe with Lev back, despite this concern that it was bringing Mason at the moment, it could ease him back on the real path he belonged on. Lev might cause him grief, but he also inspired with the way he was so passionate and determined to do what he wanted, to live his life how he deemed fit. I was hoping once Mason got past this aspect of Lev's return, that he'd be drawn to that other aspect.

"Even if they are excuses, what does it matter? We have him back with us."

"What does it matter? You know how he is, Colt. I mean, yeah, I'm happy he's here, but if you think that won't come without complications, you're really packing on the denial. He's up to something."

"Well, it has been too easygoing and kind of boring since he's been gone. He does bring the fun."

"Fun?" He scoffed. "*Anarchy* is more like it."

"Well, he is nicknamed *Hellraiser* for a reason."

He grunted, then gestured at his dick. "Sorry tonight isn't working out. Maybe call up one of your groupies, have them take the edge off."

"No fucking way. I want *you* tonight. Although, I could call one of them in to join us if you want? Carly, maybe? Hayley?"

While I was bisexual, Mason identified as heterosexual to the outside world and the only guy he fooled around with was me, and just once in a while. Even when we shared women together, he wouldn't touch me then in front of them because of his issues there.

45

More repression from him.

He was unbelievably tightly wound.

It was a mixture of him being uncomfortable in his own skin with everything, his father's overbearing influence, and also the fallout from the *incident*.

"No, I'm not in the mood for anyone else to be here with us." He went to sit up, saying, "I'll go down some liquor and then—"

"No. Only sober with us, remember? I won't have it any other way." And it shouldn't ever be any other way.

"Colt—"

His words caught in his throat as I shucked off my leather pants, my hard cock springing free.

I shoved him up the bed so his legs were no longer half hanging off, then I pounced on him.

"No more thinking. Just feel," I said, a moment before I descended on him with fervent, erotic licks, the stud in my tongue rolling over his pecs, down his chiseled abs, making him undulate beneath me.

"Damn, gorgeous," he groaned, fisting a hand in my hair and angling me where he wanted me, getting into it.

Yeah, he loved it when I was all over him.

Rather than just down by his spread thighs and teasing his cock, he enjoyed being consumed, surrounded by the all-encompassing warmth of skin on skin, the feel of a hard body on his.

I took it further in the next second, rubbing my cock against his inner thigh.

He hissed at the sensation, his fingers tightening to a white-knuckle grip in my hair.

That's right.

While he was immersed in that, I snatched up a condom packet I'd left on the sheets earlier, ripped it open, then rolled it down over my shaft.

Then I grabbed the bottle of lube that I'd used to tease his hole with my curling fingers earlier, and I made my cock nice and slippery.

I broke his hold in my hair and lifted my head as I rose up on him, sliding my cock along his that was now deliciously hard and straining for release.

I ground back and forth until his breathing was strained and ragged, then I teased his hole with my crown.

"Yes," he gasped, rolling his hips and trying to take me in deeper. "Colt."

I eased back and stroked his thighs up and down, staring into his beautiful espresso eyes that were now glazed with pleasure and rapidly escalating need.

"Love it when you whimper my name, darlin'." I added more lube all over my shaft after I'd left a trail all over his when we'd ground together. "Are you gonna open your sweet ass to me, let me hit that spot nice and deep that makes your thighs shake?"

"Fuck, gorgeous, yeah," he breathed. "Give me that big cock."

I breached him, the pressure out of this world as he bore down around my tip.

The sensations were heightened by his eyes rolling back in his head and the way he bit his lip, a sexy groan rumbling from him.

"Ungh, Colt," he uttered as I sank in deeper, real slow and easy, wanting him to feel every inch of me taking his hot ass.

I leaned in and nipped at his jaw, then licked away the sting. "That's right, let it all go."

"Fuck, yes," he moaned as I pushed in the last couple of inches, then settled, waiting for him to adjust.

He turned his head and he licked my lips, then curled his tongue around mine, kissing me sensually, falling under the heady spell we always ended up immersed in when we came together like this.

The moment I felt his tight ass start to relax around my invading cock, I moved, sliding almost all the way out, then teasing him with shallow thrusts.

Our kiss became frantic and he bucked on the bed, reaching around and scratching my back, making me hiss at the awesome light pain coming into play against the pleasure.

He spread his thighs wider, wanting more, and I picked up my pace, taking it deeper until I was slamming into his sweet spot over and over.

"Ah! Fuck me. Fuck, Colt! *Fuck!*" he roared out into the room.

Goddamn, the way he was losing it had sharp spikes of pleasure assaulting my nerve endings all fucking over.

His reactions always took it to another level for me.

I snagged his hand and wrapped it around his cock, then moved our fingers together, fisting his cock roughly.

I power-fucked him up the bed.

Harder.

Rougher.

Faster and fucking faster until all I could hear were his growls and the slapping of flesh.

His cock was hot to the touch, much like his perfect ass.

Pleasure was building higher, almost making me delirious with it.

I released his hand and watched him take over, matching the roughness I'd used.

Shit, it was a hot-as-hell sight to behold.

"Yeah, rough up that big cock for me, darlin'."

"Ungh... Jesus... yeah!"

I angled my cock slightly and it pushed him right over the edge.

"Hell fucking fuck!" he roared, a moment before he stiffened then came all over himself in a hell of a mouth-watering sticky mess.

I was right behind him as he milked my cock, squeezing so deliciously, ecstasy took me.

As I pumped my cum deep in his ass, the sight of his own stickiness all over his stomach sparked that dirtiness in me and as I pulled out, I sat back between his thighs and slicked my fingers in my hot cum trying to leak down his ass crack.

I gathered it and started to push it back in, delighting in Mason trembling from the oversensitivity.

The door flew open and Levi strolled in the very next second fully dressed in his go-to black camo pants and his hoodie.

He smirked as he caught sight of me between Mason's spread thighs, my fingers in his ass pushing my cum back inside, while Mason was lying spent after making a sticky mess all over his abs.

Lev focused on that last part. "That's a lot of cum. Been playing the abstinence game for way too long again, Mason?"

Mason grunted and went to pull the covers up to shield his naked body from Lev's view, but I was there in the next second before he could. "We're not completely done, darlin'," I said, as I leaned in and started licking up all the cum off his abs and some leaking down his shaft.

"Ah, shit," he groaned, his thighs shaking in that sexy way.

When I was finished, I pulled the covers up to conceal his nakedness, and, holding them to his chest, he eased into a sitting position.

I was just pulling on my leather pants when Levi jumped on the bed beside Mason and leaned back with his hands clasped behind his head. "Right there with you on the dry spell situation."

Mason frowned. "Impossible."

"Yeah, Mason told me you've been street fighting again since you came back. Figured you'd be inundated with those *fight bunnies*," I said, settling on my back at the foot of the bed and turning my head toward them as I chilled and basked in the rest of the afterglow.

"I was. Sammy had a great homecoming for me. After that first *business-only* fight, anyway." He shrugged. "I didn't feel like it, though. Not for the last year, actually."

Mason and I exchanged a look.

That was… off.

Levi Knight wasn't exactly one to turn down admiration or worship—in any form.

We had that shit in common.

"Want me to throw you one?" I asked, grinning at him. "Give me a couple of minutes, and I'll get right on it. I assume you'll wanna top?"

He grinned right back at me. "Appreciated, cupcake, but you know it's not my scene."

I chuckled.

"Love it when I call you that, huh?"

"*Sweet as icing sugar and just as appealing to the masses too*," I said, reciting his own words back to him.

He winked. "Damn straight you are, brother."

Mason glared at him. "You're buttering him up."

Lev removed one of his hands from behind his head and slapped it to his heart. "I'm hurt, Mason. Accusing me of not being genuine, especially to our sweetheart here."

Mason rolled his eyes. "Lev."

"I'm serious. Are you still sore because the nickname I use for you is *Killjoy?*"

"Best stick with his *Hex* nickname," I suggested.

"When I see the infamous *Scourge* back in action, I will," he said, the challenge in his tone not lost on me, and definitely not on Mason, judging by the stone-faced look he gave him. All my hard work relaxing him was quickly being undone.

I pushed into a sitting position and refocused the conversation before the antagonism ramped up even further, asking Lev, "Why are you fully dressed? We figured you'd crashed a couple of hours ago."

"I had. I woke up. Took a ride."

"What?" Mason said. "The security system didn't sound indicating you'd come in and out."

"Of course not. It's *my* system. I have full control. I wasn't gonna risk it disturbing the two of you."

"More like you didn't want us knowing you'd left in the middle of the night."

Lev blew right past that accusation and said, "I came back a few minutes ago and I was gonna crash, but then I heard you two were still up." He smirked at us. "Literally."

I chuckled.

Mason shook his head in dismay.

"Then I heard Mason's usual *'Hell fucking fuck!'* when he climaxes, so I knew you guys were done, so I could come in here. I thought it would be the best time with Mason at his most relaxed, but clearly that's an impossible feat." He eyed me. "Even with your sexual talents in play."

"Jesus, Lev, what the fuck do you want? We're looking to crash, don't draw it out. *Or*, novel idea… wait until tomorrow at a more appropriate hour? Hmm?"

"No can do. I want to know now. About *Hex.*"

"It's been a couple of days since you asked, only a couple of days since we reunited."

"Yeah, exactly. Two whole days and still no decision from you."

"And *I'm* the one with ADHD," I said.

"Lev is a whole other thing," Mason groused.

"Either way, what's the word?" Lev pushed, completely unaffected by any personal slights as usual.

"Fine. We'll get *Hex* back up and running," Mason told him. "You were right about that frat issue, for one thing. And another, it'll at least serve to keep you occupied. With it being *Hex*, I can also keep a close eye on you too."

Lev ruffled his hair. "Sure, we'll go with that." He pushed off the bed. "Good decision. Can't wait."

I went to move into his vacated spot beside Mason, but Lev told me, "I need a favor, if you're up for it."

"So you *were* buttering him up," Mason accused.

"I was calling it like it is. But I wanted to run something by him, yeah. The other reason I came in here."

"What's up?" I asked, sounding way too eager to be part of one of Lev's plans that usually involved a shitload of fun and some major adrenaline high too. Right up my alley.

There was a glint in his eye as he registered my favorable reaction.

"Brianna Walker. You've crossed paths with her, yes?"

I thought for a moment.

"The app queen?" Mason asked.

"Ah, but that's not how Colt knows her." He eyed me. "Is it?"

"Nah, girl's got one hell of a voice."

"Right. Karaoke night at *Nirvana.*" Mason said.

"Yeah, she came in with her friend who's helped me out with some promotional stuff before, and she got up and sang. Girl even looked stone-cold sober when she did it —that takes guts for non-professionals."

"What do you say to considering a duet?" Lev proposed.

"What?"

"An edgy ballad, perhaps."

Huh. "Could be ace."

"Why?" Mason demanded, before I could say much more about it.

"She sparked my interest when I saved her from one of your frat assholes at that party a couple of days ago. *But* with my rep and given how skittish that crap fest made her, it's doubtful she's gonna be receptive to me making my interest known directly. I need a little something to soften things before I approach her. Get her here and I'll take it from there."

"Wait, so there won't really be a duet?"

"That's up to you. I just want her here with nowhere to run to or make excuses out of fear. The rest is up to you—just keep it friendly, nothing more."

"*Nowhere to run to?*" Mason said. "Sounds like the stuff toxic and twisted romances are made of."

"Well, you know me, *Killjoy.*"

Mason growled low in his throat.

Completely ignoring that, or maybe not even registering it at all, Lev asked me, "Well? You up for this?"

"It's been a long time since I've been involved in a Levi Knight sponsored plan. Count me in."

"Colt—" Mason started.

"It'll be fine. Plus, if there *are* any issues that crop up, you're here anyway, right?"

"Dammit, fine."

"Nice," Lev said. "Thanks, cupcake."

"No worries."

As he turned to go, Mason called out, "What's the real deal with you and this girl?"

"I told you. She sparked my interest."

Before he turned his back and headed to the door, we both caught that dangerous dark look in his eyes.

It had Mason worrying his bottom lip between his teeth, while, for me, excitement bloomed for the first time in a long fucking while.

Things definitely weren't boring when Lev was around.

And it looked like he was about to prove that really quickly.

Welcome home, Hellraiser.

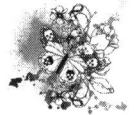

7

~Brianna~

"All right, just call me when you get back. Or, better yet, come by my place so we can actually talk in person. I don't like that the last time I saw you was for a brief five minutes before you headed off in your mom's town car. And then the longer time before that was you pissed drunk at that frat party and then—"

"I get it, Bree. It's okay," Chloe assured me down the line.

I grimaced. Was it okay?

It certainly didn't seem like it.

And, worse, it certainly didn't seem like she was going to sort it out either.

She might be a spitfire and somebody who lived their truth, marched to the beat of their own drum and all that, but it completely went out the window when she was facing down her fashion mogul mom, Celeste Anders. In fact, the way Chloe was around me and the students of Stonewell University was very clearly a case of overcompensation for that.

When she was in her mom's orbit, there was some

major regression involved. She became disturbingly subservient to that overbearing woman's demands and decrees.

The night she'd texted me that she was ready to talk, I'd finally found out what had been eating at her and had her drinking herself into a stupor at the homecoming party. Although she'd claimed that she hadn't texted me, I'd arrived just in time as she'd been headed out of her apartment.

Because I'd been right there in her space, she'd actually told me what was going on.

Apparently, her mom didn't think Chloe was making enough *traction* in her career through her studies here, not getting enough notice and attention. So she'd hooked her up with a prestigious *right-out-of-the-nepo-babies-handbook* opportunity where she'd work at her mom's design firm while also studying at a private fashion school.

It was odd that it had come out of nowhere.

It was even stranger that her mom was suddenly seemingly worried about such a thing, seeing as though she'd been fine with Chloe coming here to Stonewell to study and she'd been applauding her designs and studies all of last year. Her main goal was to learn, not to garner attention all over the place. That would come in senior year once she had the knowledge to back her up, once she'd learned what she needed to in order to become a designer worth noticing, when she was actually ready to get her name out there.

This turnabout with Celeste made no sense. Not just because the timing of the first week into her second year was messed up. But also the fact that Chloe had thrived at this college because she could be herself away from her mom's influence. She'd grown into herself here.

And now, unless Chloe could stand up to her and stick to what *she* wanted, she'd lose that.

And we'd lose each other.

I'd offered to go with her, but she'd refused, wanting to handle it on her own.

I shook my head to myself as we said our goodbyes on the phone and I returned to reading over the assigned chapters in my textbook on data structures, while also finishing up eating my meatball sandwich. *God*, the marinara sauce was to die for. It was definitely going in my sandwich recipes book.

That's right, I had a recipe book just for my sandwich experiments.

I was a major fan of them—different types of bread, different and mixed ingredients, often with what would be seen as strange combinations to a lot of people. Sometimes I ate a sandwich for breakfast and lunch. At least I hadn't crossed over to dinner with it too.

I swallowed my last bite, then started packing my Tupperware back into my fluffy pink messenger bag, because my next class was in ten minutes. Usually I got excited at the prospect of an upcoming class but, this time, as I looked around the quad from the uttermost far back picnic bench out of the way of everybody else, it was bittersweet not having Chloe here.

Sure, we weren't in the same program, but we'd always plan things between our class schedules where we'd meet during the day for lunch—like we would've just now—or fun we'd have later at night. It sounded strange, but I could feel the emptiness without her here.

That was probably being compounded by the utter shock of running into Levi Knight after all this time.

He'd been gone and he was slated to be for a good long

while—enough time for me to get my degree and be on my way out of Stonewell without ever encountering him.

Then he'd gone and thrown me for a loop. His friends too, from what I'd observed and overheard that night.

I didn't want to uproot my life yet again and start all over somewhere else.

At least not until I had my degree. Until I was ready for the next chapter.

I wanted to settle here for a while. Have some stability.

But with him being here, it put all that in jeopardy.

Unless I could get him off my radar, get him far away from me.

If we only passed by on the way to classes, I might be able to handle that.

But any more than that and it would be difficult for me to continue as I had been without what seeing him again represented to me—pain and darkness.

"Admit that you remember me."

No.

I couldn't.

I wouldn't.

Not to him.

And especially not to myself.

I rose from the bench and slung my bag over my shoulder, making my way around the edge of the quad away from everybody else, including the foursome who were tossing a freaking football around right in the middle that was flying through the air like a missile with those playing clearly having no idea what the hell they were doing. They'd already smacked a poor passerby's coffee out of their hand.

I didn't get very far before a shock of platinum-blond suddenly filled my vision, making me pull up short.

I jolted and abruptly found myself face-to-face with none other than Colton Sharp.

He shoved a hand through his wavy mohawk and grinned at me.

Oh no.

What the hell did he want?

It had to be wishful thinking to hope it was just a coincidence that a friend of Levi's who had never said more than a word to me last year had walked right up to me out of the blue.

He was dressed in his usual rocker chic way with his heavily-studded black leather jacket, a pair of tight navy jeans with what looked like a scarf covered in skulls as a belt and a partially shier metallic looking tee beneath.

"Can I help you?" I asked, hiding the edge that was just beneath the surface.

If I'd actually taken my normal route through the much more visible and populated areas of campus, then this wouldn't have even been possible. His popularity and star power would have ensured there were tons of students swarming around him.

The only time I'd ever seen that not happen was when he was with Mason Hall. Although, he was often just a silent observer in crowded situations, he had an eerie edge to him and a threatening sort of presence that managed to keep people away without him needing to say a thing.

"Well?" I pushed, when he just continued standing there and roaming his eyes over me in an oddly studious way, some sort of curiosity sparking as he did.

My black hair was loosely curled today and falling about my shoulders and I was clad in my pink houndstooth jacket and matching mini-skirt, along with a silk scoop neck tank beneath and a pair of black knee-high boots.

"I need your voice."

I started. "My… what?"

"Your voice," he repeated, as though the ask wasn't the least bit odd.

"Are we talking in a Little Mermaid way here?"

He frowned for a moment, then that movie star grin was right back, lighting up his pretty-boy-with-an-edge features. "Right, no stealing it or anything. Although, likening me to that sea witch is something I'm down with. She's a real badass."

Interesting way of looking at it.

Maybe *interesting* wasn't the right word.

He took a step closer, making me tense. "It's for a song I'm recording. A ballad. Yours has a unique quality and a timbre that will mesh well with the grittiness of mine." Off my surprised look, he explained, "When you sang karaoke at *Nirvana*, it stood out. So much so that it inspired the song I'm talking about."

"I'm not a trained singer. Nowhere close."

"That's fine. You have raw talent, something I can work with."

"I'm sure there are plenty of others who'd sell their souls to contribute to your work."

"*Unique quality* isn't something that there's an overabundance of."

"Then broaden your search."

He took another step closer and my back pushed against the building wall. "I want yours."

I sucked in a steadying breath, quickly wishing I hadn't when his scent wafted over me in a far too appetizing way.

"Ocean Breeze body wash," he told me, and I grimaced internally when I realized he'd caught me sniffing him.

He ran his tongue over his teeth as his smoky gray eyes fixed on me, and I took in his tongue piercing.

Don't focus on it. Look away.

I blinked and followed his attention that was drawn to my necklace, the one I wore every day, my blue and green all-seeing eye pendant.

It didn't exactly match that well with what I was wearing, but I couldn't go a day without wearing it.

To say it had sentimental value didn't begin to describe it.

"The Eye of Providence," he uttered to himself, before his eyes snapped back to mine. "You're a bit of a contradiction, aren't you, cutie?"

"I'm just me."

"Nah. You've got the whole Barbiecore thing going on, but then there's an edge to you too. This necklace, the tattoos I laid eyes on with the strappy tank you were wearing at the bar." He reached out and fingered my silky black hair. "The way you sang *Hurt*, the Leona Lewis version, like you were breathing it in and fueling it with a whole lot of heart *and* pain that night."

Crap.

I swallowed hard. "You're reading a lot into nothing."

"I guess we'll see when we work together."

I batted his hand away from my hair. "I'm flattered, but I can't. I have a lot going on. I know you'll find someone else easily."

"Playing hardball… that's new for me. Kind of invigorating, honestly."

"That's not what I'm—"

"I'll post Chloe's latest designs all over my IG. Endorse them myself, even do a Live if she's down with it."

Oh my God. He had hundreds of thousands of followers and given that he had connections to the celebrity community, that would undoubtedly be huge for Chloe, getting some real attention to her fashion designs.

This could go a long way to helping her to stay here.

Hold on a second. "Why offer this now?"

"Why not?"

"You know why she's not here right now?"

"Of course. It's all over her IG."

Oh.

"You'd know that if you were a little more sociable on there. Your last post was weeks ago sometime in the summer when you were close to finishing that fashion app." Off my look, he told me, "I was gonna message you to ask you about this until I realized you're hardly on there. Hence me approaching you in-person instead."

"I see."

"So? What do you say?"

Dammit. The bastard had me backed into a corner.

I couldn't let this opportunity pass by for her. She'd worked so hard and she'd been fighting to gain traction for the last few years since she'd started making her own clothes as a teen. I couldn't let her be wrenched from the life she'd been so excited about here in Stonewell. And this was my shot to prevent that from coming to pass.

I nodded. "Okay. Deal."

"And you?"

"Me?"

"Yeah, what do *you* want, cutie?"

"Nothing. I'm fine as is."

He cocked an eyebrow. "Everybody wants something."

"There is one thing."

"There it is." He folded his arms across his chest. "Go on, hit me with it."

"Keep Levi away from me."

He cocked an eyebrow. "Why is that?"

"It's my ask. End of story."

"Yeah, the thing is, asking me to make Lev do anything is like asking for the goddamn world."

"Then I guess we have a problem and—"

"Hold up. Look, we'd be doing this thing at our new place. There's a recording studio there. So you'd have your own chance to tell Levi to stay away. I'll be there as a buffer or whatever the shit."

"Hmm."

"It's seriously the best I can do when it comes to him."

He leaned in, catching me off guard, so much so that I couldn't even react as he breathed me in. "You should know, he's got his eye on you. And when Lev locks onto something, he doesn't just simply let go. Although, this is the first time that the target of his fixation has ever been a person. It's usually some lofty goal or dangerous objective. This is hella interesting, cutie."

A shudder rolled through me.

This wasn't good. Not at all.

I had to shut it down.

I figured the best way to do that was to make Levi believe that there was no connection on my end at all, to make it clear that he'd be slamming his head against a brick wall trying to access anything like that from me when it came to the past.

It was dead to me and that was all it could ever be.

I needed to make that clear ASAP. Especially if he was truly as obsessive as Colton was making him out to be.

"Fine. I'll take it."

"Good. Give me your number."

He pulled out his phone and I reeled it off to him. "Thanks. So, I'll get those posts out and tag the shit out of them for Chloe while you're in class." Pulling back in the next moment, he told me, "You smell real good, by the way. Mmm. Can't wait until we hook up." Off my scowl, he added with a laugh, "For the song, of course."

And, just like that, he was off with that swagger of his out in full force.

I slumped against the wall to take a beat and get myself together.

This year really wasn't getting off to the best start.

So many complications and surprises.

Two things I hated with a vengeance.

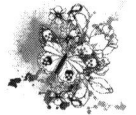

8

~Mason~

Lev leaned against the doorway of the guy's locker room, his arms and legs crossed as he stood there in a casual stance, despite the blood dripping down his fists.

Their blood.

"Efficient and appropriately ruthless," I commended him as I passed on by.

He gave me a chin lift, looking mighty pleased with himself.

More than that.

There was a sadistic gleam in his eyes mixed with excited anticipation as he watched me venture further into the space where five guys were sprawled out, two groaning as they laid on their sides naked and bloodied, while the other three were on the floor between the lockers and the benches incapacitated, yet possessing enough awareness for me to communicate my message.

Despite this being the first burst of violence that Lev had partaken in for *Hex* in over a year, he hadn't lost control or taken things too far. He'd actually followed my orders precisely.

None of the punishment he'd dealt out was life-threatening and he'd only gone after the five targets I'd specified, not going beyond that, and even luring the five to this location at the same time through some impressive manipulation of their communications via their phones and social media.

"Your attempts at a power grab are over," I spoke, walking amongst them, my voice booming through the still room and echoing nicely off the walls, adding to the ominous nature of my words. "Fraternities and football stars don't rule Stonewell U. *Hex* does."

Wide-eyed expressions followed at my declaration, a couple of them even shuddered.

The power of eliciting those reactions rolled through me in a way I hadn't felt in too long.

I'd missed the taste like no other.

"Now, this was merely to get your attention."

"With a little punishment and humiliation thrown in," Lev spoke.

"That too." I kicked the thigh of one of the frat heads in the shower. "After all, you all deserved a taste of your own medicine after the twisted operation you had running in regards to making victims out of the sophomores here."

"Third years too, I heard," Lev chimed in.

I nodded. "Word was spreading, giving Stonewell U a bad reputation. But you didn't consider the big picture at all, did you? It was all about instant gratification."

"Thinking solely with your dicks," Lev said, shaking his head. "Amateur hour."

"You're going to assist us with turning things back around. I know what you're thinking: why should we? You've taken your beatings and once you walk away from this you'll make plans to come at us en masse, yes? Something along those lines?"

"More shortsightedness," Lev chimed in. "Piling on the pathetic."

"The thing is, that won't be happening." I pulled out my cell phone and scrolled to a video I'd had one of the sorority heads secretly make with the tech I'd outfitted her with. I played it and held it out to one of the frat heads in the showers. It depicted him and the two others who were also in the room arguing with the sorority head as she'd confronted them as per my instructions. They'd thought so little of her power compared to theirs, believing themselves to be untouchable that they'd arrogantly ended up confessing they not only knew about what she'd been accusing their fellow frat members of, but that they'd actually orchestrated it together to both *get pussy* and wield power over the girls who'd all been *chosen* for their parents' connections that the frat heads had planned to use to their full advantage under the threat of revealing the girls as *cheap sluts for our boys.*

The only sluts were them.

Curses sounded from two of them, a defeated groan from another.

"That's right. We own you. Effective immediately, the three of you are the property of *Hex.*" I leaned down and jerked on the blond hair of the football captain draped at an awkward angle over a bench beside his starting quarterback. He hissed as I pulled at his pretty boy roots. "As for you and your quarterback here, fixing games against our very own Stonewell Lions just to line your pockets, and trying to elevate your own standing in spite of that by undermining your own team members through fucked-up means like rigging drug tests and manipulating them into unsavory situations. That's over and done with. You'll help to undo it all, in fact. I'm certain you'll be highly motivated to do so after *Hex* obtained evidence of you both testing positive for performance enhancing drugs multiple times last year and during your return this year too."

"That's not true," the captain grunted.

"You know what they say, the truth is what you make it," Lev called over.

"What *Hex* makes it," I clarified. "Like I said, boys, we *own* you." I took a moment to enjoy their pathetic states and having them at our mercy, and then I turned and walked back to Lev, throwing my hand over my shoulder as I ground out, "Spread it around. *Hex* is back in power."

As Lev and I walked out of the locker room and made our way through the back exit of this side of campus, he smiled at me. "Nicely done, brother. It's the first glimpse I've seen of *Scourge* in a long while since you shut down *Hex* shortly before I left. How did it feel to go there again?"

"Good," I admitted. "Really fucking good."

His smile widened and sadism danced in his eyes. "Glad to hear it."

We stepped out of the building and Lev's phone buzzed. He pulled it from the pocket of his hoodie. In the next moment, he was grinning devilishly as he took in the message, then typed back. "Well done, cupcake," he murmured to himself.

"What was that?" I asked, as he pocketed his phone, his whole being now brightened.

"Just Colt seeing to that favor for me."

"With the girl?"

"Brianna, yes."

"And?"

"And what?" he asked innocently.

That was a dead giveaway that something was off, because there was absolutely nothing *innocent* about Lev.

"Why are you going to all this trouble for her?"

"Trouble? Asking Colt to get her to the mansion isn't trouble. It's nothing."

"It is for you. You don't chase, you're the chased when it comes to women."

"Maybe I'm looking to chill."

"You mean, settle down?"

He lifted a shoulder.

"I'm not buying it, Lev."

He didn't say anything and we just continued walking through campus in silence for a while.

It gave me time to think back to the night of the homecoming party when I'd seen him with her, to analyze every little thing.

It took me time to weed through everything that had happened, given what a busy night it had been for me through orchestrating those takedowns.

But then I had it.

"The girl… Brianna… she was having an episode… what we used to call your anxiety attacks."

I noticed him tensing.

"Wasn't she?" I pushed. He was the best person to recognize those signs.

"Yes," he hissed through his teeth. "Your point?"

I rounded on him, forcing him to pull up short. He blew out a breath of frustration—another sign that I was getting to him and hitting at something real with him for once and not just the façade he put on. "That's why you made a connection to her out of seemingly nowhere. You recognized in her the same thing you used to suffer through."

He stared at me for a moment.

"Well?" I pushed.

"Yeah, you got me, Mason. That's what got under my skin about her."

"It's a dangerous connection to make, to pull on, Lev. Especially with your history."

"I'll be fine. Besides, I haven't had an *episode* in forever."

"It doesn't mean—"

"Leave it. I've got it under control."

"I guess we'll see when she comes by the mansion in a couple of days."

I saw him register the challenge I was throwing down.

As usual, instead of backing down like he should have, he rose to it, grinding out, "I guess we will."

Son of a bitch.

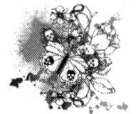

9

~Levi~

"A bit cheesy, isn't it?"

"It's a ballad, Lev."

"It's supposed to be an edgy rock ballad," I countered.

Colt snatched the piece of paper back from me with the lyrics he'd shown me for the song he was going to be working on with my girl. "You gave me two days to pull a song out of my ass, a song that was never supposed to exist. It'll have to do."

"Seems like it."

He slapped my bare chest. "Don't be a shit."

I chuckled. "My bad, you know I like teasing you, cupcake."

"You're not the only one," he said, pressing his hand to my pecs. "You've been working out. In the gym downstairs?"

"Nah, working out in a gym is Mason's thing. It's the street fighting. And woodworking, somewhat."

"Mmm," he said, sliding his palm down over my abs.

He lingered on my gunshot scar to the left, teasing it

with his thumb, before continuing down to the waistband of my black pants.

I snatched his hand before he reached the target of his interest. "Uh uh. It's not hard for you."

"I didn't expect it to be. It is hella interesting, though. That's how much you're into this girl? Sporting a hard-on for her before she even gets here tonight?"

"You know how the anticipation of a scheme coming together gets me off."

"Seems more than that. Seems all about *her.*" He eased his hand from mine, but not without giving it a kiss. "I can see why."

I tensed. "What?"

"She's got a real powerful aura about her."

Him and his *aura* shit.

"I'd say yellow with the confidence and peace in herself that I felt from her, combined with green with the kind and loving heart of hers that I picked up on. But there's also some black, because I was sensing a blockade— walls she's put up to protect herself from something, or because of something."

All right, he was pretty damn good. "You got all that from briefly talking to her to invite her here?"

"To coerce her here for you was more like it. And it wasn't exactly that brief. It was fascinating talking with her. She hides it behind that bubbly and bright Barbie-like personality she puts out there around campus and town, but there's a harder edge just below the surface. I was only able to bring out sparks of it, but it was there all right. It's gotta be what's got *you* drawn to her. Although, if that's the case, Mason isn't exactly gonna be on board. Having that from her and the vicious edge in you coming together could be explosive, in the worst ways for Mason, causing a fuck load of chaos."

I lifted a shoulder.

Let them both think what they wanted. Their theories on why I was drawn to Brianna Walker were just pieces of the overall big picture. It was so much more than that.

But until I was able to get through to her and pull her close, I wasn't ready for either of them to know the truth. It would only complicate matters and likely create more *barriers* in my path. After years of waiting for the time to be right to do this, to approach her like this, there was no way I was willing to risk more complications or possibly deterrents from them getting in my way.

So I did all I could do in this particular moment.

I redirected. "You're circling around it, but it sounds like *you've* taken a liking to her."

"And if I have?"

"We don't share women. Not like that at least. You and Mason have your threesomes once in a while, but that's all superficial."

"What if we did share?"

I shifted my weight and folded my arms across my chest. "You're serious?"

"Why not? You know I'm not set in my ways, I like branching out, exploring new avenues and passions. And you know I'm not gonna step on you, because I like you leading the way with other things. I'll just follow your lead with this like I do with everything else. Plus, if we bring Mason in on this, it could really help him to finally relinquish that insane control that's slowly killing him. It could help him to let loose like he's needed for a long time."

"I hear what you're saying, brother," I said, laying my hand on his shoulder. "But she's not just a girl to me. There's more here, more I can't get into yet."

"We'll see how it pans out then, take it slow."

"You do realize that she's an actual person? Not a doll to be played with?"

"*I* do, but the fact *you* seem to is shocking to say the least, Lev. It's not your usual way of doing things. You've always been a *hit-it-and-quit-it* type. Those *fight bunnies* were just warm holes for you to get off with."

"I don't think I was ever that crass about it."

"Debatable. But either way, seeing as though you seem to be showing genuine care toward this girl, I'm gonna help you out in any way I can."

"You are?"

"Damn straight, brother. I'm retracting my initial worry about this. I've never seen you like this before. And as long as you can tone down the vicious and *Hellraiser* side of you, this could actually be really good for you. It'll take some of the worry when it comes to you off Mason too, which I'm all for."

"Well, thanks. I really appreciate it."

He stepped close again and fingered my vibrant red and black all-seeing eye tattoo on my left shoulder. "You know, she's got a necklace like this?"

Oh, I was well fucking aware. "She does?"

"Yeah. Weird, huh? The coincidence of it?"

"Uncanny."

He frowned. "You knew, didn't you? Is that why you stripped down to this shirtless state, rather than actually getting dressed for her arrival? You wanted her to see that the two of you have this in common?"

"Anything I can do to ease her skittish state."

"Damn, that's really sweet of you. *Especially* for you."

Sweet. It was far from that. "Well, contrary to popular belief—Mason's included—I am actually human and I can demonstrate that once in a while too."

He laid his hand on my shoulder. "I know you can.

And I'm really glad you're back here with us." He cupped my cheek and emphasized earnestly, "Really glad, Lev."

I stroked his fingers on me. "Right back at you, cupcake."

The sound of the doorbell downstairs by the lobby had us both pulling back.

He adjusted his silky shirt—this time a tiger print number—along with his leather pants, then told me, "The show is on. Here goes nothing."

Thankfully, Mason was occupied elsewhere at some sort of get together with a group of his law buddies who were working on this semester's big project—or case. I hadn't bothered to get the details because my main focus had been this evening and making sure he wouldn't be here to get in my way and especially not to get the chance to figure out what my fascination with Brianna was all about.

I couldn't have that.

He'd find a way to put a stop to it before I even got anywhere with her.

As Colt headed on out of my bedroom, I hung back and sucked in a centering breath, fighting to tamper down the electric anticipation coursing through me with Brianna Walker about to enter our home, with me so close to having it out with her and doing what I'd needed to for so fucking long—pulling her close to me, fucking well binding her to me forevermore.

Just a little while longer.

All I needed to do was wait for Colt to get her into a calm and relaxed state where her walls weren't up and where she wasn't defensive.

I walked out to the landing and peered over the railing as she stepped into the house with Colt speaking words I couldn't hear from this far out.

Her silky black hair was pulled back into a bouncy ponytail that swung from side to side whenever she moved her head and, in this case, scanned the immediate area of the mansion trying to take it all in.

She had that pastel-pink three-quarter-length coat on over a white tank with butterflies lining the bust, dipping low enough to highlight her perky breasts as well as the necklace of hers that was a blue version of my tattoo. It gave way to a gray mini-skirt. The heels of her knee-high boots that matched her coat clacked on the black marble floor.

But, despite all of that being a fuck of a lot to take in, it was her eyes that drew my attention the most.

Those enchanting whiskey pools.

They were what I'd remembered the most about her.

What I'd seen staring back at me all those years ago, what I'd seen staring through me in my dreams and nightmares alike since.

I forced myself to push away from the railing and tracking her movements and guarded interaction with Colt, and then I made my way into my bedroom to fire up the surveillance I had in the recording studio—and wherever else she ended up venturing to while she was here in my home.

———

"I'VE BEEN STANDING in the shadows/ Willing the blackness to pull me in/ A place where nobody else knows/ I'm barely holding on, barely surviving."

Colt's powerhouse vocals rang out, that rough grittiness out in full force with that signature growl along for the ride, and giving him that special edge he'd worked hard to develop and capitalize on over the years.

I'd heard it thousands of times and not just with his live performances, but through him singing around the house, belting out pieces of songs he'd been working on over and over, but it still impressed me.

I thought nothing could top that until another voice joined in on the chorus wrapping around his.

"It was easier not to open my eyes/ It was easier not to feel a thing/ Until you/ You came into my life like a hurricane/ You eased away the pain."

Soft and delicate, yet also somehow notably powerful with a stirring and melancholic feel.

Brianna's voice.

It pulled me out of the moment, off mission, as it rolled through me.

The way it sounded combined with Colt's was out of this world.

The idea of the duet had begun as a farce, as a means to an end—*my* end. But hearing this now, there was absolutely no way it could remain purely as that.

It needed to be the real thing.

It wasn't just the sound either.

No, it was the look on her face, the raw emotion all over her. An odd mixture of vulnerability and ferocity she was somehow able to achieve and communicate all at once.

I was abruptly snapped out of my reverie when she faltered, then stopped singing altogether, stepping back from the mic with a curse.

Colt lifted his headphones off, the corner of his mouth turning up as he told her, "You didn't trust yourself to hit that note. You could've done it, you've got the range."

"Maybe," she said, pulling her headphones off too and stepping away. "Let's take a break. I need some water."

"Sure thing. You hungry too?"

"I could go for a snack. Do you have chocolate chip cookies?"

"Cookies, huh? Yeah, we've got a load to choose from. Mason's got a thing for snacking."

"Great," she said, leaning against the wall and folding her arms across her chest, looking a world away from the confident, caught-in-the-passionate-moment demeanor she'd had a moment ago.

It was pretty much how she had been when he'd first walked her in there. All nervous and out of her element, on edge, even. But a little while after they'd gotten started, all of that had fallen away and she'd come out of her shell.

And in those moments I'd gotten a glimpse of that fireball I remembered.

The one who haunted my dreams.

"You all right?" Colt asked, noticing right away.

When she just gave a slight nod, he told her, "The fact you can't read sheet music and just picked up the melody from me playing it once, then being able to run with it... it's majorly impressive."

"I'm good with patterns."

"Patterns?"

"Yeah, putting bits and pieces together into a whole. Kind of like coding, programming an app and that sort of thing."

I started. Interesting way of looking at it.

"Well, that's fucking awesome," he told her, brimming with excitement. He strolled across the room to her with all that swagger of his. "So, why the long face? Looking so out of sorts? You should be on a high after that performance. I know I am. Singing with you was something else, cutie."

Cutie?

"I need to see him."

"Lev?"

"Yes."

My breath caught in my throat.

Was it really finally happening?

She was actually asking to see me, so desperate to, in fact, that it was causing this noticeable reaction in her?

"Drawing it out is impacting my concentration. *That's* why I didn't hit that note."

"Well, I did promise you a shot. But like I said, when Lev is laser-focused like this, getting him to step back is next to impossible, so I can't guarantee the outcome you're hoping for."

I narrowed my eyes. She wanted me to back off? That was the deal he'd struck with her? He'd told me he'd offered to get her friend some major exposure for her fashion designs. He'd most definitely omitted this part of their deal.

"That's fine," she told him. "I'll handle it from here."

A dark look flitted across her face.

It was very brief, but also very noticeable.

It didn't just soften the blow of her intent to shut me down, it also had my dick reacting in an almost violent way.

That was what had been missing from her during my observations and her activities here that I'd been keeping an eye on for the last year.

And now I had confirmation that it was still there, still a part of her.

Nice.

"Damn, that's some eerie confidence you've got going there. Fucking hot, to be honest."

She rolled her eyes. "Is this you trying to delay so you can figure out how to go back on what you promised?"

"No, cutie," he said, drawing close and literally breathing her in. It had my fingers clenching into fists.

"Just calling it like it is. Credit where credit is due." He reached out and played with a strand of her hair and twirled it around his finger. "You know, blowing him off may not be the best way to go. It'll just antagonize him. Letting it play out is your better option. Go along for the ride. And, believe me, it will be a hell of a ride at that. You'd be missing out on an experience you'll never forget. Lev doesn't do things half way. He'll give you his all."

She stared at him for a moment and it really looked like she was considering easing up with her fight.

But then she blinked and batted his hand away from her hair. "Do you really think I was fool enough to believe it was merely a random coincidence that you invited me here to record this duet? The coincidence of Levi crashing into my path wasn't lost on me for a moment. You brought me here to lull me into a calm state so Levi could then use it to his advantage. You're working together."

I saw Colt looking stumped that she'd figured all of that out, that she'd apparently played him at his own game.

Fortunately, he managed to get it together and recover quickly. "That's quite the theory. And if it's to be believed, why did you agree to come here?"

"To minimize the collateral damage when I cut this weirdness off at its knees before it can go any further. I'm not stupid. I know about *Hex* and the brutality and damage it brought to Stonewell when it was operational, when the three of you were at your most malicious and dangerous. I'm also aware that Levi was the driving force behind that sadistic side of it, while you were just along for the ride, and Mason was trying to control and reel things in."

"Interesting deductions, cutie. The thing is, all that is from an outside perspective. Things aren't always what they seem. I wasn't just *along for the ride*. I can be a vicious fucker when I'm in that zone. And on the flip side, Lev can be the most easygoing fucker around. *Unless* he's provoked. That's when he becomes the bane of your existence."

"Advice duly noted."

"Good." He stepped back. "Now, I'll go get you that water and some chocolate chip cookies." He gestured at the seating area off to the side of the studio, a white wrap-around couch complete with a couple of matching over-sized chairs. "Take a beat and chill before we get back down to it."

With that, he walked out.

I shut my laptop screen, closing down my real-time view inside the room, then stepped away from my desk, absorbing everything that had been spoken between them.

I was so caught up in my thoughts that several minutes went by without me even realizing it, and then Colt was bursting into my room with a plate of chocolate chip cookies balanced on one hand as he clutched a bottle of water in the other.

"All softened up and ready for you, brother," he told me with a sly wink.

"Nicely done," I said, taking the plate and bottle from him. "Although, keeping from me that part of your deal with her included giving her the opportunity to blow me off leaves a lot to be desired."

"Please. It was for your own good. If I'd told you beforehand, before I'd brought her here, you would've done something extreme and ill-advised and it could've fucked everything up."

He knew me well.

"Point noted." I kissed his cheek. "Good work."

Before I could pull away, he grasped my bare shoulder and licked the scar down the left side of my throat, the stud in his tongue rolling over it. "Just helping you get in the zone, Lev," he said with a smirk as he eased away.

Sure that was all it was.

I returned his smirk. "Much appreciated."

As I headed past him, he called out, "Don't scare her off. That duet is on for real now."

"No promises."

"Lev."

I lifted my shoulder. "It depends how she reacts."

"Aren't you the master of determining how others react —always in your favor?"

"Not this time. Not with her."

"Actually, yeah, I'm getting that. Her responses to different provocations are difficult to determine and antici-pate. Woman's more complicated than she seems on the surface with that whole bubbly Barbie thing she's got going on."

"Sure is."

He didn't know the half of it.

Hell, he didn't know a mere fraction of it.

There was a whole lot more than met the eye with Brianna Walker.

And I couldn't wait to immerse myself in it all, in everything that she was.

Be ready for me, Wildflower, because I'm not backing down.

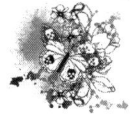

10

~Levi~

"Order up," I spoke as I approached the seating area with her water and snacks in hand.

She was lounging back in the middle of the wrap-around couch, her legs tucked underneath her and an arm slung over the white leather as she played with her hair.

I saw her noticeably tense as I drew close, then put the plate and bottle down on the gold-rimmed glass coffee table in front of her.

Her gaze left me briefly as her attention went to the cookies for a moment.

And when her focus returned to me, a different type of tension took her. She gave herself away as a pink tinge colored her cheeks, while her eyes roamed over my bare chest, taking in every chiseled inch of it, before zeroing in on my all-seeing eye tattoo on my shoulder. Her breath caught in her throat as she obviously recognized it was the exact same design as her necklace, except for the coloring.

She blinked and averted her eyes as though the sight was too much to behold.

I bet it was with all that denial she had going on.

And it was exactly what I'd intended to pull from her.

A shock to her system.

She sucked in a breath, then went to reach for one of the cookies on the plate.

I caught her hand before she could and her gaze snapped to mine.

"Why do you think I have this tattoo that matches the design of your pendant?"

She stared at me for a moment, before answering all matter-of-fact and coldly, "A lot of people have those tattoos."

I scoffed. "You really think you can put it down to a mere coincidence?"

"What else would it be?"

"You know very well."

She snatched her hand back. "All I know is that you had me lured here via Colton under the guise of the duet and helping my friend out as part of the deal, that you think you made some sort of connection to me at that party. So, with that in play, the only deduction I can make is that you've become unduly and very quickly obsessed, you noticed that I wear this necklace all the time, and you had this inked as a result of that obsession."

"It's not freshly inked. Weak try, *Wildflower.*"

"I'm not your wildflower."

I took a seat beside her—right beside her—so that my pants brushed against her bare thighs. "Oh, but you are."

"I'm not your anything," she insisted. "And that's part of the reason I agreed to come here—and to help out Chloe. That's all. To tell you to back off before things go any further and become unpleasant for us both."

"Unpleasant? Hmm, no, we certainly don't want that, do we? Well, you don't. I do well with unpleasantness."

"Is that a threat?"

"I only issue threats when they're absolutely needed. Otherwise they lose all meaning. And they're not going to be needed here, are they, Brianna? You're going to give me what I want now you've had time to digest it all, aren't you?" I sidled closer to her and stroked a finger down her cheek. "You're going to be my good girl, yes?"

A stilted breath escaped her at my touch.

"Well?" I pushed, adding my thumb to the mix and softly stroking her jaw too.

Her eyes fluttered closed for a moment and I could feel her heat, see that need there sparking to life. For *me*.

But then she went to pull my hand away.

I held fast, not allowing it.

"Stop. I'm not…"

"You're not what? A good girl? Well, I do know there's a lot more to you than that."

"Not yours."

I ground my teeth at her continuing to play hardball.

It had me forcing her hand to the side of my neck, right over my scar. "You know where and how this came about. Admit it."

"Stop it," she said, slapping my hand away, then scrambling to her feet.

She snatched the water bottle off the coffee table and screwed off the lid, taking a couple of big gulps as she backed away to the other side of the room.

"You stop it," I snapped.

All my patience, all this time I'd put into this thing, and she couldn't offer up anything in return? No. It was bull-shit. I wasn't having it.

It had me storming over to her, grasping her arms and slamming her up against the wall, crowding her with my body.

"You were there! Six years ago, you were there! Fucking well admit it!"

"Don't push this."

It was both a plea and a warning.

I leaned in closer, breathing at her ear, "I can't let it go. I never have. What you did... what you did for me... it's stayed with me. I've given both of us time to get our shit together, to rebuild after what happened, so the time is ours now."

She trembled as I drew my lips over her throat, breathing her in, tasting her just a little.

Just enough to tide me over and tamper down the rage and pain threatening to clash in a majorly destructive way with her infuriating reactions and denying the very thing that had made me who I was today, denying that fucked-up experience that had changed me forever.

"I remember," she murmured.

I stilled and eased back just enough to look into her eyes.

There was a chilling, haunting look there.

And agony. So much fucking agony.

"You... what?"

"I remember everything."

"You remember *me?*"

"Yes." She sank against the wall, the tension and resistance leaving her as she admitted with a heavy sigh, "I thought denying it would stop you in your tracks. But you're like a dog with a bone. So now I'm telling you the truth, okay? And hopefully that will make you see that we can never have this conversation again. We can never talk about anything at all related to that depraved experience we both lived through." She shoved me back, catching me off guard as her words cut into me. "You need to back off and stay the hell away from me."

"What?"

"That was the worst time of my life. I don't want to think about it. I don't want to relive it. Not with myself and certainly not with you. It's dead to me." She gestured between us. "So, you see? There's nothing here. No connection. I don't feel a thing toward you, so this pursuit of yours, this obsession because of what happened back then, is futile. There's nothing available on my end. It's dead to me." She glared fiercely at me. "And so are you." She brushed past me, "Tell Colt the duet's off. Both of you stay the hell away from me."

"That's not fucking happening."

She spun back. "Living in the past means you'll never be able to build your future. Don't make that mistake. Leave this be."

As she went to throw open the door I was there, slamming it closed and pushing my bare chest into her back, effectively pinning her there.

I grabbed a fistful of her hair and wrenched her head back, making her gasp, as I breathed at her ear, "I've been patient. In fact, I've been really fucking nice, a lot nicer than I usually am. I don't *do* nice and gentle, *Wildflower.* But I made an exception for you. If you choose to go this route, though, if you choose to fight me on this, you'll leave me no choice but to resort to much more unpleasant methods."

"I just told you—"

I slapped my hand over her mouth.

"Shh, baby." I breathed in her sweet coconut scent. That combined with her squirming as I held her still was a hell of an aphrodisiac and it had me grinding my painfully hard cock into her ass through her sexy skirt. She whimpered into my hand, and I saw her eyes flutter closed for a moment. *Mmm.* She was definitely affected.

She slapped her free hand that wasn't holding the water bottle to my thigh, digging her nails into my pants.

And then I felt her push back against me.

Christ.

I ground harder and she moved with me.

I slid my free hand up and under her top, feeling the lace of her bra.

When I snuck two fingers beneath the cup, she jolted against the wall.

Instead of making a move to stop me, she dug her nails harder into my thigh, like she was holding on for dear life and begging for more at the same time.

I slid my fingers over the soft flesh of her breast then rolled her nipple between my fingers and she bucked against me, grinding roughly against my cock.

"Oh God, Levi," she moaned, the sound rolling through me like the sweetest fucking music.

I sucked on her neck, then growled at her ear, "Is this how Tommy touched you? Nah, let me guess, he was really soft and careful with you, treating you like you were breakable, yes?"

She murmured something into my hand.

"What's that?" I asked, removing my palm.

"How do you know about that?"

"I know a lot of things. So, answer me. Was it like that? Too sweet and gentle? I can tell from your reactions to this brief little tease that you don't like it nice and easy. Isn't that right? You've been craving the rough and wild touch of a vicious bastard like me, haven't you? You want to be consumed, utterly owned. But you're also afraid, because you've never met anybody who could understand what you went through back then. Until me. I was there. I *know*, Brianna. And I know how to make it better, to give you what you need without triggering you. You're claustrophobic, yet you haven't reacted negatively to me pinning you up against this wall. Quite the opposite, wouldn't you say?"

"I… I can't," she choked out.

"You already are. I'm certain if I reached under your skirt and dipped my fingers beneath your panties, you'd be soaking wet for me too."

"It's… it's not about *you.* It's just been… it's been a long time. It could be anyone causing these reactions in me."

What. The. Hell?

A dangerous growl escaped me and I ripped my hand from beneath her shirt and ceased rolling my hips for her.

Slapping my hand back over her mouth, I hissed, "*Listen.* Very carefully. I've waited. I've been nice and given you a lot of time, allowed you your freedom. But I'm here now. We're here now together. So if you run, I *will* chase. If you make the wrong choice to fight me, I will chip away at that wall of yours right down to the bedrock. I'll come at you with absolutely no mercy, and I won't fucking stop. It won't be pleasant. I don't want to employ harsher methods, but if you continue to force my hand, I absolutely will. Final warning."

I sucked in a breath and removed my hand, then stepped back. "What will it be, *Wildflower?*"

She turned around slowly, breathing heavily, struggling to get a hold of herself and come down from the heady sensations I'd made her feel.

And then she unscrewed the cap of her water bottle.

Assuming her throat was parched and she was going to soothe it by taking a sip, she instead surprised me as she thrust it forward and poured it all over my face and chest.

I hissed and jerked back as the ice-cold water had me shuddering.

And that was all she needed to make a run for it and burst out of the room.

She was almost through the door when Colt came striding in.

She collided with him, choked from the impact, but managed to shove him aside and bolt away.

"What the shit was that?" he asked me, eyes wide with a whole lot of confusion.

I stared after her and rumbled menacingly, "It means, game on."

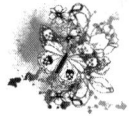

~Brianna~

That bastard had left his mark on me.

In more ways than one.

I dabbed more concealer over the right side of my neck from where he'd sucked on the skin so hard he'd left a very visible hickey.

I could still feel it, still feel him.

His touch.

His warmth.

The intensity that had taken me over when we'd collided.

The thrill as well at the strange ease with which we'd fit together.

The physicality of it hadn't been awkward at all. That was a hell of a thing considering what I was used to in that respect. Because of my issues when it came to being touched sexually it had always been really awkward for the first little while because the guys I'd been with didn't know how to handle that sort of thing. Not even Tommy and he'd been there at the end of that nightmare, he'd been on the team that had burst in to rescue me—and Levi.

Urgh. Because of that asshole bringing all of that up again, I'd been having nightmares like I used to, for the last couple of nights, reliving it over and over again. The exact thing I hadn't wanted, that I'd been guarding against for years.

And with one majorly intense confrontation, he'd ripped all of that right out from under me.

As only he could.

He was the only one who knew, that was why.

The only one who'd experienced it alongside me.

Well, the only one left alive, anyway.

I finished hiding the marks and stepped out of my apartment bathroom just as my phone buzzed on my bed.

I snatched it up, a smile spreading over my face, as I took in the message there.

Chloe: OMG! Thank you! My IG is blowing up! So many messages! So much exposure! You're amazing, sweetie!

Brianna: Just hope it helps with your mom.

Chloe: It's got one hell of a shot. Showing her when she gets home tonight.

Brianna: *crossing fingers emoji*

Chloe: *heart emoji*. TTYL.

I went to put my phone down when something stopped me.

I didn't know what the hell it was.

Maybe the fact that I was out of sorts after barely getting a couple of hours' worth of sleep last night? Maybe that bastard unearthing things I'd thought I'd long buried?

Either way, whatever it was, it had me reading over the texts that had come in from Levi Knight last night—a whole twenty-four hours since I'd poured water all over him before hightailing it out of his swanky mansion.

He'd somehow gotten my number—not just from

Colton. No, he'd actually managed to save his number into my freaking phone!

I'd run one of my security programs to try to determine interference, but it had turned up nothing.

It didn't mean there wasn't any, because obviously for him to have entered in his number there was. What it really meant was much worse—it meant his skills were off the charts. Better than mine.

As if that bastard wasn't dangerous enough without having those abilities.

I mean, I'd known he'd been studying Computer Science at Stonewell U, but not all students had an insane level of hacking ability. It wasn't as though it was a given.

Anyway, I had other ways to determine that sort of thing *and* once I figured out how he'd done it and which methods he'd used, I could then create a program to keep him out in the future.

It was just a matter of time, unfortunately.

For the time being, I'd altered his name in my contact list to something much more appropriate.

I chuckled to myself as I took it in, just before I read over his messages.

Hell Spawn: Still got your marks on my thigh. Is that how you'll grab my cock when the time comes?

Hell Spawn: Keep picturing your little ass grinding back on me. Those sexy whimpers are stuck in my head and on permanent repeat. Next time, you'll give me your screams.

A shudder rolled through me, just like had happened last night.

If only it was merely a shudder of *revulsion*. It would all be so much simpler.

Urgh. Stop looking at it.

I actually deleted both messages, then took in the time.

Crap. I was already running late as it was.

I'd missed my first class. Me? I was always punctual and on top of everything. I took my classes seriously. I knew how fortunate I was that I was actually able to do this and go to college, living my life free in this way, given my tumultuous background and insane upbringing. I didn't take that for granted and I got everything that I could out of it.

But because of those nightmares, I'd ended up sleeping in.

And if I didn't hurry and get in my car within the next ten minutes, I'd end up missing another class too.

I was just about to grab my coat off the hook by the front door, along with my messenger bag, when my phone buzzed again in my hand.

Expecting it to be another quick text from Chloe, I was startled to see that it was *him* again.

Hell Spawn: I know you're reading my messages. I don't like being ignored. If you're too skittish to respond to the fun ones, how about you give me that apology you owe me? You know, for drenching me in ice-cold water?

Seriously?

Brianna: You deserved it. No apology for you.

Hell Spawn: Ah, there you are. Knew you wouldn't be able to resist that one.

Dammit.

Brianna: We're done here then. Stop texting me or I'll block you.

Hell Spawn: That won't stop me.

Brianna: Then your own sense of decency should.

Hell Spawn: Not something I possess.

Brianna: Find yourself another obsession. This is already getting old.

And it was already beginning to impact me.

In ways I didn't want to admit to either.

Hell Spawn: Yeah? Shame, because I'm just getting started.

Brianna: There's nothing here for you and there will never be.

Hell Spawn: The way you reacted to my teasing the other day proved otherwise.

Brianna: Get over yourself. Like I said, it could've been anybody.

Hell Spawn: For someone with so many walls up and wholly intent on self-preservation, you'd think you'd know better than to provoke me.

Brianna: You should worry about provoking me. I've been trying to let you down nicely.

Hell Spawn: Because you don't want any trouble.

Brianna: I don't.

Hell Spawn: Too late. I gave you a choice. You chose wrong.

Brianna: You think you can bully me, you've got another thing coming.

Hell Spawn: There it is. That's the side of you I've been waiting on. Come out and play, Wildflower, then we can dispense with all this bullshit you're pushing me to employ.

Brianna: You don't scare me.

Hell Spawn: I'm not trying to.

Brianna: These threats would indicate otherwise.

Hell Spawn: Not threats. Promises.

Brianna: What exactly is your strategy here?

Hell Spawn: To inundate you.

Brianna: With you?

Hell Spawn: Me. The version of you that's been left behind. Our shared past. All of it that you've been trying to foolishly bury.

Brianna: Don't do this. I can't.

Hell Spawn: You need to. You'll recognize it soon enough.

Brianna: You do this and you'll regret it.

Hell Spawn: See? I'm already making strides. There's my girl.

Brianna: Not your girl.

Hell Spawn: Watch this space.

"Argh!" I yelled, smashing my fist into the wall by the door.

Then I shoved my phone into my bag and stormed out of my apartment.

IMMERSING myself in what I enjoyed and what I was also damn good at was really helping to take the edge off the other insanity.

Granted, it had taken years of practice and constant learning, as well as keeping up with developments to bring this about. But now I was at a point where it was most definitely my jam.

It was why, even with barely any sleep, I was still able to kick ass in my coding lab and even push ahead of where we were expected to be at this early stage of this new academic year.

I finished typing the last piece of code, then ran the program to test it.

Perfect.

No bugs.

It was doing everything it was intended to do, and it was doing it well. I'd made sure of it.

Despite this... setback... with Levi, then Chloe being on the verge of slipping away too, at least I still had the stability of this. And it was exactly what I needed to throw myself into.

My career path.

My future.

I continued working away, the sound of the rapid clacking of fingers flying across keyboards filling the room, one of my favorite sounds. It had a sweet, meditative-like effect on me.

I was fully immersed and in the zone, enjoying every moment of the work, the challenge before me.

So much so that I startled when Professor Martina Ruiz came up on my side.

I jolted and looked up to see her studying my screen. Her dark curls were cascading about her face and brushing the collar of her sleek pastel-blue pantsuit.

"An impressive solution to the problem you were given," she praised. "Intricately coded too."

"Thanks," I said, smiling up at her. "It's getting there."

"It's far more than that. You're first up to share with the lab."

"I am?" This was a far cry from last year where I'd run into problems and been admonished for my code not being clean, for it being written in an overly complicated way that had only been readable to me. Over the summer I'd spent a lot of time working on that. Although it seemed like a small issue, when it came to the bigger picture, it could actually become a major one when you got into creating larger programs with pages upon pages of code. I'd actually learned that the hard way when I'd tried to create my first app.

It just showed how far I'd come that now I was being asked to present my code first. Usually when we had one of these show-and-tell coding mini-presentations, I was near the last up and everyone had tons of notes for me.

"Absolutely," Professor Ruiz confirmed, smiling.

I couldn't believe it.

I pushed out of my seat and grabbed my laptop, taking it with me as I walked up to the front of the massive lab full of almost forty students, and set about connecting my laptop to the HDMI cable so my screen could be displayed on the big screen at the forefront of the room.

"Out-of-the-box thinking can go a long way," I heard the professor saying, as I got ready. "Pay attention to the novel workaround Brianna has found to the problem I provided for you all to overcome."

As my code appeared, I was about to start walking them through my reasoning when something suddenly flashed on my screen.

What the—

In the next moment, an audio file started playing of its own accord.

A chill ran down my spine as Levi Knight's voice emanated.

"You're going to be my good girl, yes?"

"Oh God, Levi."

"You don't like it nice and easy. Isn't that right? You've been craving the rough and wild touch of a vicious bastard like me, haven't you? You want to be consumed, utterly owned."

It was from our encounter in the recording studio at his place the other day.

No. No.

He hadn't even distorted his voice or anything.

Of course not. He wanted people to know—or to believe—that I was his.

While embarrassing me at the same time.

Well, *embarrassing* me didn't even cover it.

It was absolutely humiliating.

"Oh God, Levi."

"I'm certain if I reached under your skirt and dipped my fingers beneath your panties, you'd be soaking wet for me too."

"Oh God, Levi."

Those three words kept playing over and over, my breathy, turned on voice blaring out into the lab for all the students to hear.

I felt my cheeks heating—more like on fire—as I scrambled in a major panic to locate the source to shut it down.

Professor Ruiz ran over and pulled out the HDMI cable, but the recording could still be heard.

"I'm so sorry, I don't know how—I'm being set up and—"

"I'm getting that," she said, kindly.

I muted the volume, then slammed my laptop lid shut.

An awful silence filled the room and I looked out into wide-eyed expressions, some students laughing into their hands to hide their amusement, and others giving me the eye and clearly having enjoyed the sexual content of that way too much.

I cursed under my breath and then it was all a blur as I snatched up my laptop and rushed back to my chair, grabbed my bag, then ran out of the room like my ass was on fire.

12

~Mason~

I stepped out of the shadows as the girl ran away down the hallway like a bat out of hell.

Her hot-pink heels clacked loudly as she went, the strappy things matching her wrap dress that had a striking studded gold belt that gave it a rocker-type edge, something I remembered seeing in the IG pictures Colt had recently blasted all over the place—an accessory design courtesy of Chloe Anders.

The girl was really going out of her way to get her friend attention, even now taking to wearing her designs around campus too.

That whole situation had appeared more than just a little strange to me when Colt had filled me in on why Brianna had agreed to come to our home and record with him.

The timing was particularly suspicious.

I was certain it hadn't come about on its own, that Chloe wasn't being urged to leave Stonewell University just by sheer coincidence.

No, it reeked of interference.

Interference from a certain someone.

And that same certain someone had been far too giddy this morning for me not to take notice.

He only got like that when a plan of his was about to come to fruition.

So, I'd first suspected him attempting to do something with *Hex* in a bid to take the wheel without my knowledge —and thereby fuck up things before it had even begun since we'd revived it.

When I'd managed to rule that out, it had led me to the girl he'd been suspiciously fixated on.

Fortunately, during some fooling around wherein I'd had Colt's lovely cock stuffed down my throat, he'd been very chatty as usual, and he'd ended up telling me all about the plan Lev had pulled him in on to bring Brianna to the house, which had ended with her running off after dousing Lev with a bottle of water.

I'd attempted to access the surveillance from the recording studio because Colt hadn't been privy to the interaction between them, but it had been corrupted. By Lev and his talents in that arena, no doubt.

He hadn't wanted either of us to know what had been said—or what he'd done to her.

That escalating suspicion and rapidly rising concern had led me here today, to her class.

I'd been watching the entire thing and I'd witnessed her ruined presentation.

It was more than a mild and intriguing attraction on his end now toward her.

The fact that he'd orchestrated that pointed to full-on obsession.

And when Levi Knight became obsessed with something, it invited a whole lot of chaos.

Talking him down or interfering in a reactive way wouldn't counter it or be able to stop it.

I knew him far better than to believe that.

No, it required a proactive approach.

But to be able to implement that, I first needed to determine the true root cause for his fixation.

I pulled out my phone and dialed Chase Arlington, the football captain I now had under my thumb. He was the heir to an oil tycoon, a billionaire who possessed a great deal of power and influence.

My father represented many just like him with his infamous law firm, *Honor Hall Law*, but fortunately, Atticus Arlington wasn't one of them. He was outside my father's usual circles, which meant my father wouldn't be able to register what I was about to do. I could keep it off his radar.

"Mason," Chase answered. "What's up?"

"Time for the start of your service to *Hex.*"

"All right," he responded nervously. "What do you need?"

"Put me in contact with your father's PI."

"That guy's really hard to get a hold of, Mason."

"Then you'd better get on it. ASAP. Set up a meet between us just outside Stonewell. No details are to go through our phones or any devices. Relay the meet information to me in person."

"Sure, yeah, I'll handle it."

"Good boy."

I hung up and pocketed my phone in my jeans.

Time to discover what skeletons Brianna Walker had hiding in her closet and, more importantly, what had Levi believing they paired so well with his.

"Mason!"

I spun around to see Colt rushing down the hallway to my left.

He was wearing that studded leather jacket of his that was a masterclass in bling in itself, along with that cropped white tank that clung deliciously to his pecs. As if that wasn't enough, he was also rocking those tight-as-sin ripped blue jeans that did incredible things for his hot little ass.

"Did you get my texts?" he asked, breathing harshly when he slowed his run to a stop right in front of me.

I dropped my voice low so the few people passing by couldn't hear. "Let's see, was it that text you sent me while I was eating my Cheerios this morning asking me if I could still taste your cum on my tongue and if it was better than adding boring ol' milk to my bowl? Or could it be the one begging me to finger you in my Porsche in the parking lot between classes?"

He grinned. "Hot, huh?"

"That's not the word I'd use to describe it."

How many times had I told him not to send me provocative texts during a weekday when I needed to focus on my classes? Too fucking many.

He reached out to touch me and I instinctively jerked back out of his reach.

Dammit.

The hurt all over his face cut into me like a dozen knives all at once.

"I'm sorry. When we're in public it's just—"

"It's a reflex, I get it. It's okay," he said, forcing a smile.

The urge to make it better properly so that his smile would be genuine and not just put on in a bid to push beyond the awkwardness of it, was right there.

To touch him in public, to show him the affection he

deserved, to show him that our relationship wasn't a dirty little secret to me... I knew that was the way to fix it.

But I just... I couldn't do it.

I couldn't push past that wall that I'd erected long ago, that I'd been shamed into erecting.

And the longer it was there, the more impossible it seemed to tear down.

There had been a time a couple of years back, but that had all gone to hell when my father had found out about it. He'd held a certain something over my head, something he'd covered up for us five years ago. It had been his power play ever since to keep me in line. It had also cost me my desired career as a tattoo artist, and forced me into Law instead.

I hadn't realized until Lev had come back just how much I'd given up on escaping the restrictions enforced by Peter Hall. I guess that was why I hadn't resisted when it came to reviving *Hex*. It was a way to reclaim power.

Or at least, a way to begin to.

I sucked in a breath and scrubbed my hand over the rough stubble on my chin. "So, what text were you talking about anyway?"

"The one asking you to throw your weight around as leader of *Hex* to make your professor allow me into your contracts class, the one that's focused on Entertainment Law right now?"

"This is about *Mythic Cry* again?"

"Yeah."

"What's happened this time?"

He'd been having issues with his band lately. While it was technically made up of three members—Colt as frontman and on lead guitar, Flynn Borman as bass guitar, and Will Matthews as drummer—all people saw was Colton. His stage presence completely eclipsed them and left them in the dust and they'd grown irritated with it, which had led to some trouble.

"I made the mistake of playing them a portion of that duet I recorded with Brianna, and they're now up in arms that they weren't a part of it. Even explaining that the song was just in the experimental stage didn't quell their upset. And now they're talking about contracts and renegotiating, wanting more power over our catalogue—songs *I* wrote alone. They even want to dictate shows, what we perform, how we perform, and where. Flynn is even talking about splitting up lead vocals with me. I mean, you've heard his nasally voice, right? It would completely alter the sound of *Mythic Cry*—in a shit-tastic way."

"I know, I hear you. We'll fix it. Now, you're going to cover this sort of thing in your Music Marketing degree program, but that won't be until next year from what you've shown me of your syllabus. So, yes, you can sit in on my class. And I'll also help you however I can."

"The professor will let me sit in? Just like that?"

"In this case, yes."

He eyed me curiously. "How? You already have her in your pocket?"

"I needed somebody with esteemed expertise in a certain area."

"A certain *legal* area you mean?"

"Yes."

"It's about your dad? You're up to something?"

"Think of it more like me acquiring my proverbial army."

"And how is she in your pocket? *Hex* has been inactive for the last year plus."

"I fucked her a couple of times."

His eyes widened. "Hold up. You and Professor Litman? Or as most of us call her, *Hot Hannah?*"

I rolled my eyes. "Terribly original, Colt."

"*I* didn't coin it. But, shit, Mason. You know she's married, right?"

"She's actually divorced now."

"After you two screwed around?"

"It was just a coincidence."

"The hell it was. Well, it's no surprise given the power of your magical cock."

"There are other ways to persuade people other than using violence, blackmail, and dangerous diabolical methods."

"Don't let Lev hear you say that."

I chuckled. "Come on, let's get to class. We've got seven minutes to get to the other side of campus." As we started to walk, I told him, "In the meantime, I'd get that duet completed and recorded before Flynn and Will try to get their hands on that too. Release it separately from the band. It'll be a backup."

"As part of going solo."

"If you have to in the meantime should things turn even more sour."

"Kind of hard to do since Brianna left our place in a hurry. I've texted her and she's shut me down, even telling me to *go to hell* a couple of times too."

"That cute little thing used those words?"

"She might be cute on the outside, but there's more to her than meets the eye, Mason. She's got a harsher edge when she's pushed a little."

Interesting.

"What?" he asked. "What is it?"

I must've failed to keep the concern from my face, given how intensely he was reacting.

"Lev pushed her today. Hard."

"So you think I should now back off with the duet?"

"The opposite. Just approach her… gently."

He smiled. "Got you."

"And do it at the recording studio on campus. Not at the house."

"You know what it's like booking that thing in advance."

"*Hex* is back now, don't forget. I'll see to it for you. You just reach out to the girl."

"Okay, yeah. Thanks, Mason."

"No problem."

Talk about killing two birds and all that.

Perfect.

This would give Colt what he needed while also antagonizing Levi, which would enable me to determine a whole lot more about his plans and intentions regarding this Brianna. Meanwhile, I'd also have somebody looking deeply into her background to put the whole picture together.

And then I'd be in a position to stop this shitshow from getting completely out of hand.

I'd have the means to rein Levi in.

Again.

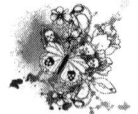

13

~Brianna~

That was how he'd done it.

The bastard had written a script on my system that had caused the audio file to play after a few seconds' delay once I'd connected my laptop to a HDMI cable—basically when he knew I was going to be in presentation mode.

Piece of shit.

It had taken me a couple of hours once I'd arrived home to locate the hidden file and erase it from my system.

Hours that could have been better spent studying and learning.

I'd already lost the rest of the day because of the humiliation of it all and left campus immediate afterward, missing three classes.

The idea of going back there tomorrow after this was mortifying.

But if that asshole thought I was just going to take this lying down, he had another thing coming.

He wanted the part of me that had been *lost along the way* then he was going to get it.

Just not in the way he intended.

So after I'd determined the source of his interference, I'd then spent the rest of my time honing in on *him* through his hack into *my* system.

The guy was good. He had many failsafes in place. Firewalls didn't even begin to cover it.

Fortunately, this wasn't exactly my first rodeo.

I'd delved into network security—or the reverse—for years after that awful nightmare that had destroyed my life. It had been my way of trying to take back control of things.

I hadn't touched it in a long while.

That didn't mean the skills weren't still there, though.

And he was about to pay the price.

"Whoop!" I cried, throwing my hands in the air as I finally managed to breach his system.

And then I sank back against my chair in the kitchen and watched as the worm I'd programmed went to work eating its way through his hard drive and decimating the thing to fucking nothing.

My stomach rumbled as I watched in sadistic satisfaction.

That was when I realized that I'd just immediately sat down and opened up my laptop about six hours ago and I hadn't moved from the kitchen since. I hadn't even taken my coat off.

Well, I had time now.

I pushed out of my chair, intending to make a sandwich—a new recipe I'd been looking forward to with cheese, ham and slices of apple—when my phone buzzed on the table top.

Picking it up, I was startled when I saw it was him.

Hell Spawn: Nice try. Color me impressed, baby.

Brianna: No idea what you're talking about.

Hell Spawn: Your denial is pointless. You think I don't have things in place to notify me of any breaches?

Brianna: I guess your detection is shit and slow on the draw.

Hell Spawn: Because your worm is tearing through my system as we text?

Brianna: Aww, payback's a bitch, huh?

Hell Spawn: It's a decoy hard drive.

I jolted.

Brianna: You're lying.

Hell Spawn: Nope. You're not the first to try something like this.

"Shit," I ground out.

Hell Spawn: In your haste to get at me, you didn't protect yourself either. You've given me the means to redirect your attack and wipe out your entire system. Fortunately, I'm in a good mood and not looking to do permanent damage to all that impressive work of yours— all those next-gen apps you've so painstakingly created. So we'll just chalk this up to a lesson you've learned. That lesson being that you can't usurp me. You can't stop me. You're just wasting energy trying to prevent the inevitable. You and me, Wildflower.

"Argh!" I yelled, slamming my fist down on the kitchen table, my laptop rocking from the force of it.

In the midst of my fit of rage, another text came in.

Colton: Please consider finishing the duet with me. It can be away from Lev. Just need a few more hours. I'm at Nirvana tonight bartending. Come by and we can arrange a time, talk.

I frowned. And not just because of the jarring difference in temperaments and approaches between him and Levi.

Brianna: Thought you just performed there.

Colton: That's because you spent most of the summer working your sweet little ass off in your apartment on those apps.

Brianna: You think I have a sweet ass?

Colton: Damn, you're actually flirting with me, cutie.

Brianna: I am.

Colton: Keep it coming, I'm all for it.

Brianna: I'll be at the bar in a few. See you.

Colton: You still drinking those Strawberry Chocolate Martinis? Or was that just a one-off for that karaoke night with your friend?

Brianna: They're my go-to.

Colton: I'll start mixing it now then.

Brianna: Thanks.

Colton: Looking forward to seeing you.

I scoffed as I put my phone down and rose to my feet. I bet he was. But not out of actually wanting to see me, nor even because of the duet, but because of whatever plan he and Levi had cooked up now.

Levi coming at me harshly and Colton coming at me so nicely… it was an obvious play they'd concocted to try to throw me off base. Maybe like before having Colton lull me into a false sense of security before Levi struck hard.

They really took me for a fool if they thought I was going to fall for that again.

The first time, I'd only allowed it because of my intent to head into the lion's den to get Levi off my scent without causing a whole thing.

That option was over and done with now.

No more nice and polite approach.

They'd already fired the first shot.

I wasn't going to let them get a second one in.

At least not without doing some damage myself.

Time to hit back.

111

⊏⊐

I WATCHED COLTON'S FIRM, sculpted ass moving in his black leather pants that were basically painted onto his skin. He had a skull and crossbones scarf looped through the belt, the way it was falling at the front highlighting a particular attribute. The way he moved was so sleek and fluid, like a jungle cat—a puma, maybe. He had a metallic silver tank on that was partially sheer and both of his tattoo sleeves were in full view.

I hadn't allowed myself to notice it so much before because I'd been so worried about the Levi bullshit, but... hot damn... he was really something.

I forced myself to look away and I focused on my surroundings instead.

The place was a multicolored neon heaven, the bar stools, the tables, even the fairy lights hanging around the edges of the window frames green, pink, orange neon. Everything was bright and bold and edgy—perfect for a college haunt.

He finished serving a group of girls, flashing them a movie-star-worthy smile, then came back to me and leaned up against the bar again, shoving his elbow onto the bar top and resting his head in his palm in a relaxed yet flirty way. "So, have you made your decision about the duet yet, cutie?"

"Maybe you haven't plied me with enough alcohol yet."

"I definitely haven't. That's still your first and you're only halfway through it after a whole twenty minutes of you being here."

Yeah, I needed to keep my wits about me.

"Aww, my bad."

He grinned. "You know, I don't think I need to be

doing that, considering I've caught you checking out my ass several times when I was serving customers."

I brought my glass to my lips to hide my guilty reaction and took my time having a sip.

He kept his gray eyes on me the entire time in playful challenge, cocking an eyebrow expectantly for my confirmation.

When I put the glass down, I gave it back to him, "As if I haven't caught you staring at my boobs too many times to count."

He slapped his hand over his heart. "I'm wounded, cutie. That's such a pessimistic way of looking at it. I was merely admiring that dress." He gestured at my pink and black glitter mini-dress with the flared sleeves that I'd paired nicely with a pair of knee high black studded boots.

"Well, it is definitely worth admiration," I jested.

"The way you wear it is where the admiration's at."

"Wow, you're laying it on thick. You really want this duet, huh?"

"I do, but it's not just about that."

I cocked a highly skeptical eyebrow.

"Nah, I like you. You're growing on me with our every additional interaction."

"That's high praise, especially when you have a whole campus worth of fans available to you. It doesn't exactly fit with your *Maverick* moniker either."

"Well, you're one of the few who's talked with me like I'm actually a human being and not some fake fantasy they usually only tend to see. It's either the *Maverick* thing or the frontman of *Mythic Cry* rockstar dream they see."

I frowned. That was… heartbreaking.

"It seemed like you reveled in all of that."

"It might sound like bullshit, but it's my music that I revel in, losing myself in it when I'm songwriting or letting go up on stage. The rest... the admiration... it can be nice in small doses, of course. I know how to work it. But keeping up that image all the time... it gets a little much." He shrugged. "But who am I to complain? It's a small price to pay for success, right?"

"In a way, but it doesn't mean you have to settle for a life you don't entirely want. I didn't."

"No?" he asked, looking all curious.

I took a sip from my drink, then told him, "I reinvented myself and now I'm a far cry away from what I grew up with." I blew out a breath. "And I'm trying to keep it that way, despite some stubborn interference."

"Lev."

"You didn't even need to ask, huh?"

"No, cutie. Like I told you, when he gets a target in his sights, he doesn't stop. It's just hella weird that it's a person this time and not just a goal or an injustice of some sort." He studied me intently. "There's something about you that he can't let go of. It's crossing into obsession. Bad for all of us. Especially Mason."

"Mason? Your elusive third?"

"He's not that elusive. He just tends to keep to himself. He's not the in-your-face type like Lev and me are."

"He's not down with Levi's antics then?"

"Let's just say, he's not a fan of chaos. He likes to keep things in line. And doing that with Lev, especially when he's in one of his obsessive modes, isn't exactly easy."

Noted.

"You telling me this means you didn't actually call me here *for* Levi then?"

"What? No."

"It wasn't another joint operation between you like before to get me to the mansion?"

He pushed off the bar and held up his hands. "No, I

swear. It was about the duet and… you know… getting to hang a little with you too."

Oh crap.

My phone chirped and I rummaged in my fuzzy purse and pulled it out to see that the program I'd been running since I'd walked in here had now completed.

"Is that a text?" Colton asked. "Him harassing you again?"

No. It was another way to turn the tables on that bastard.

Unfortunately, when I'd thought Colton had been working with him again, I'd considered it fair game to use him to achieve it.

I'd hacked into his phone and planted something on there that, when it came within a few feet of Levi's, would give me access to his GPS, so I could track him wherever he went—no more surprises.

"No. Not this time."

"Chloe?"

I shook my head. "I haven't heard back from her since she thanked me for the IG thing that you pulled off."

He smiled. "Yeah, she thanked me too. My inbox was blowing up for hours with her gratitude."

I laughed. "Sounds like her."

"You must be lonely without her here. If you want—"

"Lonely? Nah," an irritatingly familiar voice sounded a moment before Levi was there sliding onto a stool to my left beside me. "Not lonely, are you, Brianna?"

I ground my teeth. "What the hell are *you* doing here?"

"Wasn't me," Colton said quickly, before glaring at Levi. "Come on, brother, give the girl a break."

"A break?" Levi responded with a noticeable edge.

"Yeah, I heard about the shit you pulled in her class earlier."

"Hmm. Makes me sound like an asshole, doesn't it?"

"Honestly, yeah. What's going on, brother?"

"Same question," Levi said, glaring back at him.

"Just working and chilling every few minutes here with her to keep her company."

"And how did she come to be here, hmm?"

Colton rolled his eyes. "Obviously you already know. Read my texts again."

"Ding ding. Right on the money, cupcake."

"Then you'll know I asked her down here to talk about finishing the duet. Something that you've made a hell of a lot harder with what you've been up to."

"And something that wouldn't have happened at all if it wasn't for my suggestion."

"Jeez, you need to chill. Big time, *Hellraiser*." Colton laid his hand over Levi's on the bar top and I watched curiously as he stroked his fingers softly. To my utter surprise, I saw some of the tension leave Levi's shoulders, his jaw unclenching too. "Vodka neat?" Colton asked after he noticed it too.

"Yeah, all right. Thanks."

As Colton headed off to take care of the order, I took in Levi out of the corner of my eye as I sipped at my drink.

He wasn't wearing the usual black hoodie and cargo pants that I'd come to think of as his uniform.

Instead, he was clad in a pair of black jeans with a bold red zig-zagging design down the legs that matched with the V-neck muscle tee he had on that was clinging a little too appealingly to his basically carved-from-stone torso. I had to blink away images of seeing it in all its glory a few days ago. His curly hair was wilder than usual—crazier. There was days' old stubble covering his jaw and he rubbed his hand roughly over it back and forth, something it appeared he was doing to try to calm down a little more.

Suddenly, his striking pale blue eyes snapped to mine.

"Colt doesn't spend more than a few minutes talking to an outsider. Unless he's fucking them."

"An outsider?" I asked, ignoring that last part.

"Anyone who's not me or Mason. Means he likes you."

"And that's why you're pissed?"

"I was until I realized something as I observed the two of you while I was distracting you with some bullshit arguing."

"You're another level of manipulative, you know that?"

"I can be if it proves necessary. And I told you, you're making it necessary."

I rolled my eyes. "And what is it that you supposedly realized?"

The corner of his mouth turned up. "That him liking you is actually an asset."

"In what sense?" I asked, worriedly. Really worriedly when I saw that creepy glint in his eye quickly follow.

"To me with you, of course."

"What?"

"You're comfortable with him. Rare for you with a man."

"You don't know—"

"Vodka neat," Colton's voice came as he returned and slid a glass across to Levi, who caught it easily in his palm, then snatched it up and took a couple of large gulps.

"Mmm, top shelf. Nicely done. Appreciated, cupcake."

Colton beamed at his praise and gratitude.

That was an interesting dynamic.

"You two seem... peaceful," Colton said, looking between us.

"On the surface," I couldn't stop myself from biting back as I glared at Levi.

He smirked at me. "You like me being the asshole,

huh? Lets you keep the innocent princess title. It's a real shame, because we both know you're a whole lot more than that." He leaned in and grasped my hand on the bar top, making me jolt at the searing contact as the warmth of his skin burned into mine. "You think you're living your best life, but you're only standing in the shadow of it because of what you've closed off, what you've tried to bury."

I went to pull my hand away, but he held fast. "If you don't let yourself acknowledge the pain, the wounds will never heal."

Our gazes burned into one another's as his words hit home in an intense way that had me frozen into inaction for several moments.

"What pain?" Colton asked, thankfully cutting through the weird and overwhelming moment. "Something else you did?" he demanded of Levi.

"No, so don't get your skintight leather pants in a bunch, cupcake." Levi sucked back more of his vodka, right down to the last drop actually. Then he pushed it away and said, "As for me being painted as the asshole here, let's clear that up, shall we?"

"Oh, jeez," Colton breathed.

Undeterred, Levi shifted on his stool to face me head-on. "How about you being completely dismissive of me? Unappreciative of my efforts to make sure our first encounter was comfortable for you and that you were put at ease? Unappreciative of the pleasure I gave you at a slow and easy pace? Then dumping ice-cold water on me for my efforts too. Then let's not forget you trying to completely wipe out my hard drive in a vicious attack."

"Wow, that's… you two have certainly been going at it," Colton commented.

"And because it's not in the way you want, *asshole*, you

keep coming at me," I bit at Levi. "The texts. Leaking that audio to my entire class during my presentation and fucking humiliating me."

"You shouldn't be embarrassed, that breathy voice of yours as you cried out *'Oh God, Levi'* was the sexiest thing I've ever heard."

"You piece of—" I grabbed the umbrella out of my drink and went to jab it at him, but he caught my wrist before it could make contact.

"Love the fire," he said, like he'd planned the entire thing from start to finish in order to get this exact reaction from me. "Keep it up."

"If you continue like this, *you* won't be keeping it up ever again."

Colton let out a low whistle. "Damn."

I yanked my hand free of Levi's and pushed off my stool, shrugging my bag on over my shoulder. "I'm headed to the bathroom." I told Colton, "If you're inundated when I get back, just text me some times when the recording studio is free—on campus only—and we'll finish the song." His eyes lit up, but I turned away and glared at Levi. "As for you, don't be here when I get back. And stay the hell away from me going forward."

"And like I've now told you repeatedly, no can do."

Urgh.

I turned my back feeling their eyes on me as I went.

I pushed my way through the crowded bar and all the revelry taking place all around me.

It seemed like a metaphor for my life.

Never quite able to be a part of it, always holding back, always feeling like I needed to, that it was the only way I could actually be.

"You think you're living your best life, but you're only standing in the shadow of it."

Damn him and his relentless bullshit.

He was starting to get inside my head.

And not just there either.

This was becoming a serious problem.

Him touching me—even if it was just my hand—really hadn't helped matters.

And those enthralling blue eyes of his burning so intensely into mine just added a whole other level to it all.

It was why I'd excused myself claiming I needed the bathroom.

What I had really needed was to take a beat in order to get a fucking grip.

———

I STEPPED out of the bathroom after spending what had amounted to fifteen whole minutes just leaning against the stall wall trying to get myself in check and trying to figure out how to stop Levi and take him down without giving him what he wanted and letting him break what I'd worked so hard to create.

A new me.

A new life where the past simply didn't exist to me at all.

But every time I came into contact with him, even via text, I felt him smashing up against that and trying to tear it all down.

That was why, as I went to peer around the corner back at the main area of the bar, I stopped myself.

While it had actually been nice to hang out with Colton and have somebody to talk to and everything with Chloe still away, there was too much baggage there for it to be more than an one-off. And I didn't want to risk facing off with Levi again.

I couldn't trust myself with him.

"You've never met anybody who could understand what you went through back then. Until me. I was there. I know, *Brianna. And I know how to make it better, to give you what you need without triggering you."*

Those words of his had been haunting me ever since he'd spoken them in hot words at my ear.

Because, as much as I really wanted to deny it and just shake them off, they were true.

All too true.

And I didn't want them to be.

I didn't want that to be the case at all.

It couldn't be.

Shaking my head vehemently as if that could dispel it all, I spun and rushed out through the rear emergency exit.

Thankfully, as I stepped out into the back alley it was well-lit just like the rest of Stonewell tended to be at night. Probably with it being a college town. In a bid to help out drunk college students milling about at night and trying to find their way home.

I made it halfway down the alley, taking the roundabout route to the parking lot where I'd left my Charger, when that comfort was suddenly ripped away.

The lights went out.

A chill ran down my spine and I felt that familiar panic start to rise.

No. No. Stop.

I blinked a few times, both in an effort to try to push it away and to also acclimate my vision to the sudden darkness.

I was able to see my way forward. Just not anything else around me.

I continued walking, hurrying my pace.

And that was when I heard it.

Footsteps.

Heavy footsteps moving at a determined pace.

Adrenaline pulsed, reverberating through me.

Just keep walking. You're being paranoid.

Of course I was. It was just my terror of the dark skewing things.

I was just starting to spiral. It wasn't real.

I forced myself to remain calm even as the adrenaline didn't dissipate and, instead, started to climb, making my hands shake with it.

I turned the corner, going the opposite route to the parking lot, this way leading to nothing. Whoever was behind me should then pass right on by, then I could relax and come out, and not be in a highly-strung state by the time I reached my car and needed to drive.

I squinted through the dark, the faint glow of moon high in the sky providing just enough light for me to see a shrouded figure nearing the corner I'd just taken.

My breath caught in my throat when they slowed down instead of continuing on.

And then they turned, coming the same way I had.

Coming toward me.

I used the darkness and shadow to my advantage, ducking into a slight alcove and flattening my back against it.

They were actually following me.

It was a fact now, not merely a paranoid delusion.

As my anxiety threatened to take the wheel and make me useless and likely freeze up, I channeled the adrenaline into something else altogether.

I focused it into strategizing, into what needed to be done.

I also reminded myself that I had the skillset to defend myself and to dispose of a threat. I wouldn't let myself freeze up and compromise that. I wouldn't let fear rule me.

I wouldn't let it hurt me.

Not anymore.

I was sick of it.

So fucking sick of it.

The heavy footsteps drew closer.

Closer. Closer.

As soon as the figure was within reach, I struck, snatching their arm, using it as leverage to yank them into me as I bent at a ninety-degree angle, then used their weight combined with the momentum to haul them over my shoulder.

Satisfaction surged through me as the stalker landed with a brutal thud on the unforgiving concrete, grunting as the wind was knocked out of them.

It had taken me ages to learn that move and I'd only employed it once in a real life fight prior to now.

I didn't have too long to bask in the success of it and the power I felt as a result, I needed to incapacitate the offender quickly before they were able to recover.

Pouncing, I straddled them, driving my knee brutally between their legs, feeling my knee cap grinding into a hard cock. He grunted again as I brutalized his balls in the process too.

I used the opportunity to pin his hands down with one of mine against his chest, digging my nails into his palm.

Then I reared back with my free hand to deliver a knockout blow to his temple.

I never made contact.

My wrist was snagged before the blow could land.

"Impressive."

Panting and hopped up on adrenaline and a whole lot else with everything having moved so quickly it had basically been a blur, it took me a moment to match the voice to the man.

I shoved his low-hanging hood with my other hand, pulling it from his face.

"Dammit. Levi."

"Hey, *Wildflower*."

I slapped his chest. "What the hell are you doing?"

"Me? Just innocently walking to the parking lot when a sexy thing jumped me."

"Bullshit. The lot is the other way. You were stalking me."

"I just wanted to make sure you got home safe."

I scoffed. "You're really trying to paint yourself as some chivalrous gentleman?"

"Is that really so hard to imagine?"

Was this guy for real? "Yes," I ground out.

"Before we get into this, you mind moving your knee?"

I looked down to see that one of my knees was still shoved between his legs, while I had the other bearing down on his ribs. "My bad, does that hurt?" I couldn't help taunting.

After everything he'd done, he was damn lucky this was the extent of it. So far.

"It's slightly bothersome."

He was barely showing it, just the slight tightness of his jaw giving away that he was actually feeling any pain.

I applied more pressure, shoving harder. "Better?"

"Last chance."

"In case you hadn't noticed, I'm the one with the upper hand here. You're not in a position to demand anything."

"You don't think so, hmm?"

"No. Not to mention, you absolutely deserve it."

"Debatable."

"The hell it is."

"Don't make me use unpleasant methods again. You didn't like the last time I took it there."

"You—"

My words turned to a squeal as he executed a series of lightning-fast moves that broke my grip, forcing me onto my side, where he then hauled me to my feet and ran me into the brick wall.

I choked from the severe winding sensation of the jarring movements as he closed in around me, crowding me against the wall with his knees trapping my legs and one hand wrapped threateningly around my throat.

"I did warn you," he said, off my stunned reaction. "Yet, once again, you chose the hard way." He studied me up close. "I'm starting to think you like it that way. Harsh and heavy-handed, being dominated by me. Is that how you want it, Brianna? Is that the only way you can let go?"

"You're sick," I rasped against the constricting grip he had around my throat.

"Oh, baby, don't kink shame."

"It's not a kink. Not for me."

"Don't be so sure."

When I went to throw another biting response at him, he tightened his hold around my throat, then leaned in and whispered hauntingly at my ear, "When the lights went out, did you see the demons?"

Oh my God.

"Is that… is that what you call them?"

"Yeah."

When I didn't respond, he asked, "You?"

"I don't call them anything."

"How about in your head?"

"I don't think about them… about it."

"Impossible."

"It's not. It's in the past. Far in the past."

"What about your nightmares?"

"Stop," I said, struggling against him. "Get off me."

"Are you sure that's what you want me to do?" he said, rolling his hips.

A gasp escaped me as I felt his hard cock rubbing against my inner thigh. "How… how are you hard after I brutalized your balls and dick alike?"

He ground harder against me, making me feel every impressive inch of him.

God.

"My pain tolerance is spectacular." He slid his free hand down to the hem of my dress and fingered the material. "You know what else is spectacular? You in this dress." As he started inching it up and exposing more of my thigh, he spoke at my ear in a low rumbling sexy tone, "Most spectacular of all, though, is how you react to my slightest touches."

Shit.

Goosebumps broke out at the point of contact, my core clenching at his teasing.

"Your pulse is pounding," he said, stroking the sensitive skin of my throat and adding yet more stimulation to the mix.

He took it further as he nibbled at my ear lobe, sending sparks of intensity through me.

"Levi…" I thought I meant it as a protest. I thought I'd intended the word *'stop'* to follow right after. But it just ended on a soft moan instead.

"There it is," he said, lifting his head, his face so close to mine it felt like his striking blue eyes were melding with mine.

His hand left my throat and trailed down, across my collarbone, to the tops of my breasts. At the same time, his other slipped right under my dress, his fingers gliding all the way up my thigh to the edge of my panties.

Sparks of need spread everywhere then, heat engulfing me, and I couldn't look away as the sensual intensity trapped me in his spell.

And then he slid two fingers beneath the silk.

It had me bucking against the wall.

A sexy groan emanated from him. "Christ, you're soaked," he growled, as he dragged his fingers through my folds.

The sure and sensual way he touched me had me sinking into it, into him, and the long-denied pleasure he was eliciting.

He brushed his lips over mine and spoke in hot, consuming words, "Admit it. Admit it couldn't just be anyone. Say it, say this is all for me, for what only *I* can do to you."

I gasped as he yanked my panties down to my thighs. "Tell me you feel it, this connection between us."

"I…"

My words caught in my throat as he thrust two fingers inside me.

"You need more convincing, got it," he said, smirking, then slicking his tongue over my bottom lip.

Recognizing how… favorable my reactions were, it had me snagging his wrist and stilling him beneath my dress.

This was dangerous, a really bad idea.

"This is… it's… too much," I only just managed to get out as he started curling his thick fingers inside me, unable to thrust because of my grip on him.

"Then tell me to stop."

"And… and you will?" I choked, barely able to speak as his talented fingers caused a storm inside me.

"I will. I'll release you, step back, and walk you to your car and that will be it."

"You'll also leave me alone going forward?"

He grasped my jaw with his free hand. It wasn't harsh, but gentle instead, and he stroked my cheek with his thumb, back and forth, soft and slow. "No. I can't. But I won't touch you again unless you beg me to." He released my jaw then started playing with my hair, running the black strands through his fingers. "*Or*, you could stop stabbing your nails into my skin and let me give you what we both need."

"What's that?" I rasped.

His eyes were on fire as he uttered on a primal growl, "To make you shatter for me, *Wildflower*. To feel your sweet cunt squeezing the fuck out of my fingers and watch you come apart for me. To taste you on me. To feel you shuddering in pleasure and screaming out my name. To have you need me so fucking bad and finally recognize it as you let go of everything else."

Crap, his words were… something else.

The way he looked at me, like he needed to devour me, like he needed *me* so fucking badly… I'd never felt anything like it.

Dangerous and uncontrolled… there was just so much intensity coming from him, coming from *us* whenever we came into contact. It was virtually unbearable.

It was more than sexual tension, but that was a big part of it still.

And maybe… maybe giving into it now would kill his obsession with me, or at the very least tamper it down until *I* found a way to kill it for him.

At least that reasoning and excuse was what I told myself as I released my death grip on his wrist and dropped my hand down by my side.

What appeared to be an actual genuine smile spread over his face and a little bit of surprise too, like he couldn't quite believe it was actually happening.

"Fuck, baby," he groaned.

Then he yanked my panties the rest of the way down my legs and I stepped out of them.

I'd only just managed it in my shaky, overwhelmed state when he roughly grabbed one of my thighs, hooked it around him as a form of support, then pulled his fingers out of me almost all the way before ramming them back deep inside.

I screamed and arched my back as he hit a spot I hadn't allowed him to before when I'd been trying to hold off.

"Right there, hmm?" he breathed at my ear.

"Yes," I moaned. "God, yes."

He didn't stop then, finger-fucking me with wild abandon.

Hell, the way he filled me with just his fingers, the way he moved, curling and thrusting with such ferocity and passion... it took me over and I threw my head back and started fucking back against him, moving with him, until I was completely immersed in just the moment, just him and me.

I was barely aware of what else he was doing, until his rhythm broke for a second, and then I noticed that he was no longer grabbing my thigh, but using his hips to support me while he made me come undone. And then I felt it.

His big cock grinding along my inner thigh.

I jolted, snapping out of my bliss haze.

"We... can't... not here... not..."

"Shh," he crooned, brushing his lips over mine. "I'm not gonna fuck you."

I frowned, not understanding.

"I know you're not ready for that."

He did?

The surprise must have been all over me, because he brushed some strays strands of my hair out of my face in an unprecedented tender gesture as he said, "I told you, I know how to make it better, to give you what you need. Just try to trust me."

He brushed his thumb over my clit, sending sharp sparks of pleasure through my body.

His eyes darkening, on me the entire time, he sped up, until he was brushing then flicking, then pulling, while his fingers ravaged me, his cock so close to all of it as he ground his shaft against the sensitive flesh of my thigh harder, more determinedly, like he wanted to make damn sure I couldn't forget that it was there, not even for a moment.

I was drowning in his attentions, drowning in his gaze, losing myself to the building pleasure.

Moans were spilling from my lips and needy sounds I couldn't control for the life of me.

The next thing I knew, I was letting go and grabbing his nape, then yanking his mouth to mine.

I took him in a bruising kiss, pouring all my confusion, frustration, and long-denied need into it. A dark laugh rumbled from him as I lost it and thrust my tongue into his mouth, tangling wildly with his. He let me dominate, explore, and relish it, while he stepped up his torment down below until I was thrusting my hips wildly, and fisting my hand in his tee, holding him to me, needing him against me.

Closer, closer.

The wave hit me without proper warning and I was ripping my mouth from his then and shrieking out into the night, my body convulsing with the power of it as it tore through me.

"Fuck, the way you come... out of this world," I heard him say as I was in the throes of it.

He shifted his weight, roughly grasped both my thighs, then grunted, a moment before warm liquid sprayed over my inner thigh.

I choked out a gasp.

Had he actually—

The smirk on his face said it all.

Sadistic satisfaction lit his rugged features as he lifted my dress and made me watch as he smeared his cum all over my pussy.

Before I even had a proper chance to register that, he snatched up my panties and eased them back up my legs, fixing them into place. "You'll keep me there as you drive home. Preferably through the night too. But I doubt you'll go that far. No matter, we'll work up to that." He released my thighs and tucked himself in, then stroked my hair. "My *Wildflower.*"

Still dazed and trying to get a handle on what had just happened, all I could manage to ask was, "Why do you call me that?"

He smiled. "One, because I know about your tattoo of the dandelions. Two, and most importantly, because people think wildflowers are fragile and weak, but they actually survive brutal weather and awful conditions and somehow manage to thrive in the worse situations and environments. They're also beauty amongst brutality." He kissed my cheek softly. "And you, Brianna, you were an angel among demons. That's what I saw six years ago and what I still see now, despite your attempt to hide it."

Oh my God.

All I could do was stare back at him as his words rolled through me.

And then his arms were around me, pulling me into him, holding me protectively. "You're marked now."

"Levi—"

He gripped me tighter, urgency spilling from him. "You. Are. Mine."

Oh no.

What the hell had I done?

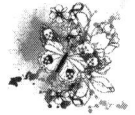

14

~Colton~

Hell had frozen over.

Lev had actually slept through the night.

He'd even slept in actually.

He was usually the guy who would go for a run, shower and dress and even make breakfast by the time Mason and I rolled out of bed and stumbled downstairs into the kitchen.

But here he was just walking in now to the kitchen shirtless and in a pair of just his deep-red satin boxers as Mason and I sat at the table eating our breakfast fully-dressed and ready to get our days underway.

Well, he wasn't just walking—he was skipping, really.

And to add to the shock of it all, he was also whistling.

Mason looked up from the papers out in front of him, spinning his pen in his hand in a casual way that I knew was anything but casual. It was more like a tic with him, when he was worried or agitated. He either did that or stress snacked on Cheerios. Seeing as though he was making his way through the omelet he'd cooked for us, the latter wasn't an option right now, so he was settling for the whole spinning pen thing instead.

"Nice of you to finally join us, *Hellraiser,*" he spoke.

I grimaced. Using that name was him calling Lev out.

It had me tensing as Lev walked to the table and leaned against the back of the chair opposite me and beside Mason.

But then he smiled.

Genuinely.

Not in the usual conniving or sadistic way.

Was he actually... happy?

"Some sweet dreams kept me asleep a little longer than usual." He gestured at our plates. "Sorry I didn't get down here in time to make breakfast, but you clearly had it covered." He eyed me. "Well, fortunately, it was Mason who had it covered, or there'd be food poisoning all around on the menu this morning."

"Hey, that was one time."

"One time too many," Mason grunted.

It had Lev laughing.

Again, a real, heartfelt laugh.

Mason and I exchanged a look. What the shit was going on?

He pushed away from the chair, then went to grab himself a coffee, starting to whistle again.

Words churned in my head at the sound, matching to the melody.

It was easier not to open my eyes/ It was easier not to feel a thing/ Until you/ You came into my life like a hurricane/ You eased away the pain/ Until you.

"You're whistling to my duet?"

He lifted a shoulder as he made his coffee. "Am I?"

"Yeah, you definitely are."

"Guess it's caught in my head from the other day."

"How? I've been singing a bunch of my others since then."

"Because of the girl," Mason said, focusing back on his papers.

"Her name is Brianna," Lev bit back with an edge this time, as he returned to the table with the coffee.

I shifted forward on my chair. "Holy shit, you fucked her, didn't you? Outside the bar or at her place?" I eyed Mason in question because he'd been home that night. "Or here?"

Lifting one eye off his papers for a moment, he answered, "Not here."

"No fucking was had," Lev said, waving his hand dismissively. "Not in the technical sense."

"Technical sense? What does that mean?" I asked.

Mason slapped his papers down and glared at Lev. "It means he fingered her up against the wall of the bar then marked her."

"Marked her? Like *Hex*-wise? He likes her, it's a little hard to believe he would—"

"He came on her," Mason told me.

"Huh, marked her in that sense. Got it." I licked my lips. "I like it."

"Of course you do," Mason grunted. "Dirty slut."

I grinned. "That I am, darlin'. And don't you forget it." I looked at Lev who was noticeably less upbeat now, some major tension having taken him over. "Although, I am a little hurt, you didn't invite me, Lev. You saw that I've got a rapport going with her now."

"You might have a *rapport* but you don't know her. Double-teaming at this stage would have terrified her and fucked up everything."

"At this stage? So you *are* actually considering my sharing idea then?"

Before he could answer, Mason ran right over that and demanded instead, "And what might that *everything* be?"

Lev glared at him fiercely. "How do you know what went down?"

"Hmm, let me see," Mason said, sitting back in his chair and clasping his hands on his lap. *Oh shit. Not good. Very not good.* "Could it be that your mysterious behavior of keeping to the shadows, combined with your even more mysterious return necessitated me putting eyes on you? Could it also be that one of those sets of eyes reported a very localized blackout at *Nirvana* right after Colt texted to tell me you were on your way home? A blackout that took out the lights just on a couple of the exterior walls of the building and also downed the security cameras? Gotta say, Levi, that was an impressive feat. It required interference from several different sources as well, and to pull it off in perfect synchronicity like you did... another level. Your skills have clearly grown substantially since you've been away. Strange, isn't it, that your internship didn't include any of that sort of thing?" When Lev just continued glaring at him, his fingers tightening around his mug to a white-knuckle grip, Mason went on, "I had one of my people get the security cameras up and running again and link me to the feed. *That's* how I saw."

"Hmm."

"That's all you have to say for yourself?" Mason demanded.

Lev sucked in a harsh breath, then narrowed his eyes. "No. Far from it, *brother.* You're so afraid of not being in absolute control of every little thing that it's become a sickness. A worrying and really fucking sad sickness."

"Lev—" I started to warn.

He ignored it and pushed harder, "You're so stifled that I was stunned that Colt was able to get you off. I mean, props to him, that's a major feat. The guy's got skills, we all know that, but with you that's not even a given. It's slamming up against some real deep-seated repression." Lev scoffed. "You don't even know who the fuck you are. I mean, shit, you can't even acknowledge him in public—or around anybody outside of the three of us—you leave him relegated to just some friend. You just don't see how much that hurts him every fucking time, is that it? Or you don't care? *Or* is it because you're so emotionally stunted these days that you really don't register it?"

I slapped my hand to my face and slumped back in my chair. "Shit. Stop this."

Mason sneered at him. "Your attempt to redirect was admirable, yet majorly transparent."

"Just stay out of my business and keep your focus on that," Lev told him, gesturing at the papers surrounding him. "Got your army in place yet?"

"Working on it."

"And then what? You're gonna hit at Daddy Dearest?"

"One step at a time."

"You chickened out the last time around."

"Because you left."

"That's your excuse. You made the decision to call it off before I even announced I was taking off for a while. But you can't stand failure in any fucking thing, so you leveled it on me because I'm an easy target as I don't care about blame, insults, or any of that shit."

"Right."

"You're actually admitting it?"

"No. I'm talking about you being right about you not caring or having a reaction to normal human things. So why are you now?"

"What?"

"You're reacting, Lev. In a major way. And it's because of this girl, isn't it?"

"If I'm reacting then *you're* reaching. Majorly."

"Nah," Mason said, shaking his head. "It's clear as day to me. This girl's a threat."

Oh no. "She's not, Mason," I interjected. "She's a sweet thing and—"

"She's a threat in the sense of how she's affecting *him,*" Mason clarified.

"The fuck she is," Levi bit back.

"The way you're reacting to her, the lines you're crossing, the obsession she's clearly become for you... it's dangerous, given what and who you are. And it won't be tolerated."

"What does that mean?"

"What do you think? She has to be dealt with in the way *Hex* deals with all threats—absolute decimation."

Before I could object, Lev shot to his feet and slammed his hands down on the table, rattling our plates. "You stay the fuck away from her," he seethed at Mason.

Mason didn't so much as flinch, eyeing him steadily. "Give me a reason to."

"What?"

"Explain to me why she's so special, why she's under your skin, and why you're going to such lengths with her."

Lev's jaw worked as he stared Mason down.

As the seconds ticked by and he didn't say anything, didn't offer anything up, Mason told him, "You have forty-eight hours to give me the truth, or she's marked by *Hex.*"

Levi stormed around the table and snatched the papers from the table. Looking them over rapidly, he muttered, "Twenty-five recruits since we restarted *Hex.* All loyal to you through fear, intimidation and blackmail."

"That's the way we do it."

Lev pulled out his phone and took rapid photos of each piece of paper with the list of names Mason had along with the details involved in what he had on each of them, what he was holding over their heads, as well as the assets and connections he wanted them for, what use he had for each of them. Then he threw the papers on the floor out of Mason's reach and leaned in and growled in his face, "You strike at her and I'll annihilate every single fucker on this list. Mark my fucking words. *Don't* test me."

With that, he pulled back, then did something we hadn't seen from him in years.

He lost his temper.

Snatching up his mug, he let out a roar as he tossed it across the kitchen, wherein it smashed against the wall and shattered to pieces, coffee spraying everywhere.

And then he stormed out of the kitchen, slamming the door shut with such force it shook the entire fucking room.

I cursed and rounded on Mason. "What the shit are you playing at? Why did you provoke him like that?"

"I needed to test a theory."

"And what theory was that? The damage he'll do if he loses his temper? You remember the last time, yes?" I gestured at his right shoulder. It was covered by the gray henley tee he currently had on *and* his skull with wings tattoo beneath that, but it was never really out of sight to me. "You got shot. And so did Lev." I lowered my voice. "The two of you murdered five guys. Your dad put you on a leash."

"I'm well aware," he gritted out. "Well fucking aware, Colt."

"Then why do this now? I mean, shit, didn't you see how happy he was when he first walked in here?"

"I did and you know as well as I do how worrying that is with him. All the signs are there like they were five years ago. You haven't been looking as closely at it as I have, namely because you've been caught up in helping him here and there with the bits and pieces of a much bigger picture he hasn't let either of us in on. *That's* why I did what I did, to see exactly where he's at. Last time, neither of us acted it time to stop all that hell from breaking loose. I'm not gonna make that mistake again."

"I get that, but *you* need to get that there are other ways to approach this." I rose to my feet. "And your way, the brutal way you just attacked and threatened somebody he clearly cares about… all it's gonna do is risk driving him away again. For good this time. I don't want that. And as much as the two of you butt heads, I know you don't actually really want that either. He's our brother, come what may."

"I'll do what I have to do to protect us, Colt."

I shook my head at him.

"Shit, Mason."

With that, I walked out without another word.

There was no point.

He was clearly in one of his hardheaded moods right now.

Any pushing would just further entrench him in his current position.

I'd have to try again when he wasn't so worked up, come at it another way.

———

I FOUND Levi in his workshop.

He was staring at an intricate carving in front of him on one of his workbenches.

Holy shit. It was incredible.

He'd carved a one-foot butterfly, the wings with some amazing detailing and patterns etched into them.

"Wow," I uttered, approaching it. "This is some of your finest work. Maybe *the* finest."

As I came within reach, I went to touch it, but he snapped his fingers a fraction of a second before I made a move. "Uh uh, no touching works in progress."

I pulled my hand back. "Right. My bad. I forgot. It's been a long time since I've been around you doing your woodworking—or carving, in this case."

He was now dressed in his black cargo pants instead of just his boxers, but still shirtless, and I took note of his hoodie thrown over his laptop bag by the opposite door that led out through the side entrance to the mansion. There was a small garage out there too where he parked his Harley, separate from Mason's Porsche and my dark-blue Mercedes. Lev liked to come and go without notice, so he set things like that up where he wouldn't disturb us when he did. The same with him having control of the security system here. From Mason's pessimistic view of it, he believed it was Lev looking to keep whatever trouble-some things he got up to off our radar.

I got that it could be worrying with Lev. Of course I did. But Mason often forgot—or didn't like to think about—what Lev had suffered through six years ago. Something that had completely changed him, *shattered* him. And when he'd tried to put the pieces back together they hadn't fit together the same way. I guess, he hadn't really wanted them to.

He'd become volatile and malicious.

Well, that was what people saw from him. All they really saw.

They didn't know him like I did.

He was just so tormented, in so much pain, and that was how he handled it, by becoming that.

But Lev had a good heart. He did care. A lot.

It was just really fucking sad that Mason couldn't see it anymore like I still could in him.

His fear of losing control and losing grip on controlling Lev warped so much for him.

I took note of some hardware—wires, connectors, some sort of battery thingy—and went to pick it up to get a closer look.

A sharp slap to the back of my hand had me jerking back. "Ow!"

"I told you, no touching."

My lips quirked. "Come on, you know how much I like to touch."

He patted my cheek. "Tone it down, cupcake. I'm already worked up. Not a good idea to throw any kind of provocation my way right now."

He moved away from me and settled behind his bench, fiddling with some tools I had no clue about as he worked on the connectors and a battery-type of thing.

When it came to my music, I was king. But this sort of stuff, the technical know-how it required—a different kind to my field of interest—it was way beyond me.

"I've told you many a time that I can teach you if you give it a chance," he said, catching me looking on curiously.

"My focus, Lev. It wouldn't be possible."

"You've done it with your music, with the band."

"In my better moments, yeah."

"Nah, more than you realize. I've seen you doing it with that duet, your persistence with it, with trying to get it done, the fact you were able to put it together so quickly."

"I put it together in one of my obsessive, determined modes."

"Yet, you're still pursuing it." He looked up at me, pausing what he was doing. "You don't give yourself enough credit." He shook his head to himself. "Not surprising when you're going up against Mason's intensely controlled and anally streamlined bullshit. Nobody can match that. For the record, not even him."

I shoved my hand through my mohawk. "Look, I know you're upset—"

"Don't defend him to me, Colt."

"That's not why I came in here."

He cocked an eyebrow.

I held up my hand. "Just hear me out before you fly off the handle."

"Not flying off the handle, working," he said, focusing on putting together… whatever that hardware in front of him was.

"All right, good," I said, dropping my hand and leaning against the workbench on the opposite side to him. "Because I think you should just put it out there… whatever your true interest is in Brianna."

"Hmm, so you're not defending him, but you're advocating for me to give him exactly what he wants?" he spoke in that deceptively calm tone of his that really meant there was bubbling anger just beneath the surface, ready to unleash in a full-on tidal wave at any second.

"You're looking at it the wrong way. The stubborn way —which is something both of you have in common, by the way. This is best for both of you."

"Cupcake, I get that you're not normally the strategist amongst us, but this is another level."

"It's not. *Listen*, Lev."

He sucked in a breath and returned to working. "Fine. Hearing you out."

"You tell Mason what's really going on and it will cut through all the worry he's currently feeling with your mysterious return and all the things not adding up about you becoming fixated on Brianna Walker out of the blue. It will calm him down, Lev. Meaning, it will get him off your back. It could even lead to him helping you, rather than being a thorn in your side to your plans. He won't feel the need to exert control, he won't throw obstacles in your path, and he won't go after *her* either."

He blew out a breath and stepped back from his work. Shoving a hand through his wild curly hair, he looked me in the eye and told me, "I didn't just become *fixated* on her *out of the blue.* There's much more at work here. It's complicated. The kind of complicated that Mason will never accept. So, you see, even if I reveal the truth to him and I'm transparent about the reasons behind my recent actions, he won't be on board. In fact, the threat he made over breakfast will seem like nothing in comparison."

"No, if he's aware of what's coming, he can work with you. He'd be willing to. It's the not knowing that amps him up and brings out his dictatorial side."

"Sorry, brother, I know you're trying so hard to make peace, but I can't allow interference."

"Lev, what could be so bad that you'd cut us out of it completely?"

"*You're* not cut out. I like you growing closer to her, I'm all for it."

"As pleasantly surprising as that is, I meant in the big picture."

He folded his arms across his chest and leaned against the wall beside a peg board full of his many tools. "Because the fundamental difference between Mason's approach versus mine comes into play in a big way here. While he has been known to take what he mistakenly terms calculated risks—the kind where it's not even really a risk at all because he's already planned moves ahead and manipulated the outcome he wants—*I'm* prepared to truly risk and wager everything to get what I want, and to cross any godforsaken lines in the process too. *I* don't have any limits."

"Holy shit, this is like a call to war. But against who? And where does Brianna fit in to all of this?"

"There's a difference between wanting to know and needing to, Colt. Trust me, you're better off where you're at right now." He pushed off the wall and came to me, telling me, "Believe me, this is me protecting you." Reaching out, he cupped my cheek. "Okay, cupcake?"

"Lev—"

"Hey, don't you need to get down to campus? Your first class of the day starts in fifteen minutes."

"Of course you know my class schedule."

Both him and Mason made a point to. It was an effort on their part to ensure I kept to it and wasn't late, or missing classes entirely because of my *focus issues.*

"Why did Mason let you come in here when you should've been on your way down to class already?"

"He was pissed about what went down in the kitchen *and* I was pissed at the way he tried to handle you, so he took off without me."

He shook his head. "Get your bag and I'll give you a ride."

"On your Harley?"

"Sure, if you don't mind riding bitch. Either that, or you let me drive your Mercedes. There's no way I'm getting in the passenger seat with you behind the wheel."

I chuckled. "A year away and you still haven't moved past those minor issues."

"Minor? Sure, we'll go with that."

"I'm fine riding on the back of your bike. I'm hella secure in my masculinity."

He grinned. "Don't I know it."

I watched him walk to his bag and hoodie. He slipped the hoodie on over his bare chest, unfortunately hiding the gorgeous sight. As he slung his laptop bag over his shoulder, then opened the door so we could head to his bike, I gestured at the butterfly he'd made.

"What's it for?"

"It's a night light."

"Oh, that's the stuff you were fiddling with to add to it? LEDs?"

"Nah, the LEDs are the easy part. What you saw me doing was rigging the hardware there to be able to send signals and work with an app I created."

"To what end?"

"So the recipient in question can use their phone to turn it on and off at their will, and also schedule it too."

"That's neat. I would ask if it was for you, but you're not into butterflies. But Brianna's butterfly tattoo comes to mind here. You actually made that for her?"

He lifted a shoulder. "She doesn't like the dark."

I frowned. "But Mason said you caused a blackout around her?"

"I needed her in the right frame of mind."

"And scaring her was the way to go about that?"

"Unfortunately, yes. She insists on pushing me to employ unpleasant methods."

"Jeez, Lev."

He ruffled my mohawk. "Relax, it worked the way I intended. All is well."

"And what if she has second thoughts in the light of day?"

"That's not an option."

"It's not an—"

"Come on," he said, nudging me. "Go get your bag and I'll fire up the Harley. Two minutes."

I stared at him for a moment.

"Go," he pushed. "I won't let you be late."

I guess that was settled then. *Not an option.*

Holy shit.

15

~Brianna~

I groaned at the sound of my phone alarm cutting through my peaceful reverie of numbness.

Lethargically, I reached over and shut it off.

It was one of those mornings where the hangover from the sleeping pills I'd had to take last night was making it harder to get going and start my day. They—and maybe a sedative too—were the only reason for the peaceful sleep I'd had. Most often when I took them, I didn't have my nightmares and I just experienced a dreamless sleep. A desperately coveted numbness.

When I'd arrived home last night after that… experience… with Levi, I'd had a bad reaction, some fallout to it all. Flashes of the past had inundated me.

Of him.

Of me.

Of us in that hellscape.

I hadn't been able to shut it off, even with trying to refocus my mind through doing some of my origami—fashioning a bunch of butterflies. The symbolism I took from those beautiful creatures was the sense of freedom and of personal change and growth. That brutal time had changed me and my life forevermore and making the butterflies had been me trying to focus on that part, what had happened after that awful experience, not what I'd been subjected to during it.

But it hadn't worked, so I'd had to use alternate methods just to be able to relax and manage to sleep.

I guess being with Levi like that had awakened it. The act itself, maybe. But more so that it was with him, and that he'd brought up the *demons in the dark*.

My phone kept buzzing even though I'd shut off the alarm, so I snatched it up.

Squinting for a few moments, I was able to see that a text message had come in an hour ago and it kept vibrating like it always did until I acknowledged the notification.

I swiped it open and found a message from the man who was now equally a part of my fantasies and night-mares alike.

Hell Spawn: You were the star of my dreams last night. You were riding my cock like a feral thing while I sucked on your breasts making your nipples red-raw as you shrieked out my name loud enough to wake the fucking dead.

Crap. So much for him losing interest.

I didn't respond and put my phone back down on my nightstand instead, trying to ignore the tingle his words had caused between my thighs. *Damn him.*

I scrubbed my hand over my face, then went to sit up, only to knock something off onto the floor in the process.

I peered down the side of the bed to see that my big book of fairytales had dropped.

That was weird. I kept it on the opposite nightstand after I was done reading a story to help me sleep. And with the medicine I'd needed last night, I hadn't even read it.

I picked it up and that was when I noticed that my bookmark wasn't in there. Something else was.

I stilled for a moment as I took in the lavender and dandelions being used as a marker instead.

"What the hell?"

I hefted the book back onto the bed, then opened it at the place the flowers were thrust between. I started as I found a folded piece of paper there marked in elegant handwriting, *For Brianna.*

Opening it, my breath caught in my throat as I read the contents.

Prince Charmings are highly overrated. A possessive villain is much more arousing. He'll give you the dark thrill you crave.

Sweet dreams, Wildflower.

"Oh my God," I choked, slamming the book closed with the flowers and the note still inside.

Levi Knight had been here in my apartment.

In my freaking bedroom!

Last night!

He'd been right up close to me as I'd slept heavily under the influence of the meds.

My phone buzzed again.

I found another text from that clearly unhinged—more than I'd even realized—maniac.

Hell Spawn: Can't get the sensation of your needy cunt strangling my fingers off my mind.

Before I could even process *that*, he sent another.

Hell Spawn: You're reading but not responding. I'm hurt. I was actually hoping for a good morning text from you after last night.

Hell Spawn: Colt's here with me. We just got to campus. You're running late, want me to cover for you with our professor?

Our professor?

Brianna: You're in my Operating Systems class?

Hell Spawn: Sure am. You coming?

How was he—he was coming back as a fourth year. That class was for sophomores.

Brianna: You were in my apartment last night. My bedroom.

Hell Spawn: The fact you know that means you got my gifts. You like?

Brianna: You crossed a line.

Hell Spawn: How? You're mine. Last night cemented it.

Brianna: It didn't.

Hell Spawn: This push and pull of yours is becoming grating. And it's coming close to upsetting me.

Brianna: Upsetting you? You broke into my home!

Hell Spawn: For your own good.

Brianna: WHAT?

Hell Spawn: Wanted to make sure there wasn't any fallout for you after what we did outside the bar. And I left you the note and flowers as a comfort in case there was.

That would've been almost sweet if he'd gone about it another way.

As it was, he hadn't.

Brianna: You did it to mark your territory.

Hell Spawn: I already marked it. Don't tell me you don't still feel me deep inside? Delectably sore this morning, aren't you?

Brianna: Go to hell.

Hell Spawn: Been there, clawed my way back.

I stilled as I read those words.

Hell Spawn: You're mine. Stop this denial bull now. It's settled. You gave yourself over to me last night. I felt it. I know you did too.

Brianna: It was a mistake. Don't come near me again.

Hell Spawn: You do this and you won't like how I respond.

Brianna: Like I said, go to hell, you fucking maniac.

Hell Spawn: Bad move, Wildflower.

I gritted my teeth, then blocked his number.

And then I forced myself out of bed and fired up my laptop to finalize what I'd set in motion last night with the program I'd written to access his phone via a backdoor method so I could track his movements from here on out.

No more surprises.

Once again, thanks to that asshole, I was going to be late to yet another class.

Well, more like miss it entirely.

For once, I was partially glad, though, considering it meant I wouldn't have to see him there.

———

I'D FINALLY MADE it to Stonewell U for my second class of the day, Algorithm Analysis.

I hadn't had a chance to make my lunch like I usually did, so I'd picked up a Greek salad from the college cafeteria and brought it out to my usual spot on the bench at the far edge of the quad, out of the way of everyone and everything. I didn't think I could eat a sandwich right now or anything heavy with the nausea that had been plaguing me ever since I'd woken up to discover Levi had broken into my apartment and been there while I'd been asleep. *And* since I'd actually registered the fallout of my bad decision to give into his seductions last night.

This salad had a lot of feta cheese all over it, one of my favorite cheeses. Well, at least that was what I'd asked for. I hadn't actually seen the cafeteria server scoop it because I'd had my back turned as I'd answered a text from Colton about confirming a time to finish that duet. I'd also ordered a strawberry chocolate milkshake to take some of the edge off. Chocolate was good for a lot of things, including trying to bury very recent salacious memories of a certain maniacal stalker.

I checked my phone and my spirits rose when I saw a message from Chloe that must have come in while I'd been in the busy cafeteria.

Chloe: Coming back next week! Can't wait to see you! *Oh my God!*

Brianna: That's amazing news! I can't wait either!

Chloe: Thanks, sweetie. Your IG campaign really helped me out. Get ready to get your celebration on when I return.

Brianna: I absolutely will.

I smiled to myself and tucked my phone into my pink and silver jacket with lots of studs, buckles and embellishments. It was the only part of my outfit that was bubbly and colorful today. With the way I was feeling—on edge and stressed by what had been happening lately, and feeling the haunting of that nightmare six years ago, thanks to Levi fucking Knight—I was wearing just a pair of black jeans, block heels, and a lacy black tank to complete my look. I'd only bothered to put my hair up in a loose ponytail. I even had heavily tinted sunglasses on because I wanted to stay inside my own bubble as much as possible and block out the world when in between classes, like now.

I sighed heavily, then opened my salad container.

A scream ripped from my throat and I shot to my feet away from the salad as I stared at the worms, maggots, and whatever else crawling through it and slithering all over the place.

It took me several moments to reach out to the milkshake and open the top.

I gasped as saw it was very far from a milkshake—and smelled it too now the lid was off. It was a cup full of urine.

Urgh.

I jerked back, breathing heavily, adrenaline making my pulse thrum like crazy.

It really didn't help when I looked out across the quad to see several students looking my way, my scream obviously having drawn their unwanted attention.

Dammit.

I forced myself to sit back down, but on the other side of the bench which was preferable both because it was away from the bugs and urine and because it had me sitting with my back turned to the rest of the quad.

As the shock of it wore off and I was able to think, I analyzed the situation.

My first suspect was obviously Levi.

Our last conversation, in particular came to mind.

Don't come near me again.

You do this and you won't like how I respond.

It should be a slam dunk deduction pointing to him being responsible.

But how could he have done it?

Although I had been distracted as the food had been made, it would've had to happen really quickly and within my immediate vicinity. It wasn't like it was my usual order, so it would've needed to happen on the fly. And now I'd put my program in place and I was tracking his phone, an alert went off when he was within a few feet of me. That hadn't happened earlier.

Sure, he could've had somebody do it for him.

But he'd definitely proven himself as the kind of person who preferred to do their own dirty work and not delegate tasks.

Also, it really didn't seem to be his style.

On some level it was a comfort that it hadn't been him. And that was something I was trying not to think about… that I actually cared about him not being responsible for this, that I didn't want him to be. The bastard was definitely in my head and crawling under my skin too.

What had happened outside the bar had been a dangerous and really fucking foolish move on my part. I'd given in. Hell, I'd succumbed. And instead of dousing the fire on either of our parts, it had made it a whole lot worse. Now it was raging flames.

Fortunately—as fucked up as it was—finding out he'd broken into my apartment while I'd been sleeping was managing to keep them at bay and to keep *me* from doing anything even more stupid, like falling for him all the way, or letting him draw closer to me.

But this… this act of bullying… it meant he wasn't the only one targeting me now.

It meant, it was becoming dangerous in a whole other way.

And now, I couldn't just retaliate in a one-shot way when an attack came, as much like an afterthought, while I kept my primary focus on college and the life I'd been building here.

I had to pull much more of my focus into dealing with this.

Shit.

My phone sounded and I pulled it out of my bag to see a text.

Blocked ID: You've been marked by Hex.

I'd heard rumors that *Hex* had been restarted and even that their tentacles were spreading all over the campus and the surrounding area of the town already. While it was known that Levi, Mason, and Colton had been the driving force before, the actual members were more on the down low, so unless you were one of them—one of their soldiers —it was difficult to discern who they were.

That meant anyone could have done this to my food.

It could've been one of the onlookers in the quad moments ago.

What I knew for sure, however, was that once you were marked by *Hex,* you were done for, your life cursed and ruined beyond repair.

Brianna: What was my offense to warrant this?

Blocked ID: Leave Stonewell or this will just be the beginning.

I glared at the message, my initial freakout replaced by seething rage.

The hell I was going to be forced from the life I'd managed to create for myself, this fresh start that I'd fought tooth and nail to obtain in the first place.

By a bunch of college bullies who were basically some low-down new adult mafia.

Before I could contain it, I was texting back rapidly and definitively.

Brianna: The hell I will.

Blocked ID: So be it.

I glared at the ominous words.

I'd made a promise to myself last night when I'd left the bar that I wouldn't allow fear to rule me anymore, that I wouldn't freeze in the face of it, or duck and hide until a threat passed on by. It was stifling me.

And, more than that, it was causing me to be unprepared to respond to threats, as things lately had served to highlight in one hell of a brutal way.

No more.

These assholes were about to discover how much of a mistake they'd actually made with targeting me.

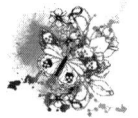

16

~Mason~

I hadn't waited forty-eight hours.

After Levi's reaction during breakfast the other day, it had become extremely apparent that immediate action was required, that there was no time to wait.

Besides, the deadline I'd given him had now come and gone anyway and he hadn't come to me with the truth. Just as I'd anticipated.

Offering him time had just been my way to test the waters with him at that juncture.

And he'd failed spectacularly.

I sure as fuck wasn't going to sit back and allow him to become unhinged again. We'd all suffered for it five years ago and I was still paying for it more than most.

I watched from the shadows as two of my soldiers slammed into the girl in the corridor, knocking her fluffy messenger bag from her shoulder and her along with it. They walked away as had been instructed and she scrambled there on her knees to retrieve her bag and a couple of things that had fallen from it in the scuffle. She hadn't noticed what one of my guys had slipped in there during the stereotypical bullying move I'd had staged. As if I'd settle for such a pedestrian tactic—at least not without following it up with something much more glorious.

She rose to her feet and squared her shoulders as if nothing had happened, then continued on her merry way.

Hmm. She certainly wasn't as meek and as pliant as I'd taken her for.

She'd shrugged off all the minor acts I'd had visited upon her over the last few days.

It was clearly time to step it up a notch.

And, although, they had been minor—messing with her food, having her cornered on campus with my soldiers uttering threatening words about her being marked by *Hex*, spilling an ice-cold coffee on her, having her tripped up the steps, taking one of her beloved jackets while she'd been immersed in a coding lab and having it trampled then half buried in the dirt—it served to pile on the pressure and to inundate her.

I'd kept it to small infractions so far to keep it off Levi's radar.

With my eyes on him, I'd managed to inflict the minor but continued damage upon her when he was out of range and none the wiser. From my observations of him, it had become apparent that he hadn't made contact with her since the morning after their finger-fuck session outside *Nirvana*. Knowing Lev as well as I did, it was clearly him gearing up to something big.

The girl had to be on the verge of breaking now, so stepping it up should finally push her to give it up and actually transfer out of Stonewell.

I wanted that to happen before Levi's *something big* came about.

She'd scheduled her time with Colt today to work on their duet, so once that was out of the way, I'd move to more damaging tactics. Let him have his time with her to get that done. It would assuage his worries about *Mythic Cry*. The fact that he hadn't understood my contracts class at all had meant I'd taken on his case myself and determined the other two couldn't touch most of his catalogue. I'd found proof that he had written ninety percent of the band's songs himself, and I was in the process of working with Professor Litman to draw up something official. If they proved resistant to it, my next move was to use the soldiers I'd acquired via *Hex* to remove them forcibly from Colt's vicinity and ensure they remained that way—fucking exiled. He'd worked too hard with *Mythic Cry* to suffer for their jealousy and ineptitude. I wouldn't allow it.

I made my way around the other side of the music building where Colt spent most of his time, meaning I knew it so well that I was able to approach the recording studio from a side entrance that most didn't know about without being bothered.

I opened the door a little so I could hear inside as I also peered through the small window in the door. Fortunately, it was at an angle where I could see them there in the heart of the recording studio, while they couldn't see me clearly.

I wanted to see how the girl reacted when she wasn't under fire from my assault.

And, yeah, I also wanted to see how she was with Colt —and how he was with her.

Lev had mentioned that Colt had taken a liking to her. I needed to understand how much my plan to remove her from our vicinity would impact him so I could manage the fallout. I was hoping that it was just fleeting for him like his interests in his many other conquests over the years had been. This was hopefully just lasting longer than usual for him because it was intertwined with his music—his ultimate passion. It was likely why he'd managed to maintain his focus on her for longer than I'd ever witnessed from him before.

Settling against the door, I looked on as Colt walked to her while frowning at her bag.

"What happened?"

"What?" she asked, following his line of sight.

"All the dust and dirt, even a scuff mark. Did somebody step on it?"

"Slammed into me, knocked my bag to the ground, and stepped on it in the process, sure."

"What? Who? When?" Colt asked.

She eased the bag away. "Don't worry about it, I'll clean it off when we're done here." She moved away then and headed for the microphones.

Colt grasped her arm in a much more careful manner than he was known for. "Hold up. Talk to me, cutie."

Cutie?

She stared—or glared—at his hand on her arm. "I'm here because we have a deal and I don't want to make things worse than they already are."

"What things? With Lev?"

"No. I haven't heard from him in days. I even saw him in class a couple of times and he didn't even acknowledge me, so I guess his threats were all about switching to the silent treatment."

Interesting. For one, that wasn't Lev's go-to. Not in the fucking least. And, another, she looked upset about it, like she was missing him.

Fuck it. This was worse than I'd imagined. He was already affecting *her* now. Yeah, I definitely needed to escalate and speed things along.

"That's… weird. Really weird. Do you want me to talk to him for you?"

"No," she said. "Absolutely no way. I'm glad he's leaving me alone. It's what I wanted."

As she shoved her hand through her hair and cut eye contact, Colt frowned. "Are you sure? It doesn't exactly seem like it."

To her credit, she managed to steel herself, her pretty features hardening, as she told him, "I have other things to deal with anyway."

"Yeah, these things you're worried about making worse. And I ask again, what things?"

She glared at him. "Come on, don't play all innocent. You already know."

"Know?"

"About *Hex* targeting me. I'm sorry—*marking me.*"

That's right, get the terminology right, troublemaker.

Colt's unadulterated shock blazed through clearly.

And then I waited to see how he'd respond.

It would tell me everything I needed to know about his true sentiment toward her.

"Are you fucking kidding me?" he yelled, surprising me at the vehemence of it.

The girl looked more than a little taken aback, reading his reaction as the genuine truth that it was. "You didn't actually know then."

"That you've been marked? Shit, no. What the shit is going on?"

"You're part of *Hex.* How can you not know?"

"I'm on the periphery. Especially with this new revival. I've been dealing with issues with *Mythic Cry* and working on getting my GPA back to a respectable level. I haven't even been tasked with anything concerning *Hex* yet." He took her hands in his and leveled with her. "I swear it, Brianna. I wouldn't… I wouldn't do that to you."

She stared at him for a moment. "You really wouldn't, would you?"

"No. Of course not. I told you at the bar that I liked hanging with you, connecting with you. I don't fake that kind of thing. I don't fake anything."

"Well, it's fine. I'll handle it. I'm working on it."

I tensed with the challenge she'd just thrown down. That tension quickly became something much more, though, as I took in the fierce look in her eyes, the fire and determination shining forth. It was intrigue, admiration… something more? I wasn't sure.

"No. Don't… don't retaliate," Colt urged her.

"Why not?"

I narrowed my eyes. Was he going to sell me and *Hex* out to a girl he'd only known for a few weeks and tell her about our covert protocol?

Fortunately, he merely ruffled his mohawk and told her, "I'll sort it out for you. I'll speak with Mason. Something might've gotten lost in translation, some mix-up."

He played with her fingers in his and she smiled, returning it, making his eyes spark with something softer than his usual blatant and unmistakable lust.

"I don't need you to do that. It'll be fine. But thanks for offering. It's actually really sweet."

"Uh uh. I said I'd do it and I will. It's all good."

"Why?"

"Why what?"

"Why go out of your way for me? Especially about this?"

"You went out of your way with this whole duet thing. It's not your thing or what you want to be doing, yet you're still here showing up to help me out."

"Well, we had a deal."

"And I already paid my side of it, so you could've walked away."

"I wouldn't do that."

"Yeah, I get that about you. You're sweet and honorable."

"I'm not sweet."

He stepped closer until their joined hands were pushing against both their chests. "Are you sure about that?"

"You tell me."

In the next moment, Colt sank his fingers into her silky black hair and eased her to him as he took her mouth.

I took note of her freezing up for a moment, before she was able to get into it and kiss him back, hooking her hands around his neck and sinking into him.

He wrapped his free arm around her and held her tightly to him as he kissed her with all the passion I knew well from him, yet also with a much more careful edge with her.

Gritting my teeth now I'd gotten my intel, I turned and walked back the way I'd come.

Not the way I'd needed things to go.

It was becoming apparent that this girl was nearing the unpredictability level of Levi.

Troublemaker didn't even cover it.

Son of a bitch.

17

~Levi~

They thought Dear Old Dad had called me home.

Well, I had little doubt he would once Mason ran his standard check into my whereabouts by calling him up to confirm. As soon as my dad found out I'd lied about heading to the family estate, he'd suspect that I was up to no good, then make a move to tug on my reins.

It was a small price to pay as a cover for what I was really doing.

It had also gotten Mason's human surveillance off my back.

And it had put some distance between me and Brianna.

As much as it had killed me, I'd realized from her reactions the morning-after that I'd needed to give her some space to absorb it all. Inundating her and continuing to come at her had just been seen as a threat by her and something to battle against, so it had created an automatic antagonistic response in her.

Fortunately, it had come at just the right time.

Because I'd finally gotten another lead in the crusade

I'd been on for the last three years ever since I'd gotten out from under my dad's invasive supervision and moved to Stonewell for college. This *crusade* was why I'd taken a supposed internship last year. *Supposed* being the operative word. No time to get into that right now… later.

Right now there was this—me lounging back in a booth in the far corner near the bar of strip club, *Ravage*. It was a couple of hundred miles away from Stonewell and my family home in the college town's neighboring City of Tolhurst.

It straddled the line between actual strip club and whorehouse. This place was off-the-radar with patrons needing to be on an exclusive guest list in order to gain entry. Those patrons being seedy businessmen. Real slime balls. It had been made clear to me from the moment I'd walked in after *editing* myself onto the guest list for tonight, that the place had no limits.

It was sleazy as fuck.

It fit well with its owner, Jeff Hurst.

At least that was the name he went by nowadays.

He'd had to go into hiding six years ago from my dad.

And me.

He just didn't know that last part yet.

It wouldn't be long now, though.

My intel had determined that at the start of every night he would review the guest list, then personally greet and schmooze any new blood. It was his way of being attentive in order to boost the expansion of his clientele.

He'd realize I was here soon enough.

I took another sip from my vodka and lime.

I didn't actually like the lime aspect. I always favored my vodka straight without any *adornments*. But I'd requested the lime for a specific reason.

I tried to ignore the uncomfortableness of being clad in

a suit. Really not my thing despite my dad's many attempts when I was younger to make it so. I was all about casual, through and through. But this had been the required dress code. So here I was clad in a sleek black Armani suit, even a pair of designer Italian loafers on my feet instead of my usual boots. I even had product in my hair instead of leaving the curls wild and free as usual.

I finally caught sight of my target venturing out onto the club floor, enjoying the spectacle of the three topless women—one redhead, one blonde, and one brunette—grinding and working a pole on the stage.

He was in his late thirties now, still sporting that same slicked back hair that had so much gel in it that it looked greasy—I hated that look. Or maybe it was more about the memories I had associated with it when it came to him specifically. He hadn't lost his bulky, roided out shape. The cheap gray suit he was wearing was pulling taut across his frame, too tight and looking like the seams would burst at any moment with the struggle of containing all that mass.

After a few moments he drew his attention away from the strippers and adjusted his pants obscenely, then turned to one of his staff members beside him, wherein they passed him the guest list, the thing on some ridiculously fancy gold-leaf paper.

I saw the moment he registered my name.

Well, my dad's.

There was no way any venue would dare to deny the almighty Roman Knight entry.

Me, on the other hand? Well, I was a wildcard. More than that in this case, that bastard and I had a bad fucking history. The bastard *I* knew as Kyle Trass, his real name.

I watched him rapidly scan the room, his eyes wild, really showing the fear.

I drank it in like the sweetest fucking nectar.

Considering our history, it was incredibly satisfying in a sick thrill kind of way.

Finally, his gaze landed on me at the far back of the establishment.

His wild eyes widened, his shock and fear at it being *me* sitting here and not my dad who was far more reasonable and controlled in his actions than I would ever allow myself to be.

I smirked and raised my glass, tossing him a wink.

He pulled at his tie and swallowed hard, then raised a palm toward the two security guards with him, gesturing for them to remain where they were.

And then he approached, one wide stride at a time.

I kept my unflinching gaze on him the entire time.

He couldn't manage to do the same, breaking eye contact. Whether it was shame or fear—possibly a bit of both—I couldn't tell. Yet.

"Levi," he uttered unevenly as he finally reached the booth. "How did you find me?"

"The more pertinent question you should be concerned with is '*why?*'"

He cleared his throat. "All right, what do you need?"

I downed the rest of my vodka, then rose to my feet. "We'll talk in your office."

"Here is fine."

"I won't do business on the club floor of a seedy strip joint."

I could see his first reaction was to resist, but he made the right choice and gave a nod. "Sure. My office it is then."

He tried to finagle things so I was walking ahead of him, but I made it clear it would be the other way around.

As if I'd be fool enough to allow anyone to be at my back.

Sure, thanks to my many years street fighting, my reactions were lightning-fast, but you couldn't stop what you couldn't see coming.

I followed him off the club floor and down a poorly lit corridor all the way to the back where my research had already determined his office was.

He took a moment to unlock the door, then he opened it and stepped inside, gesturing for me to do the same.

"So what can I do for you?" he asked, trying to feign a casual air as he tensely walked behind his desk and took a seat as I shut the door and approached.

I took a seat in one of the two chairs opposite him and kicked my feet up on the desk.

He glared for a moment, not liking the insult of it, but he didn't speak to it.

"Your former boss has been underground for years. For as long as you've been hiding away actually."

"Malcolm Lynch?"

I only just managed to suppress a shudder at the mention of that fucker's name. No matter all the preparation I'd done through knowing it would come up, it was still a bitch of a thing to suppress a reaction.

I ground my teeth. "You know it's him I'm talking about."

"Fine, yeah. But, underground? He's dead."

I clasped my hands in my lap. "Yes, what a well-fashioned coverup that was."

"Coverup? I don't know what—"

"Your denial is futile. You helped with his escape from my father's wrath."

"Levi, I—"

"I have proof, *Kyle*."

He scrubbed his hand over his clean shaven jaw. "He forced my hand. Our hands. Me and—"

"Royce Humphrey. I'm well aware you were both involved."

"Look, even if that was true, that we helped get him out, thinking he survived much beyond that night is a whole other thing. Roman Knight and Curt Walker were after him, for fuck's sakes."

"*You* survived. For the last six years too."

"I was just following orders along with Royce. Your old man and the girl's knew that's all it was on our end."

"On your end, perhaps. Royce was another story. Malcolm might have been the big boss back then, but Royce was his right-hand and overjoyed to be so." Overjoyed by a lot of what had gone down in that hellscape, what he'd inflicted upon us. "I understand why you're defending him, though. After all, you have all of this because of him. His resources and the protection of that militia he's running these days ensure your safety and that you can actually have a life after what you did for that sadistic madman."

I put my legs down and pushed to my feet, noting Kyle eyeing me warily.

Shoving my hands into the pockets of my suit jacket, I commented, "Also, in order for you to remain safe, you need to remain a step ahead. That means knowing where your enemies are at all times. There is absolutely no doubt in my mind that you know Malcolm is alive and well."

"Listen, kid—"

I slammed my hands down on his desk, rocking it under the force of my strength. "I've laid eyes on him, you fool!"

He choked. "Jesus. How the hell did you manage that?"

"That's for me to know." I pushed off the desk. "Just like I also know that rumors have been circulating in underground circles you're still connected to concerning the *reawakening of a sleeping giant.* Moves have been made, deals struck by a shadowed organization with no apparent name. Power plays are being made all over the place. They've tried to fool people into believing they were separate acts and moves committed by different groups and individuals, but I've managed to connect them to a single effort. This is one organization trying to rise, to exert influence, and claw its way to the top within the criminal underground."

"And you think it's Malcolm?" He shook his head and rose to his feet. Starting to round his desk, he told me, "Look, Levi, I get you heading down this path. But it's not gonna turn out well for you at all. I've just confirmed to you that Malcolm Lynch is alive. Let's leave it at that, yeah?"

"You didn't confirm anything. I told you I already knew."

"It's all I know too."

"I understand."

"I'm glad."

"So, you really have nothing else for me, hmm?"

He held out his hands either side. "I really don't."

"I see."

"So, we're good here, yeah?" he asked, walking to me.

"We'll never be good."

"You know what I mean."

"I do." I held out my hand, giving him my best *performance* smile.

He hesitated for a moment, but as I kept my hand out steadily, he did what weak shits tended to do and gave into the pressure of social expectations, and reached out to shake it.

The moment we connected, I used the hold to yank

him to me, deliver a chop to his throat that had him choking and disorientated, and I took advantage of it to haul him around, using his weight as an asset for me as I forced him down into a bent position over his desk.

As he struggled, I swiftly drew a blade from the inside pocket of my suit jacket and then drove it through the back of his hand, crucifying it to the desk.

Take your punishment, bitch.

He squealed like the fucking pussy he was and flailed on the desk, thumping his free fist down on the oak in agony.

"Christ! We check for weapons... how did you get the knife through?"

"My vodka needed a lime. The bartender turned their back to serve other patrons, giving me the opportunity to lift it."

"Fuck. Take it out. Please," he begged.

"Please?" I hissed. "Did you pay any mind to *my* pleas in that hellscape during those two weeks of torment? To hers?"

"I... couldn't. Malcolm wouldn't allow it... would've killed me."

"He still will if he learns where you've hidden yourself, this new identity you've used as a smokescreen. All his accomplices from the kidnapping were supposed to be annihilated. But two of you survived and scurried underground like the rats that you are."

"Don't... don't out me. I'll... whatever you want... it's yours. I swear."

"The name."

"Name?"

I twisted my knife, making him squeal again. "The name of the reincarnated version of *Lynch Corp*, you fuck!"

I needed it to be able to move forward with my investigation, to take it the last leg.

I'd known that would require insider intel only those closest to that motherfucker would be privy to. While Royce was that person through and through, he wasn't as easy to approach—not singlehandedly at least—as Kyle was. And, fortunately, I knew Royce would keep his old buddy abreast of all intel concerning Malcolm for his own safety.

Kyle Trass was the weak link.

I shifted my grip, fisted my hand in the back of his hair, then used the hold to smash his face into the hard wood of the desk.

A satisfying crack sounded as it shattered his nose, blood spurting, as a nasally cry tore from his throat.

"Name! Now!"

When he still resisted, I wrenched the knife from his hand, enjoying his screams.

They evolved to pleas all too quickly when I shoved the flat of the blade between his legs.

"No! All right, fuck! Please! I'll tell you! I'll fucking tell you!"

I pushed harder so he could really feel the cool metal against his balls. "Still not hearing a name."

"*Osiris!*" he called out frantically. "That's it, I swear!"

I frowned, taking it in.

"You believe me, right?" he asked, worriedly.

According to Ancient Egyptian mythology, Osiris was the ruler of the dead and underworld, their judge as well. Definitely fit with Malcolm Lynch.

I released him roughly and pocketed the bloodied knife.

"Nice doing business with you," I seethed, as I strode to the door.

"You pursue this and you're a dead man," he warned. "You won't get the closure you need, he'll never allow it. You'll just end up suffering even more than you and the girl already did."

I paused at the door.

"I'm not that little boy anymore. *He* needs to fear *me*. It's time for a motherfucking reckoning."

With that, I threw open the door and walked out, leaving that pussy reeling with the damage I'd inflicted.

The only reason it had been limited and he was still breathing was because he could prove useful as a source of intel down the road with my crusade.

Once that stopped being true, however, and he'd outlived his usefulness, he'd suffer the fate he'd long deserved.

Extermination.

18

~Colton~

My Mercedes screeched to a halt outside Frat Row—what we called the block that housed three of the five fraternity houses of Stonewell University.

I hadn't seen Mason for two days even though we lived in the same house. He'd been strategically avoiding me. And ignoring my texts and attempted calls.

And I knew why.

With his eyes everywhere now, he was aware that I'd found out about him marking Brianna as a *Hex* target.

He was fucking lucky that Lev hadn't.

The only reason for that was because he wasn't here right now.

I'd thought it really strange when Brianna had reported to me that Lev had been giving her the silent treatment and staying away. He was an extremely proactive guy. He didn't fold and he didn't do things quietly or carefully. So when I'd approached him about it, I'd found out the reason for him withdrawing was because he'd been called back home by his father, Roman Knight, the business tycoon and owner of the multinational conglomerate,

Knightsridge Engineering. When Daddy Knight called, there was no choice, Lev absolutely had to go.

Knowing their usual get-togethers, Lev would be back within a few days.

Long enough for me to stop Mason in his tracks before Lev found out about it and all hell broke loose.

As it was, I'd already intervened in more of *Hex's* attempted strikes against Brianna.

After she'd told me she'd been marked, I'd been keeping a closer eye on things. I'd stopped two of Mason's frat boy soldiers from slashing her tires, and I'd also stopped three of the football players also in his employ from trying to corner her one night when she'd been leaving campus late. I'd recognized the *Hex* formation they'd been taking, wherein they would've then crowded her and threatened her. I hadn't told Brianna about it because it just would've scared her, so I'd interrupted their attempt by wrapping my arm around her and staying right beside her, making it clear their attack couldn't happen.

Ever since then Mason had been avoiding me, knowing I was aware of what he was doing.

Or what he was ordering his soldiers to do, because he liked to keep his hands clean.

As I climbed out of my car, I took in the mayhem all around.

The members of all three houses were gathered around the front yards of their mansions, looking freaked out, displaced, and up in arms all at the same time.

Through the chaos, I caught sight of Mason standing rigidly by the front gate of the middle house—the one we'd been a member of not too long ago—as he spoke with Rosemary Reitner, the head of the one of the sororities. She was dressed in her favored sundress look, this one a demure pale blue. Her blond hair was big and wild in its permed style.

I'd found out that she was also one of Mason's *captains* of several of the sorority members also operating as *Hex* soldiers now. The girl's mother was a partner in a rival law firm to his father's. And Mason was obviously intending to use that connection in his upcoming war against Peter Hall. *Shit*, it was brazen of him. All of it was. With him restarting *Hex* and Levi only participating a little, it wasn't evened out like it had been before and the power of it had clearly gone to Mason's head. He was getting involved in dirty dealings that Lev would normally nix. Lev didn't like us going that route, he usually handled that sort of thing on his own and he was much more accustomed to it than Mason. Because once Mason got a taste of power after it being so long denied him and him being so subservient and restricted by his father, he couldn't hold back, it became addictive to him.

As it clearly was doing now.

I jogged up to them and Rosemary eyed me. "What you doing here, rockstar?"

Her displeasure at my presence was obvious. And it wasn't just because they were in the middle of something. It was because she wanted Mason all to herself. After I'd rejected her because she was one of the most manipulative people I'd ever met—something she had in common with Mason when he got into this kind of phase, she'd turned her attentions to Mason for the last couple of years to spite me. She'd somehow discovered that he and I had a casual thing going on and she kept doing whatever she could to remind me that he'd never acknowledge that outside the bedroom, yet he would with her if she got close enough.

"Fuck off. I need to talk to Mason. Alone."

Mason turned to face me, agitation and surprise warring. "Busy, Colt."

"You'll make time," I bit back. "*Scourge.*"

When I folded my arms across my chest and made it clear I was settling in and not going anywhere until he finally had the decency to hear me out, he blew out a breath and told Rosemary, "Give us a moment."

"Sure thing," Rosemary said. Her gaze swept over me. I was wearing my special pair of custom-made gold leather pants with studs all over them, along with a black metallic tank and a black shimmering cropped jacket over the top. "Maybe you should save those sorts of outfits for the stage. Bit too flashy for everyday wear, don't you think?"

"Like I said, fuck off, *snake.*"

She sneered. "Sure thing, pretty little rocker."

Urgh.

When she walked away into the crowds of the sorority members who'd also gathered around at the calamity taking place, I stepped up to Mason. "What's happening here?"

"Infestation."

"What?"

"One house was swarmed by red ants a couple of hours ago. Another was crawling with cockroaches. And the third has a rat epidemic."

"Wow, that's one hell of a coincidence. All at once, different creatures."

"It's far from a coincidence."

It hit me all too quickly.

"It's fine. I'll handle it. I'm working on it."

Shit. Had she actually done this? Had this been her way of fighting back against *Hex's* bullying?

"It is?" I asked, feigning cluelessness.

"Of course. This was a coordinated strike."

"Huh… that's some crazy shit."

He gave me a withering look. "This was your little girl-friend, Colt."

"My girlfriend? Last I checked, I was relationship and strings free."

"I saw you. I saw you in the recording studio with her."

I shrugged. "I was comforting her."

"Looked like she was comforting you too about you not being happy that I've had her marked."

"I'm *not* happy about it. In fact, what you're doing is both unfair to her and dangerous in the grand scheme of things. You need to stop before Lev comes back. You're living up to your *Scourge* name way too well right now."

"No can do. I want her gone before he gets back."

"What? No. You can't do that to him."

"To him? Or to you?"

"Excuse me?"

"You've clearly taken a real liking to her. I saw you with her, remember? You're enamored. As for us living up to our nicknames, you're doing the opposite, not holding true to your *Maverick* persona at all, in fact. Putting your attention all on one person, cutting back on the partying."

Before I could get a word out about that, he went on, "Well, I'm not going to jeopardize all of us based off some new feelings you have for a girl you've only known for a few weeks. The fact is she's trouble where Levi is concerned, so she needs to go."

"Mason, this is the wrong way to go about it and you know it. Just fucking well talk to Lev, all right? Solve it from that angle. Don't punish Brianna when she's not at fault."

He gestured angrily at the frat houses behind him. "I just told you she did this. Not at fault? Bullshit."

"Even if it was her and you're not just being ridiculously paranoid, it would only be retaliation for what you've already done to her." I laid my hand on his shoulder and dug in so he couldn't instantly pull away, not while I needed to drive my point home. "Come on, brother. Do the right thing and back off, yeah?"

He stared at me for several moments and I really thought he was seeing reason and the error of his ways.

But then his phone rang, shattering the hold I had on him, and he pulled away and fished it out from the pocket of his snug navy jeans.

He swiped it open and answered, "Chase?"

Chase Arlington? The football captain?

He was on his payroll too? A member of *Hex?* Shit, Mason was really going for it. Chase's father was a rival of Mason's father.

"What situation?" I heard Mason asking down the line. "Paramedics in the locker rooms? What? What about the showers? Fine. I'll be right there."

"What's going on?" I asked, as soon as he hung up.

He scrubbed his hand over his face. "Another fucking strike. This time at the players on the team who I've also recruited into *Hex.*"

"What do you mean another strike?"

"Chase was too worked up to give me the necessary details. Weak fuck. Something we need to work on. I need to head down and find out for myself."

As he went to take off toward his Porsche that was parked a couple of hundred feet in the distance, I called out, "I'm coming with."

He was too worked up and focused on the immediate to protest.

───

HOLY SHIT.

Paramedics filled the corridors near the locker room and stretchers with several players on them were being wheeled out and rushed toward the lot where I'd seen a bunch of ambulances parked when I'd arrived on campus just behind Mason.

Speaking of Mason, I hadn't seen him for at least twenty minutes since he'd dipped inside the guy's locker room to find out what had happened.

Students, professors, maintenance staff, and even the Dean were all flitting about in a panic, the Dean trying to contain the shitshow, along with the medical professionals who'd been called in.

I grimaced as I took note of another football player with burns to his face, neck, chest, and hands, being wheeled past on a gurney. Second-degree burns, if I had to guess.

Finally, Mason emerged. I stepped out to meet him. "What happened?"

"Some malfunction with the showers. The water was scalding-hot and the taps wouldn't turn off once they were turned on, so the players were stuck in there subjected to those temperatures." He lowered his voice and pulled me with him away from the crowds as he told me, "Six of my *soldiers*. Just them. The other players weren't even in there. The chances of that… it's next to none. Another setup. Another fucking strike against *Hex*. Against me."

"I guess some people aren't happy about *Hex* being revived, or the moves you've been making."

"Some people? Come off it, Colt. It's clearly her."

"Brianna? No fucking way."

He shook his head at me in dismay. "Either way, I'll find out. And whoever it is, they'll be punished. Severely."

With that, he stormed off down the corridor.

This whole thing was growing out of control more so with every passing day.

I'd thought Lev not being here right now would be a good thing, so I could reach Mason and have him call off the mark against Brianna, but clearly that wasn't going to happen. Mason was being beyond his usual stubbornness right now. So far beyond. All of this was.

While I'd failed to get through to him, our dynamic clearly not making it possible, Lev *could*.

Shit, I needed him back here ASAP.

19

~Levi~

I stepped out of the Science and Technology building on campus now that I'd retrieved the class notes I'd missed while I'd been away for a few days due to a faux *family emergency*.

As I made my way around to the north lot where I'd parked my Harley, my phone buzzed in the pocket of my well-worn leather riding jacket.

I pulled it out and swiped it open to see a text from Colt.

Yet another one.

Colt: Are you back yet, Lev?

Colt: Hellraiser, this is urgent, text me back. Better than that, get back here ASAP.

He'd sent a dozen of them while I'd been gone, but I hadn't responded because I couldn't risk having my focus divided while I'd been dealing with Kyle and obtaining that information I'd needed.

I'd made it back into town ten minutes ago and after visiting campus, my plan had been to head home anyway.

Lev: Just got back, Maverick. On campus. Be home soon. Chill, brother.

Colt: Oh, thank fuck.

Lev: Missed you too, cupcake.

Colt: Well, I always miss you, but this is actually more business related. We have a problem.

Lev: Just take a breath, we'll see to it. I've got you.

Colt: It's actually about me having your back this time.

I frowned down at his message.

Having my back about what?

Colt had been clingy since I'd returned after being away for a year. He hadn't wanted me to take off even for a few days, so I'd figured his texts had just been about that, his way of trying to make sure I came home as quickly as possible.

But with that last text, it suggested there was actually something serious going on.

So serious that he hadn't wanted to tell me via our phones.

Thuds and yells caught my attention and pulled me from my thoughts.

I spun to my right and I was surprised to see Brianna there with her driver's door open as she was half in and half out of the car, slamming the steering wheel and dash while cursing.

Her silky mane of black hair was wilder than normal and I could see why as she shoved her hand through it in her agitated state. There was less of her bubbly pink going on. In fact, her boot cut pants were plain black, along with a lacy tank, the only signs of her favorite go-to color being on her leather jacket which was predominantly black but with pink stripes adorning it, along with some studs.

What was going on?

I pocketed my phone and strode over there quickly.

"Fucking shitheads!" I heard her seething as I reached her and her Charger.

I leaned down and spoke through the open window of her passenger door, "Hey."

She started and swung her head my way. "Jeez, maniacal stalker, make a sound, would you?"

"You wouldn't have heard my approach with all the hitting and cursing anyway."

She narrowed her eyes. "What do you want?"

"Just got back into town. I had to drop into the Science and Tech building and as I was leaving I heard this going on."

She just grunted, then tried to start the engine again.

The failed results of that made it clear to me what was happening.

Or, what wasn't happening.

"You're gonna damage the fuel pump," I warned.

"What?" she snapped.

"You keep trying to start the engine while you're out of gas and it could fuck up the fuel pump."

She blew out a breath, then slammed the door shut with a brutal thud. "Sons of bitches actually siphoned my gas!"

"Yeah, I'm getting that."

She shot me a look over the hood. "I don't need your sarcasm right now."

"That was my creepy calculative tone, *Wildflower.*"

Her eyes lit with mirth and a slight smile curved her lips. "Oh, shut up," she said, but there was definite humor there in it.

I walked around the car to meet her on the driver's side. "We both know that's not possible for me."

"Never have truer words been spoken."

I chuckled and she actually joined me.

The sound was… incredible.

But it came to an end all too quickly as her focus returned to this bullshit that had happened to her car.

It was *Hex*.

Hex had happened to her car.

It was Mason through and through.

The motherfucker had targeted her while I'd been gone.

It was one of his go-to tactics.

I pulled out my phone. "I'll fix this."

"I'll handle it. It's fine. Now I'm past the initial rage, it's onto the problem-solving part of this shit show."

"While I don't doubt your ability to take care of it yourself, I have connections here in Stonewell. I can get you the gas and have your car moved to your apartment complex too."

She eyed me skeptically. "And what's the price going to be?"

"Price? Nothing. Like I said, *connections.*"

"I mean your price, Hell Spawn."

I smiled to myself. I knew that was what she called me in her phone. "Nothing."

"Nothing?"

"This is my fault. The least I can do is fix it."

"Your fault? You weren't even here."

"Mason is doing this because I pulled you close to me, because I'm showing a lot of interest in you."

"Why is that his concern?"

"It's a long story."

"One I want to hear. But not right now." She reached into the backseat of the car, then pulled out her messenger bag. "I need to see if I can still catch Professor Ruiz before she leaves. She's known for staying late. I need her help fixing the other attack from *Hex*. As much as it pains me to say it, I wasn't able to do it myself."

"Fix what? What other attack?"

She blew out a breath of frustration and reached into her bag.

In the next moment, she was pulling out a small silver cube the size of a golf ball, a piece of hardware I recognized all too well.

"That's mine."

She frowned. "You weren't around, so Mason stole it from you while you were gone?"

"Looks like. Is your laptop in that bag?"

"Yeah."

"Shit." I reached out and took the device from her, studying it. "You already switched it off."

"Yeah, I figured that much out. Although its off-switch really wasn't easy to find. It's hidden in the design really well."

"That was the goal when it was developed by *Knight-sridge Engineering*. This is actually an early prototype. The ones these days are much smaller—easier to conceal."

"For cyber terrorism? It's scrambled all my files, even programs, every single thing on the local network."

"It didn't just do that. It siphoned everything first, made copies in essence, then *scrambled* it, as you put it."

"I see. So *Hex* is looking for intel on me as well as trying to bully me out of here."

"I'll handle the former and as for the latter, there's no way that's happening."

She adjusted her bag on her shoulder and folded her arms across her chest. "Right. So you can do it yourself."

"I did gather intel on you, yes. But not for nefarious purposes. To protect you and to get to know you, so I could approach you in the right way."

"That sounds beyond manipulative."

"No. In the *right way* meaning so as not to hurt you—emotionally. After what you endured six years ago, I knew there'd be scars. I wanted to make sure I understood those and the way you wore them before I came into contact with you."

She arched an eyebrow. "Is this your maniacal and twisted way of saying you were afraid of scaring me off?"

"Actually, yeah." I stepped closer, aware of her tensing, so I pulled up shy of her personal space. "As for bullying you, that wasn't my intention at all." I shoved a hand through my hair. "It was because I saw you, *Wildflower*. I saw you standing in the shadows of who you were, afraid to be that person again because it was attached to all that trauma. I saw you hurting. And that hurt was ruling your every action. You don't even talk to your father anymore because of it, because he's a reminder of that time, of the pieces of you that you lost during that hell and were too afraid to recover all of this time." I took a risk—something I normally had no qualms about, but something that had proved different when it came to her and had me holding off on going all out as I normally would with little concern for the fallout—and grasped her hands, holding them between us.

She didn't pull away.

"And I see all that because it was me for a long time too. I went the other way eventually. Too far, some might say. Maybe even me sometimes. So much has been about trying to prove I'm not that naïve and helpless kid bound in that room unable to save himself—unable to save *you*."

"Levi," she uttered sadly. "It wasn't your job to save me. You *were* just a kid then."

"But it fell to you. And what you did for me, it hurt you."

She squeezed her eyes shut for a moment as she uttered, "It was my choice to make and I don't regret it. It spared you. That's what mattered." When she opened them, they swam with agonizing emotion. "I don't talk about it, I don't like to think about it, and sometimes I pretend it wasn't real at all. *Because* the truth is, I *do* see them when the lights go out." She squeezed my hands. "I see the demons."

"You remember me calling them that during those two weeks," I realized aloud.

She nodded.

I watched her suck in a breath and take a moment, clearly needing to say more.

I waited, trying to maintain patience that normally didn't come easy to me.

And then she told me, "I saw you as a threat when you first showed up in front of me. I thought having you around me or anywhere near at all would unearth all that trauma and pain I'd spent so much energy trying to bury. But being around you, our interactions, it started to make me realize that I hadn't really buried it at all. I'd been running. I hadn't actually faced it." She smiled sadly. "And you... you're the only one who knows what happened to me, to us. The only one who could ever hope to understand, somebody I don't need to confess it all to. And you were right, there is a connection between us all these years later, because what happened bound us together in a way that nobody else can understand."

"More than that, Brianna. The way I handled it and you handled it were polar opposite approaches, from one extreme to another. But together there's a balance neither of us were able to strike individually."

"A chance at peace, you mean?"

"Very possibly."

She pulled her hands from mine and sank against the side of the Charger. "You're dangerous, Levi."

I joined her, settling beside her, and turned my head to tell her, "As are you. You've just been hiding it in those shadows you've gotten far too comfortable immersing yourself in."

Her lips quirked as she noticeably avoided eye contact. "No idea what you're getting at."

I laughed. "Actually look at me when you say that."

She did, turning her head. "I may have flexed that *dangerous* muscle while you were gone."

I cocked an eyebrow. "Seriously?"

She nodded. "I struck back against *Hex.* Twice."

Christ. "How soon after they hit at you?"

"Quickly. I couldn't allow escalation without punishment. They were seeing me as a victim, thinking they were winning the battle they started. I couldn't accept that."

"I get that, but with the timing, Mason will know it was you. This gas siphoning is just a warmup, he's just hitting the on-ramp."

"Then it's a good thing I *am* actually dangerous then, isn't it?"

I reached out and slid my fingers into her soft, silky hair, playing with the black strands. A calming serenity took me over as she sank into it and angled her head toward me, a little sigh of contentment escaping her.

"You don't need to worry about this. I've got it from here. I also have the means to reverse what was done to your laptop." Off her incredulous look, I explained further, "When I discovered that my dad's company had created something so devastating, I worked on an antidote of sorts to the tech. As for the data taken from you, I've already put something in place that will corrupt it once Mason opens it on any device within our home."

"That's… a lot to absorb. As for the data protection, are you telling me you wrote a program to flag any intel related to me and destroy it from others' view?"

I winced because with her knowledge being similar to mine on such things, I knew she'd understand how I'd been able to go about it. "Yes."

"Shit, breaking into my apartment was just the tip of the iceberg when it came to your stalking tendencies toward me, huh?"

"I couldn't take any chances—either with messing up things between us, or with Mason getting wind of who you really were to me and interfering." I ground my teeth. "As it is, he's already interfered in another way by coming after you."

I expected her to pull away, to tell me to go to hell again, to scream and curse me out at the very least.

But, instead, she drew closer to me and a little smirk spread over her face. "I would've done the same thing."

"You… what?"

"You said we reacted to what happened in polar opposite ways. Well, if things had been reversed and I'd responded like you, I would have done things the same way in my pursuit of you."

I couldn't believe it. She was bringing out the person I remembered, the person she'd buried for far too long, but whom I'd still seen in spite of that attempt.

"*Wildflower.*"

"*Hellraiser,*" she responded, all breathy.

The surprises kept on coming as she pushed into me, grasped my nape, then dragged my mouth down to hers.

It wasn't an out of control explosion of passion like it had been the first time I'd kissed her.

No, this time it was intense in a whole other way.

Slow, easy, soft, and so incredibly raw that I felt it down to my bones.

I closed my eyes, savoring her taste, her lips on mine, her finally wanting me without any convincing on my part, actually truly connecting with me.

When I went to ease away because I felt myself getting worked up, the urge to escalate things when that wasn't what this was about in this moment, she chased my lips.

I grinned and grasped her hips, holding her at bay.

"Lock up your car, I'll give you a ride home."

"Yeah," she rasped, still caught in the moment. "Take me home."

Christ.

———

I HADN'T WANTED the ride to end.

It had barely been ten minutes having her on my bike, her chest plastered against my back, her arms linked tightly around my waist, as her sweet coconut scent wafted over me and her heat had rolled through me. Halfway through she'd even tightened her hold around me, and then I'd felt her cheek pressing against me as she'd drawn ever closer, like she hadn't wanted the ride to end either.

Something had fallen into place between us in that campus parking lot, something that hadn't been possible before because of so much resistance and fear on her end.

But now that had shifted in her—or at least begun to.

It was just a shame that it had taken *Hex* coming at her to jar that into being for her.

The idea of anyone coming at her made me sick to my stomach and infected me with a rage so pure the whole fucking world should cower at the mere sight of me.

The fact that it was Mason behind it caused a complication that didn't compute with my automatic protocol to decimate in the face of such an offense.

It posed a barrier.

I didn't care for barriers. I mowed them the fuck down.

And I was a vengeful fucker by nature. My years-long crusade being a testament to that.

If someone came at me, I struck back tenfold and razed the threat to the goddamn ground.

No matter the consequences.

Something Mason hated with every part of his hollow vacuum of a soul.

Yet, him being who he was to me, he'd forced me into a state of inaction—at least the immediate kind. He'd forced me to tone down an immediate brutal response, and to finagle another way to go about delivering punishment for the offense and, more importantly, protection for my girl from anything further being levied upon her.

I swallowed down the rage, placing it into a box for the time being. Because what mattered right now was *her*. This connection I'd felt snap into place between us earlier.

I couldn't allow anything to mar that or take precedence.

I'd waited too fucking long.

It wasn't just *Hex* inadvertently pushing her to embrace that which she'd denied for so long. It was also my absence giving her time to come to terms with things I'd brought back to life and thrust right into the forefront for her. Who knew the act of essentially doing nothing— giving her space—would actually prove such a powerful aid?

I pulled into the rear lot of her apartment building.

Her apartment was on the fourth floor facing toward this particular lot, and the forest flanking it.

As I dismounted my Harley, I went to reach out to help

Brianna down, but she swung her leg over like a pro and did it herself.

I watched enraptured as she pulled off my helmet and shook out her long silky black hair like something out of a shampoo commercial.

She passed it to me and I stowed it in one of my saddlebags.

"It's been a long time since I've taken a ride."

"In any sense, as I understand it."

Expecting her to bite back at me or tell me I was disgusting, a pervert, or something along those lines, she defied my expectations as she had been doing a lot tonight and instead stepped up to me with a suggestive glint in her eyes, as she admitted, "In any sense, yeah."

She was showing me the woman I knew she was, the parts of herself that she'd lost along the way when she'd driven herself into the shadows and reinvented herself without key aspects of her personality.

And I was absolutely here for it.

"Is that something you want to remedy?" I asked, sliding my hands down to her hips.

A soft moan escaped her at my contact, and it was all I could do to leave it at that, holding her at arms' length. It had to be her decision. Her clear choice, no hesitation.

If not, it would fuck up everything.

It would taint our connection.

Something I would never allow.

I'd already come too close when I'd teased her up against the wall of *Nirvana*. That hadn't been the same as going all out with her, though, of properly claiming her as mine where there was absolutely no question as to who she belonged to.

Absolutely no escape for her.

Besides, she'd most definitely wanted it then. She

hadn't just submitted, or been putty in my hands, she'd risen to the challenge of it and given it right back to me.

Good fucking thing. I didn't want submissive. At least, not from her. Not from something that was so fucking real to me. So important to me.

The women I'd fooled around with—mostly *fight bunnies*, as Colt called them—had only been a means to an end, to physical release. It had basically been a transaction and nothing more, to all parties involved.

But this, with Brianna Walker, it enveloped me mind, body, and goddamn blackened soul. It was all-encompassing.

Every. Fucking. Thing.

She stepped back, easing from my grip and ran her hands through her hair.

Not in a frustrated way, though. No, in a freeing way.

She let out a peaceful sigh, her beautiful whiskey eyes lit up. "I made myself forget how liberating riding is," she said in a thoughtful, faraway voice. "How much I really missed it."

"Well, you were born into it, raised in it. It's a big part of you."

"A part I've denied for a long time."

"It's okay. You're coming out of it now. It just took a little push."

"A little, huh?"

"Well—"

She jolted toward me and fisted her hands in my hair, cutting my response to the quick, and sending a shock of twisted bliss through me. Driving my already semi-hard cock even fucking crazier in the process.

"If I wasn't still high on the amazing ride, I'd slap you for downplaying your bullshit."

"Then slap me once you come back down to earth." I winked. "I like it rough."

Her hands slid from my hair, down to my shoulders, coming to rest on my biceps. I smiled as she felt them up, enjoying all the well-defined muscle I'd worked hard to maintain. "Interesting information."

"Good to know."

She smiled devilishly, that look doing a fuck of a lot to me.

"As I was saying about the ride… I haven't felt that kind of real freedom for a long time. The kind where I just let go, being my true self without any fallout from the trauma of the past trying to yank me back into those shadows, as you call them. The only other time in all these years was what happened between us outside the bar—kicking your ass, then… the other stuff."

"Kicking my ass… that's a rewrite of recent history right there."

She chuckled. "Have you ever lost a fight?"

"Once."

She looked surprised. "To who?"

That was a story for another day, and definitely not something I wanted to get into now. So, I redirected. "Hmm, you know about my street fighting then?"

"I do," she said, thankfully accepting the redirection.

"So, I'm not the only one with stalking tendencies?"

"I might have started looking into you once you made your presence impossible to avoid."

"You also tagged me—or more specifically, my phone."

Her eyes widened. "How do you—you hacked my phone. It wasn't just a one-off so you could enter your number."

"Had to keep an eye on what's important to me. I would apologize, but looks like we're even."

"Not even close. Plus, you deactivated the tag before you left on your recent mysterious trip."

"I did."

"Noted that you didn't deny the *mysterious trip* thing. So you didn't really go to visit your dad then, like Colt said?"

"Aww," I said, sliding my hands into her hair. "You were asking about me, hmm? Missed me, didn't you?"

"Yes," she answered, sinking into my touch and moving closer so I could get my fill of her hair.

"Wow, that was… unexpected. I thought you were going to deny the fuck out of it."

"Not anymore."

"Is that right?"

She smiled, then frowned at me.

"What?" I asked.

"You're nervous, aren't you?"

"Nervous?"

"About where this is clearly leading tonight? You swerved our conversation down a totally different path. Are you having second thoughts?"

I cupped her face. "Never. There could never be second thoughts when it comes to you, my *Wildflower.* But, yeah, I am nervous, I guess."

"Wow, unexpected," she said, echoing my words a moment ago. "Why the nerves? I mean, I know I am, but it's largely because it's been a really long time for me and I'm not exactly used to the *rough* that you prefer."

I stroked her cheek with my thumbs. "That's a shame, considering you were made for the *rough*, for letting go and unleashing that raw and too-long-repressed part of you. I'm sorry that need was never met for you. Well, a little sorry. Also happy that the real you wasn't shared with anybody else."

She chuckled. "You're another level, you know that?"

"Oh, I'm well aware."

She sobered then and grasped my hands on her face. "Why the nerves?"

I sucked in a breath and gave it to her straight, "Last time we got… carnal… you blew me off like it was nothing. Like it was just a meaningless release, an itch you needed me to scratch for you."

"I didn't mean… I was just scared… not ready. I hadn't pegged you yet. And I was still in those shadows."

"I know. And I see that's shifted for you, or it's at least on its way. I just… I've waited a long time, held off for longer than you even realize. Christ, I've been obsessed with you since I was fifteen. But it wasn't the right time then. I mean, it took me two whole years after what happened to even become stable again." I cocked my head to the side. "Well, to be able to appear outwardly stable to others, anyway. To get my father off my back and be able to live without such a short leash. And after that, it wasn't safe to approach you. Not until the last year or so."

"Wasn't safe, how?"

"It doesn't matter. It is now."

"Levi—"

I dropped my hands from her and stepped back. "What I'm trying to say is that if I touch you again like that, escalate things beyond a tease, I won't be able to give you space again, to allow distance between us. I won't be able to let you brush it off. I'll be all fucking in, Brianna. You will be mine. No fighting it this time."

"Like I was saying, both times I've felt free and like my true self was around you, *because* of you. I want more of it. I don't want to run anymore. And, you, you make me feel safe to do that, to get back to that." She smiled, her eyes swimming with emotion, though, as she confessed, "You pulled me out of the shadows. I don't *want* to fight that, to

197

fight you, or this thing between us. It's past the point of being denied, trust me."

In the next moment, she was on me, looping her arms around my neck and crushing her lips to mine.

The moment I responded, all bets were off.

She hooked her thigh around me and I took the cue, hauling her into my arms without breaking our kiss.

It was all a blur of roaming hands, fisting each other's hair, nipping, biting, and tonguing as I carried her into the building and managed to get us into the elevator and push the button for her floor.

As soon as we were inside, I slammed her up against the wall and rolled my hips, grinding my painfully hard cock between her thighs. She threw her head back, opening wider for me, inviting me in, her desperate need as acute as mine.

The doors pinging open had her pulling her mouth from mine, much to my regret.

Even for a moment.

I couldn't stand the separation.

I fisted her hair to pull her back to me, but she resisted, uttering breathlessly, "My bag. I left it in your saddlebag."

"Your keys are in it?"

"No. My jacket pocket."

"Then I'll get it after."

"After?" she asked all coyly, biting her lip all fucking sexy.

I carried her down the corridor toward her apartment door. "*After* my cock has a thorough introduction to your sweet cunt."

A little tremble of need went through her.

"Is that how you want it from me, *Wildflower?* Dirty and rough?"

"I thought you'd studied me in such an invasively in-depth way that you already knew how to *give me what I need?*" she said, grinning, so proud of herself, thinking she was calling me out.

Mmm. I loved it when her fight came out, when she spit fire back at me.

"I'm confident that I do. But this is about what *you* know, what you're ready to accept."

She reached into the pocket of her edgy pink and black leather jacket and withdrew her key. Even at the awkward angle, she was able to reach down and unlock her apartment door with it. She pocketed it, then took me in with blazing eyes. "Everything. I want it all."

"Everything, hmm?"

She leaned in, her warm breath tickling my neck and teasing the fuck out of me in the process. Her sweet coconut scent and her body wrapped around mine already pushing me right to the edge as it was. "Don't hold back," she whispered huskily.

"Fucking Christ."

In the literal next second, I shoved us through the door, kicked it shut, then roughly locked it, then strode to the nearest surface—that being the kitchen table—and put her down on the edge on her ass.

My blood was roaring in my ears.

I could barely breathe with the thick and all-consuming anticipation that was fueling my every step knowing that this was the moment I'd been waiting on for so fucking long.

Her really and truly wanting me.

Her being as desperate to have me as I was to have her.

I was shoving her jacket off her shoulders in the next second, and she was stripping me down to just my pants, the two of us in a frenzy.

I yanked down the bust of her tank, splitting it down

the middle with my roughness and a sexy little pink bralette came into view.

I pushed against her, making her lie down on her back while I stood between her spread thighs, then dove down and bit at her nipples through the lace.

"Ah!" she cried, hooking her ankles around my hips and jerking me harder to her, as she arched her back, pushing her breasts closer, silently begging me for more.

I couldn't get close enough to her fast enough. I needed to feel her skin-to-skin immediately, no fucking waiting.

I moved to reach around and open her bra so I could taste her breasts, when another idea occurred to me.

I reached into the pocket of my cargo pants and pulled out my tactical knife.

A small gasp escaped her, but as her eyes lit up with fucking flames, it was clear it was far from anything resembling fear.

It was twisted depravity just like what I had in mind.

There she is. There's my girl.

"Give me everything," she uttered on a needy rasp, referencing our discussion earlier.

"Fuck, baby." I took her in a sloppy, wild kiss and she chased my lips when I pulled away to slice my blade through her bra.

A thrill rolled through me as it fell away and she watched so intently, her chest heaving, her breathing coming fast and uneven because she could barely contain herself, getting off on it as much as I was.

I swept the pieces of her bra away and then I trailed the flat of the blade down her throat, along her collarbone.

She fisted her hands on the kitchen table either side of her, clearly struggling not to move while I teased her.

"Don't worry about a little nick here and there. I'm very skilled with a blade."

"I don't want you to be."

Our eyes locked.

"Is that right?"

She bit her lip wantonly and gave a coy nod.

"Christ."

I spun the blade in front of her and adjusted my grip and she looked on in wonder.

And then I very carefully pressed the tip to her hard, cherry-tipped nipple.

She hissed and a pearl of blood leaked onto the cold metal. I exerted more pressure until it was leaking over the curve of her breast.

And then I dove down and licked up the trail, tasting her.

Her hands fisted in my hair. "God, Levi."

I sucked on her abused nipple, drawing more blood onto my tongue and savoring such an intimate piece of her.

Mine.

Her nails scraped my scalp. "I need you. Fuck, I need you now."

I lifted my head and slicked my tongue across her bottom lip, delighting in her licking off my taste and her blood mixed together.

And then I brought my blade to her pants and cut through the soft material like butter.

I brushed the scraps away, made a little slice to her lace panties beneath, then tore them from her body with a growl, her needy pleas making me fucking crazy.

As I pulled off her shoes, and her entire body was bared to me, it was all I could do not to jerk down my pants and slam inside her, pounding her up the kitchen table, maybe even decimating the thing with the force of my out-of-control thrusts.

Because that was how I felt with her right now—out of fucking control.

I wanted to let go, to give into it, and her reactions and pleas made it clear she did too.

But I couldn't.

Not just yet.

I had to summon restraint.

For her benefit.

She needed me to straddle that line.

And I fucking would.

I wouldn't screw this up, I wouldn't scare her, not when it came to getting physical.

Absolutely fucking not.

"Christ, you're so fucking beautiful," I groaned, taking in every inch of her in all her bared glory.

A goddamn goddess was what she was.

Lying there sprawled out on the table like an offering, her breasts reddened from my erotic attentions, her chest heaving in need, shifting restlessly in her desperation to have me, to have us, and her cunt so slick she was dripping down between her spread thighs.

All for me.

I traced my fingers over her all-seeing eye pendant. "I never forgot a single detail about you, *Wildflower*."

And then it happened, she finally gave it right back to me. "Neither did I."

I lunged at her, earning a yelp, and hauled her off the table.

Gathering her in my arms, I carried her to the bedroom.

She licked my neck, her tongue teasing my scar. And then she was slicking it over my vibrant red and black all-seeing eye tattoo on my left shoulder, tracing the design with sensual licks that had a carnal groan escaping me, my cock pushing painfully against my pants.

I adjusted her weight in my arms and held her with one hand, so I could snatch her wrist and exact the same sensual torment on her watercolor butterfly tattoo on her inner forearm.

Her eyes rolled back in her head, sexy moans spilling from her lips.

I dropped her on the bed.

I kicked off my shoes and socks and almost ripped my pants and boxers as I stripped them off in record time.

In the next second, I was pouncing on the bed and crawling up her body.

"Levi," she uttered in that breathy, turned-on voice that did things to me.

She surprised me then before I could cover her body with mine, and slapped her hands to my chest, pushing me back onto my haunches.

She grasped my biceps and kissed my scar again, then her mouth was all over me, licking and nipping at my pecs, my tattoo. She scraped her nails down my abs, making red-raw marks that had me throwing my head back and fisting my hands in the sheets.

"Brianna," I breathed, as she kissed the gunshot scar over my abs, then swirled her tongue around it.

My cock jerked when she came so close and I could feel her hot breath fanning over my tip.

Her hold tightened on my biceps, then she dove down and swallowed my shaft.

Right to the fucking hilt in one shot.

"Motherfucker!" I growled.

She found her rhythm instantly, moaning and grinding her cunt into the sheets as she went absolutely feral all over my cock.

I slammed my hands down onto the bed, losing my shit as she fucking well deep-throated me like a wild thing. The pleasure was so intense, I'd never felt anything like it.

It was more than even the act, it was the need I could feel from her, between us. All fucking consuming. Transcending everything.

"Not in your mouth," I was gasping after a few minutes, threading my fingers in her hair and easing her off my cock.

She smirked up at me, her beautiful whiskey eyes glazed as she licked my pre-cum off her lips.

Christ almighty.

"Woman, you're gonna kill me," I growled, grasping her hips and tossing her up the bed.

Snarling like a fucking animal, I dove down between her thighs, holding them at my mercy as I dragged my tongue through her dripping folds.

She screamed as I lost my shit all over her, lashing her clit, biting, sucking, until she was thrashing on the sheets, her thighs shaking.

"God, Levi!" she cried in that sexy way. "Ah! I'm gonna come! Fuck! Fuck me!"

Her screams turned to shrieks and she convulsed in my arms as she came all over my tongue.

I lapped up every drop of her sweet taste.

Then, before she could recover, I rose up on her, grabbed her hips, then slammed inside her cunt, the force of it rocking her up the bed.

She went still, her breath hitching.

She was *so* tight.

Fuck, the pressure was out of this world.

Wide eyes met mine. "More," she pushed, but I could see her wincing and trying to hide it.

"Not yet," I said, bringing my hands down either side

of her head and covering her body with mine, reveling in her heat and us finally being connected like this as her gaze blazed back at me, those beautiful eyes holding me hostage. "Just relax, feel my cock stretching your sweet cunt."

"Definitely feeling it," she said, with a little grin.

"Want me to pull out?" I asked, stroking her soft black hair.

"No fucking way," she answered adamantly. "I want you to stop taking it easy on me."

"Baby—"

"No. Fuck me like a beast. I told you I wanted it all."

"It's been a long time for you, you'll hurt tomorrow."

A sly look flitted across her face. "You mean, I'll feel you every time I move?"

Fucking shit, she certainly knew how to push my buttons. That was fucking it!

"Oh, *Wildflower,* you're so fucked."

She grinned. "Good. Give it to me, *Hellraiser.*"

I slammed her hands down above her head, weaving my fingers with hers, then I pulled almost all the way out and thrust inside her, rocking her up the bed.

"Fuck! Levi, yes!"

I didn't take it easy, I couldn't anymore.

I lost fucking control and pounded into her like a madman, holding her at my mercy as I power fucked her sweet cunt like an out-of-control machine, the bed rattling at the force of my rapid-fire thrusts.

"So. Fucking. Beautiful," I ground out. "So. Fucking. *Mine.*"

I angled my cock and hit her sweet spot, her eyes shooting wide. "Ah!" she cried in rapture. "Oh my God!"

"Say it," I growled. "Say that you're mine."

Before she got the chance, the animal took control and

I was pulling out of her roughly, then hauling her around onto her hands and knees.

I slammed back inside her, and she screamed as she came, clamping down around my cock, pleasure shooting through my shaft, my balls drawing tight.

Fisting her hair, I yanked her head back so her eyes met mine. "Say it, Brianna."

"Yes," she cried. "Yours. Yours, Levi."

"*Fuck.*"

I could barely see straight as I slammed into her like a beast.

I reached under her and slapped her highly-sensitized clit. She whimpered and tried to twist away, but I held her in place with my hand in her hair.

"Let go. Let it all go, baby," I uttered through ragged breaths at her ear. "Wreck for me, *Wildflower.*"

My slaps to her wet cunt became harder and faster, rapid-fire, until she was shrieking non-stop and fucking back against me, trying to meet my powering thrusts.

And then she stilled and lurched, a sexy animalistic growl tearing from her throat as she clamped down around my cock and came all over me.

It was too much then, she milked the fuck out of me and I roared as I came with her, filling her tight cunt with my hot cum.

I felt her knees start to give way and I eased her down into the bed, keeping my cock buried inside her as I covered her body with mine.

I couldn't leave her warmth yet, couldn't break the connection.

"That was...insane," she breathed into the pillow.

"Beyond even my most vivid fantasies about us."

She chuckled, then relaxed against me.

Mine.

I stroked her dandelion tattoo on her right upper back that was concealing something only the two of us knew about—a gunshot wound she'd taken there from the demons. Trying to save us. Trying to save *me*.

I grimaced and forced those thoughts from my mind, focusing on the moment. On her. She was here with me now.

Safe and protected.

And we'd finally come together the way I'd craved for so long.

The way I'd *needed* us to.

Tonight had been more than just her surrendering to me.

It was *us* surrendering to each other.

In a way that would stay with me forever.

I tightened my hold on her and breathed into her hair, "My *Wildflower.*"

20

~Brianna~

A repetitive buzzing forced me awake.

Groaning, I turned toward the sound, only to smush myself into a wall of warm, hard muscle. I jolted and looked to see Levi still here and wrapped tightly around me, his arm around my back and one of his big, muscular legs thrown over both of mine that were slightly curled.

Levi Knight was in my bed.

Warming my sheets. Warming *me*.

That masculine sandalwood scent that had become synonymous with him for me infused my senses.

Even in his sleep, his hold around me was unyielding and possessive. Protective and needy. And it made me feel… cherished.

As fucked up as it was and with the twisted way it had come about, not to mention how things had started when he'd come at me in his maniacal way, he made me feel safe and free at the same time. Being with him made me feel alive for the first time ever.

I didn't have to pretend with him either.

I didn't have to pretend that I wasn't damaged.

Because he was too.

But when we were together, in each other's company, it became something else.

It soothed it, all that pain we carried around with us.

It was solace.

As the buzzing thankfully stopped, I eased away a little to take Levi in.

He was on his side over on my side of the bed—well what I considered my side considering the whole bed was really mine, although I only kept to the left side and slept in a cocoon-like way, something that helped to ease my anxiety a little bit so I could fall asleep. Some nights. Others, I wasn't so lucky, and I couldn't do it on my own.

But last night I'd been able to.

I'd slept really hard, really deeply.

Because of him.

He was shirtless, the covers down to the waistband of his crimson boxers. His curls were all sexy and wild, a few strands flopping down over his eye. With the way he was sleeping, I couldn't see either of the two things that had drawn us together—his all-seeing eye tattoo and the scar along the left side of his throat.

But the other scar I'd seen last night during the whirl-wind that had been the two of us was visible.

I found myself reaching out and tracing my fingers carefully over the small cross-like shape. Unfortunately, I knew my wounds. It was definitely a gunshot wound.

"Mmm, already back for more, baby?" his sleep infused voice sounded, making me jerk my hand away and choke out a gasp of surprise.

"Crap."

A smile tugged at his lips as he opened his eyes and fixed them on me. "Thought I wore you out last night?"

"Never," I said, smiling back at him.

He arched an eyebrow, not buying it.

"Maybe a little," I actually found myself admitting, my tough front melting a little.

He wrapped his arm tighter around me and pulled me into him, until his big biceps were engulfing me with my looking up at him from his hard torso. "Morning."

"Morning," I returned, grinning up at him. "Last night was…"

"Incredible? Earth shattering? The best night of my fucking life?"

"Wow, that's high praise."

"And?"

I took in the light blazing in his pale-blue eyes that were most often dancing with a heady combination of determination, ruthlessness and malice. This time, it was wholly different. There was a light there so freaking bright it hit me right in the gut. Light and excitement. He looked so happy, so content and at ease.

It had me stroking his chest and confessing, "All of the above. It was amazing."

"I'm glad," he said, nuzzling my hair and breathing me in.

We'd only just sank into the intimacy of it when his phone buzzed yet again.

He grunted.

"It keeps doing that."

"It can wait."

"The persistence suggests it could be urgent."

He groaned, then very reluctantly released me to reach over to the nightstand.

I watched him swipe open the screen and I saw there were four missed calls from Colton. There were some text message notifications too.

"Christ," Levi muttered. He eyed me over his shoulder. "One second."

In the next, he was dialing Colton, and putting it on speakerphone mode.

"Lev, finally, what the—"

"Can't talk right now. I know I said I'd be home last night, but something came up. Be back in a couple of hours."

"But it can't—"

"I'm at Brianna's, cupcake."

There was a long pause.

"Well, damn. That's… I don't know what to say."

"Good. That concludes our conversation then. Gotta go, brother. See you soon enough."

With that, Levi hung up without another word.

He put his phone down, then blew out a breath and rolled back to face me on his side. "Sorry about that."

"That was rude, cutting him off like that."

"Rude? Rude was interrupting our first morning together with his relentless calls and texts."

"Well, did you even check the texts, because you didn't give him a chance to tell you why he was being so persistent."

He lifted a shoulder. "It's not a big deal."

"How do you know?"

"Because, shortly after we fell asleep, I was woken up by my phone ringing. It was my guys telling me that your car was gassed up and in your apartment complex lot, and that they'd slid your car key under your apartment door for you. At the same time, I saw a couple of texts from Colt with him thinking I hadn't come home because I was mad at him."

"Thank you for doing that for my car," I said, stroking his arm.

He beamed out at me. "No worries."

I shifted my weight. "So, are you mad at Colton?"

"Nah. He kept apologizing for kissing you. He thought I somehow already knew about it."

"You didn't?"

"Nope."

"And now that you do?"

His lips quirked. "How did you like that tongue piercing of his?"

"I… what?"

"Adds another level of stimulation, hmm?"

"It does," I admitted. And then I was frowning. "How do you know? Spend a lot of time kissing Colton, do you?"

"Twice. After he got that piercing, he was all worried about it impacting his game and he wanted to test it out, so I helped him out."

"Wow, that was very generous of you."

He grinned. "I thought so."

With his free hand, he trailed his fingers up and down my thigh. "Forget a kiss, imagine how it would feel teasing that sweet cunt of yours."

He stared at me in that challenging way of his.

I rose to it, telling him, "It's certainly something worth thinking about."

"Yeah?" he murmured, sliding his fingers higher, toward my inner thigh and making me tremble in his arms.

"Mmm, yeah. And where would you be while that's going on?"

"While Colt's spreading your thighs wide and tonguing your pretty little clit, you mean?"

God. "Yes."

"I'll be straddling your face and feeding my cock down your throat, baby."

My core clenched at his words, the picture he'd painted heating my blood.

"You like that, hmm?" he said, noticing my reaction.

"In your wildest dreams."

He chuckled and stroked my hair, playing with the strands. "You're so adorable when you try to kid yourself into resisting me."

"And you're so full of yourself."

"Nah, I just know that this thing between us fits." He took my hand gently and kissed my palm, startling me at the sweet tenderness of it. "It feels right. So fucking right."

"As twisted as it is, it actually does," I admitted. I shifted in his hold, angling myself closer to his teasing fingers wandering up my thigh beneath the sheets. A gasp escaped me as it had them touching my bare pussy.

His eyes darkened as he felt it. "Mmm, I love how wet you get for me from just a tease."

"Show me just how right it really is," I said, rolling my hips against his fingers so they slid through my folds, the stimulation sending sparks of bliss through me that had me moaning out.

I reached up and grasped his nape, but he resisted when I tried to urge his mouth to mine.

Off my look, concern spread over his rugged features as he asked, "Aren't you sore after last night? I'm well aware that I didn't take it easy on you." He smirked. "As much as I tried, you just weren't having it."

"You did show superhuman restraint. At first."

"And I'm going to again."

"Levi."

"As much as I want to fuck you until you shriek my name, I don't want you hurt."

"You know, there is another place you haven't fucked me yet. That no one has."

His eyes went utterly black. "Fuck."

"That's the idea."

I squealed as he suddenly pounced and rolled on top of me.

Caging me in, he leaned down and growled at my ear, "The idea of sinking into that tight little ass has me rock fucking hard." I turned my head and licked the shell of his ear as I rolled my hips at the same time, and a sexy groan emanated from him, sending a delicious tremble through me, making my need climb to new heights. "But," he breathed at my ear. "I don't have any lube."

"Neither do I. It'll be fine without."

"Not for the first time. Absolutely not." He planted a chaste kiss on my lips, then eased back to his haunches, the struggle all over his face to manage it blatantly obvious. "Give yourself some time."

"Okay," I reluctantly agreed.

He stroked my calf. "There's my good girl."

I slapped his hand. "I'm not your good girl."

He smirked. "Oh, really? You sure as fuck were last night."

"Does that make you my good boy then?" I challenged. "After all, that makes more sense, I'm three years older than you."

"I've never been called *good* before. But if it pleases you, feel free to call me that. Although, *Hell Spawn* is my favorite, for the record. Actually, nothing can beat the breathy and needy sound of the way you utter *'Levi'* when you're turned the fuck on."

I kicked at him from underneath the covers. "Stop!"

He laughed and rolled out of the way, and the movement turned into some sort of partial somersault as he somehow landed on his feet in front of the bed.

Off my incredulous look, he told me, "A few gymnastics classes gave me an edge in the fight arena. It opened up a bunch of moves for me that I wouldn't have been able to pull off as easily otherwise." He waggled his eyebrows at me. "Helps out in the fucking arena too. Last night was our first time, but down the road I'll show you some things, baby."

A tremble of excitement rolled through me. "I can't wait."

He tutted. "You'll have to. I'm gonna make you a bath, then I'll see to your laptop for you."

"Oh, so you're headed home?" I asked, pushing out of bed.

"Is that what I need to do?"

"Need to do?"

"Yeah, I mean, is that how this morning-after thing works?"

Oh my God. He looked unsure, almost… vulnerable.

"I don't think so. Well, I don't have anything to gauge it by."

"What do you mean? You've dated before. One person… that slimy shit, Tommy."

"He's not slimy."

"Not from your perspective, because of the hero worship you had going on."

"What?"

"He was the first person you saw after those two weeks in that hellscape, storming in as part of the rescue crew. After that, your dad ordered him to teach you how to fight as a reaction to it all, and you developed a relationship on that highly unstable ground. He took advantage of you."

"That's not… can we not talk about that… about him, while we're standing in my bedroom both half-naked?" I winced. "Or at all, actually?"

He held up his hands. "Fine by me. Just one more

thing… so you didn't wake up beside him, hence you saying you're not familiar with this morning-after thing either?"

"Correct. It was a secret relationship. From my father, from his club. Any time we… came together… it had to be… brief."

"No stamina, huh?" he said, grinning.

"Stop," I said, grabbing a pillow and tossing it at him.

He snatched it out of the air and hugged it to him.

"You're lucky I'm too nice to snap a picture of you cuddling a fluffy pink pillow."

"Your social media is weak. It would do nothing."

"I'll send it through to Colton."

"Oh shit, you got me." He tossed the pillow back on the bed. As I walked to him, he lowered himself to one knee and bowed his head, all so dramatically. "I yield, milady."

I burst out laughing. "Oh my God, you're something else."

Grinning, he held out his hand to me. "Join me for a soothing bubble bath, *Wildflower?*"

"You want to—I thought you were going to work on my laptop?"

"The thing I need is being retrieved as we speak. We have about thirty minutes before it makes it here."

"Isn't it in your mansion?"

"Sure is. One of my *connections* is covertly accessing it. Then it will be delivered to me here."

"Wouldn't it have been easier just to go home and grab it?"

"No. Then I'd have to leave you."

My heart melted at his words, the blunt way he'd just stated that outright, like it was a given, like it couldn't be any other way.

I took his hand and smiled down at him. "Do you want to stay for breakfast after?"

He rose to his feet still holding my hand. "Sounds really nice. I'll teach you some things while we eat." Off my look, he said, "No, not those kinds of things, dirty girl." He stroked my fingers in his and drew closer. "Although, when you're no longer sore, we'll get right back to that, believe me. I meant I'll teach you how to up your hacking game. And, more importantly, your network security defense protocols."

"So I can keep you out of my phone?"

"I'm actually already out. I have been for a few days."

"Wow, that's a big step in the right direction for you."

"Well, I was giving you space in every sense."

"And now?"

"And now, I'll back off. Well, in the intrusive sense anyway."

"The *intrusive sense*. Such a mild way of putting it."

"I'm sorry."

I gave him a withering look. "You don't mean that."

The corner of his mouth turned up. "You're right, I don't. It succeeded."

I shook my head. "Toning it down is a work in progress, I see."

He reached out and stroked some strands of my hair, the way he seemed to like doing a whole lot. "For the record, I don't usually compromise. So, believe me, it's more than just a work in progress."

"All for me, huh?"

"Abso-fucking-lutely." He beamed down at me. "Let's take that bath."

I LOOKED over at Levi typing away rapidly.

I'd never met anyone who could type faster than me, at least not when I was in the zone, but here he was doing just that.

And as strange as it probably sounded to someone not in our similar fields of study, it was hot as all fuck watching him. The rapid-fire clack of the keys, the determined look on his face like he was waging war and decimating his enemies with absolutely no respite, how he was so confident like some kind of coding God working his will.

Every now and then, he'd reach out with one hand and take a bite of the fried egg sandwich I'd made for breakfast, while not breaking his rhythm with his other hand still flying across the keyboard. Then he'd return to using two like one had never left.

He'd kept to his promise of not touching me so I could have time to recover, which had been an impressive feat seeing as though we'd taken a bath together in my tiny bathtub. Wet, naked, and wherein I'd spent the majority of it on his lap. He'd wanted to be close to me, not wanting the physical separation. And, honestly, I'd been right there with him on that. Although neither of us were virgins, it had felt different and incredibly intense when we'd come together last night. It hadn't just been physical by any means. *God*, it had been all-consuming being with him, letting go with him.

Another impressive feat—on my end—was the fact that I was actually able to remain in my seat at the kitchen table and eat while he was sitting there shirtless, all that hard and defined muscle of his hot-as-sin chest on display.

I sucked in a breath, trying to push down the primal memories of last night, trying to focus.

"Still picturing it, hmm?"

I blinked to see Levi looking up from my laptop with

that devious smirk I'd become so well acquainted with.

"What's that?"

"You know very well. Or were you feeling it as well as picturing it? Vividly?"

"Stop," I said, shoving my sandwich into my mouth and taking a big bite to avoid answering.

"Saved by that delicious sandwich. Nicely done." He gestured at my laptop. "Just waiting for my program to run all the way through your system. A couple more minutes and everything will be recovered and back to normal."

I nodded and smiled as I continued to chew the ridiculously big bite I'd taken.

He stared at me as I ate, his hot gaze wandering over me in just my pink zebra-print robe, my hair mussed in its still damp state from the bath we'd taken just a little while earlier.

I finished eating, then asked, "So, who did you lose to?"

He arched an eyebrow. "What's that?"

"Last night you said that you've lost one fight in your life."

"Ah, that." He shifted his weight. "Talk about a jarring change of subject. Fighting temptation, hmm?" He thumbed his chest. "Want me to put my shirt back on?"

I rolled my eyes. "I'm fine. And I really want to know."

"My dad. It was to my dad."

A shudder went through me. "Your dad... beat you?" It didn't compute. Of course, I knew Roman Knight was a ruthless man when he needed to be. Anyone who'd been in my dad's *business* circles back then had needed to be. But there'd also been a respectful gentleness to him whenever he'd encountered me, anyone who held less power than him—so long as they weren't a threat, anyway. "The times I met him, he seemed so—"

"No. It wasn't like that. He thought it was for my own

good—the fight we had, I mean."

"How the hell could that possibly be?" I demanded, unable to check my vehemence.

"Aww, look at you getting all riled up for me."

I rolled my eyes. "Levi."

He certainly had a fondness for changing the subject when he was uncomfortable, or didn't want to reveal specific pieces of information.

"Remember me telling you it took me a couple of years to stabilize after what happened in that hellscape?"

"Of course."

"Well, a few months afterward, once I was physically healed, I was determined to find mental and emotional healing as well. For me, I believed that to be through dealing out damage to those who'd wronged us."

"Shit, you tried to go after them?"

"Stupid at my young and rather naïve age. Something my dad demonstrated to me the only way I would listen to at the time—through action."

"A man challenging a boy to combat, though? That's—"

"It was exactly his point. I *wasn't* a man. I stood no chance of being able to go up against them back then. He saved my life that day." He looked at me with a bittersweet smile. "Twice that year I had my life spared."

"Is that gunshot wound connected to that fight with your dad?"

"In a sense. It wasn't inflicted by him, though, nor actually during our round of combat."

I frowned. "Then, what—"

My laptop chirped, cutting me off.

Levi blinked, then took in the screen. "Done. Now to ensure the data that was taken is secure."

"Take a break. You don't have to do it all at once."

He looked out at me. "I appreciate that, but I need to get it done."

"It's hard for you to stop, isn't it?"

"What's that?"

"It's difficult for you to stand still, to relax, or just to do nothing, isn't it?"

He averted his eyes and I thought he was going to blow off my question or, more likely with him, redirect and possibly make a joke in the process.

But then he sucked in a breath and sank back against the kitchen chair. "I need to keep my mind busy, yeah."

"Because of them?"

"Yes."

We didn't need to utter it aloud, he knew what I meant. *The demons.*

"Even in the bath, you kept fussing with it, adding more hot water, then cold, putting in more bubble bath, then moving the actual bubbles around."

"I'm sorry."

"You don't need to be. I get it." I gestured at the three new origami butterflies in front of my plate that I'd made this morning since he'd started working on my laptop. "Do you think it'll ever stop?"

"I do."

"You sound so certain."

"They're still with us because we never had closure."

"They were punished."

"It's not enough, though, is it?"

"I don't know."

"*We* didn't get the opportunity to deal with them."

"Even if I do acknowledge that disturbing claim to have some truth to it on my end too, the fact is that the… ringleader… he's dead."

Something flitted across his features that I couldn't

quite discern because it was so quick.

"Levi, what—"

A sudden pounding on the front door brought me up short and had Levi instantly shooting to his feet on high alert.

No, it was more than that.

I recognized it as the same thing in myself—a trauma response. A symptom of PTSD that the two of us obviously shared.

It had taken everything in me not to react by lunging for the knife block and drawing a blade in the next split-second.

As it was, I managed to rise to my feet somewhat calmly, even though the sudden shock of the aggressive noise had made my pulse spike and adrenaline spark.

Shit, chill out. Get a hold of yourself, girl. It's just a knock at the freaking door.

"It's okay," I told Levi, managing to dart in front of him as he went to storm toward the door like a war machine of some sort.

I pressed my hand to his chest and his now dark gaze snapped to mine.

His heart was thumping rapidly.

"I get it, but it's just the door."

He stared down at my hand on his bare chest, then back up to my face. "Yeah," he murmured.

I smiled, then headed on out of the kitchen the very short distance to the apartment door, hearing Levi's footsteps right behind me, so close I could feel the heat from him at my back.

"That door needs a peephole," Levi groused. "Scratch that, you need a security camera and better locks. The building itself needs heavy security too."

I looked over my shoulder at him and grinned.

"What?" he asked.

"Just understanding how much you care about my well-being. Who knew with the way you came across at first, huh?"

He rolled his eyes. "Brianna."

I chuckled, then unlocked the door and opened it carefully.

The careful part fell to the wayside almost instantly when I took in Colton on the other side.

"Hey, cutie," he greeted with a smile.

But it wasn't his usual big and bright one. No, it was restrained, and there was worry there in his smoky eyes. He looked on edge, his black and gold zig-zagging printed shirt was haphazardly done up only halfway with one side tucked into his ripped gray jeans, and his mohawk was mussed.

Levi was right beside me then, his arm brushing against mine. "Colt? What are you doing here?"

"I'm here because you told me *you* were here," he answered, matter of fact. The corner of his mouth turned up as he took in Levi shirtless and barefoot and me in only my robe. "So, it was what I thought." He stepped across the threshold and fingered the scratch marks on Levi's neck and down the length of his chest. "And it was also how I imagined it would be between the two of you."

"You imagined the two of us having sex?" I asked.

"As soon as I saw Lev taking an interest in you. I imagined him fucking you, you fucking yourself, him fucking himself. Then as I started spending time with you too, it evolved to imagining me fucking you, then me and Lev fucking you, and then Mason and Lev devouring you while I—"

"Well *fucking* received, Colt," Levi cut in, batting his hand off him.

Colton blinked out of the haze of lust he'd clearly just been caught up in, and then that anxiousness was back as he shut the door behind him. "Good thing you two are late for classes. In fact, it's gonna be best if you get the material remotely for the next little while until things die down." He eyed Levi. "You, because of how you'll react to this attack. You know, with a destructive display of violence and payback?"

"Payback for what?" Levi demanded, getting agitated.

I was too, but from a rapidly rising worried standpoint.

What the hell had happened?

Colton shook his head at Levi. "This sort of thing is exactly why you need to be more active on social media. If that had been the case, you'd already know about this."

"Like I need that hassle," Levi muttered. "Now, what's going on, Colt?"

Colton looked between us. "You're gonna want to sit down."

"Sit down? Come on, brother. Just spill it."

Colton grimaced, then pulled his phone from his pants, scrolled for a moment, then handed it to Levi.

I watched Levi's expression morph from disbelief, to something a whole lot more dangerous as he swiped rapidly through whatever Colton had brought up, his free hand clenching into a white-knuckle fist.

And then his eyes went black with unadulterated fury.

"How?" he rumbled. "I had this protected."

"I heard Mason talking on the phone earlier tonight as I was passing by with my acoustic guitar to song write out in nature like I do every now and then, and he spoke the name, Rina."

"He had *her* crack my system," Levi grunted, handing the phone back to Colton.

"One of the very few people we know who actually

could. The only one we know, really, outside of your dad."

"Motherfucker!" Levi roared, and I could see the strain on him not to start punching or pounding on anything in his immediate vicinity.

"What's happened?" I asked, walking to Colton.

He handed his phone to me. "I'm sorry, cutie."

Sorry? What was going on?

Fortunately—or perhaps, unfortunately—I got the answer to my question all too quickly.

There, on Colton's screen were photos and posts of *me*. Me and Tommy. Me and Tommy getting it on. Even stills of us making out and doing more than even that.

My own private photos and videos that I'd kept out of… I don't know… maybe a connection to the person I used to be before I'd cut it all off and turned my back on that part of my life to spare myself the pain.

"Oh my God," I breathed, continuing through and noting how many likes and interactions the things had.

So many.

"It's gone viral. Not just there on IG, but all over the place," Colton told me, wincing.

"That's why you were trying to reach me?" Levi asked.

"This only happened an hour or so ago. I was trying to reach you because even though Mason knew you were back, he called a meeting with *Hex* earlier tonight. Meaning—"

"Meaning, he's cut me out." Levi's gaze strayed to mine briefly, before turning back to Colton. "Because Brianna is involved. Because he's had her marked."

"Yeah. I tried to stop him, Lev. I really did. But he's just… it's like he's power mad. I think you showing care for somebody, intense care, really freaked him out, and sent him reeling back to five years ago, and this is his response —and major overreaction."

Levi scrubbed his hand over his face, then started pacing, thinking.

Colton came to me and wrapped his arm around me, gently easing his phone from my grip with his free hand. "Don't look at it anymore. We'll fix it."

"You better fucking believe we will," Levi said, conviction and rage colliding into one hell of a vehement statement as he looked at me. "I'm sorry, *Wildflower*. I'll take care of it, I'll make it better." He addressed Colton, "I need you to head back to the mansion and retrieve my special laptop."

"Special?" I asked.

"Oh, it's the shit," Colton answered instead. "Military-grade and everything."

"It's… holy shit." I eyed Levi. "Wow, you really don't do things halfway, do you?"

"Fuck, no."

Colton kissed my cheek, then pulled away, telling us, "I'll head back and get it now. Mason's still out at this fucked-up meeting." He grasped Levi's hand. "Brother, this violation isn't gonna be the end of it."

"It fucking is, believe me. But first thing's first, get my laptop. If I step foot back home and Mason does walk in, all hell's gonna break loose on my end, and that will delay me being able to pull all the shit he's put out there in fucking cyberspace."

"I know. But after you take care of this, you and me will go to Mason together. All right? Let me be there to minimize the fallout."

Levi gave his hand a squeeze and smiled. "Of course. You've got it."

With that, Colton smiled back at him, then headed on out of the apartment.

As Levi locked the door after him and turned back to

me, I spoke, "You're not going to wait for Colton to be there, are you?"

"No," he seethed. "I'm not. Mason deserves my worst for all of this. Colt being there won't allow that to be possible."

"Because he has a soothing effect on you?"

A half-smile graced his lips. "You picked up on that already?"

"Well, I've been observing you from a distance ever since I realized your interest in me wasn't going away."

He came to me and wrapped his arms around me, holding me to him. "I'm sorry," he breathed into my hair. "I'll make it better. Don't let him win. Don't leave Stonewell. You belong here with me, *Wildflower.*"

I tightened my hold on him, feeling the vulnerability from him cutting at me. "I'm not going to let anyone force me from where I've chosen to be, where I *want* to be."

"Good," he said, nuzzling my neck. "Because I can't lose you. I can't go back to being in this alone. After all these years—"

"Shh," I said, reaching up and cupping his face. "I feel the same."

"You do?"

I nodded and stroked his skin that was hot to the touch, on account of him trying to reel in his anger with what had happened, what had been done to me, and the threat to driving us apart that he'd initially believed it to be. "Yes. We've both spent so much time drowning in what happened, having it eat at us. It was like poison, infecting us each and every day, in ways I wouldn't even let myself acknowledge. I just kept shoving it down with keeping busy, reinventing myself, and with my meds. But seeing you again, growing closer and taking the leap to allow you in, it… it's changed that… there's hope now. Because *you're* here with me, the only other person who knows what was done to us, who understands. Like you said, *together* we can find peace now."

He smiled and stroked my back up and down, soothingly. "I'll get *Hex* off your back." His eyes darkened. "Even if I have to tear my way through Mason's entire band of so-called soldiers to make it so."

"I already struck back and it's only made things escalate. Why don't you level with Mason, tell him why you were really pursuing me, tell him the truth about the kidnapping?"

"I've kept it to myself for years. So have you. To suddenly reveal it, especially under these circumstances, it doesn't sit right with me."

"I get it, but if it gets to the point where you can't reason with him without revealing the whole deal, you're going to have to. We can do it together if that will make it easier. I just don't want things spiraling out of control. More than they already have, anyway. Like I said, I already struck back myself and it clearly hasn't stopped anything."

"The fact you struck back is hot as fuck, by the way."

"Come on."

"I'm serious." He cocked his head to the side. "What *did* you do?"

As we stood there in each other's arms, I told him how I'd struck with the showers and the infestations, and his surprise gave way to a whole lot of admiration. Or, more like, adoration.

And as I spelled it out, recounting every little detail, and he hung onto my every word, I realized for the first time in years that I actually felt like myself.

More than that, I actually felt safe to be the real me.

The real me that had a much darker and harsher edge that meshed so well with the same in him.

21

~Levi~

She wanted me to reveal the twisted truth.

For six years, my brothers had believed that I'd been held alone when I'd been kidnapped that day as a fifteen-year-old clueless kid on my way home from our hoity-toity private school. The town car I'd been traveling back home to the Knight family home in had been run off the road. The ordeal had begun with the first hit of trauma when the driver's door had been thrown open and my driver had been shot through the skull, his blood and brain matter spraying all over the seats and me.

Little had I known at the time, but that had only been the beginning.

Per a deal that Roman Knight had struck with Brianna's father, Curt Walker, the fact that Brianna had been taken too that same day across our mutual home city of Tolhurst had been kept a secret. As had my kidnapping. It wasn't public knowledge. But Colt and Mason knew because they'd been in the car behind me and seen me being taken.

Both Roman and Curt hadn't wanted it to get out,

because it would have been seen as a weakness by the many other enemies they'd shared at the time that somebody had actually been able to get at their children. Worse, that the particular somebody had managed to keep them in captivity for two whole weeks before those two dangerous powerhouses had found us.

There were many reasons why I'd never spoken about it—outside of to my father—in all these years. Obviously, one of the main reasons was that I hadn't wanted to relive it in vivid detail like talking about it would have caused. The nightmares were bad enough and came too close to that as it was. Another reason was that I'd wanted to keep my memories of the one bright spark that had been there through all that pitch-black—Brianna Walker. I hadn't wanted to share that—her—with anyone. And then there'd been the two-year period where I'd tried to let it all go, to bury it beneath a shit-ton of other things, which had resulted in what my dad had called *a whole lot of acting out*. Fortunately, that had all been put down to teenage rebellion. But the worst of it had really ended when I'd stopped trying to bury it, to put those two weeks of torment behind me and all the trauma that had gone along with. When I'd had an epiphany of sorts and realized what I'd really needed was ultimate closure. And that ultimate closure could only be found in revenge and utter decimation of the bastard responsible for what had been done to me, Brianna, and the one other person who'd been there that she'd yet to talk about—her mom.

That last part was a tale for another day, though. When my *Wildflower* was ready.

The fact she hadn't brought that part up once since we'd been reunited had made it abundantly clear to me that she either really wasn't ready at all, or that she was still stuck in some major denial when it came to that aspect of what had happened. Maybe both.

Even with all of that in play, there was an even greater reason why I didn't want to go the route of full disclosure to Mason.

Since I was seventeen, for the last four years, I'd been building on my skills—what laymen called *hacking*, as well as my tactical know-how, and combat experience—all in the name of tracking down that motherfucker, Malcolm Lynch, and ending his sick and twisted life in the most painful way imaginable.

The guy had been underground all this time. It was why Brianna thought he was dead, why my dad did as well, why *her* dad did. But a few months before I'd left for a year for a supposed internship, I'd finally received intel confirming he was alive. For the last year, my *internship* had all been a manufactured façade that I'd used my skills to maintain, when really I'd been out there traveling and tracking every single whisper concerning Lynch. I'd managed to lay eyes on him once, which was a feat in itself, considering he'd gone to great lengths to maintain his ghost status. But he'd been surrounded by two dozen of his soldiers-for-hire at the time. I couldn't take him and bolting into the fray would have exposed me with nothing to show for it. So I'd had to walk away. When I'd gone back with a force at my back, thanks to Sammy, the fucker and his people had already moved on. They were always on the move. Whenever I'd moved on chatter after that, they'd been gone each time I'd arrived.

It was why I'd come back here. I'd been aware that Brianna had come to Stonewell, but I'd wanted to see to Lynch before approaching her, so I'd made myself hold off.

But with the walls I'd kept slamming up against, I'd

decided to come back to work *with* her to find him and the new organization he was building.

Unfortunately, all I'd found in her had been more walls. Denial. Reinvention. Her running from the past and not being willing to face it.

I'd managed to crack that now and she was with me, she wanted us to heal together.

She even believed that healing would partly require the kind of closure I'd been hell-bent on for years.

"They're still with us because we never had closure."

"They were punished."

"It's not enough, though, is it?"

"I don't know."

"We didn't get the opportunity to deal with them."

"Even if I do acknowledge that disturbing claim to have some truth to it on my end too, the fact is that the... ringleader... he's dead."

The problem was, she was hesitant about it. And she'd only just come around enough to admit to what had happened, to the experience that we shared, and being able to be around me.

We'd only just connected and I didn't want to risk that. It meant fucking everything to me.

So, yeah, I was stuck when it came to revealing the truth to Mason and Colt, as well as the last part of it to Brianna too.

I didn't want *her* to run from me.

And I didn't want *Mason* to get in my way, which he would absolutely do once he found out my true endgame here. He'd even bring in my dad and that powerhouse coming down on me would either end up forcing my hand away from my vengeance crusade, *or* it would lead to a war between the king and his heir.

So, there was only one thing to do right now.

Make a dent in Mason's rapidly hardening armor before it became impossible to penetrate. He'd already grown *Hex's* numbers beyond what both me and Colt had expected in such a short time. I'd seen Mason getting into it that day in the locker room, but the power had gone to his head all too quickly. His desperation for control had fueled it in a completely dictatorial way that had touched me, Brianna, would soon touch Colt too, and had already infected the campus. If it continued unchecked, it wouldn't be long before it spread through the town of Stonewell too and hit Sammy and *my* connections. The fuck I would allow that to happen. It would fuck up everything.

Mason fucking Hall needed bringing down a peg—or several—for the good of us all, including him. Most especially him. He wouldn't be able to stop on his own, we'd seen this from him a couple of times before. Nah, it required interference.

And in this specific case, a show of force.

Fortunately, that was one of my many talents.

Using a prototype that I'd *borrowed* from my dad's company just before I'd left for my fake internship, I'd managed to use its highly-advanced thermal imaging capabilities to determine the precise location of the ten frat boys within the farmhouse in the distance.

After Brianna's infestation strike against three of the houses, a bunch of the residents had been staying with the other frats until the houses were sanitized, but Mason had put his soldiers up here in an abandoned farmhouse on the outskirts of Stonewell. Actually, I'd initially thought it had been abandoned, but as I'd tracked down where Mason had put some of his *Hex* members, I'd discovered that he'd actually bought this place while I'd been away. Why, I had no clue. It wasn't as though he'd planned to revive *Hex* in this way before I'd come back and insisted upon it.

Or, had he?

The guy certainly played things close to the vest. I'd wanted him to restart *Hex* to keep him busy and off my back with what I had in the works, and also as a way to draw on more resources should I need them down the road. Instead, though, he'd gone a completely different way with it since he'd taken power.

As for the football players he'd taken on as his *Hex* soldiers, some were still in the hospital being treated for the burns they'd sustained from Brianna's hit, and the others were in special on-campus housing—too difficult to get at when they were home. I had to wait for an opportunity there.

There were also another dozen on the list I'd copied from Mason of his recruits, but they were students scattered all over—some living in campus housing, some off-campus and in the town, and a few even commuting the fifty miles from here to the City of Tolhurst. Again, more complicated to get at. That would require some manipulation on my part to have them convene in a single area. If I'd known about that meeting Mason had called last night, that would've been the perfect time and circumstance to strike. As it was, I hadn't, and now I had to wait, or create another opportunity.

If I absolutely had to.

I was hoping what I was about to do here would be enough of a blow to Mason to function as an unavoidable wakeup call. For him to see fucking sense.

I made my way through the brush, the blanket of night making it easy for me to blend into the shadows. Spinning my collapsible bo-staff around, I headed toward my first set of targets. The four frat boys I'd been able to see with my imaging device through the empty barn. They were twenty feet from it sitting around a fire pit in lawn chairs and drinking the cheap beer they were so fond of.

Two others were to the right in the main farmhouse building in the kitchen sitting around an island and having an apparent midnight snack. The remaining four were upstairs asleep, two to a room in bunk beds.

As I reached my first targets, the four of them were laughing and joking around and talking about how lucrative being members of *Hex* was, the cache it afforded them.

Not tonight, boys.

The fools were so relaxed, thinking they were untouchable now that they didn't even notice me when I was right upon them.

I twisted my bo-staff and it extended to double its length.

And then I jabbed it into the lower back of one of the guys sitting around the fire.

The force of it had him crying out and hurtling off the chair, landing on the grass just inches from the flames.

As he scrambled to get back to his feet, stumbling from the mild damage I'd done to his back, the other three shot from their chairs and spun to face me.

"Knight, what the hell?" one of them cried, taking in me wielding a weapon and the dark, unforgiving look in my eyes.

"You came at what's mine."

"We had orders!"

"Stand down now and walk away then."

"We can't do that. *Hex* members don't balk."

Heading down here tonight to inflict damage had ramped up my bloodlust, so that sick and depraved part of me was really fucking happy to hear that they were gonna go the fight route.

I stepped forward and readied my staff. "Then it's time for a reckoning, fuckers."

As they hesitated, trying to process what was happening, the brutal reality cutting into their reverie, I took advantage of their slow reactions and processing abilities, and swept my staff at the back of the closest one's legs, ripping him off his feet.

As he hit the ground on his ass, the other three launched themselves at me.

Adrenaline tore through me in the most glorious way, fueling everything and firing me up to deliver punishment and spill their goddamn blood.

I spun my staff, clocking one across the side of the head, and knocking him back as he struggled from the disorientation of the injury. Not breaking my spinning momentum, I jabbed another in the ribs, hearing a distinct crack and a corresponding wheeze from the fucker confirming I'd hit my target. With an upswing, I smashed the end of the staff into the underside of the other guy's chin. His head snapped back and he stumbled back several feet.

I finished off one of the fallen guys with a blow to the side of the head, knocking him out cold. Then, I thrust my boot into the ribs of the guy I'd already done damage there to and he stayed down incapacitated, clutching himself and wheezing.

One of the two remaining, snatched my staff, while the other tried to come at me from behind in another sneak attack. Not much of a *sneak* attack when the guy had no stealth to speak of, but whatever.

I yanked on the staff, sliding it under my arm and taking the guy who had hold of it with the jerky movement. He slammed into me and I held fast at the impact, then yanked him around and snagged him in a chokehold with the staff to his throat.

As he flailed and struggled, the final guy came at me. I dodged a kick to the ass—literally—then threw his buddy's weight in my hold around, smashing into him. As he staggered from it, I swept my boot at the back of his knee and wrenched it out from under him. The moment he hit the grass, I delivered a kick to the side of his head and knocked him out like the other guy.

It didn't take long before the guy being choked out by my bo-staff lost consciousness, and I released him and let him sink to the ground among the rest of them.

Four down, six to go.

━━━

IT HAD BEEN a whirlwind of violence, pain, screams, and a whole lot of bloodletting since I'd stepped into the farmhouse and made my presence known.

My staff was slick with blood as I strode out of the bedroom, where I'd put down two of the last four targets. One was unconscious in there, another was screaming because he'd taken my weapon to the balls after putting up a fight, instead of succumbing to my wrath like he should have. *Fucking fool.* After witnessing the damage I'd already done so far.

There was broken furniture throughout the house, holes in the walls from me slamming my targets into a few during the battle, frat bros downed and a whole lot of shattered glass all over the kitchen from me driving an opponent's head into a window to knock him out.

I spun, hearing the hurried footsteps of another guy coming at me, the dumbass thinking he'd be the hero who took me down. I spun into a roundhouse kick and sent him careening down the stairs, watching as he passed out from hitting step after step when he hit the landing.

And then I saw the final target trying to slip away, dodging past me.

I bolted forward, then swept my staff at the most opportune time, ripping his legs out from under him.

He crashed onto the landing, just a foot from making it to the top of the stairs.

I lunged at him and hauled him around onto his back, about to do some nasty damage with my prized weapon.

"Wait!" he called out as I brought the bo-staff down.

I stilled just an inch from driving it into his ribs. He was damn lucky for my quick reflexes.

Through the haze of violence, I took in the identity of a target for the first time.

It was Chase Arlington, the football captain, one of the first recruits to Mason's resurrected version of *Hex*.

He wasn't supposed to be here. He wasn't a member of the frat.

There were no accidents when it came to the moves Mason made, so he must have separated Chase from the rest of the team and relocated him out here for a reason.

"Rob!" he cried, before I could even begin to determine a reason for it.

"What?" I spat.

"Rob Brown. Your boy reached out to him," he told me frantically. "Made me put him in contact with that dangerous freak."

"And? Why does that concern me?" I had my suspicions, obviously, but I needed them confirmed.

"The girl, the one you're into… Mason has him investigating her."

Jesus.

Rob Brown was the intel man of this shithead's father,

Atticus Arlington. Rob was ex-military, a fucking shadow nowadays. And because he was, he was able to venture places that very few others could and obtain extremely hard to acquire information. Just like the very thing I was trying to keep Mason away from.

"How long?"

"A couple of weeks."

Christ. That was an age for a man like him.

It meant Mason knew something.

Just how much remained to be seen.

He would've likely discovered that she was Curt Walker's daughter, perhaps what the guy used to do before his small business empire had gotten up and running six years ago.

But even if he knew that, there was a barrier in place thanks to my dad between all of that and the kidnapping. Rob Brown was good, but I had faith in my dad's abilities too.

Even then, though, I didn't like Mason knowing *anything* about Brianna, beyond her being a student here and her field of study. To Mason, information was most definitely power and he always found the most opportune —and when he was on a tear, the most destructive—way to use what he discovered on those he'd targeted—or *marked*, in this case.

Goddammit!

With a roar, I whipped my bo-staff at the side of Chase's head, knocking him out cold.

Then I stormed down the stairs and made my way out of the farmhouse, stepping over the bloodied and beaten unconscious fools as I went, reveling in the power I'd unleashed and the punishment I'd dealt out, the eerie, stone-cold silence and the scent of blood rolling through me like the sweetest drug.

Still, it wasn't enough to quell the rage and anxiousness all of this had elicited.

Mason's moves were complicating everything and throwing up barriers all over the fucking place.

All this tonight, it was just a temporary fix. A Band-Aid on a sucking chest wound kind of deal.

But that was all I needed—to pause things, to create an interim reprieve so I could put certain things in place.

He thought he could throw up barriers at me and I'd just take it lying down because it was him, or because he had an army at his back?

Big fucking mistake.

He was about to get one fuck of a wakeup call.

Tonight would look like nothing.

Shouldn't have come at her, brother.

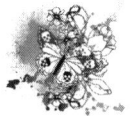

22

~Colton~

"You're making it aggravatingly difficult for *Hex*," Mason's voice came eerily calm as I stormed into the living room, the complete opposite of the faux relaxed demeanor he was putting on.

Well, judging by him sitting on the edge of the couch and working on his lock picking hobby on the coffee table, it was more like him fighting to make his fake control real. He only really brought out the lock picking when he was agitated. Considering there were four different locks out this time instead of the usual two at a time, it seemed to support my theory.

"Good," I bit back as I stopped in front of the sleek white marble coffee table that Lev had picked out, just like everything in the house. The guy had good taste, no doubt.

Rounding it to get up closer, like in his face or some shit, wasn't a good idea with how riled up *I* was right now.

I'd barely been able to concentrate in my classes all day because of all this bullshit. Sure, yeah, I had a known issue with my focus and all that, but today had been more than that. It was because of what Mason and his *soldiers* had pulled this morning. And all the shit before that too. It was all just escalating.

I'd stayed away late into the night inside the recording studio. Not even recording, because I hadn't had my time booked, just sitting in on some other students' sessions quietly—all to avoid coming home while he was still up. That hadn't exactly worked out with him still wide awake past fucking midnight. I'd known if I hadn't been able to sleep on it before seeing him, I wouldn't have been able to contain myself when I laid eyes on him.

That was how *I* calmed down, taking a nap, or sleeping it off through the night. Some people unleashed anger with violence, others stuffed their faces with junk food, some when for a drive, but mine was sleep.

"You're being fucking insane with all this bullshit, Mason!" I yelled, slamming my hands down on the coffee table and rocking his locks and all his specialized picks too.

He grunted, but didn't look up at me, focusing on the immediate task ahead of him instead.

Responding in a nonchalant tone, he said, "That's your opinion. Your biased opinion, I might add."

Urgh. I hated when he got like this, giving me that fake calm and condescending tone, like I couldn't possibly be right over him, like he was some all-knowing entity seeing things I couldn't begin to comprehend.

"You've crossed a goddamn line!"

"Please. *Hex* has committed far worse offenses against its marks before."

"Not against somebody Lev cares about deeply!"

"You mean, his latest fixation? His obsession?"

"It's never been a person before. Only a goal or a project."

"So, he's branched out. It's still beyond dangerous for

him. And if you weren't in the process of being smitten with her too, you'd be with me on this."

"What the shit do you need me for when you've got your ridiculous army of blackmailed soldiers at your beck and call? Rosemary too? Jesus, Mason. Involving that snake? Tell me it's not to gain access to her family's criminal empire?"

"Like I told you and Lev, I'm gathering my army of key individuals all recruited for specific purposes—either for their own skills and on their own merits, or for that of those closely connected to them."

"You talk about Lev being dangerous, but it's you who's crossed that line this time. You need *him* there to balance that out for you. You always have. *Hex* has never run without the two of you at the head together."

"Cutting Levi out reduces complications more than you can possibly imagine with you now standing on the periphery."

"Don't talk down to me. I'm right about this. You might consider Lev a loose cannon and volatile, but unlike you he's incorruptible. Without him there to balance you out, *your* actions have become dangerous."

When he just continued working on his lock picking and not even gracing me with his eye contact, I slapped the table again, making it rock and jostling him. "You need to back off Brianna Walker now and apologize to Lev, even swear to him that you'll never come at her again."

"The fuck, I will."

"This *obsession*, as you keep calling it, is different this time. *He's* different with her."

His head shot up. "Different, how?"

"He's… gentler with her. He even apologized to her and—"

"He apologized to her?"

"Yeah."

A deep frown etched his brow. "Lev doesn't ever say sorry. Not for anything."

"Exactly my point."

Hope sparked as it looked like I'd finally gotten through to his stubborn ass. One majorly sweet ass, no doubt, but right now the shit he was causing was dampening that for me. I hadn't even sent him a single flirty text for days on end.

He sat back against the couch and blew out a breath. "Look, I'll—"

The entrance door of the mansion slammed so hard that it reverberated all the way through to the living room.

"Ding dong, motherfucker! *Hellraiser's* home!" Lev's voice rang out a moment later.

I grimaced as I heard that dangerous and vindictive tone to it. *Oh no.*

That was relegated to the least of it when Lev tracked us easily to this room—one of three living rooms in the place, and stormed inside.

"Holy shit," I choked out at the shocking state of him.

Blood.

Blood everywhere.

It was dousing his cheeks, forehead, and even his hair.

His knuckles were covered in it too.

He was wearing one of his hooded leather jackets, the kind he used when he went out street fighting, along with a pair of black tactical pants this time, his collapsible bo-staff holstered at his right hip, along with a couple of blades secured to the legs of his pants. And all of it was splattered in blood. Especially the bo-staff that was slick all the way down.

Mason shot to his feet and rounded the coffee table, his gaze anxiously traveling up and down Lev.

"You like?" Lev asked, caustically as he caught him looking, getting off on his reaction.

"What the fuck have you done?"

Lev cocked his head to the side. "You don't remember?"

"Remember what?" Mason gritted out.

"My warning, of course. *'You strike at her and I'll annihilate every single fucker on this list. Mark my fucking words. Don't test me.'*" He slapped his hand to his heart. "My bad, you really don't recall, *Killjoy*?"

Shit.

"Lev, let's just—" I started, moving to intervene before Mason blew his top and things imploded.

But Mason shot past me and then he was slamming his hand into Lev's chest, using all that powerhouse muscle at his disposal and shock factor to run him into the wall beside the door.

Lev jarred against it painfully and Mason didn't make it easy for him to recover, keeping one hand bearing down on his chest and the other wrapping around his throat.

I shook my head in dismay as Lev choked out a wild, unhinged laugh. "That's it, *Scourge*, break for me." He wheezed, but kept pushing forward, as his maniacal laughter sounded again. "Like your fucking soldiers just did for me."

"*What?*" Mason seethed, shaking him violently.

"Get on your fucking knees, baby. Beg for my forgiveness. Suck my fucking cock for my troubles." Lev reacted in the lightning-fast and skillful way he was known for and dislodged Mason's grip in two brutal moves, then slammed his boot into his gut, knocking him back with a push kick. "Choke on it!" he roared.

Lev's insanely quick moves bit Mason in the ass again, as Levi kneed him in the gut, then used Mason hunching over in response to yank on his shoulders, forcing him to his knees.

Then he fisted his hand in his thick, caramel-brown hair and used the hold to grind Mason's face into his pants, angrily rolling his hips in the process. "Is that what you need to calm the fuck down with *Hex?* A good cock?" Lev growled. "Too much fucking denial for you!" Blood from Lev's pants smeared Mason's face in moments and as Mason struggled, Lev abruptly released him, shoving him away.

"You little fucking bitch," Mason gritted out as he pushed back to his feet.

He went for him, but I was there in the next second, holding him back with a steady palm to his chest, doing the same to Lev too.

Mason was basically frothing at the mouth while Lev's black gaze was boring into him.

"You want to hurt each other more and you'll have to go through me, you'll have to hurt *me*."

I saw a crack in Lev first, light filtering back into his eyes.

And then he took a step back and held up his hand—not at Mason, at me. "You're not getting hurt, brother."

Mason cursed, then eased off too, stepping back and folding his arms across his chest.

I didn't move, though, still standing between them as an effective barrier. I knew better than that.

Lev took my hand and pressed a kiss to my knuckles. "Sorry you were here to see that."

Before I could respond, Mason demanded of him, "What did you do?"

"Paid a visit to your lovely little farmhouse. Put a dent in your resources."

"Lev, the blood," I choked, looking him over again.

"Don't worry, cupcake, they're all still breathing. Although, I'm sure when they wake up, they'll wish they weren't for a few weeks."

"Fuck," Mason ground out, scrubbing his hand over his jaw that was stained with blood after what Lev had done.

"How many were there?" I asked him.

"Ten." He glared at Lev. "She was there too lending a helping hand?"

"She had nothing to do with it."

"Your *connections* in town then? Sammy's guys?" Mason asked.

Well, more like demanded. It sounded like he was looking for a target for his wrath.

I saw it registering with Lev too, who told him clearly, "It was just me."

"How the shit?" I exclaimed. "Ten? That's—"

"You've been training over the last year you were gone."

"Come on now, Mason, you know damn well how good I was before I even left."

"No, this is more than that. To take on ten—most of them big fucking guys too—alone like this, it's another level entirely." Realization combined with condemnation flamed in Mason's eyes. "So much for that supposed internship, huh?"

Lev didn't give anything up, responding, "I'm a spectacular multitasker."

Mason shook his head at him, then turned away, pacing the room with hard, angry steps. "Did you even think before you went on a rampage tonight? The cleanup it's gonna take to handle what you did… losing that many *Hex* members… fuck, Levi!"

"I thought about it in great detail."

Mason scoffed. "Bull. You reacted out of rage, and this was a kneejerk reaction, plain and simple."

"Nah," Lev said, coming a little closer, but stopping a few feet out from Mason when I flashed my eyes at him as a reminder to keep distance. "I thought about how debilitating it would be to your current operations against your mark. I thought about how it would fuck up your *soldiers'* faith in you and undermine your rule. I thought about how it would be a shitshow when it got back to Chase's father, in particular, given who he is. I thought about how he would likely hit back by going to Peter Hall and the glorious ways that would come back on you, especially how it would put you on a leash so you're forced to back off."

A dangerous growl rumbled from Mason.

"I warned you!" Levi yelled, undeterred. "I told you not to come after her! You don't fuck with my woman! Do you fucking hear me? If you don't back off right fucking now, what I did tonight will look like child's play. End it, Mason, lift the mark."

"Your woman? All this, going against our brotherhood, for her?"

"It's you who's gone against the brotherhood and completely lost sight of it. Your obsession with controlling every little thing has brought us here. You hurt me, you hurt Colt. And the crazy part is you can't even recognize that you've become what you're so afraid of—*I'm* the voice of reason in this."

Mason started.

Shaking his head and blinking as though that would will away the harsh reality Lev had just laid out, he turned to me. "He's wrong, yes?"

I sighed and shoved my hand through my mohawk. "No. He's not, brother. He's right on the money."

Mason took a moment, looking between us. "All right, I

may have gone harder than needed because of my worry about you being back here, Levi, and needing to reel you in again. And, yeah, the power reviving *Hex* made me feel after so long without it played a part too. But it doesn't take away from the fact that the girl is still dangerous."

"How's that?" Lev asked, and I saw his eye twitch. *Oh shit*, what was going on?

"She's the daughter of a motorcycle club president. The club princess of a one-percenter club. Steel Dawn MC."

"She's what?" I exclaimed. "Wow, I didn't get that vibe at all. I mean, yeah, she has an edge and a toughness about her, but still."

"She *was*," Lev corrected. "The club is long gone now, disbanded years ago."

"A club that was rumored to have done business with *Knightsridge Engineering.*"

"That's how I know her."

Mason frowned. "Why didn't you just tell me that?"

"Because it was six years ago, shortly before the kidnapping. I thought you'd react worse given the timing."

"No, there's something more here. And because you're so determined not to tell me, it just proves how dangerous this connection to her is to you, that it needs to be severed. She needs to go, Levi. Out of Stonewell."

"There's no fucking way—"

"Yeah, she's not going to be doing that," a voice boomed from the door.

We all spun to see none other than Brianna herself standing in the doorway.

Her fierce gaze drilled into Mason. "It's time we had words, *Scourge*."

23

~Mason~

Well, then.

Color me impressed.

The troublemaker had mustered the courage to venture into the lion's den.

The shock of her showing up so unceremoniously had even managed to cut through the rage that had infected the living room—and me.

A biker princess.

It wasn't actually a surprise that Lev would be drawn to somebody like that. He liked an edge and roughness to everything he did. And he was all about being wild and free, not living confined by society's—or anybody's—rules, which fit the whole motorcycle club thing to a T. Also, despite his upbringing being in the lap of luxury, he'd never felt comfortable with any of what he called the *hoity-toity bullshit* that went along with it, all the expectations of high society, something that was particularly prevalent for me, especially with my mom being a society queen—a famous socialite. Our attitude toward it was something the three of us had in common, something that had actually drawn us together during our school days.

The only thing Lev *had* cared for when it came to his life before Stonewell U, aside from Colt and me, was his dad.

Unlike my father, Lev's actually cared about his well-being beyond him just being a toy to him or a piece on his board. There was a real father-son relationship there. Sure, they had their ups and downs, but somehow Roman Knight had managed to strike a balance between reeling Levi in and allowing him freedom too.

My father, however? Well, he was all about control and appearances.

Unfortunately, as had been pointed out to me tonight in a very in-my-face way, it seemed I had inherited much more of the former than I'd even realized.

Fuck me, I was becoming Peter Hall.

Just what he'd always wanted.

Just what *I'd* always dreaded.

I blinked out of my thoughts and tuned back in to the whispers being exchanged between Lev and the girl, which had been going on since the moment she'd walked on in here.

Levi had pulled her to the back of the room hastily. It seemed to be more than the mere act of protecting and shielding her from me. He didn't want her here having *words* with me.

Just as I'd thought, there was something Levi hadn't disclosed to me about his connection to her.

It had to be more than him merely encountering her during shared business between their fathers. That wouldn't have led to him becoming so dangerously fixated on her *or* to him actually going against *me* in order to pursue her.

Levi had never stood against me when it came to dealing with a threat before.

But this girl, she had a hold on him, a very powerful hold.

It was fucking dangerous.

For all of us.

And because he'd refused to see it, I'd had to employ extreme methods. He wouldn't let go of her willingly, so I'd worked to force her out of his life.

And yet, in spite of all those efforts, here she was now in our home.

With everything I'd levied upon her, she should be a wreck.

But as I continued to study her, the only difference I noticed compared to before I'd had her marked was that she was wearing far less pink than normal. She had on a light-gray tiered ruffle tank beneath a black checkered cardigan embellished with sequin butterflies down the sleeves with a large one centered on the back. Navy skinny jeans gave way to a pair of pastel-pink pumps. Of course, there was also that necklace that she wore every day, with the all-seeing eye pendant that was basically a cobalt-blue version of Levi's tattoo.

Maybe the lack of her usual over-the-top pink get-up was a window into her true mental state, that she had actually been affected, but she was merely hiding it well.

So well in fact, that she looked utterly calm even as she stood in the home of an enemy, even as the whispers from Levi were becoming harsher as they argued about whatever. I'd ensure she didn't leave here until she revealed exactly what that was, and until Levi finally divulged the truth of what he'd been keeping from me.

Colt sauntered back into the room with that usual sexy swagger.

I found myself paying more attention to it that I even normally did, watching his zebra-print shirt pulling taut across his toned torso, his hard abs visible beneath the thin fabric, then his sculpted ass drawing far too much attention to it as he walked, a pair of maroon leather pants not exactly making it easy to look away.

The fact that it had been a long time since we'd fooled around was another thing not making it easy, and clearly what was making me notice every sexy thing about him in magnified detail. Just like earlier when he'd confronted me and come at me, all that passion coming off him and turning me the fuck on, at a time when I'd been trying to focus on the serious subject matter and the worrying growing tension and separation between us.

"Here, brother," Colt spoke as he reached Levi and held out a package of medical wipes, along with one of Levi's black tanks that he wore when he was practicing his fight moves before a street fight.

"Thanks, cupcake," Levi said, very slightly pulling away from the girl so he could take them.

Before he made it, though, she was there batting his hand away.

He eyed her in question.

"Go get cleaned up properly."

"Nah, I'll be fine with the wipes and the change of shirt for now."

The hell, he would. He'd get all that blood and grime over the furniture. I hated when he did it after being covered in sawdust and grease from woodworking and what-not, then came in here and lounged all over the furniture. Because, of course it was me who ended up having to clean it. Lev was too laser-focused on whatever task or *mission* he had in mind at the time. And Colt was too erratic and didn't remember if *he* made a mess.

I was about to speak to it—despite it being a bad idea when the two of us were at the height of antagonism toward one another—but I got a surprise in the next moment, as the girl beat me to it.

She stroked his hair, some with dried blood in the strands and told him in a patient and strangely soothing tone that I'd only come close to experiencing the likes of before with Colt, "This whole thing is already difficult subject matter, so you being caked in blood and dirt is just going to make it all the more uncomfortable."

"That's why I asked Colt to get me some wipes and a clean shirt."

"Not enough."

"I'm totally with her, Lev," Colt piped up.

"Then why did you get these for me?"

"Because you're a stubborn ass." He rolled his eyes, like he was so completely done with the two of us tonight. "Just like Mason. The two of you are two peas in a fucking pod on a bunch of things, more than you realize."

When it looked like Levi was going to argue his case further, the girl took his hand all stained with blood and gave it a gentle yet firm squeeze. "Please, lovely."

A smirk spread over Levi's face. "*Lovely*, hmm?"

"You want more of that, go wash up properly, no more arguments."

Shocking the fuck out of both me and Colt, Levi actually nodded and told her, "All right, yeah." He leaned down, just shy of brushing his lips over hers. "Besides, then I don't have to hesitate on touching you when all this grime and blood is off me."

"I have no problem with that, for the record."

"Shit, cutie," Colt uttered. "Don't wake my cock up right now, yeah? Tone it down."

Fuck me, I was right there with him on that. It was hot

beyond belief. In a completely twisted way, but that was kind of our thing—as a unit, especially.

I saw Levi's eyes flame.

But then his reaction with her surprised me again and that flame died out and a gentleness I couldn't believe took its place as he said, "I won't touch you with sullied hands. Not the blood of our enemies."

"So, only in-house then?" she teased.

She got more than she bargained for when Levi confirmed, "Exactly. Just the four of us." He glared out at me, acknowledging me for the first time since she'd shown up. "Well, *three* right now."

"Take that shower. It's time I introduced myself to Mason anyway."

Levi looked between her and me, then to Colt. "You won't be here alone while I'm showering, Colt will be here with you."

"Not necessary. I'd rather talk to him alone." Off Levi's suspicious look, she assured him, "Not about *that*, we do that together, like I said. Jeez, it took me a lot to convince you, I wouldn't risk messing up how we do it. You have my word."

The tension started to leave him—a little. "As you wish, *Wildflower.*"

He pressed a soft kiss to the top of her head, and then he headed out of the room, looking back a couple of times. Colt followed after him muttering something about needing a *fucking strong daiquiri after the shitshow of tonight*.

And then it was just me and her.

The troublemaker.

The thorn in my side.

The dangerous temptation to Levi.

The knife through the heart of our brotherhood.

I chugged the remainder of my scotch, then placed it

down on the coffee table and sank back against the couch, affecting a casual and calm air—neither of which I really felt.

Her eyes were on me studiously as she made her way to the adjacent armchair and relaxed into it, then mirrored my pose.

Trying to play me at my own game? Yeah, that wasn't the first time she'd done that.

She'd actually fought back and that never fucking happened—no one returned fire against *Hex*. She was the first. Completely unprecedented.

I didn't like that. Unpredictable elements concerned me. Just like Levi Knight.

Now there were two of them.

Jesus.

"Well, you're certainly doing your utmost to live up to your reputation of *Scourge*," she commented.

"Compliment accepted."

"I'm not your enemy."

I sneered. "Burning my soldiers through rigging the showers and displacing many more from their homes with various infestations would beg to differ."

"Those were retaliatory responses," she answered evenly. "Which you made necessary."

"Our marks don't strike back against *Hex*."

"Then I guess there's a first time for everything." She folded one leg over the other. "And also the first time you've made the mistake of *marking* someone like me."

"Someone like you?"

"That's right."

"A club princess?"

Her lips curved. "Took you long enough to figure it out."

I moved to respond in the decimating way I was known for when somebody challenged me.

But she beat me to it, cutting me off, "And you should have. You should have researched me before you marked me. It was incredibly dangerous to come at me, given who I am, and where I come from, who my father is. You're really lucky that I held back and didn't call on the true resources at my disposal. I held back because of him, by the way, because of Levi. And Colt, because he's an absolute sweetheart. Yet, you came at me *because* of Levi, because you're so intent—in an obsessive way, to be honest —to control him that *you* were the one who ended up completely out of control."

Jesus. The woman certainly had some nerves of steel to come at me like this.

"You don't understand the complications and dangers associated with Lev."

"As the object of his intense fixation, believe me, I do."

"Not to the full extent. I've known him for years, we've been the closest of brothers since we were kids. Believe me, there's a lot you have no comprehension of."

She shoved a hand through her silky ebony hair, then took down the harshness in her tone, telling me with an earnestness that caught me off guard and… touched me, "You've clearly been too close to it for too long, because it's compromised your ability to identify the root cause of all this animosity and struggle between the two of you."

I sat forward, clasping my hands between my knees. "Levi doesn't think about the consequences, any sort of fallout, or the big picture involved when it comes to any task or *mission* he embarks on. He gets severe tunnel vision. And we all end up paying the price. I saw him re-entering into that fixated, obsessive mode through his pursuit of you. You're a complication I can't afford, that none of us can. There are things at stake that you don't understand. Hell, there are things that have actually happened that almost destroyed all of us, because of the way that Levi is." I shook my head at her with disbelief. "So you telling me there's a root cause I'm not seeing... even if that was the case, I still need to protect us all."

"I get you wanting to protect your brothers. Club princess, remember? That was my whole life for two decades. *But* the way in which you're doing it when it comes to Levi is actually resulting in the opposite."

I thought for a moment. "Is that why you came here to talk it out, rather than responding to my escalation with another show of force?"

She nodded. "The harder I come at you, the greater the divide it will cause in your brotherhood. I don't want that." Shifting to the edge of the chair, she added with a sexy, fierce edge, "But I also can't allow you to continue to strike at me. I won't be anybody's victim."

"You were Lev's not long ago, before this coupledom I've witnessed between you tonight. You were his prey."

"He went about it the wrong way, but his actions came from wanting to draw closer to me. Affection, if you will. He became desperate because I wasn't ready at first to acknowledge what's between us. And that's the root of it for him—feeling powerless. After what's happened in his life, he can't stand that notion, he really can't stomach it. So these *missions he embarks on* are all to combat that. He needs you to understand that and work with him, not to just throw up walls in his way. You could work with him to change the way he goes about doing these things, to minimize the risk and potential fallout. And Levi can agree to tone it down and do it your way in exchange. But just getting in his way is only going to worsen everything and make him more desperate. Like what happened tonight with him taking out a big chunk of your *Hex* members. I tracked him and watched from a distance. He's in a lot of pain." She sighed heavily. "If you continue to allow your fear of loss of control to get in the way, you'll lose him, you'll lose each other, and things will spiral like crazy. I'm sure you're already seeing the results of that as it is."

I stared at her, taking her words in.

Fuck me, I was impressed.

Off my incredulous look, she grinned. "That's right, I'm a very reasonable person."

"I'm getting that."

Her phone buzzed, cutting through the understanding and shared moment between us.

She pulled it out from her pocket, swiped it open, then started typing rapidly.

After a few moments of it, I asked, "Damage control?"

She lifted her head, her whiskey eyes locking on mine.

Fuck me, they were stunning.

I hadn't seen her up close until tonight and every time she fixed me with her gaze, they caught my attention all over again.

"For the leak of my personal photos?" she responded with an edge, before returning to her typing and telling me, "That's already been dealt with. Nice try, though." She stopped typing, then stowed her phone away. "That was Levi just asking if I was okay in your presence."

"And? How did you respond?"

"I told him it's going as well as can be expected."

"Very diplomatic of you."

"I figured that was needed right now." She gestured at my cheek. "You have blood there. You and Levi came to blows, yeah?"

"Things reached an intense level before you arrived," I admitted.

"Then you're in the right frame of mind to put an end to it."

"So, this is a peace talk."

"What else could it be? If we continue in this vein, it'll end up destroying us all. And for what? Levi won't accept you pushing me out and *I* won't allow you to either, it'll create a divide between the two of you—possibly even Colton becoming involved in it too—that could prove irreparable."

"I agree."

She cocked a skeptical eyebrow. "You do?"

"Yes, you've made your case well." Extremely well, actually. But there was no need to be throwing out further compliments. That made for over-inflated egos and complacency, both hazardous things to indulge.

Her reason couldn't be denied, though.

It had already become straining commanding *Hex* while I had my active focus on her and Levi, it had compromised my studies and I was falling behind. Me. *Jesus.* I also had barely seen either Colt or Lev in the last few days because of it. And extremely worryingly, I was getting off too much on wielding the power of *Hex*. It was starting to corrupt me and I was honestly just hanging on by a thin sliver of a thread in order to avoid that happening. But if I kept it up at this pace *and* going it alone without Levi at my side to mitigate my addictive issues when it came to that sort of thing, it wouldn't be long before I fully succumbed.

In spite of all of that, it had hit me tonight that Brianna could prove useful, if I could balance the detrimental aspect she posed to Levi's stability with his obsessiveness about her. I'd watched her calm him and even convince him to do something he hadn't wanted to earlier. It was absolutely unheard of. The only way I'd managed to get him to do something he hadn't desired to was to use harsh methods. But there she'd been with a gentleness, yet firmness all at once that he'd responded incredibly favorably to.

Before I could speak more to it, Colt swaggered back in, popping a rumball into his mouth, a full packet clutched in his hand. Yeah, he was definitely pissed and agitated about what had transpired tonight. Rumballs were his stress foods, as Cheerios were mine.

He looked between the two of us, then slumped onto the couch over on the farthest cushion, making it clear he didn't want to be close to me right now. "Figured you guys were done by now."

"Not really," I responded.

"Then go right ahead, Mason," he retorted. "Glad to see you managed to summon *some* sense and you didn't hurt her."

"I don't hurt women, you know that."

"Do I? How about that attack you had set on her, that I intervened in before it could actually take place?"

"*That's* why you randomly showed up at my side that night and insisted on escorting me home?" Brianna asked.

"Damn straight. I wasn't gonna let you get hurt. I've grown hella fond of you, cutie."

As she beamed at him, I clarified, "It was a scare tactic. Intimidation. Nothing physical would have transpired."

Levi's shadow fell over the door. "Your toy soldiers would've suffered big time if it had gone down that way." He winked at Brianna. "You've got skills, don't you, baby?"

"I can hold my own," she responded, modestly. Or perhaps she intended to downplay her combat abilities to have me underestimate her in case we couldn't maintain this peace.

"I've summoned more than *some sense*, Colt," I told him. "We're making peace."

He cocked an eyebrow. "You are?" He swung his head toward Brianna. "He is?"

"That's right," she responded brightly, then reached out and gently rubbed his arm. "It's all okay. Or, it will be."

"Well, good," Colt said, brightening too, his antagonism toward me lessening a little as he looked back at me and actually smiled. "Really fucking good."

"Sorry, cupcake," Levi said, having taken a quick shower and now changed into a clean pair of gray sweats. He crossed to Brianna and perched on the arm of her chair, then draped his arm over her shoulders. I watched with intrigue as she immediately sank into his touch. "That's gonna be tested right off the bat."

Before any of us could get a word out, him and Brianna exchanged a nod of agreement, then Levi sucked in a breath and revealed, "We don't just know each other from our fathers doing business a few years back." With his free hand, he grasped her hand for obvious support. "She was there six years ago. I wasn't alone when I was taken. Brianna was with me."

"What?" Colt exclaimed, his vehement shock mirroring mine.

"*That's* where your obsession with her stems from?" I asked.

"My interest was sparked before then, but what happened during those two weeks… let's just say that it escalated that interest. Cemented it, really."

"Fuck me," I choked. "Lev, this is—"

"It's not like you think. She saved me back then. She saved my life, Mason." He tightened his hold on her and looked at her with utter reverence. "Fuck, she saved me from more than even that. She *spared* me."

Brianna grimaced as that time was referenced.

And Levi could barely hold it together, his body now full of tension, emotion swimming in his eyes that had Colt going to him and wrapping himself around him uttering words of comfort.

Lev *never* talked about that time in his life.

This was beyond unprecedented.

"You see now, Mason? You see why I can't let you pull her from me?"

"This is dangerous, that being the root of the connection and obsession, Lev."

"We'll make sure that isn't the case," Brianna said, eyeing me in reference to our conversation about my handling of Lev being detrimental.

"You don't understand," Lev insisted, pulling from Brianna and Colt and rising to his feet. He strode over to me and slapped his hands down on the coffee table in front of me. "But you will."

I tensed, preparing for another fight.

But then he pushed off the table and went another way that I wasn't expecting—there seemed to be a lot of that lately.

Too much.

"I'm gonna tell you how it was."

And then the most shocking thing of all happened.

He went back to that time and place that had marked the worst experience of his life and forever changed him.

24

~Levi~

Six Years Ago

SHE WAS SO BEAUTIFUL.

Like a princess.

She even had a jeweled tiara on to go along with it.

But the white summer dress beneath a black leather jacket... no, it was like she was an angel who'd been dragged through the gates of hell because of some awful mix-up.

I knew who she was really.

The club princess of the Steel Dawn Motorcycle Club.

I'd met her before when my dad had taken me to the clubhouse her father ran. A couple of months back. It had been part of his training, to show me how to do business, how to strike deals with dangerous men. And Curt Walker had definitely fit the bill. But so did my dad.

That made it all the harder to swallow that this had happened.

That I'd been taken.

I didn't want to think about it.

When reality was too brutal, fantasy helped you through.

So she was an angel to me. One who'd lost her way, one who the bad men would come to realize didn't belong here soon. And then they'd take me with her as they sent her back to the good place where she was really supposed to be.

I started as I watched her fingers flex in her binds, nasty zip-ties trapping her to that metal chair just like they were with me a few feet to her right.

Hope blossomed as her head moved and shifted from its uncomfortable lolled state.

And then she raised it, wincing. It had to be from the nasty bruise I'd seen on the left side of her face when they'd dragged her in here and bound her right beside me. I'd yelled so much when I'd seen them manhandling her that one of the bad men had knocked me out. Now I had a bruise the same place that she did. She also had a nasty cut down the right side of her face, though. It had to hurt. But one grimace and she seemed to just shrug it off, as she opened her eyes and fully came to.

Whiskey.

Her eyes were the color of the liquor my dad drank.

His favorite kind. Something he called top-shelf. I forgot the brand. It didn't matter, I'd tasted the stuff when he'd offered me a sip as some sort of rite of passage, and I'd nearly thrown up, I'd hated it so much.

Oh crap, my mind was wandering all over.

My dad always warned me to keep my focus, especially in tense situations. This was way beyond that, though. Way.

"Hi there."

I jolted and it took me a moment to realize that the angel was speaking to me.

Her voice was the sweetest sound.

I'd heard nothing for hours on end and hearing her… I'd never forget it.

"Curt Walker's daughter. Brianna, right?" I whispered back.

"Yeah." She took me in, noting my school uniform—black pants and a now rumpled and dirtied formerly white shirt. They'd taken my

tie, but I still had my school blazer on—royal blue with golden markings and the uppity school's crest. "Levi Knight. Roman's son."

I nodded. "Are you all right?"

She smiled and it was amazing through this awfulness. "Of course."

I frowned. "You're lying."

Her lips quirked. "Why do you say that?"

"Your eye twitched."

"Right, that's my tell."

"Like in poker?"

"In life. Say a lie into the mirror when you get home and see if you have one, then school it. Practice and no one will ever know. It'll help you out a great deal as you get older, especially in our world."

"Our world? The badness, you mean?"

She smiled, but this time it was sad. "Yeah."

A gloomy silence filled the space between us and I hated it. I couldn't take it again. So many hours of nothing but the screeching of doors in the distance and heavy footsteps all over. The bad men's footsteps.

"You're dressed so nice. Were you at a party?"

"In a way. It was my high school graduation ceremony. We were on our way to the party afterward when—" She stopped herself and looked at me. "I mean, when this detour happened."

"I'm fifteen, not stupid. We've been kidnapped."

She stared at me for a moment. And then she sucked in a breath. "We'll sort it out, get you home for dinner."

"And you to your party?"

"Exactly." She started looking all around, then studying the chair and the binds. "I'm going to hasten that along, but I need your help."

"That's dangerous. They got angry at me for trying to stop them from tying you to the chair when you were unconscious earlier. And that was barely anything. If they find us trying to escape, it won't just be a knockout punch to the face that we'll suffer."

"They did that to you?" she seethed.

"Yeah."

"You're just a kid. Those sick bastards."

"I might be a kid, but I'm also Roman Knight's heir."

She sighed. "I get it, believe me. Being Curt Walker's little princess comes with a crapload of stuff like that too. This isn't even my first time being taken. Last time was by a rival club."

"Oh my God. What happened?"

Something dark flittered across her face.

But it was only for a moment before that sunshine returned and she told me, "Nothing much. Steel Dawn MC showed up quickly and got me out."

Why didn't I believe her there?

"I didn't see who was responsible for taking us tonight. The guys that tied us up were wearing ski masks and they didn't speak, didn't come in to tell me what was going on, or how long we were going to be here, nothing."

"That doesn't bode well."

"You don't think?"

She caught herself again, forcing a smile. "We'll be fine. There's two of us, we can work well with that. Now, listen carefully, our ankles are tied with rope, not zip ties. They've used special knots, but I can walk you through how to undo it. We'll slide our chairs close enough to one another, then I'll knock my chair over so I can reach behind me to untie your feet and then—"

"And if they catch us in the middle of this?"

"Given that you're here alongside me, it's clear who took us. Malcolm Lynch and his organization. We can't wait, believe me."

"Lynch? Never heard of him."

"Then your dad has done his job well shielding you." She rolled her eyes. "Much better than mine. Lynch didn't take us for ransom or leverage. He's taken us as punishment, to hurt our fathers."

I swallowed hard.

But before I could respond, the door screeched open.

A figure came into view and we watched as he sealed the door behind him, then drew closer.

It wasn't one of the bad men this time. No ski-masks.

In his forties but well-preserved with very few age lines, the guy was built like a linebacker. He had a dirty-blond buzz cut that gave him a severe edge. Those beady eyes of his added a creep factor too. He was dressed in a pair of gray dress pants and a V-Neck muscle tee, a forest of chest hair showing through.

He smirked as he caught us looking at him warily.

He pointed at himself in dramatic fashion with two thumbs. "Malcom Lynch."

He drew ever closer with wide, measured strides. "We're going to be spending a lot of time together, so best to know whose care you're in."

"What do you want?" I found myself blurting out.

The rapidly ramping up tension combined with the hours' long wait I'd already endured was apparently making me more impatient than usual.

He looked at me and that nasty smirk spread like an infection. "Two little heirs to formidable empires," he mused, looking us over, a sadistic gleam flashing in his eyes. "That will be remedied over our time together. You'll break, and without heirs, your fathers' legacies end. Not to mention how destructively they'll react when they see what I've done to their precious offspring. Two empires will fall and with the heirs useless they will never be resurrected."

Brianna hissed. "Your plan is foolish. Neither of us are heir apparent. Steel Dawn MC won't accept a woman as President. And Levi isn't destined for the family business either, he's treading his own path. My dad showed me an announcement that Roman was a couple of days away from making to that effect. So doing this is completely pointless."

Wow, she was good. Amazing, actually. None of that stuff about me was true. My dad was training me to take his place one day, to carry on our legacy. Or, our dynasty, as he called it.

Lynch walked up to Brianna, his lip curling. "You've inherited Curt's smarts, I see. His defiance too."

I yelled out as he shot out his hand and grabbed her jaw in a painful hold.

"His overconfidence too, pretty princess."

"Get your fucking hands off me," she seethed.

"Daddy's not here to save you now, so I wouldn't be making demands if I were you."

"Get off her!" I shouted, bucking in my chair.

He swung his head toward. "Getting worked up already at this? That doesn't bode well for you, boy. I've barely touched her yet."

Yet? Oh my God.

"Don't. Don't hurt her."

"It's okay, you won't be left out. You'll get to enjoy the show."

"Take me instead. Hurt me. My father is way more powerful than hers. It'll be a much bigger coup to break me and mess with his empire."

He released her roughly and spun to me.

"No, Levi!" Brianna cried. She fought against her binds wildly. "Don't hurt him, you monster. He's just a kid! Just a fucking kid! Kidnapping him is traumatizing enough, you don't need to do more to him. I'll take it all. I'll be compliant, or I'll fight… whichever pleases you."

Lynch pulled up short and eyed her incredulously. "My, my, what an offer."

He stepped up to her and trailed his thumb over her lips, exerting painful pressure that made her grunt. "Such a pretty mouth." He ripped open his belt. "Prove to me you'll give what you've offered first and I won't touch the boy." He paused as my yells became more vehement with every passing second, his fists clenching in agitation.

Brianna noticed and tried to save me in yet another way, telling him, "Let him go."

"Can't do that. Roman needs a lesson."

"Then at least take him out of the vicinity. He doesn't need to see any of what's coming. He's already traumatized like you wanted."

"Best to take it all the way then, isn't it?"

He ignored Brianna's protests as he stormed to me and drew a flip knife from his pocket.

Before I could even react, he was sweeping it across the left side of my throat, cutting painfully through my flesh.

"Won't kill you, but it'll certainly serve as a warning for you to shut the hell up. Know that I'll do far worse if you don't."

Brianna was bucking in her chair, and shouting. She looked so pained for me, it was hard to stomach, much more than the brutal burning pain in my throat now.

With a roar, Lynch thrust his boot into my chair, sending it careening onto its side. I cried out as I remained bound tightly to it as it hit the concrete with a bone-jarring thud.

"That'll do for now," Lynch said, striding predatorily back to Brianna.

He grabbed her jaw again to stop her screaming protests on my behalf. And then, with his free hand, he opened his pants.

No. No. No!

I saw Brianna's fingers tightening around the chair arms, her body trembling, even as I could see her fighting to hide it, to muster courage.

Our gazes clashed and pain met pain.

"Close your eyes," she beseeched me.

But I couldn't.

I couldn't leave her alone in this.

So I kept eye contact with her throughout.

And it killed a piece of my soul knowing that was all I could do to help her.

I SNAPPED BACK TO REALITY, feeling my pulse pounding in my ears, my hands shaking.

Next, I would be struggling to breathe easily and sweating profusely.

I was on the verge of having my first anxiety attack in ages. *Fuck.*

I'd often thought about that time, obviously. Especially with my mission at hand, and through connecting with Brianna again. I also had recurring nightmares about it if I allowed myself to sleep for more than a couple of hours a night. But I'd never actually spoken about it or gone there in detail like I just had, I'd never recalled that hellscape to the point of basically having to relive it.

And I hadn't even covered more than a very small portion of what had gone down over those two weeks. Not who else had been dragged in there. Not how Brianna's gunshot wound scar in her back had been caused in that place. Not what else had happened to us.

I couldn't.

It should be enough to make Mason understand where I was coming from, though.

I sank against the wall, trying to stop myself from entering into a full-blown attack.

Looking out at Brianna, I saw Colt on the arm of the chair beside her now, stroking her back and whispering words of comfort to her as she leaned forward with her head buried in her hands.

I wanted to go to her, but I could barely move currently.

"It's okay, *Wildflower,*" I spoke, my voice sounding like it wasn't my own and like it was so far away. "You're safe. It's over, it's long over."

She lifted her head and instantly I saw that she was struggling with the same reaction that I was—she was having an attack. Her eyes were wide and glazed, sweat slicked her brow and down her chest, and she was panting.

Just as Colt started to talk her through it like he and Mason used to do for me when I'd had attacks regularly, a wall of muscle blocked my visual.

I blinked, struggling to make out what was happening in my discombobulated state.

And then I managed to take in Mason through my blurred vision.

"I'm sorry, Lev. So sorry you both suffered through that."

I jolted as he grasped my biceps.

"Breathe with me. Focus on me."

I couldn't speak, could barely comprehend what he was saying.

He eased me closer, making more physical contact, and it was enough to get me to focus on my breathing with him.

"Good. Very good," he spoke softly at my ear.

"Mason," I croaked.

"It's all gonna be okay. I'm fucking here now, I swear it, brother."

He wrapped his arms around me in one of his warm bear hugs, and I sank into it.

For the first time in a really long while, I let him comfort me.

I let him see the pain beneath the armor.

25

~Brianna~

As painful as it had been to relive that brutal time in our lives, it had been the right call to reveal the truth to Colton and Mason.

It had done what I'd hoped it would when I'd managed to convince Levi to tell them.

It had given Mason peace of mind with a major truth finally being revealed by Levi.

It was clear by the reaction I'd seen from Mason right afterward, that it had also taken him back to a time before so much antagonism had developed between the two of them.

It had given him a glimpse of the person he'd been so close to before so much other shit had gotten in the way and weakened their bond.

He'd taken off once Levi and I had come down from our... *episodes*... to deal with the fallout of Levi's retaliatory response. And he hadn't even made a dig or a single negative comment to him about it. He'd just gone to deal with it.

Not only that, but he'd invited me to stay in the

mansion for a couple of days, while he spread word that I was no longer a mark of *Hex*, which would result in the looks, comments, and negative attention and reactions from so much of the campus finally letting up.

My goal coming here had been to make peace, so I'd agreed, not wanting to rock the boat. It had also been clear that Levi had needed me to stay with him after the revelation and us both reliving that nightmare again. While I'd agreed, I wasn't stupid enough to give Mason my trust this early on after what he'd done, so when he'd offered to have a couple of his still able-bodied soldiers who Levi hadn't yet hit to retrieve some of my essentials for staying over, I'd declined, and Levi had sent one of his *contacts* for me instead.

I finished up brushing my teeth, and slipped into my bubblegum pink pajama pants, then pulled my matching strappy tank on.

I stepped out of the ensuite bathroom into the spare bedroom Colton had guided me to earlier, while Levi had been making the arrangements to bring my stuff over.

A gasp caught in my throat as I found Levi there, sitting on the foot of the bed.

It wasn't just the surprise of him being in the room, it was him lounging there in that sexy way of his, leaning back on his hands, while wearing nothing but a pair of crimson boxers.

"Hey," he greeted me as I walked into the bedroom.

"Hey."

"Do you have everything you need? Anything you forgot to ask for come to mind?"

I smiled. "I'm all good, thanks."

I walked to him and when I reached him, he slid his hands to my hips, holding me to him. "Mmm, this is where I like you. Here in my arms." He drew soft circles on my hips. "I can't get enough of touching you, Brianna."

"You're not the only one."

Being with him was like nothing else I'd ever experienced before.

It was beyond passion itself.

It was raw, animalistic, yet somehow I also felt safe and adored.

He slid one hand up into my hair and gave one of his sexy tugs, urging my mouth to his.

I resisted—barely. "Don't you need to crash? It's been a long night. That takedown you handled, the revelation."

"It actually has me wired. Violence and bloodletting… ah, that's the stuff." He waggled his eyebrows at me.

"I can't actually tell if you're joking or not."

"I schooled my tell, that's why, baby."

"Just like I taught you."

He smiled. "Just like you taught me."

I stroked his fingers in my hair. "You didn't tell them everything that happened in that place."

"We agreed we'd tell them enough to explain our connection. That's what I did."

"You held back for me, didn't you?"

"I wasn't sure if you were ready for everything to be put out there. I mean, you've never talked about *her*, even when we've referenced the kidnapping. It's like that part was erased to you."

"It was. At least, I tried to make it so, to pretend she'd never been there, that I'd lost her another way entirely. Not… not like that."

"I understand."

I pulled away and shoved my hand through my hair, pacing back and forth in front of him.

He didn't say anything, just watched and waited

patiently, something I was well aware from his initial pursuit of me didn't come easy to him.

Once again, he was doing something all for me.

The least I could do was fully step out of those *shadows* and do him the same courtesy.

So, I forced the words I'd long-denied breath past my lips as I came to a halt and faced him. "My mom... they brought her into that hellhole too... beat her down, then... then they killed her... right in front of me."

As the words left me, the awful confession, so did a weight I'd been carrying for so fucking long that I'd actually forgotten what it was like to exist without it.

Levi pushed off the bed and came to me, wrapping his arms around me and pulling me in close as he stroked my hair. "My *Wildflower*... so brave. I see it... I see you becoming freer, embracing the real you. I feel you, I feel you there with me now. Don't slip away again... I can't go back to the cold."

Oh my God. His vulnerability was staggering. And it hit me beyond bone deep.

I clung to him and buried my face in his bare, chiseled chest. "Me neither."

Now we'd crossed that line, all barriers down, I couldn't imagine going back on it.

I didn't want that emptiness anymore.

Letting go and coming together the other night had been a fucking revelation, an epiphany of epic proportions.

The moment took me over, his warmth seeping into me, his hands on me, his hard body pushed up against mine, the raw intensity coming off us both... *God*, it was a heady experience.

And I let it engulf me.

Lifting my head, I slicked my tongue over his jaw, then nipped at it.

A carnal groan reverberated from him, sending sparks of need to my core.

In the next second, Levi snagged me around the waist, then had me yelping with excitement as he tossed me on the bed.

As I bounced on the mattress, he was there, pouncing on too, then crawling up the bed toward me, a predatory look rising to the surface that basically had me melting into a puddle of liquid desire right there.

He straddled me and growled like an animal, before slamming his palms down either side of my head. "Let me see you, baby."

I didn't even hesitate, I just pulled off my strappy tank and tossed it God knew where across the room. I shuffled underneath him and shucked off my pants too, just my black lace panties left remaining.

His hot gaze flicked over my body, traveling up and down, taking in every inch of me "Fuck."

A zap of pleasure hit me as he trailed his thumb over the front of my panties, feeling my wet warmth through the barely-there barrier to my pussy. He hissed through his teeth, and then he went feral, unleashing his tongue and teeth all over me, trailing down my neck, sweeping across my collarbone, teasing my breasts and making my nipples pebble.

He was all fucking over me, growling, grunting, and rutting, as I undulated beneath him and fisted my hands in his hair, tugging painfully, and just ramping him up all the more with the bite of pain. Moans and cries of succumbing pleasure spilled from me almost involuntarily, as he utterly consumed me.

And then a voice cut into all the delicious intensity.

"Now this is what I'm talking about. Hot damn."

I jolted at the sound of Colton's voice, turning my head

on the pillow to see him standing there at the threshold, one hand slapped to the door, and wearing a leopard-print kimono, his mohawk in disarray and wild. It was tied so loosely that I could see it was all that he was wearing.

"Can we help you?" Levi asked, swinging his head toward him and slapping his hands down either side of me as he basically held a push-up pose, his biceps bulging. *Jeez*, these guys really knew how to turn the sexy on.

"I heard some interesting sounds coming from in here. Thought I'd check it out."

Levi told me, "His room is right next door to this one."

"Damn straight," Colton said, flashing us a shit-eating grin. "So, is this a private moment, or are you up for company?"

"You sure you can handle a threesome with *me*?" Levi asked. It wasn't arrogance, but genuine concern coming through for Colton. "I'm worked up. You join in and it's gonna get intense."

"Sounds like fun to me."

"Yeah?"

"Yeah. I'll bring my *Maverick* persona out to play."

"Mmm... very nice. But hold that thought." Levi gazed down at me. "Your call, *Wildflower*. Always your call."

"No hard feelings, honestly," Colton called over. "I'll just go play with myself to the sounds of the two of you."

"Or wait naked on Mason's bed for when he gets home," Levi said.

"God, the two of you," I groaned, rubbing my thighs together. I looked out at Colton. "Come."

His eyes flamed. "Oh, I plan to, cutie," he said, sauntering into the room toward us. "But you first. I'm a gentleman, after all." He pulled something from his robe pocket and tossed it to Levi who snatched it out of the air and put it down on the bed where I was able to see that it was a bottle of lube.

He shrugged off his robe, baring his naked inked body in all its glory, his fully-inked arms, a beautiful colorful tapestry all the way from the tops of his shoulders to his wrists. He fisted his already hard cock, stroking it roughly as he sauntered toward the bed, his eyes blazing at me and Levi.

Levi eased off me to the side and stroked my hair reassuringly as Colton climbed on.

I jolted as he trailed his free hand up my leg, all the way to my inner thigh, then brushed his fingers over my panties.

A gasp escaped me as he exerted a little pressure right on my clit, then circled right there.

"God," I cried, arching off the bed.

He smiled and eyed Levi. "Already so wet. You've got her all primed for us, *Hellraiser.*"

My heart was pounding in my chest with excitement and barely-contained anticipation.

I was sure it would have been mixed with fear too if Levi wasn't here calming me, making me feel so at ease and spelled in pleasurable need.

"More," I found myself uttering as Levi looked to me for my consent yet again. Double checking, always so careful.

Levi smirked, his fingers leaving my hair and then sinking into Colton's. Tugging him closer, he brushed his lips over his.

That quickly escalated to more than a mere brush as Colton's tongue snaked out and swept over Levi's bottom lip, his stud rolling over it and making Levi groan. In the next moment, their tongues were tangling wildly.

God.

The eroticism of it had me shifting restlessly on the sheets.

As Levi used his hold in Colton's hair to rip them apart suddenly, they were both panting.

Colton jerked forward and yanked down Levi's crimson boxers, exposing his rock-hard cock that was now dripping with pre-cum.

A tremble went through me and I licked my lips at the sight.

"Got the right idea there," Colton told me, noticing my reaction.

Levi had only just pulled his boxers the rest of the way off when Colton's hooded gaze was all over his cock.

Levi grinned, then grabbed the back of his head and shoved Colton into my breasts.

"God," I cried out as Colton's tongue went feral instantly all over them.

When his tongue piercing rolled over my nipples, shocks of intensity went through me right to my core making me drip into my panties. I reached up and fisted his hair, and I felt him smiling against my soft flesh as he let me guide him and take control.

"Mmm, she loves your magic tongue, *Maverick*," Levi said, a moment before he was down between my legs and ripping off my panties. "Spread, baby," he said.

I didn't get the chance as Colton grasped my thighs and opened them up wide for Levi. He pulled from my breasts, then straddled my stomach and took my mouth in an all-consuming kiss.

I realized it was part distraction when cold liquid dripped into my ass. I gasped into the kiss as I felt Levi's slick finger rimming the sensitive skin of my hole. The sensation was out of this world and it took me over. I dug my nails into Colton's biceps and a sexy grunt from him reverberated through our kiss.

Levi's soft, teasing touches were replaced by pressure as he began to ease his finger inside my ass, inching deeper, then drawing out, before sinking deeper than before again.

I pulled my mouth from Colton's and cried out, clawing at the sheets.

"Never there, huh?" Colton said, reading my reaction well.

"Virgin," Levi told him.

Colton stroked my cheek. "Only fingers this time, cutie. We don't want you to hurt."

"Okay," I murmured, awash in a haze and only sinking deeper as Levi's finger did the same.

In the throes of it, as he started thrusting, I curled my fingers around Colton's cock. He jarred from watching Levi's finger disappearing in and out of my ass and smirked at me. "Messaged received." And then he was straddling me backward, his cock in my face as he leaned down and lashed his tongue through my pussy.

"God!" I cried, and he took advantage of my lips parting to slide his cock into my mouth.

I took it greedily, swallowing more of him.

"Shit," he choked.

"That's right, baby, open that throat for our boy."

Levi added another finger, stretching me and pulling a long moan from me that had Colton jerking in my mouth as it reverberated along his shaft.

He started to tongue me like a madman then, his stud assaulting my clit over and over in the most incredible way, while Levi fucked my ass with two thick fingers rapid-fire.

It was sensation overload and I grasped Colton's ass, digging my fingers in, as I deep throated his cock, completely caught up in their heady spell.

The wave hit me without any warning, and I bucked on the bed, twisting in the sheets and screaming around Colton's cock down my throat as I came all over his face.

"So fucking tight," I heard Levi say as I clamped down with brutal pressure around his fingers in the throes of my orgasm.

I'd barely recovered when the two of them shifted around, Levi's fingers leaving me empty and Colton's talented tongue and mouth lifting from my pussy.

I whimpered at the loss.

"Greedy girl," Colton commented. "I fucking love it." He eyed Levi. "Damn, that was close, she almost shot me over the edge with that glorious mouth."

Speaking of being right on the edge, Levi's eyes were black with that sexy, dangerous look as he took me in sprawled out naked on the bed, my nipples and breasts marked by Colton's love bites, my pussy glistening from my orgasm.

"Lev's about to lose control, darlin'. You up for that?" Colton told me, registering Levi's state of mind too.

My answer came in the form of pushing up to a sitting position.

Levi's eyes flickered, unsure if I was turning away from where he needed to take things now that the two of them had warmed me up.

And then I bolted up and lunged at him, a snarl escaping me.

He caught me, grasping my thighs, then spinning us around and slamming my back against the wall.

And then his mouth was all over me, licking, sucking, and biting the column of my neck, along my collarbone, down to my breasts.

"Fuck, woman," he growled, grinding his big cock between my spread thighs, sliding through my folds and bumping my clit roughly with every aggressive roll of his hips.

I screamed out at the overstimulation, the wildness, and the animal in me broke free entirely, clawing at him and biting everywhere I could reach, drawing blood.

This, when we came together in this primal way, was the most free I'd ever felt.

And I needed it so badly, *we* needed it.

It became clear in the next moment that we weren't the only ones, because as rivulets of blood covered our skin and smushed together as we ground together, rutting like wild things, Colton was suddenly there back with us and licking some droplets off the side of my throat.

"Goddamn, this is what I'm talking about. Wild fucking things. I'm here for it," he breathed between us.

He grasped Levi's throat, making his eyes flame with animalistic desire, before forcing him closer, then thrusting his tongue into his mouth, making him taste the blood he'd just lapped up and gathered there.

I was right on the edge with the erotic torment Levi and I were making together, then watching the two of them clash in such a feral way, gnashing teeth and hooking tongues, the sharp smacking of wet lips.

Levi snarled and ripped his mouth from Colton's all of a sudden. He stopped grinding and told me desperately, "Need to be inside your sweet cunt. *Now.*"

Then he was hoisting us onto the dresser, spreading my legs obscenely wide, a second before he slammed me down onto his cock.

Colton was there taking over with spreading my thighs so Levi could wrap one hand around my throat in a dominant move that held me to him, while he scraped his blunt nails down my breasts and stomach, spreading the blood all the more over my heated skin.

The moment Colton dipped his head and lashed his tongue harshly through my folds, Levi started to thrust up into me, filling me deep with stabbing, violent thrusts that forced scream after scream from my throat. Colton ravaged my spread open pussy with his tongue, teeth and lips, driving me absolutely insane, especially when he then thrust a finger into my ass.

"Fuck, Colt," Levi choked.

Colton smirked. "Feel that, huh?" he asked, starting to curl it inside my ass.

"Ungh, yeah."

"Good. Feel me as you come inside her sweet cunt."

With a growl, Levi's hand left my throat and he grabbed Colton's cock.

I watched, enraptured as he began working it viciously, fisting his shaft mercilessly, so much so that Colton lost his rhythm eating me out and had to slap one hand to the dresser to steady himself.

"Lev," he gasped. "Yeah, don't stop, don't fucking stop. I'm right there. Ungh… shit, *Hellraiser.*"

Colton twisted his finger inside my ass, then tormented my clit with his tongue piercing.

I was right there too within the next few seconds just as he grunted and exploded, Levi angling Colton's cock so it shot his hot cum all over my spread open pussy.

The dirtiness of it and the added exquisite sensation sent me hurtling over the edge, and then I was coming, shuddering between them.

A roar from Levi sounded a second before he came inside me, triggering another shot of ecstasy that had me shrieking and bucking on his cock as it tore me in two.

"Holy… hell," I gasped, collapsing back on Levi.

Colton wolf whistled and slumped onto the bed,

breathing heavily and sweating. "I'd say so. Better than I'd even been picturing playing with you two."

Levi chuckled and held me closer, the animal retreating and that attentive and caring aspect of him taking the reins again, as he effectively cradled me.

"All right, Brianna?"

"Amazing," I choked out.

"Free, hmm?"

"So free."

He kissed my neck and Colton smiled as he watched his sweetness with me.

"I'm glad, my *Wildflower.*"

Then he eased me off the wall, carried me to the bed, and he and Colton tucked me in and settled either side of me, nuzzling against me.

Taking care of me.

Reassuring me.

Loving me.

26

~Mason~

Brianna Walker had proven to be an interesting and highly unprecedented development.

A *positive* one to make it all the more astounding.

I couldn't actually believe it, given how things had started, and how I'd first viewed them because of my preconceived notions of how it could only lead to a shit-show's worth of trouble.

But it was undeniable.

She'd managed to calm Lev down right after our confrontation. She'd come to me diplomatically offering a truce, not because she couldn't take the heat of the battle I'd been throwing down, but because she'd been worried about the fractures it had been causing in our brother-hood. She'd convinced Lev to tell me the truth about their connection. And even more miraculous than that was that her presence and support had led to Lev actually talking about the kidnapping, something he *never* did. It was absolutely astounding.

After handling damage control from Levi's *message*, which had taken me hours, I'd returned home in the early morning hours to find her, Colt, and Lev asleep in her bed in the guestroom we'd assigned her. An interesting development indeed.

All the more interesting had been the jab of need, regret, and jealousy that had hit me as I'd taken them in wrapped around one another. Without me.

That was the way it had been for weeks now ever since Levi's return. Me pushed apart from them as I'd worked behind the scenes in a bid to contain him *and* me becoming immersed in the power trip that taking on sole leadership of *Hex* had caused. Instead of going to such lengths to rein Lev in and protect us by extension, it had just served to pull us apart—well, to pull *me* from them.

But now, with Brianna's involvement, and her suggestion on approaching things a new way with Levi, it had enabled things to shift and to clear the way to bring me back to them as a result.

I made my way toward the kitchen for breakfast, hearing the voices and laughter of Colt and Brianna from within.

I couldn't believe it, but Lev had actually left her side and given a break to his extreme clinginess that he'd been afflicted with when it came to her.

He'd left an hour ago, sending a text message to each one of us that said the same thing, where he'd claimed he had to take some time today to catch up on his coursework and readings that he'd already been neglecting recently because of his activities with Brianna and that sudden trip he'd had to take to see his dad. He was apparently heading down to the campus library away from any distractions so he could immerse himself in the work that he needed to get done ASAP before he risked failing out after just returning. *Dammit, Lev.*

Perhaps that was why he'd been called home by

Roman. As usual, he hadn't been very forthcoming about the reason behind that trip.

Daddy Knight was always watching him to some extent. Although, over the years, Lev had learned how to evade detection when he was engaging in certain activities that he knew Roman wouldn't approve of. However, keeping tabs on his son's college grades and progress would be child's play for the tech engineering giant, so it stood to reason that he was aware that Lev wasn't doing well. Given that Levi Knight was a prodigy in his field of study, Roman would put it down to his son's focus being elsewhere—on something it shouldn't be.

I drew closer to the kitchen, picking up on the conversation within.

"That's why Lev calls you his Wildflower? Shit, that's cute. He's not just putting on the charm, you know? Despite his rep to the outside world, he actually has a really sweet side."

"Yeah, I've seen it lately. Especially how he is with you. I love his nickname for you."

"Cupcake, yep. It's because he says I'm as sweet as icing sugar and just as appealing to the masses too."

"I can see that."

"You flirting with me, cutie?"

"A little."

"I like a little flirt over breakfast."

I walked into the kitchen. "You like a little flirting at any time of the day."

Instead of rising to it, he barely gave me more than a second's glance, then clammed up and looked down at his plate, continuing to eat his pancakes.

Question answered then. He was still pissed at me.

"There's more," Brianna told me, offering me a bright smile. "Made you a plate."

I located another plate beyond the kitchen table over

on the counter, taking in the stacked pancakes with rasp-berries and whipped cream on top. They were drizzled with a deep-red syrup, which I assumed was also rasp-berry-flavored. We didn't have that on hand, so she had to have made it from scratch.

"You did all this?"

She lifted a shoulder—just like Lev did in similar circumstances. Pointing her fork with a drizzled piece of pancake on it at Colt, she told me, "I walked into the kitchen to find *Maverick* here spraying whipped cream into his mouth straight from the canister, so I knew I had to do something about it."

"Hey," Colt exclaimed with his mouth full. "Told you I'm banned from cooking."

"I remember you telling me. But you could've at least eaten one of those Granny Smith apples in that bowl at the end of the counter."

"Nah, I have way more of an intense sweet tooth than an apple can handle."

She giggled.

Fuck me. It was the sweetest sound I'd ever heard. It rolled right through me.

She was sort of dressed down compared to what I was used to seeing from her through my *Hex* observations. All right, *surveillance.* In a pair of gray distressed jeans and an off-the-shoulder baby-pink top, and a pair of block heels, it was simple for her, but she somehow made it look abso-lutely stunning. In a way, she dressed up whatever she was wearing and took it to another level. Her ebony hair was pulled into a sexy half-up, half-down do with a few strands cascading about her face.

Jesus.

I caught myself.

I was liking it too much, revering her almost.

Seeing the three of them entangled in one another had obviously gotten to me more than I'd fully realized. The need to re-bond with my boys *and* to draw closer to Brianna and have my taste like the other two had was right there at the surface nagging at me fiercely.

But before that could happen, I needed to smooth things over with Colt and Lev.

We couldn't come together as a unit until peace was made there.

"So much for me resorting to Cheerios this morning," I said, walking over to the plate she'd very considerately made for me. "This is a lot better."

"I saw the box and Colton told me they're your snack food."

I smiled, then grabbed the plate and made my way back over to them. "True. And sometimes my lazy breakfast when I can't summon the wherewithal to cook. Or if I'm in a rush." Although, that was rare, because I was highly-organized and efficient.

I took my first bite, the flavor exploding on my tastebuds. "This is amazing," I told Brianna.

"High praise," she said, amusement dancing in her eyes.

"She made them from scratch, not from a mix," Colt informed me.

"Praise all the more warranted then."

That same giggle came from her again and I watched her for a moment as she dug back into her pancakes. She certainly was a beauty. Absolutely stunning.

It had taken me until last night to acknowledge it, because when somebody was my target, physical appearance or any other positive qualities didn't register with me. In a way, they didn't really compute as being human to me, just mere threats that needed to be dealt with swiftly and brutally. Registering them as anything else risked compromising my ability to do what needed to be done.

But now that she was no longer a target, no longer a mark of *Hex,* it left me free to open up to all of that, to really start seeing her.

I settled into my meal, trying to ignore the cold shoulder coming across clearly and brutally from Colt as he kept his gaze either riveted on Brianna or his food and strategically avoided connecting with mine, and didn't actively engage me in direct conversation either.

"Is this your go-to breakfast food?" I asked Brianna, wanting to know things about her that my standard surveillance and investigative insight hadn't allowed, such as her favorite things, personality quirks, hopes and dreams, and the like.

She swallowed a piece of pancake, then held her knife and fork in hand as she looked across the table at me and answered, "I'm a fan, for sure, but I have a sandwich fetish —at all times of the day. It would've normally been a breakfast sandwich." She gestured at Colt. "But when I realized what a sweet tooth he has, I pivoted."

"Aww, seriously?" Colt piped up. "You went this way for me?" His eyes gleamed with playful mischief—a look both Lev and I knew well from him. Sure enough, the next words out of his mouth confirmed it as he asked, "Is this you expressing your gratitude for the tonguing I gave your delicious cunt last night? No need, if it is, because, believe me, the pleasure was absolutely mutual."

Brianna stilled.

I choked on a mouthful of pancake.

As I was thumping my chest and clearing my throat, he went on, "You thinking about this little devil?" He stuck his tongue out, flashing his stud.

"Colt," I rumbled.

"Curb your prudish tendencies," he bit back at me, then continued with Brianna, "No need to be shy, cutie. I'm definitely thinking about your taste on my tongue. I even considered not eating this morning so I could still taste you." He smacked his lips in a chef's kiss. "Mmm, and the way your thighs squeezed my head as your sexy body trembled, begging for more like that... holy shit... it's burned into my memory."

"Jesus," I uttered, shaking my head.

Brianna's cheeks heated and it took her a moment to absorb Colt's graphic commentary. That was about right when it came to him.

But then she stunned us both as she told him, "Actually, I was thinking about the part where you and Levi both lost control and he grabbed your cock and fisted it, making you pant and moan for him, then spray all over his fingers."

Lev had done *what?*

"Mmm, yeah. Good stuff," Colt said, doing a good job of trying to absorb how much her words had gotten to him. She'd learn his cues soon enough as she grew closer. "You enjoyed eating up every last drop of our cum, didn't you, darlin'?"

"It's definitely worth a repeat," she responded evenly. Her gaze flicked to mine and the corner of her mouth turned up, making her interest known in somewhat of a subdued way.

She was likely still wary of me.

That was to be expected given the way things had transpired.

Time would assist.

It wouldn't be enough, though, so I'd have to actively work to earn her trust.

Best start now.

"By the time Monday rolls around, everything will have returned to its status quo on campus," I informed her.

"Within just forty-eight hours?"

"It's a guarantee. No comments, no more social media activity concerning the photos I leaked, not even any looks your way. *Hex* won't come at you again."

"I would say *thank you*, but rewarding bad behavior sets a bad precedence."

"I agree. But how do you chalk up your relationship with Lev where that's concerned?"

"That was different."

"Because of your connection?"

"Something like that." She finished the last bite of her pancake breakfast, then dabbed her mouth with a napkin and sat back in her chair. "But from this moment, you and I can put what's happened with *Hex* and my strikes against you too behind us. If you're really willing to in the light of day."

I sensed Colt looking at me and I could basically feel the anxiousness rolling off him that I might back out now or something.

"Clean slates," I confirmed to Brianna. "*However*, we need to discuss Levi."

I jolted as Colt suddenly slammed down his plate, then shoved himself to his feet. "Fuck, Mason. You say all this bullshit is done with, but now you want to use Brianna to go behind Lev's back, use her to control him, I'm guessing. That's putting her in a really fucking awkward position *and* it's gonna hurt Lev badly if he finds out. You know he has major trust issues."

"It's not what you think. Calm down. Just—"

"You wouldn't listen to me about all of this before, the hell I'm gonna do you the dignity of hearing you out now." He rounded the table to head for the door, but pulled up short to tell Brianna in an attempted calmer tone that he didn't quite pull off, "Sorry, cutie. I can't. Once this is done, you need me, I'll be outside songwriting with my guitar, all right? Don't hesitate."

"I won't," she said, smiling out at him. "But I'll be fine."

"Yeah," he murmured. His eyes blazed at me in ire. "Make damn sure that rings true."

I rolled my eyes. "Of course I will. Truce, remember? You're really overreacting, gorgeous."

"Don't call me that. We're not good. You don't get to go there with me right now. Not until I'm sure you've fixed this for real."

With that, he stormed out without another word, his tight distressed blue jeans doing a great deal to draw attention to his delectable ass.

I blinked and looked away. I needed to focus, and thinking about fucking him really wasn't conducive to that.

"He doesn't like it when you and Levi are at odds, huh?"

I looked back at Brianna.

"No, he really doesn't."

She leaned forward on the table and propped her elbows on the surface. "I see that it's a lot of pressure for you, as their leader. It's much more complicated for you."

"Yeah," I murmured.

"My dad operated a lot like you do."

"Curt Walker was a micromanager with Steel Dawn MC?"

"An extreme version." She smiled sadly. "It nearly killed him."

"I'm not—"

"You're still young. My dad did it for decades and it really wore on him. The pressure and stress of it led to him suffering from two heart attacks before he was even forty. He never learned. The only thing that saved him was having to give up his club. And that wasn't exactly a good thing at the time for him and he didn't consider it as such for several years. It was painful. *You* have the chance now to recognize how detrimental your current way of doing things is before it's set in stone and you can't escape it."

I stared at her, shocked.

I'd thought she was going to go into a fierce defense on Levi's behalf.

But she'd gone another way entirely.

She was actually expressing concern for me.

Understanding that I wasn't used to.

Humanity.

"Thank you."

She cocked an eyebrow, now looking almost as surprised as me.

"No problem," she managed, a few beats later. "You know the first step is trying to share the load, right? With Levi."

It occurred to me that it was several levels beyond strange that I was actually allowing her advice to be conveyed to me. I didn't do that. I didn't share the pressures of anything with anyone. Not even Colt or Lev. I kept it to myself as I'd been *trained* to do by my father. Sometimes I needed to let it out and that was how the physical part of my relationship with Colt had been born.

But this, here, with her, it was another unprecedented thing about her.

I was seeing one of the reasons that Levi was so enamored with her. Beyond the foundation of their connection that had been established six years ago.

She was caring and empathetic. She could read people exceptionally well.

More than that, she had a gift for seeing their pain.

Even when they concealed it so well—like I always had.

And then she had the ability to put you at ease and offer advice without coming across as condescending or as the unwanted interference from an interloper.

I scrubbed my hand over my face. "I'll talk with Lev with you there."

She smiled. "Sounds good."

I took another bite of my pancakes, then rose to my feet. "Make yourself at home. I need a little time with Colt."

"You trust me to be left around the house unsupervised?" she asked with a humorous glint in her eye.

"We called a truce. To maintain that requires trust. On both sides, right?"

"Right," she said, her smile widening.

I liked that.

I fucking liked that from her a whole lot.

So much so that on my way out, I stopped by her chair and leaned in. "Thanks, dark angel," I said, before planting a kiss on the top of her head.

I turned and made my way to the door right after, not seeing her reaction.

But I could've sworn I felt her eyes on me the entire way out, before I rounded the corner onto the corridor out of sight.

I smiled to myself.

One step back in the right direction.

I CLUTCHED the papers I'd retrieved from the safe in my bedroom as I knocked at Colt's door.

Again.

It had been three times now with no answer from inside.

I knew he was in there. I'd checked everywhere else. He was no longer outside songwriting on his acoustic guitar and he wasn't with Brianna. I also knew he hadn't left the property.

No, he was simply ignoring me.

Well, there was nothing *simple* about us being at odds and barely talking.

I fucking hated it.

He and I being on bad terms twisted me up inside.

I couldn't stand it much longer.

And I was hoping that the document I was clutching would be an in toward fixing things.

I pulled my pick set out of the back pocket of my jeans. It really came in handy carrying it on me constantly.

Within moments, I breached the lock on his bedroom door, then I shoved it open and stepped inside.

And there he was sprawled out on his stomach in the middle of his bed, reading a music magazine. He jerked his head toward me as I walked in. "Crossing lines all over the place lately, aren't you? Now we've got a mix of invasion of privacy, along with B&E."

I rolled my eyes. "Seriously? Can we make some peace here?"

"I don't know, can we?"

"What does that mean?"

"Are you actually being genuine, or is this *truce* one of your high-level mind games, another way to drive Brianna away from Lev—and me?"

"It's genuine, Colt."

He put his magazine down and rolled off the bed, getting to his feet.

"I hope so, because if it's all bullshit, it's gonna hurt all of us. Beyond repair, Mason. The brotherhood won't just fracture, it'll implode."

"I get that now."

"If you'd listened to me in the first place you would have gotten it sooner. Things wouldn't have gone so far. But you dismissed me."

"I'm sorry. It wasn't about *dismissing* you. It was just that I had tunnel vision. The power trip of *Hex* because I'd taken to heading it alone this time, then my paranoia about Lev's unstable fixation with Brianna… it all compounded. I guess… it was me struggling to hold everything together."

He softened a little and stepped closer to me. "I'm here. I'm always here. Fucking well call on me, Mason. You're not alone. Please, for the love of shit, stop operating as though you are."

"I'm working on it."

He cocked an eyebrow. "Really?"

"Effective immediately." I handed the papers over to him. "And I've also come with a peace offering."

He took them curiously, then started looking through them.

That familiar warmth that always infused me whenever he looked at me in that bright way took me as I saw that from him while he read.

"You did it! This is gonna get Will and Flynn off my back entirely. I'll get to keep all the songs I've written, the name of the band, everything."

"The downside is that the condition is you go solo. No more involvement with them in any way. You've got a concert coming up at a high profile club in the City of Tolhurst. Are you sure you can put a performance together and bring in a drummer and base player in time? There are gonna be record company reps there, you can't take chances here, Colt."

"As shocking as it sounds, I've already thought it through and prepared. I have a list of narrowed down candidates for a new drummer and bass player. It'll just be me and stand-ins, hired help, different each time or something so they don't get attached or to thinking they're *Mythic Cry* alongside me."

"Perfect. I'm really proud of you for sorting that."

"I have my moments." He walked to his dresser and put the documents down. "Thanks for this, Mason. I really appreciate it."

"Anything for my brothers."

He shot me a withering look. "Don't push it."

"Are we at least on the road to being good again?" I asked as he walked back to me.

"Yeah. Yeah, we are."

I eased myself onto his bed and slumped down with a heavy sigh, exhaustion finally getting the best of me. "Thank goodness. Being at odds with you… I hated it. I always hate it."

He smiled and perched on the edge beside me. Reaching out, he stroked my hair. "Good thing it's so rare then, yeah?"

"Yeah."

I went to move, telling him, "Anyway, I'll leave you to it and—"

He grasped my shoulders. "Chill. I can see how exhausted you are. Just take a load off for a while."

Then he was easing me down into his bed and covering me with the blankets.

I smiled to myself. Tucking me in.

"Okay," I murmured.

He settled onto the bed over the top of the covers and

rolled onto his side next to me, propping his head up with his elbow on the pillow.

Reaching out and fingering my hair, he told me, "Take a nap, relax."

"Yeah, I think I will," I answered wearily.

I was spent.

I hadn't slept last night because of the damage control I'd had to do, and now it was hitting me.

My eyes grew heavy and soon enough I couldn't keep them open at all.

The last thing I was aware of was Colt nuzzling against me, before sleep took me.

THE SOUND of my white noise machine was a soothing soundtrack as I eased awake.

I slowly opened my eyes and confusion set in as I found myself tucked up tightly in his zebra-print sheets. I was still in his room then, where I remembered falling asleep in his arms.

But the white noise?

It took me a moment, but then I saw my machine on the floor beside the bed.

I smiled to myself, touched that Colt had specifically brought it in here for me to help me sleep longer and get the rest that I'd needed.

I blinked past the bleariness as I became more cognizant and awake with every passing second, and I took in his skull-and-crossbones clock high in the corner.

Wow. I'd slept for four hours straight.

So much for it merely being a nap. That was almost a full night's sleep for me.

I extricated myself from the cocoon and pushed up

into a sitting position against the headboard, noting that I felt a hell of a lot better.

I also noticed the scrap of paper on the duvet beside me with my name scrawled on it in Colt's handwriting.

I snatched it up and opened it to read:

Sleep as much as you need, all is well here with Brianna. She's gonna teach me how to make a dragon origami thingy and then I'm taking her into the studio as I work on my newest song, 'I Remember'. Didn't get to tell you about it with the distance between us, but it's about her and Lev's relationship, all shmaltzy and shit, but with my usual hard yet raw edge. Speaking of, she's a fan of my genre, post-grunge. Told me her playlists are full of post-grunge bands from the noughties. How fucking perfect, right? Anyway, rest up, brother. We're well on the way to being good now. Just keep up with what you're doing now, no more shutting down, yeah? XOXO. Colt.

Relief coursed through me.

One relationship on the mend, thank goodness.

Now, on to Lev.

That was going to be easier said than done.

My phone buzzed and I followed the sound to see it now on the nightstand on my side of the bed, not where I'd left it on the floor in my pants earlier.

I picked it up and found a text from one of my *Hex* members, one of three I'd tasked to keep tabs on Lev. Although we were working toward a truce, I couldn't simply sit back and let him run wild. I still had to protect us. Hopefully, once we sat down and talked it out, the way in which I did that could alter. Less invasive, perhaps. And for my sanity, not a constant thing.

My guy's message didn't bode well right off the bat, however, because he'd just confirmed that Lev wasn't where he was supposed to be. He'd either lied or, from a more *benefit-of-the-doubt* standpoint, he'd stretched the truth or omitted some details.

Steven: Knight spotted on outskirts of downtown. Abandoned apartment building. Been inside for five.

Mason: Good work. Send me the address and I'll take it from here. Stand down.

Steven: Got it, Boss.

Sure enough, he sent along the intel in the very next moment.

Dammit, Lev.

I hurried out of bed and threw on my clothes from last night, then hurried out of Colt's bedroom. I didn't want him or Brianna seeing me as I was on my way out. It would invite questions, the answers to which would make me look bad either way.

As I made my way through the house, I heard music sounding, coming from the recording studio. It was sound-proofed, so it meant that Colt hadn't shut the door.

Colt's voice reached me.

"I remember the nights I couldn't sleep/ The nights I was screaming out your name/ The memories made me weep/ They had me twisting the sheets in fucking pain."

He stopped singing and playing and I heard Brianna's gasp of surprise. "This is about Levi and me?"

"Sure is, cutie."

"Whiskey eyes pulled me through."

"You like?"

"It's a lot to absorb. Intense."

I just needed you to remember too."

"That's when it gets more intense. We'll leave it at that for now. Want to hear the finished duet, all polished and ready?"

"I'd love to, yeah."

I heard the smacking of lips—kissing. And then Colt telling her, "Coming right up, Bree. Hey, you okay with me calling you that?"

"My close friends do."

"We're more than that now, yeah?"

"We're getting there."

"I'll take it. Love spending time with you."

I turned the corner and even as I shook my head to myself, I also couldn't help smiling.

Colt certainly wore his heart on his sleeve. It often slammed up against the opposite in me—the closed-off stoicism I had going on.

But it also helped to chip away at that, to open me up a little more.

That had only managed to go so far, though, but with Brianna now here in the mix, I had a feeling she'd be able to assist with that. She had this uncanny way of making even an ice-cold bastard like me relax in her company.

I *wanted* to be getting to know her right now.

Instead, I *needed* to rein Levi in.

Jesus fuck, Hellraiser.

27

I'd done it.

I'd been right on the money. The intel from that sleaze-ball, Kyle, had proven to be a vital piece of the puzzle that I'd gone without all this time in my pursuit of that mother-fucker, Malcolm Lynch. I'd had to go about my mission in a roundabout way.

Sure, it had enabled me to lay eyes on Lynch and track him down once.

But beyond that, it hadn't been possible to replicate.

Until now.

Now that I had the true name of his shadowed orga-nization.

Osiris.

With the program I'd built in operation with that new intel plugged in, it had managed to pull up half a dozen mentions of that name. Places they'd been, deals they'd made, even details of a covert investigation into them from Nico Marchetti. He was the heir to the notorious Marchetti Syndicate—mafia, basically. Either he was vetting them now that they'd started making waves and looking to work with them, *or* he had a beef with Malcolm Lynch too and he'd discovered he was the man behind the operation of *Osiris*.

If it came to it, I could go through him.

Only if it became absolutely necessary, though.

Going that route came with complications for many reasons. But it wasn't merely the whole mafia thing. It was the fact that one of my contacts, Rina, absolutely despised the ruthless bastard.

Rina, who Mason had recently called upon.

To him and Colt, they believed her just to be an actual contact of mine who I'd exchanged favors with over the years. She was a *hacker extraordinaire*, as Mason put it. Her skills were equal to mine. That was on the down low, though. Her family and the circles she walked in weren't aware and she was very careful who came to know. Mason was only privy to it because of his closeness to me, some-body whom she trusted implicitly.

You see, she was much more than just a contact to me, or even an asset. We were close. We'd been friends for five years.

There was an understanding between us that was very difficult to find. She got where I was coming from with my quest, and my reaction to the kidnapping. Although she'd never actually suffered through that herself, there had been several attempts to do so. There'd also been at least three attempts on her life over the years. Her father, Santino Leone, had many dangerous enemies and as his daughter —a mafia princess—she was a chief target of those enemies.

I scrubbed my hand over my face as I focused back on my *conspiracy board*, all the clues, evidence, and key intel I'd obtained, linking patterns with red string across the cork surface, color-coding the push pins, the whole nine. I hadn't left out a single relevant detail.

"Fuck," I ground out.

There was no way around it now.

I'd reached a point where I had to dive deeper into my investigation *or* reach out to the likes of Nico to pool our intel.

With either option, it posed a risk of what I was doing finally being detected, of me exposing the fact that I was looking for *Osiris* and Lynch.

And that could very well mean them launching a preemptive strike against me before I got any closer. Before it was me on their doorstep striking.

While I wasn't above taking such risks, it wasn't just about me.

What I did would impact my brothers *and* Brianna.

So, I needed to tell them.

Things were precarious right now with Mason, though.

And then there was Brianna. I'd finally managed to pull her close to me, and the way things were between us was incredible. Even the thought of fucking with that made me sick to my stomach.

But I also couldn't let *this* go.

My phone pinged and I pulled it from the pocket of my black hoodie to see a text that I'd been expecting.

Hmm, she'd reached out sooner than I'd figured she would.

Caterina: Apologies, bello.

Damn straight.

Levi: Why did you help him? Especially over me?

Caterina: Not by preference, believe me. Necessary, unfortunately. Required an introduction to Peter Hall.

Levi: Are you in trouble?

Caterina: Aww, even though I hurt you, you're still so caring.

Levi: Our bond can weather this easily. Just give me a heads-up next time.

Caterina: Again, sorry. I was distracted when he contacted me.

Levi: By this trouble you're in?

Caterina: Not trouble, merely being prepared.

Levi: You need me, I'm here.

Caterina: I never doubted it. You too, bello.

Levi: Later, Rina.

Caterina: A presto!

I stowed my phone away.

I'd considered reaching out to her about this, but now knowing she was dealing with her own shit, I couldn't burden her with more.

"Motherfucking shit," I ground out, before smashing my fist into the wall beside the board.

"That seems like a significant understatement," a voice sounded from behind me.

Fuck.

I spun around to see Mason, the stealthy fucker, standing at the threshold of my tiny shithole apartment.

"I hate it when you pull that ghost shit, Mason."

"It comes naturally to me." He kicked the door shut behind him and strode toward me, taking in the place. Boring, beige walls, worn cheap hardwood floors, and a mattress in the corner I'd used as a bed a couple of times when I'd first come back here ahead of him and Colt knowing. My computer desk setup was the only other feature of the small space.

"Not your usual speed in the least. I thought my guy had made an error when he reported you being seen here."

"It's just a space. Purely about functionality."

"Business, not pleasure?"

"In a sense." There was no point denying it, because he'd seen the board, and he was even studying it with a furrowed brow as he drew closer.

"How did Steven detect your movements? You're stealthy too."

I lifted a shoulder. "I was laser-focused."

"Ah. The state for you where the rest of the world slips away."

"Yes," I ground out.

I stepped back from the board and shoved my hands into the pockets of my hoodie. "Let's stop dancing around it. Get to it. Reprimand me. Tell me this truce is already done with. Call me an obsessive danger to us all. Tell me that you'll—"

"This is impressive."

I started. "What?"

"The detail here, the depth of it all, so much that you've compiled over time, all these leads you've obtained all by yourself… it's impressive, Lev."

"I… what?"

He merely smiled, then studied both my board and my laptop screen for several minutes.

And *I* studied *him*.

What the *fuck* was happening?

He stepped back, then folded his big arms across his chest. "I'm sorry."

I frowned. "For what you did to Brianna?"

"That, yes. And I'm trying to make it up to you both. It's why I offered her to stay with us for a couple of days, to get to know her, to show you both that I'm going to support your relationship. But that's not what I'm currently saying sorry for." He shifted his weight, clearly uncomfortable with the emotion he was displaying, the raw honesty and regret coming off him. It flew in the face of all that stoicism he usually put forth. "I'm *sorry* that you've had to do this all alone. I didn't realize how badly you needed this justice for what happened to you. You don't talk about it, Lev, so me and Colt both thought you'd made peace with it, that you'd let that initial surging need to make him pay that you'd had after it happened go."

"You saw what happened when I talked about it last night."

"I did, but it's more than that, isn't it? It's because of *me*. You thought I'd shut all of this down, that I'd even use Roman to do it."

"Yes."

"Well, I'm not gonna do that."

"Why not?" I asked, the suspicion in my tone very clear.

"Let's just say that Brianna made me realize a few things, especially when it comes to you. *And* it's clear you need this. You need this closure to find peace." He dropped his arms and stepped right up to me. "The torment won't stop, will it?"

"Mason," I groused.

I went to turn my head away, but he grasped my jaw.

Firmly, but with no malice in it. "Lev," he pushed.

I swallowed hard. "No," I forced myself to admit. "It won't fucking stop."

"But doing this will see to it, won't it?"

"I've never been more certain of anything in my life." I grimaced. "But going any further with this—because it's reaching a tipping point—risks exposing me to Lynch and his new organization, which risks pulling you guys into it too by close association. And Brianna... she's not ready to hear about this yet. It was hard enough to get her to admit that it had even happened, to acknowledge who she really is, to get her to acknowledge *me.*"

"I understand. And I have an idea."

"What's that?"

He stroked my cheek lovingly with his thumb and I couldn't help the groan that escaped me at the calming effect it was having on me. It was similar to what he and Colt used to do for me back when my *episodes* had been much more brutal and frequent.

And then he pulled away and walked to the board, slapping his finger to a photo of Royce Humphrey with a list of details below his image. "We use this piece of shit."

"I've considered it, but he's one of those types who can't be broken—like fanatics who are so entrenched in their skewed beliefs that there's no way to sway them to any other way of being."

"No, not like that. Although, it's deliciously stimulating that your mind went there."

I stared at him. "You're still going through a dry spell, huh?"

"It's not that."

"Then you exhibiting some actual sexuality, which you rarely ever do with locking that down so tightly, doesn't make sense." I pulled up short as the realization hit me. "You want Brianna?"

"She's... really something."

"No denying that."

"And?"

"And what?"

"How do you feel about that? You're possessive over her. Clingy, even."

"Clingy? No. Having no qualms about showing how much I want and care about her? Yes."

He chuckled. "Semantics."

I leaned against the wall beside the board. "I've wanted to bring her into my world for a long time. It's happening now. You're a part of that world. Colt's also been with her —with us. She's exhibited interest in you too. Asking about you, all that shit. I'm good with it, so long as you make damn sure it's on her terms. After what happened to her, it can't be any other way for her. It scares her otherwise and it could easily trigger her too."

"I'd do nothing less than ensure it's on her terms, Lev."

"Then, good."

We stared at one another for a few moments, Mason looking as taken aback by his interest in her as I was with absorbing it. He was so closed off, the fact that he was admitting it outright was really something. She'd definitely gotten into his head—and other areas.

I smiled inwardly. That was her. My *Wildflower* had a power that she didn't even realize.

"All right then," he said, then focused back on the board. "So, Royce… there needs to be some degree of separation between your investigation and its target in Malcolm Lynch. Royce is it. according to your intel here, he's aware of Lynch's movements. So we use him to obtain the additional intel needed in order to bridge the gap and zero in on Lynch."

Hmm. "You want me to infiltrate his system?"

"Precisely. Without a trace." He raised an eyebrow. "Can you pull it off?"

I scoffed. "Please."

"I meant the *without a trace* part? Being careful, brother?"

"Whatever it takes to do this."

"Perfect, then we can work together on it."

"You're really up for doing that? Working with *me*? On this, of all things too?"

311

He laid his hand on my shoulder. "Like I told you last night while you were suffering from that attack, I'm *here*, Lev. I'm here now."

I smiled and grasped his hand on me. "Thank you"

As he smiled back at me and the moment rolled over us, I added what had been missing between us for too long, "*Brother.*"

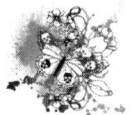

28

~Brianna~

"What's wrong with it?" I demanded with a noticeable edge.

Levi smirked as he pushed my laptop back to me, then started pulling up his own code on his. "Aww, baby, don't get worked up—at least not in that way. I said I'd teach you a few things, so here it is." He pulled up what he needed to, then pointed at a section of his code. "You see the difference? Yours left a backdoor entry point accessible. Most wouldn't be able to work with that, so it's why it's not taught to go the extra mile with this. Well, also the fact that the way I'm doing that isn't exactly on the up-and-up. But you and me, the world we walk in, *we* need to concern ourselves with the threat of the best trying to access our data and private information."

"I see it," I said, taking in his code and all its complexities. "I'm definitely better with software and programming apps than this side of things. I thought I could at least hold my own, but looking at this now, the holes you found in my code… it's clear I can't."

"No, you can definitely hold your own. But, like I said,

in our world, things need to be another level to protect ourselves."

I looked out at him, very aware of him sitting so close to me, so much that I could feel his body heat and smell his sexy sandalwood scent.

He was in a gray pair of his go-to cargo pants today, with a white muscle tee that served to highlight his boxer's physique beneath, all that hard muscle and incredibly toned abs. A gray hooded denim jacket completed his more relaxed look today.

I was dressed down too in just a pair of gray lounge pants and an off-the-shoulder pastel-pink top.

Levi might have appeared relaxed, but he wasn't. Because it was Sunday and my last night here, because I'd only be here in the morning tomorrow, spending most of the long-weekend Monday at my apartment studying and making sure I was up to date on the remote learning I'd been doing for a few days after those leaked pictures had caused such a hoopla on campus for me.

Honestly, I was a little tense about it too.

It had been a really nice experience surrounded by the three of them in this house, not being alone with my thoughts, actually having people in my corner—in spite of the fucked-up way it had all started. Since Chloe had been called home by her extremely overbearing mother, I'd been without a close friend, the *only* friend I'd felt comfortable making because of how difficult it normally was for me to hide all the trauma behind a façade of normalcy, to pretend it didn't exist. She'd even messaged me telling me she wouldn't actually be coming back now like she'd thought, that her return was being delayed, and she didn't even know for how long.

Because of Levi, he'd set things up for me with him and the guys where I actually didn't need to hide any of my trauma. More than not concealing it, they understood it because Levi had suffered from *episodes* just like me. Colton and Mason were used to dealing with it through him. And they didn't look at me differently because of it. They didn't treat me like broken glass, like I was damaged. I'd never had that before once someone had discovered my issues. Not even with my ex, Tommy. In fact, when Levi had posited that I hadn't experienced the rough, raw, and mind-numbing intensity of sex before because Tommy had treated me so gently, he'd been right on.

As much as I liked being around the guys, the flipside was that things had moved fast since that night I'd come here to talk with Mason and end his *Hex* campaign against me. I needed some space to take stock of it all away from them so I could see things in a more clear and objective way. Also, having the guys around would be majorly distracting to my studies, and I couldn't afford to screw up and fail out.

"Let's take a break," Levi said, pulling me from my thoughts.

"No, I'm good now. We can keep going."

"We'll come back to it. I've got something to show you, something for you to take home with you tomorrow."

I cocked an eyebrow. "What's that? Colt already gave me a going-home present. The recording of our duet, *Until You.*"

He chuckled. "Of course he did." He laid his hand over the back of mine on the coffee table. "It was more than even a song to him—and that already means a fuck of a lot for him. It was him connecting with you, bonding."

I smiled. "It was for me too. That's what it'll represent whenever I play it."

"Good. He'll be a happy little cupcake."

It was my turn to laugh then. I slid my fingers into his

hair, stroking softly and making him groan. "You're so sweet with him."

"Well, he makes it impossible not to be."

"I can see that, yeah. But I like it, how you are with him."

"Yeah?"

"Yeah. You're like that with me too. Sweet and attentive."

He gave my hand on the table a squeeze. "Well, you deserve to be treated like a princess. And not a *club* princess, because we're equals, and I don't want to push you to the sidelines like what was done to you with your dad's motorcycle club. A whole lot of misogyny masquerading as intense overprotectiveness."

"I couldn't have said it better myself."

He eased away from me then, and I saw him tense up. "Speaking of that, and in the name of being equal partners and transparency between us, there's something I need to—"

"Lev."

We both jolted at the sound of the voice, and we swung our heads to see Mason now leaning against the open door.

"Mason, I just—" Levi started.

"You just wanted to show Brianna that thing you made for her? That secret present you've been keeping from her until it was completely finished and polished to perfection?"

I frowned as Levi hesitated and even more so as a look I couldn't decipher passed between them.

But then Levi gave a nod and brightened again as he looked at me, then rose to his feet. "Come on. It's in my workshop."

Before I could get a word out, or question what was

going on, which seemed to be beyond the mere surprise of a present, Mason told us, "We'll have that talk right after, yes?"

"Sounds good," Levi said all too quickly.

Okay, then.

Mason fondled my hair as Levi and I passed on by, sending a tremble of awareness through me and sparking that need I'd been feeling toward him increasingly so over the last couple of days with us being in close quarters.

"Dark angel," I heard him breathe as Levi and I headed through the mansion toward his workshop.

"He's up for it too, you know?" Levi said, eyeing me as we walked side-by-side. "He's just really sexually-repressed, not at all open like Colt and me."

I arched an eyebrow at him. "Why are you being so cool with the possibility, almost wanting it to go in that direction, really?"

"I want you to have everything that you desire. Despite our recent issues, Colt and Mason are my brothers, the closest people to me. To bring you closer, I need to make you a part of that world, of the three of us. Besides, my possessiveness doesn't extend to the two of them. It's completely different."

"I see." As complicated as it was. "So, why *is* Mason like that? So repressed?" I asked. "It seems to be more than his staunch need to be in total control of every little thing at all times."

"You've read him well. It *is* more than that. A lot of it is his old man. He's all about maintaining an infallible reputation and ensuring his son doesn't impact Peter Hall's pristine, straight-laced image in any way. Mason thinks that his sexuality plays into that, that Peter wouldn't accept it. So he tries to repress it, but it's a part of him, and it keeps rising up when he tries to shove it down, hence him turning to Colt to take the edge off that's always so desperate at that point."

"That's really sad to hear. Especially in this day and age. Jeez. What about Colton?"

"His parents are the direct opposite, especially his dad. They're so free and completely supportive of everything Colt does. His dad is a former frontman of an 80's hair-band, *Epica*. His mom heads a successful Wealth Management firm, *Sharp Wealth*, but she used to be a groupie—that's how she met Oakley Sharp."

"Wow, that's an awesome meet-cute."

"*Meet-cute?*" he chuckled. "Yeah."

We reached his workshop that he'd shown me around yesterday, and he opened the door and gestured chivalrously for me to go on in ahead of him.

He walked in and made a beeline for a locked cabinet in the far corner.

"Present time," he called over his shoulder, as he opened it, then lifted something out.

He turned and placed it on a nearby workbench.

The moment I took it in, my breath caught in my throat.

It was absolutely exquisite.

So beautiful.

The skill that had gone into carving it was incredible. He'd clearly put so much effort into it.

"Wow," I breathed. "It's amazing." I took in the twelve-inch standing wooden butterfly, the intricate details of its wings, the beautiful wood he'd used to fashion it.

"It's a nightlight," he told me, flipping the switch he'd hooked up to it and I watched a warm, yellow light bathe the workshop. "I know you don't like the dark. I figured this would help and it can be programmed to go on when it suits your sleep schedule precisely. You can even switch it on via your phone before you get home, so you don't have to walk into a dark apartment ever again."

I couldn't contain myself for the life of me, and I was throwing my arms around him in the very next second and hugging the life out of him.

He laughed as I kissed his forehead, his cheeks, his nose, the underside of his chin, then squeezed him to me.

"That's it, I'm making you another dozen of these if I'm gonna get this reaction every time."

I sank into him. "This is the sweetest, most thoughtful thing anyone has ever done for me. Thank you, *lovely*."

"Of course. Now you can take a piece of me home with you."

"I already am."

"Yeah?" he asked, our gazes clashing intensely.

I smiled. "You been with me for the last six years. I've carried you with me."

"As I have you, my *Wildflower.*"

"I'm not going anywhere. I mean, yeah, back to my apartment so I can focus on college, but that's it. I like it in the company of the three of you."

"Promise. Promise me that, Brianna."

I kissed his cheek. "Promise."

━━

"WE'LL SPLIT the command of *Hex* by forty-sixty. You take more leadership, because that's how you need it to feel in control," Levi spoke. "But I'll be there to stop you from going too far and allowing your addiction to the taste of power from spiraling."

"Sounds good," Mason said.

Really easily, surprisingly.

"We'll also need a tie-breaker in effect for when we

inevitably clash over an issue or an approach toward a situation," he pointed out.

"It can't be Colt. He's doing well in college finally. This will be too much of a distraction."

"Agreed." Mason's gaze fell to me.

"Me?"

He nodded. "You're reasonable and diplomatic. You can reconcile both sides of an issue. And your ego is checked and not a problem."

"Yeah," I said. "I can do that."

"Perfect," Levi spoke.

Mason sat forward in the armchair and looked between Levi and me snuggled on the couch. "Although, there is a chance of bias."

I cocked an eyebrow. "Why is that?"

Levi rolled his eyes and answered for Mason. "He means, because you've had my cock."

I spluttered. "What?"

Mason waggled his eyebrows. "You heard him."

"Wow, you're actually openly flirting," Levi commented.

"He does that sometimes," a voice came from the living room door, and we looked to see Colton leaning against the doorway, his arms folded across his chest, looking all sexy as usual in his leather pants and a tiger-print shirt that was only done up halfway. His platinum-blond mohawk was a little out of shape and wilder than usual, giving him more of a rugged look.

He grinned at Levi and me, then said, "When he's hard-up, or really fucking turned on."

"Colt," Mason groused.

"Nuh uh," Levi said. "Don't retreat back into your repressive state. Keep it going."

I eased from Levi's hold and moved to the edge of the

chair, eyeing him and asking pointedly, "You want to fuck me?"

He started at my brazenness.

I could see his resistance, conflicted about retreating into himself, versus taking a leap and actually breaking from his control and being free for at least a little while.

"Or is it Colton you're needing?" I pushed carefully.

I could feel Levi and Colton looking on with bated breath.

The tension ramped up.

And then Mason's eyes flamed and he growled back at me. "Both."

—

MY BACK HIT THE BED.

Three shadows fell over me.

Closing in.

Threatening me with erotic torment.

Promising me twisted depravity.

Offering me the freedom of it that I craved.

That we all craved.

"Worship our girl, boys," I heard Levi say in the midst of the rustling of clothing being torn off and hitting the floor of Mason's bedroom.

There was no build up this time, and I didn't want it, I wanted to be consumed completely. I wanted them all consumed with me.

The three of them worked together to rip my clothes from my body.

"Fuck me," I heard Mason say when I was bared to them. "Stunning."

He was there then, taking me in a deep kiss. I opened and he thrust his tongue into my mouth.

I jolted when I felt another mouth on my breasts, sucking on my nipples, and I looked to see Colt there teasing me.

And then my thighs were spread wide and Levi dove between them, bringing out his animalistic side as he tortured my pussy with his lips, tongue, and teeth.

The overstimulation had me beside myself and I was thrashing on the bed within moments as pleasure built so quickly that I couldn't get a handle on it.

It happened so fast with them all over me and my entire body lurched as I came with a shriek that pulled Mason's mouth from mine.

As I basked in the slowly rescinding pleasure, I was lifted off my back, and then I was looking into Colt's eyes as Levi and Mason lowered me onto his cock.

I cried out as he stretched me open, them making me take him balls deep until I was settled all the way down and sitting on his thighs, mine wrapped around his hips as he sat up against the headboard.

Colt was gritting his teeth and looking out at the guys. "Damn."

"I know," Levi said, smirking at me, knowing how it felt to sink into me.

He was there then stroking my back, particularly my tattoo. "All right, baby?"

I smiled out at him through hooded eyes, focused on the feel of Colt's cock filling me so perfectly. "Perfect."

Mason chuckled and played with my hair, brushing some stray strands out of my face. "Remarkable woman, aren't you?"

Colt reached out and fingered my all-seeing eye pendant, smiling up at me.

Then he started rolling his hips and I threw my head back at the glorious sensation. Mason's fingers trailed down my throat, over my breasts, feeling my soft flesh, then pinching my nipples and making me tremble with the sensations and bounce on Colt as my need skyrocketed and I succumbed to the heady intensity of it all.

I grabbed Mason's cock and he grunted, instinctively drawing closer to me, wanting my touch. I stroked him, exploring his shaft, his tip, down to his balls. When I rolled them between my fingers then pinched them, his cock jerked and he groaned as pre-cum leaked from his tip.

Colt, keeping up the sensual roll of his hips, reached out and grasped Mason's ass as I was teasing his cock and making him moan for me. Colt had me jolting as he reached between us and slicked his finger in my wetness. And then a thrill ran through me as he eased it into Mason's ass.

"God," I breathed, watching the erotic show as he thrust and twisted, making Mason's cock jerk in my hold.

"That's it, darlin'," Colt uttered. "Let it all go."

And he did.

Apparently, he'd been holding back, something Colt had recognized, because then a snarl came from him and he was fisting my hair, then shoving his cock into my mouth, and fucking my throat like a wild thing.

Yes!

It was hot and domineering and vicious.

And so fucking freeing.

Just what I'd wanted from them all, from being utterly consumed by them.

I rose to it, swallowing around his crown and watching with a thrill as he recognized that I didn't have a gag reflex.

"Fuck me," he growled. "Ungh, yeah."

I felt heat at my back and then pressure at my hole a moment before two slicked fingers slid into my ass, making me jolt.

I tried to look over my shoulder, but I couldn't because Mason kept my head held in a tight-fisted grip. "Uh uh. Just feel, dark angel."

"Hell, yeah," Colt said, leaning in and slicking his tongue all over my breasts, sending sharp sparks of pleasure through me when he rolled his stud over my nipples.

Mason cried out in rapture as I moaned around his shaft pumping in and out of my throat.

The fingers in my ass started to move and curl inside me, twisting and stretching me, the burn an exquisite addition to the over-stimulating pleasure.

When they suddenly left me, I whimpered.

Mason eased his cock from my mouth and grasped my throat. "Stick out your tongue."

I just did it and he placed his cock there.

"Don't lick. Just hold," he commanded.

The degradation of it sent a thrill through me I hadn't experienced in this sort of way before.

Massive pressure at my ass had me moving and Mason squeezed my throat in warning. "Be still. Hold."

Colt's hips stilled and then he was reaching down between us and teasing my clit, rolling, pinching and pulling, then spreading my wetness all over it.

Oh God, it was amazing.

And it had me relaxing enough that the pressure at my hole lessened and then Levi's cock slipped through into my depths.

"Ungh," I grunted.

Mason grinned. "Now lick."

I slathered his cock all over, making him shudder for me.

And then he fisted my hair and drove down my throat again.

At the same time, Levi started thrusting in and out of my ass, and Colt slammed up into my pussy.

I cried out around Mason's cock and lost control, bouncing wildly on Colt's cock, then trying to thrust back onto Levi's at the same time.

It was a blur of insane intensity and stimulation that was climbing higher and higher with every passing second of having them all over me, using my body, as I reveled in every delirious moment of it.

I scraped my nails down Mason's chest, drawing blood from the viciousness of it that had him growling like an animal and sending a delicious thrill through me.

Colt grabbed his ass, not breaking his rhythm fucking me for a second as he drove a finger deep inside him again, twisting roughly, then pounding rapid-fire.

"Hell fucking fuck!" Mason cried out, a moment before he came down my throat, pulled out, then finished on my breasts.

His hot cum spraying me pushed me over the edge and I came all over Colt's cock.

"Shit, that grip," he gritted out a moment before I had him coming inside me too.

"Christ," Levi grunted, obviously having felt all of that. "Your tight little ass is killing me, baby." A telltale growl from him and a final thrust had him spurting inside my depths.

The sensation pushed me over the edge again, and then I was coming over Colt again.

He threw his head back. "Damn… yeah, that's it."

Levi slipped out of me and Colt lifted me off him.

Just as I was about to slump down onto the sheets, the three of them flipped me onto my stomach.

And then they shocked me as they all descended on me, licking, nipping and sucking every inch of my body, cleaning off their cum, pushing it back inside my ass and pussy, then eating it out of me, playing with me and driving me into utter delirium.

Oh. My. Fucking. God.

⸻

I SIPPED at my glass of water that I'd retrieved from the kitchen after waking up parched and boiling hot from the guys sleeping all over me.

I'd intended to head right back to Mason's bedroom, but as I passed by an open door that I hadn't been in before, I caught sight of several bookshelves. A library in the middle of the mansion? Yeah, that sort of thing fit well.

I walked inside to find a room with floor-to-ceiling sleek black and white bookshelves, one hell of a library containing hundreds of volumes, with a cozy saucer chair in the corner for reading, no doubt.

There were many Law books, all heavy stuff, on one bookcase. But the rest lining the shelves were quite different. I looked through the titles and a pattern emerged regarding the authors of Mark Twain, Hemingway, Faulkner, F. Scott Fitzgerald, Theodore Dreiser.

"Twentieth Century American literature," a voice sounded, making me jump.

I turned to see Mason strolling in, just a pair of black boxers on, all that ink and muscle on display. His brown hair was all wild and sexy.

"Satire and cynicism?"

"There's that through them, yes. But I'm focused on the freedom and sense of individualism. That's why I like them."

I smiled sadly. "Something you aspire to, but don't believe you can actually touch?"

"Pretty much." The corner of his mouth turned up. "Although, last night certainly flew in the face of that."

I smiled. "It did."

"You had a similar existence when the Steel Dawn Motorcycle Club was operational, yes? Levi told me a little bit about it."

I nodded. "There wasn't a lot of freedom back then. As club princess, it was all about being secured and protected, pushed off to the sidelines and kept away from everything. I was basically a porcelain doll to them all."

"And your biker boyfriend? You weren't free with him?"

"Not really. It wasn't like that. He was my assigned protection and also the first person I saw when my dad and Levi's dad raided that hellhole we were being held in. So, the relationship started from a messed-up place. *I* was in a messed-up place, and I was desperate to erase what had happened to me there. Tommy became the vehicle through which I did that—or tried to."

"I'm sorry," he said, reaching out and cupping my cheek in a tender way I never would have imagined from him a few days ago. But, as he'd shown me recently, and last night, Mason Hall was capable of a lot more than he let on.

I smiled up at him. "Your situation isn't permanent either. Things changed for me because I fought like crazy to be able to leave all that behind, to come here and do what *I* wanted to do with my life, instead of working under my dad as an assistant or something in one of his small businesses."

"I appreciate you saying that, but the time was right for you when you made those moves. For me, it's a lot more complicated. My father sees to that."

Realization hit me. "He has something on you, doesn't he?"

He tensed, then eased his hand away, and slumped against one of the bookcases. "Something that I couldn't just walk away from. Something that impacts Colt and Lev too."

"What is it?"

"Revealing that would require a mass amount of trust."

"I already know about *Hex,* how it works and even exactly who your members are."

"My members? How?"

"When an enemy comes at you, it's pertinent to gather all that you can on them."

"Fuck me, why didn't you say anything when Lev and I were having our peace talk and discussing *Hex* downstairs?"

"It could've been read as a threat. I didn't want to destabilize our new truce. Now you're talking about trust, though, I needed it to use as an example of what I'm already being trustworthy with. If I'd wanted to, I could have easily finished what Levi started and taken every single member out. The shower attack I only knew those members. And the frat infestations, I wasn't sure who exactly among them were members, so it had a lot of collateral damage, displacing many, instead of the few I now know were members."

"Jesus, that's something else."

I fixed my pink robe around me that was coming loose and winked at him. "I know."

It took him a moment, but then he settled in against the bookcase and told me, "Five years ago, I was on track to becoming what I really wanted to be—a tattoo artist. And then something happened. Well, Levi Knight happened. He was sixteen at the time and it was one year after the kidnapping. He'd hid it well and we'd all thought that he'd moved past it and dealt with the trauma, but he hadn't. Colt and I found it out the hard way. Lev had been sublimating by training hardcore in various forms of combat in secret."

"So he could street fight?"

"No, this training… it was to *kill.*"

"Jeez."

"Yeah. So, one night, Lev headed out to an abandoned mansion on the outskirts of the city. Colt followed him, unbeknownst to either of us at first, because he thought Lev was headed to a secret house party. Back then he used to get invited to everything, his whole mysterious vibe really making him popular, along with his father thrusting him into the public eye as his *heir* a lot—overcompensation for the kidnapping, we believed, with him wanting to reinforce the stability of the Knight empire." He scrubbed his hand over his face. "But it wasn't a party. Lev had got a lock on an up-and-coming gang of drug dealers and rapists and he was using his rage and pain of his trauma and dialing it to violence, intending to beat the five of them down and dispense some frontier justice, and run them out of the city. Anyway, it didn't exactly go to plan. Lev hesitated when he found Colt there. But it was too late to back out when the guys came at them. I'd been tracking Colt's strange movements with our friend GPS app he and I had. I arrived to a bloodbath. *The enemy's.* Lev was tearing into them like a madman, roaring and growling like an animal. One of them had ripped off Lev's balaclava, so it was too late, they'd seen his face. So the bloodbath escalated to a whole lot more. Between us, Lev and I murdered the five of them, while Colt went into shock on the sidelines. In the middle of it, I got shot." He gestured to the scar in his right shoulder. "That scar over Lev's abs was him taking a bullet that night too."

"Oh my God," I breathed.

"After that, Roman and my father worked together to cover it up. My father has used it to control me ever since. I had to give up my tattoo artist career and go into Law as he'd wanted. He kept evidence of that night as a threat that constantly hangs over my head if I fall out of line. Lev has tried to get to it before, but it's not kept on any of the *Honor Hall Law* servers. It's a physical tape of that night from the security system the guys had installed at the house."

I frowned. "So, what would he do if you did fall out of line? Release it? How would that help him if his son is taken down?"

"He'd disown me. As long as I do what I'm told and I'm useful to him, I'm his son, and his heir apparent. I don't and he'll have no use for me… he'll burn me."

"Fuck," I choked. "That's demented."

"No arguments here. But it's also my reality."

That explained the full extent of why things were so antagonistic between him and Levi.

Wow.

"Reviving *Hex* in the way I did, was me trying to build contacts and assets to be able to counter my father's threat, to find something on *him.*"

"To regain your freedom."

"Yeah."

"And Levi? What were the consequences for him?"

"Roman loves his son deeply. There weren't any brutal threats or force from him, but it did begin Roman's very close watch over Lev. But Levi learned to become extremely resourceful and he's able to evade that and throw up smokescreens, like that internship. And Colt, well he didn't murder anyone. His parents encouraged him to pursue music and stick with it, they opened a lot of doors for him. They are the most laidback people you'll ever meet. It's likely why he's able to be so incredibly free and light."

"He's a perfect counter to you."

He smiled. "Yes, he is."

I closed the distance between us and stroked his arms. "I'm really sorry you've had to suffer for that."

"Thank you. So, that's where I'm coming from when I clash with Lev. He's my brother and I love him, but there's also that."

"It's complicated, more than I even imagined."

"Yeah," he murmured, easing from my hold. "It is."

He looked a world away from his usual in-charge, steadfast self now. The pain of recalling such an awful time and how it had continued to impact him to this day had taken that spark out of him.

It cut at me, because I knew that sort of pain all too well.

I didn't want him to be alone in it.

"My mom was there," I ended up revealing in a burst.

He cocked his head to the side. "What?"

I fingered my all-seeing eye pendant. "This was hers. She gave it to me shortly before it happened for a graduation gift. She said it had served her well over the years, a symbol of security and protection, and of her watching over me wherever I went in life." I sucked in a breath. "She was there during that hell. During the kidnapping, Levi and I weren't always the only ones there."

I sucked in a breath and then the words came tumbling out, the recollection spilling forth.

. . .

I COULD HEAR Levi screaming as I was dragged from the chair by a big guy I'd learned was named Kyle.

I was exhausted, barely lucid. I was beyond sore between my legs, raw, really. And I was bleeding from the brutal abuse. It trickled down my legs as they dragged me barefoot and in what was left of my now shredded and dirtied white dress.

A pained cry from Levi had me only just trying to turn my head.

And that was when I saw the other guy, Royce, kicking and beating him on the ground, then shoving the toe of his boot into his mouth until he gagged and retched.

"Stop!" I cried. "Leave him! He's a kid! Stop!"

"Boss will only leave him when he shuts the fuck up and stops trying to save you. He wants him to learn not to keep fighting," Kyle told me quietly, like he was trying to help. But how could that be? He was dragging me back to that madman, Malcolm Lynch. "He needs to break. Or pretend to. When you get back, tell him that. He won't make it out alive otherwise."

Before I could get a word out, I was dragged toward that awful interrogation room again where bad things had been done to me. Where Malcolm had first made me bleed for him, taking from me what should have never been for him. It was supposed to have been a special time, but it had all been torn away.

The place we were in seemed like an abandoned police station, or something. There was that two-way glass stuff in the interrogation room where Malcolm had whispered to me that we were being watched as he'd... defiled me over and over again.

This time, I was dragged into the viewing room, not the interrogation room.

I shuddered as Malcolm stood there in just a pair of dress pants, his dick already hard and prepared for another awful session.

He yanked me from Kyle and ordered, "Leave us."

"Boss, listen, I think this is enough. They're already really fucking traumatized. Mission accomplished, yeah?"

"I'll say when it's enough, now get the fuck out. Tell Royce to bring our guest in."

Kyle hesitated, his gaze meeting mine.

But then he sucked in a steadying breath and walked out, slamming the door behind him.

"There's my pretty princess," Malcolm said, breathing me in. "Mmm, you smell like me. All fucking over."

I cried out as he pushed me over to the two-way glass.

I threw my palms out to stop myself from smashing my face into it.

And then his body was pushing into mine, while his hand reached under my dirtied dress.

I shuddered as he whispered hauntingly at me ear. "Watch the show and be my good whore and I won't have hands laid on the boy for two whole days."

When I didn't respond, he yanked on my hair at the roots, making me hiss at the biting pain.

"Deal?"

"Yes," I gasped.

"Good pretty princess." He played with my hair in a creepy way that had another shudder rolling through me. "Now, you've proven far too resilient and I need to remedy that. Can't have you coming out of this unscathed, can I? What would be the point in all the effort I put into pulling this off? The boy is already close to breaking, now it's your turn. And lucky for me, Mommy made the foolish mistake of trying to find you on her own, independent of Curt and Roman's efforts."

A chill ran down my spine. "Mom?"

"Yes, Penny Walker, the queen of the Steel Dawn MC."

"No… what have you—"

He slammed inside me, filling me brutally, making me shriek.

Clamping his hand over my mouth, he rocked into me as the door to the interrogation room opened.

My heart lurched as Royce appeared and dragged my mom in.

Her jeans and t-shirt were caked in mud, her leather jacket even torn, and her black hair, just like mine, was matted.

"Baby girl!" she shrieked, staring at the glass.

"She can't see you," Malcolm told me. "I've just had Royce tell her you're here being railed by me like a good little whore bitch."

I couldn't even fight as he tightened his grip on me, then fucked into me like a madman, as Royce slapped my mom hard across the face.

I screamed into his hand as he started beating on her until she collapsed onto the concrete.

"All this fear from you is turning me on. Go on, squeeze my cock, and I'll make it quick for her, no more drawing it out."

I couldn't process any of it, I just shrieked and bucked in his merciless hold.

And then Royce drew a gun.

I couldn't do a fucking thing as he fired off a shot right through my mom's skull, blowing her away right before my eyes.

I screamed and screamed, tears pouring down my face.

"Ah, fuck, yeah, that was the shit," Malcolm grunted as he spilled inside me, then ripped me off him and tossed me onto the concrete on my hands and knees.

"That's for giving Roman's heir hope. You're fucking up my plans. There's no hope here. You're my whore, your mom is dead with a failed rescue attempt, and the same will happen to Roman and Curt when they come too." He yanked on my hair as I balled my eyes out, shuddering and choking on my tears. "Break, bitch," he spat, then threw open the door and commanded to one of his guys, "Get her back to the chair."

I SNAPPED BACK to the immediate moment, working on controlling my breathing, in a bid to prevent another *episode* from befalling me.

"After that, he threw her body in with me and Levi for a couple of days. All in his attempt to break us."

"Jesus fuck," Mason rasped.

And then his arms were around me, holding me tightly to him, up against his warmth.

"You did it," Levi's broken voice sounded, before he joined the embrace and the two of them gave me the comfort I'd never really had, that I'd never really allowed in all the years prior.

"Thanks to you all," I murmured against them. "You're freeing me. Thank you."

"The thanks is all owed to you, *Wildflower.* All to you."

In the middle of it, I caught Levi and Mason exchanging a fierce resolute look, communicating something intense to each other.

I couldn't even ask, because I was too caught up in the moment, and liberating myself from the memories I'd kept to myself like poison for so long.

So fucking long.

29

~Colton~

"It's called *Headstrong,*" I told them as we walked through the quad, a whole lot of eyes on us. I was more than used to the weird attention, so it just rolled off my back, and I continued, "It's about you, cutie."

Bree turned her head to me as I walked on her left side holding her hand, while Lev was on her right, his arm wrapped around her and his fingers tickling the back of my neck because the three of us were smushed so closely together. Mason was right in front of us like some sort of sentry, parting the crowds for us. He was in extreme protective mode. I mean, he always was with us—his brothers. But he'd been even more protective of Bree since the morning-after our first night together as a foursome. He'd even been upset about her going back to her apartment the other day. It had led to him insisting the three of us walk her to and from classes all day long.

Strangely, Bree hadn't even protested one little bit.

She was clearly sinking into it, into us.

And I was loving it.

Having her with us was bringing things to a balance

we'd had trouble striking before because of Mason and Lev clashing so much since the *incident* five years ago.

"About me?" she queried with mirth dancing in her eyes.

"Yeah, you being a badass bit—"

"Colt," Mason admonished.

I held up my free head. "Right, my bad. I meant badass *babe.*"

"I've gotta hear this one," Lev said, excited by it.

"You haven't heard my other one yet, *I Remember.*"

He looked between me and Bree. "You told me not to, *Wildflower,* right?"

"I did." She flashed her eyes at me. "Remember, Colt?"

Colt. I loved that she was calling me that now.

She still didn't call Levi, *Lev* though. She liked using his full name. I guess it was how they'd always known each other, with him still calling her Brianna too.

And Mason, well he went with *Bree* too now. Major for him, because he was usually way more standoffish with anyone outside our threesome unit. It meant she wasn't *outside* it to him anymore.

That morning-after something had happened between them—not sexual, but some sort of deep understanding, and it had changed everything, it'd had him letting down his guard with her and everything.

He'd even shown me and Lev up accidently one morning when we'd—well Lev had, but I'd been *assisting*—been cooking her one of her favorite breakfast sandwiches, and Mason had walked in with a half dozen different ones he'd ordered in for her, and then he'd even baked her some double chocolate cookies too.

He was smitten with her.

Hell, we all were.

And she was with us.

When she'd gone back to her apartment, she'd been basically texting us all night in the group text we'd set up.

One night, we'd even been on video call and each of us had taken turns reading lines from one of her stories in her fairytale book that Lev had told us helped her to sleep. We'd watched her fall asleep over video, and it had been the cutest thing ever. Just like her with her pink, Barbiecore thing and that soft heart of hers.

"Right, yeah," I said. "I forgot. So, you two are in the same class this morning? *Operationals?*"

Bree chuckled.

Lev grinned. "Operating Systems, cupcake."

"Boring as fuck. I don't know how you guys do it."

Mason spun and gestured at himself as he walked backward. "Hey, no one has drier classes than me. I'm the king there."

"No argument here," Lev agreed.

"Glad you can finally joke about it, brother," I pointed out.

He shrugged. *Shrugged?* Mason fucking Hall. Like, all casual and relaxed. I caught Lev's eye and he was as shocked as me.

"So, we're all still on for tonight at *Nirvana,* yeah? My first live show test thingy without those fucker former bandmates of mine?"

"Of course we're gonna be there, brother," Lev said.

"Locked down," Mason confirmed.

Bree kissed my cheek. "Absolutely, *cupcake.* "

I burst out laughing and so did Lev.

Even Mason grinned from ear-to-ear. "That's about right."

"Fine with me," I told them. "I'll be the sweet one,

Mason will be the hot hardass, Lev will be the smoldering dangerous one, and Bree will be the edgy Barbie."

She looked down at herself dressed in one of the outfits I liked best on her, a gray mini-skirt with pastel-pink knee-high boots that matched her long coat, and a white tank with butterflies across the bust that really made her all-seeing eye blue pendant pop.

"Where's the *edgy* part?" she asked me.

"Your grit and determination, your fearsome attitude, your *headstrong* thing."

"He's right on, *Wildflower.*"

Unfortunately, we reached her class in the next couple of seconds and it was time to say goodbye and get on with our days.

As we were doing just that, I felt a squeeze to my ass.

It wasn't from her and I spun to see Mason right there winking at me.

Holy. Hell.

He'd just grabbed my ass in public!

I couldn't believe it.

As Lev and Bree headed into class, Mason leaned into me and brushed his lips over my cheek as he whispered in his turned-on, husky voice, "Fuck you later, gorgeous."

"Shit, darlin'."

He chuckled at my ear. "Either after the show or during intermission. But definitely at the venue."

Heat rolled through me, my cock reacting almost violently to his erotic promise.

Before I could get out a response, he kissed my cheek again, then disappeared into the crowds, leaving me staring after him in a mixture of shock and wonder.

Well, damn.

I WAS KILLING IT.

Okay, *now* I was.

It had taken me two songs to get into it and lose the nerves.

Even with me doing my usual ritual of kissing all the tuning pegs of my guitar.

When going on stage with the band, I usually only got a couple of minutes' worth of stage fright right before we went on, then we'd do our backstage ritual, and it would quiet down.

But this time, without the backing of the band, and the energy of a party-type crowd, it had thrown me off and taken me a while to get into it and lose myself to the music.

Doing an acoustic set was way more intimate too.

It had made me feel more exposed.

Fortunately, I'd quickly realized that I hadn't actually been alone at all when I'd looked out at the middle booth near the stage and I'd seen the smiling, supportive faces of Mason, Lev, and Bree right there.

I'd focused on that and them, and then I'd managed to let go and revel in the vulnerability of it and the special edge it was bringing to my music and performance tonight.

"This is for our girl, Brianna!" I called out, as I shifted my weight on the swivel stool and got ready to launch into one of my new songs, after giving the more well-known hits around campus some attention to get the bar hopping and in good spirits.

I grinned as I looked out to see Bree slapping her hand over her reddening face as Lev hugged her to his side, and Mason held her hand.

I let go and allowed the music to roll through me, feeling the melody and lyrics alike as I gave it my all vocally and via the playing of my Gibson Hummingbird.

"Like a thief in the night/ You tried to steal me away/ From

everything I'd been leaning on/ You thought you could handle it/ That I was just another play/ Too bad you didn't count on my might."

I looked out to see Bree smiling as she noted the lyrics.

"Watch out/ Watch me/ I'm coming for you/ Beating you at what you do/ You see, I'm headstrong/ Headstrong/ And you're dead wrong."

Lev and Mason gave me a side-eye at that last verse, knowing it was about them coming at her, and her being tough enough, smart enough, and just plain awesome enough, to turn it around on them and fight back.

Hey, I was an artist, I called it like I saw it, and interpreted it as I experienced it.

I chuckled into the song, then managed to make it through to the end.

And then it was time for my fifteen-minute break to soothe my throat and chill for a bit.

Before I could get off the stage to reach my people, a bunch of students from the crowd gathered all through the bar, even many standing up, surged toward me, all over me asking questions, chatting it up, the whole nine.

By the time I was done and I made it back to the booth, Mason and Bree were gone.

Lev was sitting there looking his usual impatient self and trying to hide it—for Bree's sake as I'd noticed him doing a lot for her—while he tasted some of her drink, her go-to Strawberry Chocolate Martini. I chuckled as I saw him grimace, then quickly put it down and sip at his vodka to take away the taste.

"Worth a try, huh?"

"Already regretting it. Damn, it's sweet. Right up your alley, though."

"Nah, I'll stick with my daiquiri when it comes to liquor, thanks."

"That was ace, Colt," he said. "Really amazing. The songs you've been working hard on, the playing, your voice, all that passion coming through. You've got this without those fuckers, brother."

"Thanks, Lev," I said, slapping his shoulder. "Where's Bree and Mason?"

"Brianna went to the bathroom." He smirked. "And Mason? Well, color me shocked, but he told me to tell you to meet him out by the delivery entrance."

My pulse picked up. "Seriously? You better not be fucking with me, Lev."

"*I'm* not fucking with you, but it sounds like he's gonna be."

Hell, yeah. "Fifteen minutes... best way to spend the break."

I rushed off then, weaving my way back through toward the bar. I managed to sneak past and head on through to the storage area, then I pushed on out to the delivery entrance.

I'd only just made it out when my arm was snagged and I was spun around and shoved up against the wall of an adjacent alley.

"Hey, gorgeous. Right on time. For once," Mason said, right in my face as he slammed his palms down either side of my head and caged me in with his big, hard body. "Time for your reward."

In the next second, he was grinding his cock against mine through our pants, real rough making me moan out. "Yeah. Shit, yeah, Mason."

He nipped at my jaw, sending sparks of need through me that had me rolling my hips harder, all needy for more friction.

"There's my gorgeous boy," he whispered sexily at my ear, before licking the lobe, then trailing his tongue down

342

my throat, sending shudders of sensation through me. That, combined with his closeness, his body plastered against mine and our cocks roughing together, his sexy citrus scent infusing me… it had me beside myself.

He read my growing desperation well and ripped me around, pushing me against the wall again and then yanking down my leather pants to just below my ass. I was going commando as I often did for a show, so the cool air whispered across my exposed ass in the most amazing way.

He slapped my cheeks in turn and I jolted in surprise at his aggressive playfulness, eyeing him over my shoulder.

"That's right," he said, smirking at me. "It's like that."

Before I could register it fully, I was jolting as the cold, slippery feel of lube was squirted into my hole and along the crack of my ass.

I hadn't even seen him pull it out, he'd done it so fast. Damn, he was really on point right now.

In the next moment, he was sliding his rock-hard cock along my crack, teasing my hole.

"Ah, Mason, please," I whined as he continued on and on, teasing, while slathering his cock in all the lube he'd dripped there.

"Please, huh? You need my cock that bad, gorgeous?"

"Yes," I groaned, digging my nails into the wall in front of me and pushing my ass back against him. "Fuck me. Rail my fucking ass, darlin'."

An animalistic growl sounded at my ear, and then he breached me, making me cry out at the suddenness of it.

He drove all the way in and I threw my head back in ecstasy at the delicious roughness, the way he was bringing the domination this time.

"Ungh. Fuck, yeah. Fuck!" I gasped.

He fisted his hand in my mohawk and used it to yank my head back, nipping and licking at my throat and jaw as he pulled almost all the way out, then slammed back into me, hitting that sweet spot so fucking amazingly that the intense pleasure had my knees threatening to buckle.

His other hand suddenly cradled my cock and he growled at my ear, "Fuck into my hand."

I did, I just did it, pumping my hips almost violently.

Pleasure built so quickly. So fucking quickly.

"Shit! Shit!" I gasped out. "Oh my God, Mason!"

"I know," he groaned. "Tight fucking ass. Hot fucking cock."

He picked up his pace even more until he was jack-hammering into my ass and I matched his pace, feeling his fingers vibrating all over my shaft as I rammed into them.

It hit me so quickly and he clamped his free hand over my mouth as I screamed out my release, pumping into his hand.

"Yeah… hell fucking fuck," he choked, and I felt him spill inside me.

"Eat," he commanded, slathering his fingers dripping with my cum all over my lips, pushing them into my mouth and coating my tongue too. *Shit*, it was hot as hell and it had me shaking with it.

I almost lost it completely when he took it to another level, spread my ass open, then started licking up all his cum spilling out of my ass.

When he was done, I was boneless, slumped against the wall. "Fucking shit," I breathed. "We're doing it that way again."

"Although, not in five minutes from now, which the glint in your eye is suggesting. You have a show to finish."

"Show… yeah… the show," I murmured, trying to recover.

He'd really brought it, and I was still even fighting to register the fact that this had happened at all, that he'd taken me in public like this. I'd even been vaguely aware of people nearby while it had been going down. While that never bothered me, it usually did for Mason—in a big way.

Things were changing.

And I couldn't be happier.

———

I STUMBLED BACK into the bar and Mason caught my elbow, grinning. "All right there, Colt?"

"More than all right. I can't believe you just did that with me. A few people were walking by and you didn't even stop."

"I know. I didn't want to. I didn't feel like I needed to."

"Yeah? How come?"

"I'm not sure. I just… I feel… freer, I guess. I mean, it's definitely a work in progress, but still."

"It's a major deal, Mason. You moving along the path of being true to yourself and who you really are… it's what I've wanted for you for so fucking long."

We made it back to the booth and I found Lev alone again.

"She's still not back?" I asked, as I slipped in opposite him, and Mason joined me. "I mean, I know we only had time for a quickie, but it wasn't *that* quick."

Lev tensed right up. "What? You didn't see her on your way in?"

"No. Why?"

"She said she had to return a call."

"To who?" Mason asked.

"I don't know, I'm trying not to be so invasive with that sort of thing when it comes to her anymore."

"Fuck, neither am I. Bad timing or what. Clearly that was a mistake."

I held up my hands. "Chill, guys. Maybe she just moved off to the side to take her call?"

It didn't work, the two of them shot to their feet.

"Colt, just finish your set," Mason said, before eyeing Levi. "Lev, hack the cameras the way you did last time and try to pick her up from there. I'll physically search around the property."

"Got it," the two of them said in unison.

And then they were darting off.

Hell.

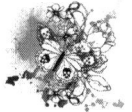

30

~Mason~

My pulse was spiking like crazy.

She wouldn't just leave for this long.

Not on her own.

Not of her own free will.

She couldn't get enough of being close to the three of us right now, just like we couldn't with her.

All four of us were caught up in some sort of honeymoon phase at the moment.

Even though she'd managed to go home, because she hadn't wanted to lose focus on her studies, her program meaning so much to her, it had still been hard for her to be away from us, and we all connected all the time via text and call and video.

Even if her call tonight—whoever it was to—had taken longer than she'd anticipated, she would have at least texted us.

Fuck me. Where was she?

I'd already checked the bathrooms and the east, south, and west side of the building—even down the alley Colt and I had just fooled around in.

I still couldn't wrap my head around me instigating that. I was glad that I had, it was just surprising for me. Bree being with us… it was loosening me up more than I'd ever thought possible. She was inspiring hope in all of us in different ways.

For me, it was the notion of being who I really wanted to be. Bit by bit.

The addition of her to our group had managed to restore the camaraderie we'd lost for a while, to bring us closer together, and for there to be many more lighthearted and jovial moments that we'd been without for too long.

So where the fuck was she?

I neared the north side of the building when I picked up on a commotion.

"Get the fuck off me, you skank!"

I frowned at the familiarity of the voice.

Rosemary?

A thud sounded and her pained cry rang out.

Then a very familiar voice eclipsed hers.

"It's bad form to slut shame someone in this day and age. Even more reprehensible is doing it as a sorority head with young women under your charge who look up to you. Don't be sore that someone has beaten you at your own game. Did you really think you could double cross Mason that easily?"

"I would have if you hadn't interfered."

"The moment Colt told me about you, it raised suspicion. So I kept an eye on you. Or, my girls kept an eye on you. You actually thought you could weasel your way into being a member of Hex just so you could report on what Mason was doing to use it as blackmail to be with him, or threaten to report your findings to his father should he refuse? That would destroy him. As it is, now it will only destroy you."

What the fuck?

I peered around the corner and found Brianna there

pinning a flailing and really pissed Rosemary up against the wall as she spoke in that calm and reasonable manner of hers—all class—while Rosemary hissed and struggled in a completely undignified manner.

Brianna turned her head toward me right away, obviously having sensed my approach. *Damn,* she was on the ball. In more ways than one, clearly.

"Hey, babe," she greeted, casually, like she wasn't pinning somebody against the wall and conducting covert business like a seasoned pro at this sort of thing.

"What's—" I started, but Rosemary's whine cut me off.

"Mason, this little cunt—"

"Shut your fucking mouth," I rumbled dangerously, and it literally had her lips slamming closed.

I stepped forward, but Bree held up her hand, signaling that she had it.

In the next moment, she released Rosemary roughly.

"We're not done," she warned when Rosemary made a move to take off.

I watched, more than a little curiously, as Bree reached into the pocket of her jacket, then withdrew her phone. She scrolled for a few moments, then flipped the screen for Rosemary to see.

"A single word to Peter Hall through any means—even via your sorority members—and this hits *Reitner and Simmons* immediately. I really don't think your mom will take well to photos of you snorting a line of coke off some random guy's abs, *or* to this video of you fucking one of her business partners."

"You cu—"

I cleared my throat roughly.

Rosemary bit her tongue.

"Get gone. *Now,*" I commanded.

Bree stepped aside and pocketed her phone, and Rosemary ran off into the night.

"How much did you hear?" she asked, walking to me, as we met halfway.

"Enough to know how far you went to protect me." I screwed up my face at the guilt that plagued me like a bitch of a thing. "After what I did to you? I don't—"

She took my hands in hers. "That was then. It was through a massive misunderstanding based on your flawed perception of Levi. We're allies now, right?"

"More than allies."

She nodded with a sweet little smile. "And I protect those closest to me."

"How did you even—how did you stop what she was attempting to do?"

"Well, if you hadn't come at me, I actually wouldn't have been able to. Not fast enough. When you marked me, I mobilized my girls to investigate you and to turn up intel. Once we became allies, those that I had in place were shifted to protective mode on your behalf, Levi's, and Colt's."

"Wow, that's… beyond impressive."

"Well, I'm not just a sweet, innocent girl with a pretty face."

"Believe me, we're all well aware you're much more than that, even without this. We wouldn't be so enamored with you otherwise. You're complicated, multifaceted." I stroked her fingers. "You're extraordinary."

"That she is," Levi's voice came from behind us.

We pulled apart as he stepped out of the shadows, grinning from ear-to-ear. "I accessed the cameras and picked you up here right in time for that show with Rosemary." He came to us and wrapped his arms around her, pulling her in for a tight hug, his hands shaking a little and belying just how freaked out he'd been when we hadn't been able to find her for those few minutes. "Nicely done," he said, as he eased away just a little, still staying close, like I was to her.

It was very noticeable that he didn't say anything about her taking off without telling us what she was doing and making us worry.

He was really trying so hard not to be so invasive and clingy with her, trying to give her the space and freedom that she needed. After all, he knew better than anyone from knowing her in the past, seeing her club life, and doing *so* much in-depth research on her, that she'd been denied that freedom for so long, a compromise she wasn't ever going to make again.

"Did you know about her *girls*?" I asked him.

He lifted a shoulder, then beamed at her, answering non-committal, "I know a lot about our woman."

"Who are they?" I asked.

The two of them exchanged a look, then Bree pressed her hand to my pec. "All in good time," she told me, planting a soft kiss on my cheek.

"Let's head back inside. Colt needs us," Lev said.

"Yeah," I agreed, re-centering myself after all the worry and the shock of what I'd walked in on. "Yeah, he does."

We headed back in, my hand on the small of Bree's back, and Levi holding her hand as he played with her hair.

We'd just sat down at the booth as Colt was finishing up another song.

And then he surprised the fuck out of us by snatching up a spare microphone at the edge of the stage and pointing it at Bree. Off her surprise, he chuckled and spoke out into the bar for everyone to hear, "That's right, cutie, time to debut our duet. Everyone will melt at the sound of your sexy voice."

She hesitated.

Lev stroked her shoulders, encouraging her, "Being free, remember? This is a great step toward that."

"Sink into the song, block out the crowds. Just focus on Colt," I added.

It took a moment as she looked between us, the students packing the place who'd come for Colt's special show, and the microphone he was still holding out to her, but our words proved to be enough to bolster her when she rose to her feet.

Applause and wolf-whistles of encouragement from the audience sounded, egging her on, and then she was sauntering up to the stage.

Colt wrapped his arm around her and gave her a sweet kiss on the top of her head, then handed her the microphone, as he started off the song.

"I've been standing in the shadows/ Willing the blackness to pull me in/ A place where nobody else knows."

As he sang, Lev snagged my glass of scotch across the booth between us to get my attention, halting it just shy of my lips. "I want to tell her."

"About our tracking of Lynch?" I whispered back.

He gave me a withering look. "What else, Mason?"

"I don't know, I was hoping for anything but that."

"You saw her earlier. She can handle it. I don't want to keep this secret from her any longer. My plan was always to tell her once she'd come around and accepted the real her and stopped hiding. And she clearly has."

"These *girls* she has in place… it poses a danger, not just to what we're doing, but to her if she gets them and herself involved. After earlier, I can absolutely see that happening, something she'd do in a bid to protect us."

"Mason—"

"Just wait until we have something concrete, all right? Once you're able to leverage your recent infiltration of Royce Humphrey's security network toward finding Lynch."

I could see his resistance, his need to share this with her.

But he surprised me when he took the cautious and careful route and gave a nod. "Okay, yeah. It will be best for her if there's something concrete when I reveal that Lynch didn't actually perish six years ago."

"After what he did to her, I have no doubt. Knowing he's out there with no current way or strategy to take him down… it will torment her."

"Yeah," he murmured, a dark look flitting across his face, as he obviously started to recall that time.

Fortunately, the sound of Bree starting her verse of the duet managed to pull us both from our current conversational path, and jar him before he slipped into an *episode*.

We turned to watch as charisma came off her in waves and she sank into the moment with Colt and the song.

"It was easier not to open my eyes/ It was easier not to feel a thing/ Until you."

She really was something.

Fuck me, that didn't even cover it.

She was fast become *everything* to us.

31

~Brianna~

Life was good.

My classes were going well.

After that duet a couple of weeks ago, it had drawn a lot of attention to me and the students on campus had made the connection to my apps and now I was labeled *App Girl*, with hundreds of people wanting the app. It was a major deal and it was all thanks to Colt.

Actually, my upbeat mood was thanks to all three of my guys.

My guys?

I couldn't believe that was where we were at now.

Things were going so well.

We'd fallen into a really nice rhythm too.

I felt freer than I had in... ever.

I was happy. Actually happy.

I shrugged my fuzzy pink messenger bag onto my shoulder as I stepped out of my coding lab, headed for the café to grab a quick bite for lunch before my next class.

Usually, me and the guys would meet at this point to hang out. It was like the halfway point through our days.

Then at night we'd hang at their place, or sometimes mine. Levi had helped me to make dinner at my apartment two nights ago and it had been cute seeing three big guys filling the small space. What had happened afterward had been far from *cute,* though, as the four of us had basically dirtied up my bed all night long.

But today, it was just me for lunch because Mason had a mock trial he was prepping for, Levi had a call with his father, and Colt was interviewing a bass player and drummer.

I ordered a coffee and a special meatball sub from the café then made my way out to my favorite bench at the back of the quad out of the way of everything to decompress and chill out before my next set of classes.

The café never used to carry this sort of special sandwich, but after Mason had found out it was one of my most favorite sandwiches, he'd thrown his weight around as co-leader of *Hex* and had not only made them carry it, but he'd also ensured it was always ready for me on Tuesdays and Thursdays when I ordered it. They even had freshly baked chocolate chip cookies now too.

And the bench we ate lunch at together now was always unoccupied unlike before when I'd only been able to gain access to it two out of five times a week. I'd found out from Colt that it had been Levi's doing, using *his* power as co-leader of *Hex* to keep everyone away and mark it as off-limits.

Just like *I* was now.

Nobody bothered me or even looked my way. Things were so peaceful for me, so nice.

So life really was good.

In a completely different way to how this academic year had started off.

Because of *them.*

355

As I placed my bag down beside me on the bench and then unwrapped my sandwich and savored the first bite, my phone buzzed in the pocket of my pink houndstooth jacket.

I pulled it out and blinked in surprise at a text from Chloe.

I'd been communicating with her a lot via text, but she'd barely been replying.

For the last couple of weeks, I'd left her alone, figuring she was upset and dealing with the issues with her mom and needed some space from me and the reminder of this place in order to do that.

I opened it with bated breath.

Chloe: Sorry I've been AWOL, Bree. Lots been happening here. Are we still good?

Brianna: We're good. I get it, no worries.

Chloe: Oh, thank fuck. I thought you'd be pissed at me for basically ghosting you. It really wasn't intentional, I swear. Life just got in the way, all the craziness, you know?

Oh, I did know. Definitely.

Brianna: Totally understand. Things have been crazy on my end too.

Chloe: I'll say. I heard the rumors and the talk all over the campus social media. You're dating the leaders of Hex? That's some insanity right there. The hot kind, no doubt.

Before I could figure out how to respond to that, she sent another text.

Chloe: I want to hear all about it. Every dirty little detail too. I'm coming back tonight! For real this time. You up for meeting for a coffee?

Oh my God.

Brianna: Of course! Send me the details and I'll be there.

Chloe: Yay! See you soon, babe.

I couldn't believe it. After all this time, I was finally going to see my friend again.

And, boy, did we have a lot to talk about.

She had been the only thing missing from things being perfect, so with her coming back now everything could fall into place.

I fired off a message to the group text with the guys.

Brianna: Need to raincheck tonight. Chloe coming back into town. Meeting for coffee.

Colt: I'm bummed we can't hang, but happy you get to see your friend again. It's been way too long for you guys.

Brianna: Thanks, cupcake.

Colt: Love you calling me that.

Brianna: Well, it's so accurate, I can't help it.

Levi: Chloe Anders is coming back here tonight? Why?

I figured he wouldn't be pleased we had to cancel our date.

I might have noticed him going to a lot of effort to tone down his intensity so it didn't come off as overbearing, and him also loosening up a little there, but it wasn't going to disappear entirely, it was a part of him, of our dynamic.

Brianna: Didn't say exactly. Just happy I get to see her.

Levi: Right, sure.

I frowned at that. Levi was usually so supportive with absolutely everything. Maybe it was just about me having to raincheck things?

Before I could think more on it, a message from Mason came into the group chat.

Mason: Have fun with your friend. We'll come by your place for a nightcap.

Colt: Translation: we'll fuck you to sleep, cutie.

Mason: Do you have to be so crass?

Colt: You know you love it. You're just pissed because it's making your dick hard while you're in your mock trial thingy.

Mason: Fuck, Colt.

Colt: LMFAO. Wanna step out and I'll give you some relief?

Mason: Stop.

Levi: Save it for later tonight once Brianna is done with her fair-weather friend.

What the hell?

Colt: What's up your ass, brother?

Brianna: Seconded. You don't care for Chloe?

Levi: I don't care for her screwing you around and getting your hopes up about coming back.

Brianna: I'm a big girl.

Levi: Still don't want you hurt.

Mason: Let's tone it down. Bree, have fun with your friend. We'll come by later and I'll make sure Lev is in a better mood.

Colt: Me too. I'll cheer him up.

Brianna: Thanks. TTYL. Get back to your stuff.

We finished texting and I pocketed my phone and settled into eating my sandwich, pushing Levi's strange reaction to the background and focusing on the fact that I'd get to finally see Chloe again tonight.

"I WAS SURPRISED when you wanted to meet over coffee, not booze or hard liquor," I said, eyeing Chloe across from me in the little coffee shop in downtown Stonewell.

Her short purple hair was striking against the black

lace dress she had on that was held together with safety pins and what appeared to be buckles. A pair of silver, shimmering denim boots added an extra edge to her look.

"Not exactly my preference, but my mom is sending two movers down early tomorrow to pack my stuff up for me so I can't exactly be hungover and useless."

I choked on my sip of coffee. "What? This isn't you actually being back then? You're really done here?"

She smiled sadly. "Yeah, I am. I tried everything, but her mind was made up."

"Jeez," I groused. "It's not the way I thought it would go, especially with the spotlight on your designs that we were able to get for you all over social media."

"That was the sweetest, so thank you. Thank you so much for trying for me, Bree. But my mom just turned that around, citing that I'd been noticed by fashion influencers and a couple of designers looking for fresh talent, so I needed to capitalize on it by attending the hoity-toity design school in the city."

"Shit. I'm so sorry, Chloe."

She shrugged, clearly resigned. "It is what it is." Laying her hand on mine, she told me, "I swear we'll keep in contact. Much better than I have been at it too, once I get settled. We can visit each other too. We won't lose our friendship."

"I'll make sure of it."

"I know you will. You're cool like that. Caring too. You've got a lot of that to go around." She winked. "Enough to give to three guys."

I chuckled. "Yeah, that came about completely unplanned."

"I always thought those three were nightmares walking. Well, except for Colton. Are they nice beneath the hard surface then? Like, actually human, after all?"

"They are with me, yeah. We mesh well together somehow."

"Well, damn, I honestly didn't see this coming. I didn't see any of this coming, anything that's happened to the two of us when we started back at Stonewell U this year, you know?"

"It's certainly been full of surprises, for sure."

Intensity took her over and she leaned in closer, dropping her voice to a conspiratorial whisper. "Just be careful with them, okay?"

I frowned. "Is there something specific you're worried about?"

"I want you to be happy and I get that it's hard for you to let go and all that, so the fact that you have with them is a big deal. But the thrill and relief of that might be clouding some things for you."

"Like?"

She blew out a breath. "I know who bent my mom's ear about pulling me out of here. I'm sorry, Bree. It's one of your guys."

I tensed and a chill rolled down my spine at the accusation, and the corresponding awful implications.

"I guess they wanted me out of the way so they could have a clear shot to you or something. Either way, it's fucked-up, so I wanted you to be aware."

"Of course, yeah. Thank you. Who was it?"

"It was Levi Knight."

Son of a bitch.

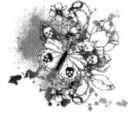

32

~Levi~

The big motherfucker went down hard again.

Thanks to me.

More specifically, thanks to the wrath I was channeling all my frustrations into.

The secret I was keeping from Brianna was weighing on me more with each passing day.

I'd listened to Mason's logic and reason, things that I'd normally refute and go with my instincts instead. But because of the agreement we had and the way things were going so well with the two of us, and all of us lately, I hadn't gone that route. I'd held back.

And it was killing me inside.

She deserved to know what was going on. It had a direct impact on her. It was as much a part of my dark and fucked-up past as it was hers.

Now there was another complication that had been thrown into the mix in the form of Chloe Anders. Her fucking timing of returning—even temporarily as I already knew it to be—couldn't have been worse.

The fear rolling through me of her fucking things up was a living breathing thing twisting me up.

And when I got like that, I tended to be... destructive.

So I was channeling it into a little street fighting.

Something Sammy had been really happy about, because I always brought in a hell of a crowd—and money for him—and I'd been away for a while immersed in Brianna and our foursome awesomeness.

The roided-out monster of a guy tapped out instead of getting up and coming back into the fight.

Pathetic.

Sure, he had a broken nose and bruised ribs, but that was nothing in terms of the damage I could really do.

As one of his buddies helped him to head out, I stepped out and walked to Sammy.

"That was a hell of a fight. You're really bringing the wild tonight," he said, slap-shaking with me, then tossing me a ratty towel to wipe my bloodied face. My eye was a little sore from a nasty hit I'd taken, and it was gonna leave one hell of a bruise. I'd wake up with a black eye tomorrow, no doubt. But it was nothing compared to what I'd sustained before during my training years.

And it certainly wasn't enough to purge what I needed to tonight.

"Give me another," I told Sammy.

"You sure?"

"You want to make money, or you want to worry about me?"

"Both, my friend."

I tossed the towel back to him. "I'm fine. Hit me up."

"All right."

I turned away and strode back into the fight space.

It wasn't two minutes before another guy joined me.

A guy about my size and a few years older with shaggy blond hair.

Sammy had just called the start of the fight when a sharp whistle rang out that stilled both my opponent and me.

I got a hell of a shock when I saw Brianna pushing through the riled up crowd.

I growled low in my throat when a bunch of them checked her out in her little pink skirt and her leather jacket, with a scoop neck hot-pink top beneath that did amazing justice to her breasts.

That antagonism was replaced by yet more shock when she stepped into the fight space and walked right up to my opponent.

I watched her slap a wad of bills into his hand and tell him something quietly.

He grinned happily, then gave her a chin lift and took off.

Then *she* moved into his place.

To take me on?

What was happening?

"*Wildflower,* what are you doing?"

"What do you think?" she bit back at me with an aggressive edge.

"I'm not fighting you. Ever. Step out."

She stormed toward me instead.

"How could you?" she yelled irately.

No, it was more than anger. It was… pain.

Disappointment and hurt—in me?

"Brianna, what—"

Her fist came at my face, the surprise of it actually managing to make me stumble back a step. And, damn, she had a solid punch. There was a lot of power in it, no doubt.

"You took my friend from me! Another mindfuck? Seriously? After everything we've been through, everything we'd worked through, and you do *this?* It's beyond fucked-up, Levi!"

I wiped a trail of blood out of the corner of my mouth. "It's not what you think."

"It's exactly what I think!"

"*Wildflower*—"

"Don't call me that!" she screamed. "And don't come by my place tonight! None of you!"

Before I could do a thing, she thrust her foot between my legs, making me choke and collapse to my knees.

And then she was storming off and disappearing through the crowds.

Motherfucker!

—

I SWUNG my leg over my bike, finally able to ride out of the fight venue now the abuse to my balls had eased off enough.

I stilled on firing up my Harley and checked my phone again to see if she'd responded to any of my *many* text messages.

Nothing.

Fuck.

I was about to put it away and head back to the mansion to get Mason and Colt's input when my phone did buzz.

Instead of it being the one person I desperately wanted to text me back, though, it was something else entirely.

Blocked ID: You come after me, kiddo, I come after what you love. Just like back then.

A chill rolled down my spine.

Kiddo.

It's what he'd called me in that hellscape.

Levi: Royce.

Blocked ID: Clever boy. What's not clever is you coming at me and threatening to fuck me over with Malcolm. Bad move. You need a lesson.

How did he know? I'd been really careful like Mason had asked me to be.

Motherfucker, it had to be Kyle. He'd told Royce about my little visit, and it had enabled him to put the pieces together.

Levi: Cut the cryptic.

Blocked ID: I already told you. Coming after what you love. Still such a pretty little thing, isn't she? Even more so. Come at me again and the damage will be permanent.

Fucking Christ.

Brianna!

To be continued in **WHEN KINGS FALL**

Next Book in the Series

WHEN KINGS FALL

Vicious Things, Book 2

Six years ago, my life was shattered to pieces.
Now it's happening all over again.

I thought information was true power.
But as awful secrets come to light, it's clear it's also pain.

He's pulled me back in.
He's started something that can't be undone.

Now they're coming for us.
History is repeating.
They want us to crawl.

But we're different now.
This time, monsters will weep and false kings will fall.

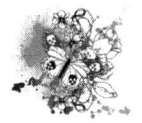

Vicious Things

THEY BREAK BEAUTY
WHEN KINGS FALL

Connected Series

VICIOUS THINGS & COVETED KINGDOM

<u>VICIOUS THINGS</u>
Brianna, Levi, Colton, Mason
THEY BREAK BEAUTY
WHEN KINGS FALL

<u>COVETED KINGDOM</u>
Caterina, Nico, Emilio, Julian
WHERE THE WICKED REIGN
VICIOUS LITTLE PRINCESS
THEY MAKE MONSTERS

WALKING WITH MONSTERS & TWISTED TORMENT

<u>WALKING WITH MONSTERS</u>
Aurora, Asher, Killian, Jonah
LOCK UP THE DARKNESS
SCARS RUN DEEP
BURN IT DOWN

<u>TWISTED TORMENT</u>

Skylar, Bastian, Caleb, Caspian
WRECK ME
HATE ME
CRAVE ME

Leia King Library

WALKING WITH MONSTERS
LOCK UP THE DARKNESS
SCARS RUN DEEP
BURN IT DOWN

TWISTED TORMENT
WRECK ME
HATE ME
CRAVE ME

VICIOUS THINGS
THEY BREAK BEAUTY
WHEN KINGS FALL

ELECTI ACADEMY
WICKED HEIRS
CURSED HEIRS
FALLEN HEIRS

COVETED KINGDOM
WHERE THE WICKED REIGN
VICIOUS LITTLE PRINCESS
THEY MAKE MONSTERS

KNOT YOUR QUEEN

OMEGA FALLS

IMMORTAL PASSIONS
IMMORTAL BURDEN
REIGN OF THE BEAST
FALLEN ANGEL
OUT OF ASHES

IMMORTAL FLAME
HARBINGER
LEGACY

KING

About the Author

Where Damaged Heroes and Badass Heroines Collide.

Leia writes edgy and emotional stories across multiple genres. She enjoys crafting flawed heroes with a dark side and strong women who hold their own.